DEATH TO PAY

A DRAMATIC THRILLER WITH AN
UNBELIEVABLE TWIST

DEREK FEE

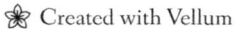 Created with Vellum

For Aine, Bobbie and Sean

CHAPTER ONE

Lizzie Rice stared at her image in the mirror of the toilet at The Star Bingo Club and pouted. 'Hello beautiful.' She could hear the caller in the main room as his amplified voice announced the numbers in a monotonous tone. Lizzie was anything but beautiful. Millions of cigarettes and thousands of cans of lager had taken their toll on both her face and her body. The crags on the face that stared back at her resembled the figures on Mount Rushmore. The radial lines emanating from her lips were a testament to her addiction to nicotine. Her rotund body was crushed into her Union Jack-patterned jacket, although she would insist to her friends that she could still fit into the clothes she bought twenty years previously. She removed her mobile phone from her purse and flipped open the Union Jack-patterned cover. No missed calls and no messages. Bugger that fat bastard Billy. He didn't give a shit for her now that she was over sixty. She coughed up some phlegm and spat it into the hand basin. Fucking men. They were keen enough to get into her pants when she was slim and lithe. To hell with them all. She replaced the phone in her jacket and fingered the twenty quid that she'd won at bingo. She fluffed up her thinning blonde hair. Time to get a move on. When she got to the door of the building on North Street, she found her two friends had already fired up the ciggies and were standing in the doorway puffing away. They stood back and gave Lizzie pride of place between them. Lizzie Rice was somebody in west Belfast. The Protestant newspapers painted her as a kind of Joan of Arc during the 'Troubles'. When her husband had a pair of balls and a dick that functioned, he'd been one of the leaders of the Ulster Volunteer Force. Now Billy was just a fat old drunk, and it was her son, who was one of the men who ran Belfast.

'Ciggie,' one of the women proffered a packet of cigarettes.

Lizzie pulled a cigarette from the packet, and a match instantly appeared in front of her lit by the second woman.

'Not a bad night,' the woman said as she lit Lizzie's cigarette.

Lizzie removed the twenty pounds from her pocket and waved it in front of her friends' faces.

'Lucky bitch, 'the first woman said. 'I'm down a fiver.'

Lizzie looked along North Street. It was empty except for the groups of women sheltering in the two doorways of Star Bingo. 'Time to hit the road, girls,' she said waving her winnings in the air before depositing them in her pocket. 'I'm a bit fucked.'

'Chance'd be a fine thing,' one of the women said and laughed.

Lizzie shot her a glance and the laughing stopped abruptly. She took a long drag on her cigarette and tossed it into the drain at the edge of the path. It was a bit of a walk to her house. If Billy was any bloody good, he would have been there to drive her home. But right now, he would be so drunk he wouldn't even know his name. It was either a taxi or a twenty-minute walk. Hell, she was going to walk it.

BILLY RICE CRUSHED the empty lager can and dropped it on

the pile of empties beside his chair. He tried to focus on the television screen at the other side of the room and smiled before leaning forward to pick up another can from the pack at his feet. He had no idea what programme he was watching, and he didn't give a damn who or what was on the screen. It was simply noise and a substitute for actual human company. He ripped open the lid of the can and poured a generous measure straight down his throat. He leaned back and flicked up the footrest on the lazyboy chair. He was just settling down when the doorbell rang. 'Piss off,' he shouted but since he was already drunk, it came out more like 'Prisof'. The doorbell rang again more insistently this time. 'Bollocks,' he said rising from his chair with difficulty. He was going to give the bugger at the door something he would remember. If it was one of those fuckers from Salt Lake City, he was going to be knocked into the middle of next week. Billy shuffled his large body down the corridor and opened the door. He was about to shout a few obscenities at whoever might be on the doorstep when a spray hit his face. His open mouth wanted to scream, but it couldn't. Every sinew in his body was concentrated on the pain in his eyes. As Billy raised his hands to his burning eyes, he felt a hand push him back into the corridor. He stumbled backwards trying to make sense of what was happening, but his brain was addled and unable to function. He was being pushed all the way back into the living room. 'I'll kill you,' he mumbled just before an electric shock hit him in the neck. He dropped his hands from his eyes to his chest as electricity coursed through his body. Then the lights went out.

LIZZIE RICE OPENED the door to her house. Her feet were killing her. Although the distance from the bingo hall to her house in the Shankill was only one mile, her feet were twenty years too old for the pair of high heels she'd been wearing. She kicked off her shoes, and as she did, she saw an open can of lager lying on the corridor carpet. "I'll kill that auld bastard someday," she thought as she bent to pick up the can. Spilt lager lay in a pool on her carpet. She draped her jacket over the bannister of the stairs and marched towards the living room. Her husband was lying asleep on one of the chairs, his two feet stuck out in front of him. She looked at the accumulation of empty cans at his feet. The television was blaring from the other corner of the room. As Lizzie entered the room, the door closed behind her. Something hit her on the back of the head and there was an explosion of pain in her brain. She fell forward onto her knees. A second blow struck her head. She fell further forward, and the pain stopped as her brain ceased functioning.

THE MURDERER STOOD above Lizzie Rice and looked at her smashed head. Two additional blows to the already dead woman reduced the head to a blonde hair topped by a mass of bone and brain. The murderer dropped the ball hammer into a carrier bag and removed the plastic apron from around her neck. The apron was covered with blood, and she wiped it on Lizzie's clothes before balling it up and placing it in the carrier bag beside the hammer. The bag would be in the Lagan within the hour. She glanced once more at the body lying at her feet. It was time to get out of there.

CHAPTER TWO

Recently appointed Detective Superintendent Ian Wilson was carrying out one of his new duties. He was seated cross-legged on the king-size bed in his apartment. His partner, Kate McCann, lay in front of him wearing only a pair of panties. Normally, this level of undress would be enough to turn Wilson's thoughts to shagging, but it was not a normal situation. The bump now very visible above Kate's panties contained their embryonic child. Wilson poured some warm oil over Kate's stomach and began to gently massage it in. He couldn't get over the vanity of women. Kate wanted desperately to have the child, but she didn't want to have the stretch marks that might go with it. The leader of the pre-natal classes had suggested that the new fathers should show their concern by a nightly massage session. As soon as she found out that she was expecting, Kate had immediately started a regime of diet and exercise that was aimed at keeping her figure as trim as possible. Four months later, it was not possible to tell that Kate was pregnant without seeing her naked. Wilson glanced at the Polaroid-style photo on the bedside table. It was the photo of their child taken by the gynaecologist at the first scan. No matter how many times he looked at the photo, and despite half a dozen explanations from Kate, he still couldn't see the outline of a child in the triangle of light. He finished massaging Kate's stomach and moved on to her thighs. Despite his best efforts to concentrate on his stretch mark-busting job, he could feel himself hardening.

'No,' Kate said keeping her eyes closed.

'What do you mean no?'

'No, you can't screw me.'

'How do you know that I want to screw you?'

Kate opened her eyes and stared at his crotch. 'I'm psychic,' she smiled.

'You have no idea how difficult this job is on someone like me,' he returned the smile.

'After the baby is born, I think that we might continue with the massages. I could massage you, and you could return the compliment.'

He stroked her legs with the oil. 'We might never get to the part where you get your massage.'

Kate sat up and kissed him lightly. 'Put your friend away for now and get me a coffee.' She picked up the photo from the bedside table and looked at it for what must have been the hundredth time. 'They'll be able to tell us the sex at the next scan.'

'Do we really want to know?'

'I suppose not,' she continued to stare at the photo. 'I'm more interested in having a healthy baby than in knowing the sex.'

'You'll excuse me if I mention the unmentionable,' Wilson disentangled his legs and climbed down from the bed. 'You seem to be busier than ever although somewhere in the not too distant past you promised me that you'd start taking things easy.'

Kate sighed, dropped the photo and slipped into a silk kimono. 'That was the plan, but the work just keeps coming.

From a career perspective, I can't just turn work away. After the baby is born, I'll have to get back to work pretty sharpish.'

Wilson stood directly in front of her. 'This work issue is not going to go away. We both have careers that we care a little too much for, but soon there'll be someone else to think about, and that could seriously affect our current lives.'

'Let's cross that bridge when we come to it,' Kate dodged past him. 'Looks like I'm going to have to get myself that coffee.'

Wilson turned, and they both raced for the kitchen.

AFTER THEY'D DRUNK their coffees, they had nestled down on the couch to watch a taped episode of the 'Graham Norton Show'. Wilson was aware of Kate glancing at regular intervals at her briefcase. An evening rarely went by without Kate seated at the desk in the living room examining legal type papers tied with different coloured ribbons. Although she was in great shape physically, Wilson had noticed that she was looking tired and sometimes when he woke, he found her already at her desk. Work was the elephant in the room, and they were going to have to confront it sooner rather than later.

WILSON WOKE to the insistent ringing of his mobile telephone. He was still sat on the couch, but Kate was no longer by his side. He looked across the living room and saw that she was sat at her desk. She turned as he came out of his nap.

'Wilson,' he said into the phone.

Kate watched him as he listened.

'I'm on my way,' he said as he shut the phone down and stood up. It was eleven o'clock at night, and he assumed that he had been asleep for more than an hour.

'Serious?' Kate asked.

He moved behind her and kissed her on the top of the

head. 'Armageddon, or something like it. You'll be reading about it in the papers. I want you in bed by eleven thirty. Chances are that I won't be back until early morning, and I don't want to find you with black circles under your eyes.' He slid his hands down and around her slightly swollen stomach. 'We want Junior to pop out on time and in good condition. Do I get a promise?'

'I promise,' she said quickly. 'What is it?'

'Someone just murdered the wrong person and created a shit storm in the process.'

CHAPTER THREE

A crowd was already gathered outside the Rice home in Malvern Street. A wide area around the small red-bricked house had been cordoned off by crime-scene tape. Wilson had already called his detective sergeant, Moira McElvaney, from the car, but she hadn't yet arrived. Five uniformed policemen from the station stood around the Victorian red-bricked house. An officer holding a clipboard guarded the entrance to the house. Wilson signed in, picked up a plastic jumpsuit and put it on.

'Bit of a mess inside, boss,' the senior uniformed officer said as Wilson finished the operation of putting the jumpsuit on.

'Is Billy inside?' Wilson asked.

'He's been shipped off to the Royal. His eyes're in a woeful state.'

Wilson stared at the policeman.

'Tear gas or something like it,' the policeman said by way of explanation. 'He got it right in the face from close range.'

'And Sammy?' Wilson asked.

'In Spain by all accounts, but you can expect him here tomorrow. Lizzie and he were close, very close.'

'So I've heard.' Wilson was aware of the role the Rice

family had played in the various Loyalist paramilitary organisations in the Shankill. Sammy Rice was no longer involved in paramilitary activities but used the skills he'd learned during the 'Troubles' to establish a criminal organisation. Lizzie and her son wielded enormous power in the area they came from. 'Let's get on with it.' Wilson pushed open the front door. He was about to step into the narrow hallway when he saw a pile of vomit directly in front of him.

'The attending officers didn't make it to the street,' the uniformed officer said.

Wilson stepped around the pile of sick and made his way towards the living room. There were two easy chairs, a small coffee table and a television. Family photographs dominated the wall space. A laminate wooden floor was an addition to the original house. The body of what was Lizzie Rice lay prone on the floor. The back of her head was gone, and the floorboards were littered with broken bone and grey slivers of watery brain. Her blonde hair was stained red with dark cranial blood and had fallen forward over the crown of her head. She looked like a broken doll. Her Union Jack plastic handbag lay beside her. To the left of her head was an enormous pile of sick. Wilson turned to the uniformed officer who had followed him into the room.

'That's Sammy's,' the policeman said. 'Looks like he was well into the cans before Lizzie got it. By the look of it he had pizza for tea.'

'Boss,' said Detective Sergeant Moira McElvaney as she stood in the doorway of the living room. She had already donned her plastic jumpsuit.

Wilson turned from the body in time to see Moira retching. 'Take it outside quick.'

Moira disappeared from the doorway, and Wilson could hear deep retching from the street. 'What's the mood of the crowd?' he asked.

'Ugly, but its early doors. The news in going around like

wildfire but nothing'll happen until Sammy gets back. Then, all hell's going to break loose. We'll be breaking out the riot gear over this one.'

'Sorry, boss.' Moira reappeared at the door. Her face was ashen, and she was wiping a gob of spittle hanging from her mouth.

'No disgrace,' Wilson said joining her. 'Someone really wanted Lizzie dead. Any sign of forensics or the pathologist.'

'Both on the way,' Moira said. 'I've never seen anything like that.'

Wilson moved into the rear of the house towards a small kitchen. There was no sign of activity. The kitchen units needed updating, and the fridge and cooker had seen better days. The family Rice didn't benefit greatly for their dedication to Ulster Unionism. He went back into the corridor and climbed the stairs to the two small bedrooms. The front bedroom measured twelve feet by nine and contained a double bed, a tallboy and a wardrobe. Wilson opened the wardrobe and saw it contained an assortment of winter clothing and a few items, mainly female, with the Union Jack motif. Billy and his wife would have required a visit by their local haberdasher if they received an invitation to the Queen's Garden Party. The back bedroom measured nine feet by seven and contained an old wooden single bed that had been slept in recently and not made up. Perhaps this was Billy's room after an evening on the cans. It was nothing out of the ordinary for the average working-class Belfast family. It was apparent that all the action had happened downstairs.

As Wilson descended the stairs, Moira was talking to a young woman clad in a white plastic over suit in the hallway. The woman was carrying the obligatory black doctor's bag.

'Boss, this is the pathologist, Professor Reid.' Moira stood aside.

'Detective Superintendent Ian Wilson,' he proffered his hand. 'Where's old Carmody?'

'Somewhere up the Zambezi,' Professor Reid took his hand. 'Gone for a year at least to help our African colleagues discern the cause of death of their stricken citizens.'

Wilson sized up the new pathologist. She was about thirty-five, had a good figure, and she was certainly attractive. She wore her curly blonde hair short. Her skin was either naturally sallow, or she had recently acquired a tan. Either way her skin colour contrasted very well with her blonde hair. 'You look too young for this game. Most of our pathologists have been old codgers.'

'Your reputation precedes you, Superintendent.'

'All good I hope,' Wilson said.

'Probably deserved,' she lifted her bag. 'Now that we've observed the preliminaries, perhaps we had better get to work.'

'I thought you were spoken for,' Moira said as soon as Reid was out of earshot.

'What?'

'There was more than a bit of flirting going on there. I don't think your very pregnant partner would appreciate it.'

'That American psychologist boyfriend of yours is having a negative effect on you. I suppose it could simply be the Catholic upbringing that sees sin everywhere you go. Get Peter on the phone and have him organise the house-to-house. Harry can set up the murder book as usual. I was thinking of making you SIO (Senior Investigating Officer) on the next murder case, but this one is too big.'

'What's with the crowd outside? And he's not my boyfriend.'

'If you want to continue to work in west Belfast, you're going to have to get up to date on your Loyalist iconography. That dead woman was once one of the most powerful women in this community. She headed the Shankill branch of the women's UVF, and she was at the front of every demonstration that took place in the 1970s and 1980s. Her husband, Billy, who is currently in the Royal Victoria Hospital where we are going next, was also a major character in the UVF but even more importantly her son, Sammy, is the current bull goose in this area.'

'That's why the crowd?'

'That's why the impending evening demonstrations just around the corner will make the fracas about what flag is flying over city hall look like a church picnic. Get on with the phone calls.'

Moira moved to the front door while Wilson returned to the living room. A forensic technician was photographing the body and the room in general. Professor Reid was standing by the door.

'No problem with cause of death,' she said as Wilson joined her.

'But I want to know what particular blunt object caused it and I want to have a decent idea of what time it happened. Her husband will be no good on time of death. Whoever killed her sent him bye byes. How soon will you have her out of here? I'm a bit nervous about the crowd. The sooner we have these people back in their houses the better.'

She nodded at the photographer. 'As soon as he's finished, we can bag her and tag her.'

'And I want those photos on my computer first thing tomorrow morning,' said Wilson as he saw the photographer toss his eyes towards heaven but decided to ignore him. He turned to Reid. 'You've covered a lot of these cases.'

'You mean why didn't I throw up like half the people who've seen her?'

Wilson thought of Moira's reaction. 'Sort of.'

'Two years with Doctors without Borders in Goma in Northern Congo can have a very serious effect on your sensibilities. This is basic stuff in comparison to the aftermath of a Mai-Mai raid on a village. The first few times I got sick and despaired of the human race. Then I just got down to the work of cataloguing the depravity.' She turned to the photographer. 'You finished yet?'

The photographer sighed, packed up his gear and headed towards the door.

'First thing tomorrow morning on my computer,' Wilson said as the photographer passed him.

'We'll have her shipped to the Royal Victoria,' Reid said. 'I'll try to schedule the autopsy for tomorrow morning, and I'll get a tech on the job of identifying the blunt object. Don't send one of your more squeamish colleagues. It could be messy. Now I'd appreciate it if you'd piss off. There's a lot of bone and brain fragments to collect. I'm sure you have something more useful to do.'

So much for the flirting, Wilson thought as he made his way back into the hallway. Maybe Moira should have seen that conversation. On second thought maybe it was better that she hadn't.

CHAPTER FOUR

Billy Rice was still in A and E at the Royal Victoria Hospital when Wilson and McElvaney arrived.

A young Pakistani doctor holding a clipboard met them at the entrance to the ward area. 'Someone sprayed his face with what was probably Mace, but we can't be sure what the composition was because it has all evaporated. However, Mace would be a good guess considering the state of his eyes. They've been burned, but they'll recover. He was so inebriated when he arrived that we had to put him on a drip. There's a mark on his head where he received a blow. It wasn't a heavy blow, and I don't think it was inflicted purposely. It's probably the result of a fall. There are two marks on his neck and some localised burning. I would estimate that he was hit with a disabling weapon like a Taser. I've seen similar marks in Pakistan.'

'A Taser, are you sure?' Wilson asked.

The young doctor nodded.

'What would the effect of being hit by the Taser be?' Moira asked.

The doctor looked at Moira. 'I thought that you people were trained on this stuff.'

'Humour me,' Moira said.

'Different people have different reaction to being Tasered. However, I assure you that it's uncomfortable. Some people compare it to touching a live electrical outlet except that it's not localised to the point of contact. It has a fuller body effect where muscular control is limited for the duration of the cycle charge. It is normally described as 'muscle lock up' because you're generally unable to move. The whole effect is not about pain but incapacitation in order to keep someone down and away from you. The pain generally goes from mild to moderate depending on the charge from the weapon.'

'But it's impossible to obtain a Taser in Great Britain,' Moira said.

'They can be bought in most of the US states,' the doctor said. 'You can even go on *YouTube* and learn to build your own. It doesn't take a genius to put a few proprietary items together, and you have the added advantage that you can add a bit of zing to the customised weapon.'

'And was Mr Rice hit with something having a little extra zing?' Wilson asked.

The doctor thought for a moment. 'Difficult to say. The fact that he was already heavily intoxicated would not have helped. That and the blow to the head could have kept him out a little longer than normal. I'm sorry, but I can't be more exact than that.'

'So, what's his condition?' Wilson asked.

'In general, his injuries are fairly light. He should be discharged sometime tomorrow.'

'Good then there's no problem in interviewing him,' Wilson said.

The doctor shook his head and pointed at the last cubicle.

Wilson pulled aside the curtain to the cubicle and ushered Moira inside. The air was redolent with the smell of stale beer and fresh farts. Billy Rice had been in the cubicle only a few hours, but he had already established his own unique environment. Lying on the bed, he resembled something like Ayers Rock. His stomach, which had always been significant, had reached gargantuan proportions since Wilson had seen him last. Two large gauze circles covered his eyes, and a drip had been inserted in his right wrist. There was a plaster on the side of his head.

'It's Detective Superintendent Wilson. How are you, Billy?' Wilson said easing the curtain around the cubicle back into position.

'Fuck you, how do ye think I am?' Rice shouted while remaining immobile. 'Lizzie's dead. Some bastard caved her head in. That boy doesn't know what they've done. Just wait till Sammy hears.'

'What happened?' Wilson asked.

'Fucked if I know. I was watched the TV, don't ask me what was on I never take a blind bit of notice of the damn thing. There's a knock at the door, and I tell them to piss off but they're not listening. I get up and open the door. As soon as the door opened the bastard sprayed some shit in my eyes, the pain drove me up the wall. They pushed me back into the living room and hit me with some electrical gizmo.'

'Lizzie wasn't at home?'

'Bingo, every Wednesday like clockwork. She normally gets home before ten.'

'And what time did the doorbell go at?'

Rice thought for a moment, and the effort seemed to tax him. 'If I'd been payin' closer attention to the TV I'd have a guess, but I was into the cans.'

'How many were there?'

'I have no idea. The minute I opened the door I was hit in the eyes. Then I was electrocuted or something, and everything went blank. It's the fucking Taigs. Lizzie was a thorn in their side for years. You drag a few Taigs into the station and beat the shit out of them until they squeal. If you don't Sammy will.'

'Why didn't they hurt you, Billy? You were heavily involved yourself.'

'Hell if I know,' some tears flowed out of his right eye.

Wilson wondered if it was the result of the spray or was Rice crying for his dead wife. If he were a betting man, he would have chosen the spray.

'Lizzie was the target. Any idea why?'

'Who can tell with the Taigs? Bloody vermin.'

'Sammy having any business problems these days?' Wilson asked.

'My son doesn't have business problems for too long. He takes care of business problems.'

'No reason why some of his associates would target Lizzie?'

Billy Rice snorted. 'Whoever did this is mad or crazy or both. You don't bash in Lizzie Rice's skull and make any long-term plans. The word'll be out on this tomorrow, and the whole of the Shankill will be looking for the bastard. And when he's found, we won't be needing the help of the peelers.'

'We'll be in touch,' Wilson said pulling back the curtain and allowing Moira to leave.

'Piss right off.'

'Just what we don't need,' Wilson said walking along the passageway between the cubicles. 'A load of idiots trying to ingratiate themselves with Sammy Rice by bringing him the head of some poor unfortunate who had nothing to do with murdering Lizzie. However, Billy is right on one count. Whoever killed Lizzie Rice is one crazy bugger. It was a high-risk murder right in the middle of a staunchly Protestant area of Belfast. It either took amazing guts or more than a little fool-hardiness.'

'What about the method?' Moira said as they made their

way to the car park. 'Surely if someone wanted to kill her, they could have used a knife or a gun.'

'That's been bothering me too. Lizzie's head was smashed to a pulp. The question is why?'

CHAPTER FIVE

Wilson's in-head alarm clock woke him at seven thirty exactly. He managed five hours of fitful sleep and had only begun to sleep properly just as his brain told him it was time to get up. He extended his arm to find that he was alone. He left the bed and without showering or dressing headed for the living room. Kate was sat at her desk a cup of steaming coffee within reach of her right hand.

'How long have you been up?' He wrapped his arms around her neck.

'Maybe twenty minutes,' she tilted her head upwards to see him.

'Liar, liar. If you don't stop, Junior is going to come out thinking lying is okay.'

'No, I'm serious. This is my first cup of coffee,' she turned to face him. 'You were remarkably quiet coming to bed last night. How did it go?'

'I'd be happy if it turns out to be just Armageddon,' he pulled her to her feet and kissed her. 'Work's finished for you this morning. Get me a coffee while I take a quick shower, and I'll fill you in.'

They sat at the breakfast bar directly across from each

other while he told her of Lizzie Rice's murder and the visit to the Royal Victoria.

'How bad is it?' she asked when he'd finished.

'There'll be people on the street tonight, a couple of cars will be burned, and some police and protesters will be injured. Tomorrow night will be worse, and things will escalate until we manage to apprehend someone.'

'And what are the chances of that?'

'Your guess is as good as mine. I hope we'll have something from forensics today, but I'm not counting on it. This murder was planned. The killer, or killers, knew when Lizzie was due home. Billy was dispatched to the fairies and the killer waited quietly until Lizzie came home. Then he smashed her head in. It took planning and daring. We're not going to find whoever did it that easily.'

Kate finished her coffee and stood up. 'I'm sorry for your trouble but I've got a busy day ahead. I'll be in court until at least four o'clock, and then I have some client meetings. I hope to make it home by eight.'

'Remember our little talk about cutting back on work, and please try to be home before the riot starts.'

LIZZIE HAD MADE the front page of the *Belfast Chronicle* and was the first item on the TV news channels. Sky even managed to get their national crime correspondent to Belfast in time to report on the early-morning news. Wilson could only imagine the level of activity at PSNI HQ. The Chief Constable and his minions would be pissing themselves at the expected fallout.

'Christ, boss,' Detective Constable Harry Graham said as Wilson entered the murder squad room at the station in the heart of the Shankill. 'Twitter is going crazy. If the idiots who create these social network sites could see the uses that they get put to, maybe they'd have had second thoughts. The riot for tonight is already organised and Sammy hasn't even appeared on the scene yet.'

'Tell me something I hadn't expected,' Wilson said heading for his office at the end of the room. He closed the glass door and laid a copy of the *Chronicle* on the desk. The details were sketchy, but the central point was that a major Loyalist figure had been brutally murdered in her home. In these days of sound bites that was all the balaclava-wearing rioters would need to know. He stared out at the five members of his team. They were all busy on their computers, but he knew that they were all waiting for him to get them into gear. Although he had been promoted to Detective Superintendent for several months, the sign that some wag had erected at the end of the room with the legend 'KEEP CALM THERE'S A NEW SUPERINTENDENT IN THE HOUSE' was still in place. He turned on his computer and looked at the list of e-mails. An e-mail from Forensics told him the crime scene photos would not be available until ten o'clock. The autopsy on Lizzie would begin at 10:30 at the Royal Victoria according to an e-mail from Professor Reid and he had a feeling that it meant 10:30 and not 10:31. And there was the frantic e-mail from his boss, Chief Superintendent Spence asking him to brief him as soon as possible since Public Relations had been banging on his door about a press conference later in the day. The forensic report would not be available until sometime during the evening. It had been given the express treatment, and if it could be sent earlier, it would be. The last e-mail he opened was from Human Resources reminding him to keep control on the overtime costs. That was a major laugh. He left his office aware of five pairs of eyes following him as he made his way to two whiteboards at the side of the room.

'Gather round children,' he said. He picked up a felt pen and wrote 'Lizzie Rice' on the top of one of the whiteboards

His team comprising Detective Sergeant Moira McElvaney and Detective Constables Harry Graham, Peter Davidson, Eric Taylor and Ronald McIver made a semi-circle with Wilson at the centre.

'Moira, briefing please.'

Moira pulled out her notebook and gave a succinct briefing of the finding of the body of Lizzie Rice at the Malvern Street house and the interview with Billy Rice.

'I have no need to remind you that this is probably the highest profile case we've ever handled,' Wilson said when McElvaney finished her briefing. 'The photos will be on the computer in an hour and the autopsy starts at 10:30. The forensics are promised by this evening.'

'You want me on the autopsy, boss?' Graham asked.

'Thanks, Harry, but I'll handle this one myself. I want you to put the hustle on the forensic guys. The sooner we have the results the better. Even something preliminary would be helpful.' He turned to Davidson. 'Peter, the house-to-house?'

'We tried to get something going last night, boss, but conditions weren't ideal. I have four uniforms available, and we'll be doing the streets in the neighbourhood in half an hour.'

'Eric, Lizzie was at the bingo last night. Check it out and see if anything out of the ordinary happen there.'

Eric Taylor nodded.

'I don't have to tell you that we're all going to feel some pressure on this one.'

'What about the overtime, boss?' Graham asked.

'More school uniforms to buy, eh Harry?' Wilson smiled. 'Although I have no confirmation from above, my guess is that overtime will not be an issue on this case.'

CHAPTER SIX

W ilson entered the Royal Victoria Hospital complex from Grosvenor Road and made his way to the car park at the rear of the mortuary building that was itself located at the hindmost section of the complex. The red and yellow brick construction of the mortuary was very much in keeping with the 19th century origins of the 'Royal' as the locals call it. Wilson entered by the portico door and was shown to autopsy room No.1, where he found Professor Reid. The corpse of Lizzie Rice was laid out naked on a stainless-steel table with channels all round to direct the flow of fluids.

'Will you stay here, or do you prefer to watch from above?' Reid nodded towards the viewing area at the end of the room.

'And good morning to you too, professor.'

'Up or down, your choice. But if you decide to stay here, I suggest you gown up. I'm not an expert on men's fashion, but that suit looks like it might have cost more than a few hundred pounds. It'd be a shame to wreck it in the name of justice.'

Reid's male assistant already held a green set of surgical scrubs in his hand, and Wilson quickly climbed into it.

Reid pulled down the microphone that was located above the table. 'This is the autopsy of Elizabeth Rice. The subject is a female of approximately fifty-five years. Although the injuries she sustained, which caused her death are to her head, I will begin by examining the internal organs.' She picked up a scalpel and made a long incision straight down the corpse's sternum. Then she picked up the rotating saw.

One hour later, Reid pushed up the microphone and moved towards a rack of washbasins in the corner of the room. She removed her surgical hat and gave her blonde hair a toss. Then she removed two bloodstained gloves from her hands and tossed them into a bin located beneath the washbasin. She removed the rest of the surgical garb and thoroughly washed her hands.

'A very professional performance,' Wilson said dumping his scrubs into a basket.

'You got the gist I suppose,' she said.

'You mean the bit about the tumour in the lungs and the embryonic tumours in the pancreas.'

'Elizabeth Rice would have been dead in six to twelve months if someone hadn't bothered to murder her. '

'Unfortunately, they weren't to know that, and they wanted to make sure that she died. Do you have time for a coffee?'

'Sorry, the next client is about to be wheeled in. This one appears to have died naturally, but we shall have to wait and see.'

'What about the blows to the head?'

'They accomplished their purpose. My assistant will take an impression, and we'll send it to the pathology lab. We should have some idea of what the blunt instrument was, but I wouldn't like to speculate any further except to say that it was something very heavy. Given that the impacts came from behind and the strikes appear to have been right to left. I'd say you're looking for someone who is right-handed. But you'd already deduced that from my commentary.'

'I'm at least that much of a detective. Anything else worth noting?'

'Other than the fact that this woman ruined her body with cigarettes and booze?'

'Yes.'

'I'll review the transcript of the tape later and if anything strikes me, I'll get on to you. '

They both turned as a gurney entered the room with an enormous naked man on it.

'Duty calls,' she said accepting a new surgical outfit from her assistant. She nodded at the man on the gurney. 'And somebody is wondering why he got a massive heart attack.'

CHAPTER SEVEN

The crime scene photos arrived, and a set was already attached to one of the whiteboards. Wilson went into his office and opened a copy of the photos on his computer. He went through them one by one, enlarging them as he went. He didn't note anything of significance, but he decided to wait for the full forensic report. He was still examining the photos when his phone rang.

'My office, now,' Chief Superintendent Spence, the boss of the station was not noted for being long winded.

Two minutes later and three flights of stairs higher, Wilson knocked on Spence's office door and entered. The Chief Superintendent was seated at his desk. He had dispensed with his uniform jacket, his black tie was loosened, and the top button on his shirt was open. Things were indeed serious when the Chief Super could be considered to be casually dressed.

'What a royal screw-up,' he said nodding at the chair in front of his desk. 'Please tell me that we're making some progress.'

'I'm just back from the autopsy,' said Wilson as he flopped onto the proffered chair. He had worked with Spence for five years, and they were not only colleagues but also friends. And given Wilson's relationship with PSNI HQ, he needed every friend he could get. Spence was eight months away from the compulsory retirement age of sixty-five. He had a full head of grey hair, and his obsession with golf had kept a paunch at bay. 'The bloody bugger jumped the gun,' Wilson continued. 'Lizzie was riddled with cancer and would have been dead in six to twelve months. Peter Davidson is organising a house-to-house but since I haven't heard from him, I must assume that nothing has surfaced so far. There are no CCTV cameras in Malvern Street, but we're checking the available CCTV in the area. I wouldn't hold out too much hope though.'

'You mean to tell me that someone just breezed into the Shankill and killed a prominent Loyalist and then buggered off and nobody saw anything.'

'That conclusion is a bit premature. We have all our resources out there, but it doesn't look fantastic.'

'The DCC has organised a press conference for 1500 hours. He wanted to catch the late editions of the newspapers.'

'And the six o'clock TV news, no doubt.'

Spence smiled. 'We'll need a statement, so draft something positive that the DCC can say. We hear that there'll be two to three hundred rioters on the street tonight. Send me the draft and I'll forward it to HQ so that the spin doctors can get at it. Any news of Sammy?'

Wilson stood up. 'We're expecting the explosion any minute.'

ALTHOUGH WILSON WASN'T aware of it, the explosion was already taking place four floors below in the reception area of the station. Wilson's mobile rang as he was descending the stairs to the murder squad room.

'Help,' the desk sergeant said simply.

A mini riot was taking place in the reception area by the

time Wilson arrived. Sammy Rice's blond locks were in full flow as he flung every manner of invective at the desk sergeant. The former leader of the UVF in west Belfast was surrounded by five of his leather-jacketed troops who were adding to the commotion as much as they could. The desk sergeant who was no shrinking violet himself had stood back from the counter separating him from the mini mob.

'OK, everyone shut the hell up,' Wilson shouted at the top of his voice. 'Everybody out except him,' he pointed at Sammy Rice. For a moment, there was a stunned silence. Just as the shouting was about to begin again Wilson said, 'I'm going to arrest every man still in the reception area in one minute and charge them with affray. Sergeant put Mr Rice in the 'soft' interrogation room, and I'll join him there in five minutes. If these men are still here in one minute, call out the station and have them all arrested including Mr Rice.'

Wilson waited until he saw Sammy give the troops the signal to disperse.

WILSON CARRIED two cups of coffee as he entered the 'soft' interrogation room. He placed one in front of Sammy Rice and one on the other side of the table. He held out his hand. 'Condolences on Lizzie. I'm sorry for your trouble.'

Rice took the proffered hand and shook it.

Wilson sat down and blew on the coffee before tasting it. 'Canteen crap,' he said nodding at the cup. 'The coffee machine is bust.' He looked at Rice – the blond hair, the tan, the designer jeans and leather jacket. Rice had put on a bit of weight since Wilson had last seen him. The additional weight gave Rice's unlined face a cherubic look. It was a face that totally belied the nature of its owner. Rice wouldn't have got to where he was without being a thug. But he was a thug with a brain. Wilson knew that men with that combination could be very dangerous. Right now, Rice was taking on the mantle of the grieving son.

'She was a feisty auld mare,' Rice said lifting his coffee cup and followed Wilson's example by blowing on the liquid before tasting it. 'But she didn't deserve to be battered to death in her own home.'

'I know it's no consolation, but she was on her way out anyway. The pathologist did an autopsy this morning. She was riddled with cancer and had six months, maybe twelve. I'll get you a copy of the findings when it's available.'

'When can I see her?'

'She's in the mortuary at the Royal. I'll make the arrangements whenever you're ready. I'd wait a while if I were you. I'm afraid she's not a pretty sight.'

'I already talked to the auld boy,' he sipped the coffee. 'I hear that she's a bit of a mess.'

'That's putting it mildly. We'll get whoever did it.' Wilson tried to put a confidence into his voice that he didn't feel.

'Aye, you'd better. Because if you don't, I will and the kind of people I'll put on the streets won't be wearing kid gloves. The point here is not that someone waltzed into the Shankill and murdered Lizzie Rice. The point is that someone waltzed into the Shankill and murdered Sammy Rice's mother. That can't be allowed to happen.'

'Was it about you or her?'

'You think the Taigs were involved or one of my associates maybe?'

'What do you think?'

'Count the Taigs out. They wouldn't bother with yesterday's news. Lizzie might have been a target twenty years ago but not today. And I've no problem with the Taigs right now. Killin' each other is bad for business. I'll be checkin' out my associates myself. Ye haven't a fuckin' clue, have ye?'

'It's early days. We're still looking at possible lines of enquiry.'

Sammy drained his coffee cup. 'You're not a fool, Mr Wilson, far from it. The boys'll be on the streets this evenin'. There'll be some ruckin' and a few motors'll be burned. They'll be out there every night until you catch the bastard who murdered my mother. My advice is to get your arse in gear and get someone behind bars.'

'I think it would be more useful if we didn't have to expend vital resources keeping your people in check. Why don't you call off the dogs until the funeral is over?'

'You people need to feel the pressure,' said Rice as he stood up. 'You're right, shit coffee,' he said on the way to the door.

CHAPTER EIGHT

W̱ilson's team assembled at two o'clock in the afternoon to review the progress on the case. The whiteboard now contained a picture of Lizzie as she had been before someone had cleaved her head in. A selection of crime scene photos of the living room was set out beneath and a map of the area around Malvern Street.

'Peter, nothing from the house to house?' Wilson asked.

'Not a sausage, boss. All sorts of people were going hither and thither, but nothing concrete.'

'Moira, what about CCTV?'

Moira moved to the whiteboard and pointed at the map. 'Nothing inside the streets behind the Shankill. The first CCTV point is where the Shankill Road meets the Westlink.'

'The city fathers don't give a bugger about the Shankill,' Harry Graham said. 'The Safer Belfast CCTV scheme covers only the area around the university. Let's take care of the students but leave the other poor buggers with no cover.'

Wilson turned to McIver. 'Ronald, anything on threats to Lizzie?'

McIver coughed to clear his throat. 'She's been out of the public gaze for a while except for a few sorties during the flag protests. It's all the young people now, boss. Nobody has given a shit about Lizzie for quite a long time.'

'Keep on it. Check with her friends. See how things were with Billy. It's a bit convenient him being sprayed with Mace and then conked out during the murder. We need to know everything about Lizzie. She was the target and there must be a reason. We need to find that reason.'

CHIEF SUPERINTENDENT DONALD SPENCE stood next to Wilson as both watched Deputy Chief Constable Roy Jennings press the flesh of the large contingent of reporters gathered in the press centre at PSNI headquarters. Judging from the number of journalists present, and the number of TV stations represented the world had not forgotten Lizzie Rice or her fight to keep Ulster British. Her murder and its method were big news.

'That's the way to make it in our game,' Spence said nodding in the direction of Jennings.

'That's the way to make it in every game,' Wilson said. 'The shit always rises.'

'Some day, Ian, someday,' Spence said. 'That wee bastard is going to have your guts for garters.'

'Aye, but I'll be ready to go by then. And he'll not have an easy ride.'

It was five minutes to three o'clock, and the PSNI press officer was gradually getting the assembled journalists to take their seats. The hubbub was decreasing when Jennings indicated to his junior officers that they could join him at the top of the room. The DCC was wearing his dress uniform as was the Chief Super. Wilson was dressed in plain clothes, that is if one could consider a white Boss shirt with a blue Armani tie and a grey Canali suit plain. Jennings led the way to the top of the room followed by Spence with Wilson bringing up the rear. An outsider might think that the line-up had been decreed by height rather than status. Jennings stood at five foot six in his platform shoes; Spence was a healthy 6ft while Wilson towered over both at 6ft 3ins. They reached the podium and sat behind the cardboard triangles bearing their names. Jennings had centre stage.

'Ladies and Gentlemen,' he began. 'First on behalf of the Police Service of Northern Ireland I would like to extend our condolences to the family of Elizabeth Rice. We are appalled that such a prominent member of the Loyalist community could be so viciously murdered in her own home.' Jennings allowed a pregnant pause for his words to sink in. 'As many of you will be aware, the Senior Investigating Officer on the case will be Detective Superintendent Ian Wilson, head of the murder squad. Superintendent Wilson is one of our most experienced officers and is currently following several lines of enquiry. We are hopeful for an early arrest. I would like to take this opportunity to request the Loyalist community to remain calm. Early indications are that there is no sectarian aspect to this heinous crime. A disproportionate response from the Loyalist community will not help this investigation and will only divert resources from crime prevention. I would, never-theless, call on any person who has direct or indirect informa-tion concerning this crime to phone the Crime busters phone line. Thank you.'

Wilson was pleased that he hadn't been called on to say a few words since there was very little he could have added. He would have sprouted the usual tosh about his team being totally committed to solving the Elizabeth Rice murder. He looked at the mass of journalists who started to raise their hands, and he saw a figure he recognised. Maggie Cummer-ford, the former crime reporter of the *Belfast Chronicle*, was staring directly at him. Wilson hadn't seen her for months and had assumed that his insistence that she retract an article concerning a Professional Services Division investigation into his handling of the arrest of his former boss put paid to her career. Their eyes linked together, and she slowly raised her right hand and made a childlike goodbye wave at him. Wilson simply smiled and turned to see that the DCC was fielding questions. This was a risky business, but every answer from Jennings would prove just how on top of things he was. Wilson was tempted to stand up and leave, but that might be seen as a sign of disdain for his superior. Fuck it, he thought and stood up. He walked slowly out of the Press Room leaving Jennings in full flow.

CHAPTER NINE

The meeting of the Murder Squad team at six o'clock that evening represented the end of the first day of the investigation into Lizzie Rice's murder. The riot, or more correctly the embryonic riot, had already kicked off in the Shankill and rush-hour traffic was being diverted. The signs were ominous. It was going to be a long night for the thin blue line. Wilson hadn't heard from Kate, and he was hoping that she was following his advice concerning getting home early. He also hadn't eaten and was equally hoping that Kate had the foresight to think about dinner. Since they both had taxing professional lives, the fridge was generally found wanting when an impromptu meal had to be put together. Thank God someone invented takeaway.

'Peter, anything?' Wilson asked.

Peter Davidson didn't even bother to answer. He simply shook his head.

'The forensic report has arrived, boss,' Moira said. 'There's a copy on your computer, and I've been going through it for most of the afternoon. It looks like Billy Rice's evidence was on the spot. They found evidence of a mace-like substance on the door. There is evidence of someone grabbing at the wall in the hallway corroborating Billy's statement. Most of the finger-prints in the house were Billy's and Lizzie's although there are quite a few others. Eliminating the other prints is going to be a nightmare, although four sets of the fingerprints found belonged to Sammy Rice and three of his cronies.'

'Check them out for alibis,' Wilson said.

'Already on it, boss,' Moira said. 'There was a mass of blood around, all of it Lizzie's. There were as we know no defensive wounds on her hands so it's safe to say that she was attacked from behind. There could be no resistance after the first blow.' Moira was about to continue when her mobile phone rang. She pressed the green button and listened, then cut the line. 'Pathology lab. They've been in contact with forensics. It appears that your new best friend, Professor Reid, sent them a cast from Lizzie's head wound. They haven't completed their investigations, but it looks like the assailant used a ball hammer, whatever that is.'

'It's a very wicked tool and an interesting choice of weapon,' Wilson said. 'I have only three preliminary conclusions. One, Lizzie was the specific target. She was not a victim of circumstance. Billy was lying prone on a chair, and he wasn't harmed other than being zapped with a Taser and possibly given a blow to the head. Someone wanted Lizzie and Lizzie alone. Second conclusion concerns the wound and the choice of weapon. The murderer wanted Lizzie's head caved in. There was no stabbing or shooting. It was a premeditated attack on the head. Why only Lizzie and why was the head so important? If we can answer those two questions, we will have some idea who the murderer might be. Three, the use of Mace and a Taser-like weapon to disable Billy. This is someone who either knows something about physiology or who has done some research. That means it could be any of the million people in Northern Ireland who can use the Internet. Personally, I don't think that any of these questions will be answered easily. That's where we must go. It's in Lizzie's background. Now we must find it. Anything else?'

The team remained silent.

'First thing tomorrow morning, we start on Lizzie. I want to know everything about her from the day she was born until the day she died.' Wilson returned to his office and switched on his computer. A list of fifty e-mails ran along the page.

'Want to see the press conference?' Moira asked from the door.

Wilson glanced at his watch. 'It's over.'

Moira held up a tablet computer. 'The wonders of technology.'

They watched a rerun of the press conference. The TV camera caught his departure and DCC Jennings' reaction to it.

Wilson smiled. 'I'm going to pay for that.'

'You're incorrigible.'

'That's a big word like arsehole.'

'There are ladies present. How's the baby coming along?'

Wilson explained the photo from the scan and his difficulty discerning a baby in it.

'You're not only incorrigible; you're also a Neanderthal. You know the guy I've been seeing lately.'

'The good Dr Guilfoyle.'

'It's Professor Guilfoyle to you. He'd like to meet you.'

Wilson raised his eyebrows. 'Surely a member of your own family should handle the 'my intentions are honourable' conversation.'

'He's a clinical psychologist, and he's done some work for the FBI.'

Wilson's eyes rose for the second time.

'I know how you feel about profilers and the like, but Brendan is just interested. I think he finds the criminal scene in Belfast a little tame and Lizzie Rice's murder is a bright spot in his otherwise boring lecture schedule.'

'Not a consultation,' Wilson said. 'A drink.'

'Agreed. Can I show him the crime scene photos?'

'If you take them home this evening to examine them, make sure nobody outside the team sees them.'

'Understood. Tomorrow evening for the drink.'

'Unless the Loyalists set the town on fire.'

Moira exited the office, and Wilson was left alone with his thoughts. And those thoughts turned to riots. Every time either the Loyalists or Republicans didn't like something they would take to the streets. Groups preparing to riot throughout the world should first employ one of the professional rioters from Belfast to train up the learner-rioters in their country. A subject for the riot was not necessary. The recent 'flag riots' were one of the best examples. The streets of Belfast were turned into a mess because the city fathers had decided to fly a flag only on certain days of the year over city hall. So what, said the majority of the population. Not so, said the professional rioters. Their itchy fingers sped to their mobile phones or their tablets and Twitter was alive with arrangements to riot. Times and places were transmitted and for the uninitiated rioter, a Google map could be appended. Technology was shown to be riot-friendly. With great reluctance, Wilson returned to his computer. He would give the blasted e-mails one hour of his time.

CHAPTER TEN

Sammy Rice walked away from the mortuary at the Royal Victoria Hospital. He hadn't liked what he had seen. Someone had really gone after the poor auld biddy. They had cleaned her up and they had tried to hide her injuries by covering the back of her head, but he had insisted on seeing the full extent of the damage. He was no stranger to death, but this was something else. A bullet in the back of the head was Sammy's style. He didn't hold with the hands-on stuff, although he had those in his employ who would positively salivate when they got the opportunity to inflict pain. Lizzie wasn't the best mother in the world, but she'd been his mother and that's what counted. She had fed him and clothed him and, on the weekend,, she'd combed the lice out of his hair and squeezed them between the nails of her thumbs. She brought him up as a good Loyalist. He believed Wilson and the pathologist about the cancer. Lizzie smoked like a chimney and drank like a fish, so he supposed it was inevitable that some form of cancer would catch up with her eventually. He hadn't shed a tear over her not because he didn't think it was manly, but because he hadn't felt grief at her passing. He was more pissed that his holiday had been interrupted than at the fact that he had seen the woman who had bore him lying on a cold slab. The fucked-up holiday wasn't the only thing that was pissing Sammy off. His control of the Loyalist enclave of West Belfast and the financial benefits that flowed from that control depended on his personal prestige. His position as a Godfather had been established and cemented by the ruthless way he climbed the ladder and how he dealt with pretenders to his throne. The fact that someone had the audacity to murder his mother was a direct threat to his prestige and by extension his position. He would have to be seen to deal effectively and viciously with whoever had killed Lizzie. That meant he would have to get his hands on the murderer before the peelers. He would have been confident of that if it was anyone other than Wilson who was investigating the murder. He had several informants in Wilson's station, and he owned them body and soul. He would get his people on the ground to start beating the bushes to see what they might flush out. He would find out what track Wilson was on and he would try to get ahead of him. And when he found the fucker who tried to piss in his ear, he would hand him over to people who would do things to him that would make him wish he had never been born.

'IT'S KICKIN' off,' Ivan McIlroy, Rice's lieutenant, said with a smile as he entered the back room of the Black Bear public house which was Sammy Rice's office.

'Fat fuckin' good it'll do,' Rice said

'The boys are out to make a point,' McIlroy sat down at the table with Rice. 'You can't swan into the Shankill and kill a Loyalist. It also gives them a bit of diversion. Are you goin' to turn up?'

'Are you out of your fuckin' tree? I'm grievin' for my poor dead mother.' Rice lifted a glass of whiskey and downed the contents. He looked over at the corner of the room where Billy

Rice sat slumped in a chair. 'What a fuckin' lump of shit. That I would end up like that. Toss a whiskey into the cunt.'

McIlroy nodded at the barman who brought a whiskey and laid it before Rice's father.

'We have a real fuckin' problem here, Ivan. That tosser,' he nodded in the direction of his father. 'Has no fuckin' idea what happened. He saw nothing and heard nothing. Drunk as a skunk. He's about as much use to us as a fridge is to an Eskimo. We must get to our people in the peelers. We need to know exactly what Wilson is up to. I want a copy of everything that he has. The photos, the forensic report, what line of enquiry he's following. Everything. We'll keep the pressure up with the riots every evening except on the day of the funeral. I want you to spread the word among the troops. Anyone who brings me information about the murderer will be taken care of.'

'What about the Taigs?' Ivan asked.

'It's possible but why would they bother? What would they have to gain? It's more likely someone on our side. Maybe McGreery wants to muscle in. Maybe he'd like to show that I'm not the force I once was. '

Maybe if you didn't spend so much time in Spain, McIlroy thought but didn't say.

'You should have seen her head, Ivan. Someone wanted her dead very badly.'

'If he's out there we'll find him.'

'I don't just want to find him. I want him here and when I get him, I'm goin' to put his balls in a vice and squeeze until they burst.'

CHAPTER ELEVEN

It was nearing eight-thirty when Wilson opened the door to the apartment he shared with Kate McCann. Since a mini-riot was taking place on the doorstep of the police station, it had taken him some time to get away. The riot hadn't really developed along the usual lines and had consisted more of a protest by residents that one of their own had been murdered in her home. There was a storm out there, and it probably wouldn't burst until the killer was found. As Wilson opened the door, he heard voices coming from the living room. That could only mean that Kate was holding a meeting. Which meant that it was probably the committee she formed to pressure the Northern Assembly and the British Government to set up a Truth and Reconciliation Commission. It was a subject on which they had opposing views, and he needed to listen to her committee's ramblings like he needed a hole in the head. His heart sank and for a moment he thought of retracing his steps and heading for the local hostelry. Instead, he simply sighed and marched straight into what he perceived to be the lion's den. There were three strangers seated with Kate at their living-room table. A series of papers was spread out across the table and for a few moments the group were unaware of his presence so engrossed were they in their meeting.

'Ian,' Kate finally noticed his presence. She tried him with her most dazzling smile. Please don't make a scene, it said. 'We're just about to wrap up.'

'Don't let me interrupt you,' Wilson said.

'Let me introduce you to the other members of the committee.' She turned to the three people at the table. 'This is George Carney from the Human Rights Group, Greg Ferris from Worldwide Watch and Ellie Smith, who has just joined us from South Africa. My partner Ian Wilson.'

'Pleased to meet you,' Wilson said pleasantly. He was a little dismayed that one of Kate's hobbyhorses was raising its ugly head again. From time to time, she and other like-minded citizens would attempt to repeat the South African example of dragging the miscreants responsible for the 'Troubles' before a committee of their peers and have them recant their evil ways. Wilson didn't think she had a hope in hell of getting such a committee off the ground. Ulster was not South Africa.

The group at the table were clearing up their papers. The two men packed their briefcases, briefly shook hands with Wilson and departed. Wilson noted that the woman, Ellie Smith, hung back slightly.

'Ellie wanted specifically to meet you,' Kate said as the two women approached him.

Wilson looked at the woman at Kate's side. She had dark hair cut in pageboy fashion and an angular face that obviously didn't smile too much. No feature stood out. Her eyes were brown but not sparkling, her nose was neither big nor small, and her mouth was a thin line with virtually no lip showing. The one feature that struck Wilson was her physique. She was at least five feet nine and had shoulders to match. He guessed that she was somewhere in her late thirties.

'Oh, and why is that,' Wilson held out his hand.

'Two reasons,' Ellie Smith had a distinct South African

accent. She took his hand and shook it vigorously. 'I was brought up in the Transvaal and you know how we are about rugby. I saw you play for Ireland when you toured SA. You were way ahead of your time.'

Wilson had heard this so many times that he didn't bother to blush. 'And the second reason?' he asked.

'I'm a criminologist, and I hear that you're the top gun in the local detective world.'

Wilson glanced at Kate. 'And who might have told you that?'

'It's the word around,' Smith said smiling. 'Don't worry Kate is a paragon of discretion when it comes to you.

'Ellie worked with the South African Truth and Reconciliation Commission, and she's also a bit of an athlete,' Kate said. 'She swam for South Africa internationally.'

Ergo those shoulders, Wilson thought.

'I saw you on the television this evening,' Smith continued. 'You're the SIO on the murder of that woman in the Shankill. The killing is still going on here?'

'I don't think that this one is sectarian,' Wilson said simply. 'It's always a possibility. I'm sure scores are still being settled in South Africa. What about that Terreblanche fellow?'

'Some resentments run deep,' Smith said. 'Our psyches are strange things. That's what reconciliation is all about. Unless we can reconcile the hurt that's been done to us the wound festers, and bad things can ensue. I've outstayed my welcome. You really were something on the field.'

'I was my pleasure and a lot of fun,' Wilson said.

'I hope we meet again,' Smith said. 'We could have a good natter about rugby.

'I am going to have to tie you up,' Wilson said to Kate as soon as they were alone. 'You're supposed to be slowing down not taking things on, and this Truth and Reconciliation thing is going precisely nowhere. You're twenty years too late. Most of the principals on the Ulster side are dead, and most of the principals on the mainland are tending roses in Sussex and have no interest in exposing their wrongdoing. Unlike the South Africans, the Irish don't want to remember: They're still busy trying to forget.'

'That's so bloody typical of you,' Kate was more than usually brisk in stuffing papers into her briefcase. 'Anything I believe in doesn't count. You're trying to control me. You've made me pregnant and now you want to decide what I should think. Soon you'll want me to give up my stupid job so that I can stay at home and take care of your child.'

'You're a brilliant barrister with a fantastic future but this reconciliation idea is a caprice,' he hoped this would soothe her. He wasn't ready for a session with an angry Kate McCann. 'Stick to what you do well. Our lives are about to change in a way that neither of us can understand. We're going to have a real living breathing other human being to take care of. Right now, you need to be making allowances for the future by focusing on what's absolutely necessary.'

'And, of course, I suppose you're the judge of what's absolutely necessary'. The colour rose in Kate's cheeks. 'I saw the way you preened when Ellie mentioned your television appearance. I suppose that was part of your focusing.'

'Think about it, Kate. I know you believe in what you're doing but the powers that be don't want it. They've never wanted it. Sometimes you have to let something you really believe in go.'

'And you've experienced this?'

'I wanted to get the people behind some of the murders I investigated but for various reasons, they were not to be got. I believe in justice, but we can't always have it. I'm a pragmatist.'

'Or a coward.'

Wilson was stunned.

'I'm sorry,' Kate said quickly. 'That was supposed to hurt, I shouldn't have said it. You're the finest and most honest man I've ever met. It's just that I want to contribute.'

'You will. But not by tilting at windmills.'

'How about this is my last tilt?'

He smiled and threw his arms around her and kissed her hard on the lips. 'The last tilt, OK,' he said when they disengaged.

'I'm sorry about the preening remark. You looked very handsome on TV.'

Wilson did his best impression of someone preening. 'Now I definitely need my pre-dinner drink.'

'Oh, dinner?'

CHAPTER TWELVE

Brendan Guilfoyle, Visiting Professor of Psychology at Queens University, sat cross-legged and naked on the bed in Moira McElvaney's apartment. He and Moira had eaten dinner and then made love and now he was sitting examining the Lizzie Rice murder scene photos.

Moira ran her fingers along his back. 'I think you only came here this evening because of those photos.'

'Nonsense,' he turned a photo over. 'I needed dinner because I hadn't eaten all day.'

She pulled him back onto her making sure not to damage the photos. She loved the soft lilt of his Boston accent. 'I am going to kill you, Brendan Guilfoyle.'

'Well if you do, please choose another method than our friend in these photos.' He kissed her lightly and put the photos carefully on the floor beside the bed. 'Round two,' he announced as he pulled her on top of him.

'Now that's what I call a good old-fashioned murder,' Brendan said when they had finished making love. 'I love a bludgeoning. It's so basic, so much a part of our simian past. And very, very personal.'

'Wilson wasn't totally convinced about meeting you,' she puffed up the pillows behind her head.

'And I cannot wait to meet him. I'm sick of hearing about the great man. And I'm more than a little jealous. You have blown this guy up so high that I feel like accusing you of hero worship. You haven't fucked this guy, have you?'

Moira looked harshly at him.

He smiled. 'OK, you haven't fucked him, but you've wanted to.'

Moira reddened.

' My God I'm right. I bet I'm right.'

'You self-righteous American bastard. You can psycho-analyse your students but keep your grubby mind off me.'

'I saw the guy on TV today, and I don't really blame you.'

She aimed a playful punch at him.

'Seriously, he looks the part. The other two guys were hogging the limelight especially, the little guy who looks like a leprechaun on speed. Your buddy dominated the screen. I bet every lady in the audience was ogling him. And you say he's smart too. My God, how did you manage to keep your hands off him?'

'He's spoken for,' Moira swung her legs over the edge of the bed. 'His partner is beautiful, sexy and one of the top barristers in Ulster. And she's pregnant.'

'Barrister, that's a lawyer, right?'

Moira smiled and nodded. She was getting very fond of Brendan Guilfoyle. He was intelligent and funny and a whole lot better in bed than her ex-husband. Sometimes she wondered where it was all going. Brendan was only in Belfast for one year. Then he would be returning to his real life at Harvard, while she would still be chasing miscreants around the dingy back streets of Belfast. She was happier than she had been for some time. Although she was enjoying the banter with Brendan concerning Wilson, she was also realising that there might be something to it.

Maybe she spoke too much about him to Brendan and God forbid some of her colleagues. Wilson was always going to be out of reach for her. Brendan was her here and now, and she was going to enjoy every minute with him.' Coffee or round three,' she asked.

'What's that expression you guys have 'need you ask'?'

CHAPTER THIRTEEN

Wilson rose earlier than usual. He had been awake since six o'clock and had decided to get up and go for an early-morning jog along the Embankment. He loved it not only because it blew away the cobwebs of sleep, but he was able to mull over what was on his mind as his feet pounded the pavement. Although he had learned to disguise his limp when he walked, he had never, and would never, regain the fluidity in his running style he had had before his injury. As he started his run, his mind was focused on Lizzie Rice's murder and the possible motivations behind the killing of a woman in her mid-sixties who had been for some considerable time in the waste basket of Ulster's politics. He would have to put the issues of motive on the backburner until he knew more about Lizzie's life. He was quite sure that there was more than one skeleton in Lizzie's cupboard, and he would have to dislodge them all before he could discount them as possible motivations. As his feet pounded the concrete, he considered the past day and the information they had gleaned. He concluded that they were no nearer to finding the killer than they had been the previous morning. Murder investigations were a process, and as with any process there had to be forward momentum. Standing still was not an option. Every day would have to show some progress in identifying the killer. He was well into his fifth kilometre when his mind switched from Lizzie Rice to Kate. Their conversation of the previous evening troubled him. Was his concern with Kate's working life really centred on the well-being of their unborn child or was she right in thinking that he was trying to control her? He was in no doubt that she believed it was the latter although the accusation had come out in the heat of argument. He tried to examine his motives. Did he really want to curtail Kate's professional life because he wanted to turn her into a wife and mother? She was one of the most brilliant lawyers of her generation. She would, in the not too distant future, be offered a place on the Bench with the possibility to contribute not only to the dispensing of law but also to the making of law. Did he really want to deny her that future? He was still struggling with the answers to these questions when he reached their apartment. He would have time for a shower, and then he'd make Kate breakfast as a peace offering. The smell of frying eggs greeted his nostrils as he pushed open the door to the apartment.

'You're just in time,' Kate called from the kitchen. 'Ham and cheese omelette alright?'

'Perfect, along with a coffee. Let me get out of these sweaty clothes and grab a quick shower. I'll be with you in five.'

He was still perspiring when he joined Kate at the breakfast bar in the kitchen.

'My perfect wife,' he said kissing her on the lips.

'Let's not go there. It's only an omelette and coffee.'

He looked at her and was delighted to see that the smile was not only on her lips but also in her eyes.

'What's on the agenda for today?' he asked.

'Court, court and even more court. I have a nice juicy drugs case, and I'm meeting a client in Government later who is having trouble explaining away some of his expense claims.

Apparently, the prosecution would like to lock the poor chap up just because he stole a lot of taxpayers' money.'

'How inconsiderate of the prosecution. Don't they know the reason that most people enter politics is to rip off their fellow citizens?'

'You're a cynic. They enter politics to serve. What does your day look like?'

'More of the same although I hope that we'll be spared another press conference. Has the *Chronicle* arrived?'

Kate retrieved it from the shelf under the bar. 'I was hoping to avoid this,' she said placing the newspaper on the bar beside him.

The mini riot in the Shankill pushed Lizzie off the front page of the *Belfast Chronicle*. Lizzie's murder had, of course, been mentioned as a major contributing factor to the riot but the article pointed out that the spokesmen for the rioters voiced several other issues of concern to the Loyalist community. The report on the PSNI press conference had been relegated to page three, and the accompanying photo had been a stock shot of Wilson. That would not go down well with the powers at HQ.

'Don't forget that we're expected at the opening of that new art gallery in Donegall Street. Seven o'clock, latest.'

Wilson closed the paper and put it away. He forked a piece of omelette into his mouth. 'It looks like my day could be even worse than I anticipated.'

CHAPTER FOURTEEN

Wilson held a briefing at nine o'clock in the squad room. There was nothing new to report overnight. Moira had been put in charge of looking into Lizzie's life, and she had delegated much of the work to Ronald McIver, who was the 'Mister Research' of the team. Peter Davidson was out on another round of house-to-house enquiries while Harry Graham was following up on the forensics report. Wilson was worried by the lack of progress. There were no sightings of people going in or out of the Rice house. There had been buckets of blood flying all over the place and there was no doubt that the killer would have got some of it on his clothes. The mace, pepper spray or CS could have been brought in from abroad or could have been manufactured at home from components bought at a local Tesco. The same could be said for the Taser so pursuing them would be a dead end. The only avenue of enquiry was Lizzie herself.

Just as Wilson was about to delve into the pleasures of his administrative tasks, his phone rang. 'You and I are wanted at HQ,' Chief Superintendent Spence announced. 'I'll meet you outside in five minutes.'

Wilson took one look at the e-mails on his screen and for once wished he had been left alone to deal with them.

A copy of the *Belfast Chronicle* sat on Deputy Chief Constable Jennings' desk when Spence and Wilson entered. The DCC did not invite either man to sit, but Spence took the initiative and sat in one of the chairs in front of the DCC's desk. He looked at Wilson, who was still standing and then put on a pleading face. Wilson understood and sat in the other chair.

'First thing this morning I received a call from the Chief Constable,' Jennings began. 'The Secretary of State for Northern Ireland, and the First Minister, already called him. Then I received a call from the Minister for Justice.' He tapped the front page of the newspaper. 'They all want to know what we're doing about these riots. All I can tell them is that my SIO is wandering around in the dark with his proverbial thumb up his arse.'

Wilson stiffened and Spence rested a hand on his arm.

'I briefed you last evening, sir,' Spence said in his most moderate and diplomatic tone. 'The whole resources of the Murder Squad and many uniformed officers are committed to the investigation. So far, we've a drawn a blank on the house to house. The victim's husband has been unable to provide us with any clues as to who the assailant might be or what the motivation for the attack might be. You're right, for the moment, we are wandering around in the dark.'

Jennings looked down from his desk. The DCC was short at five feet six but had arranged for his desk and chair to be elevated above his visitors. He pinched the top of his nose. 'Perhaps nobody has told you that there are rioters on the streets. And there will continue to be rioters on the street until you get your act together. I want Lizzie Rice's killer found and put behind bars before things on the street get out of hand.'

'We're currently looking for a lead to follow,' Spence said.

Jennings looked directly at Wilson. 'And what leads would they be, pray tell?'

Wilson would have preferred to let Spence carry the ball. 'The crime appears to be centred on Lizzie, so we need to know why the killer picked her in particular. I have my team trawling through her life looking for someone who might have a reason to kill her.'

Jennings sneered. 'Try half the Catholic population of Belfast. The Rice family have been synonymous with attacks on Catholic homes. I assume that you have pursued this particular line of enquiry?'

DCC Jennings had never led an investigation in his twenty-five years on the Force, and Wilson was about to tell him so when he felt Spence's hand on his arm again. 'We don't think that the crime was sectarian,' he said simply.

'But you can't say for sure. I would be grateful if you pursued this line of enquiry at least.'

Again, the pressure on Wilson's arm. 'Yes, sir.'

'I've been in contact with the coroner,' Jennings said. 'He's already received the report from the pathologist, and of course he intends to hold an inquest. However, I have prevailed on him to release the body for burial. He can hold the inquest later, but it's important that we get this wretched woman in the ground as soon as possible. Maybe that will put an end to the riots.'

'Fat chance,' Wilson said quietly.

Jennings stared at Wilson. 'You said something, Superintendent?'

'Well done, sir,' Wilson said.

CHAPTER FIFTEEN

B elfast, 1983

THE WOMAN HELD the young girl by the hand as they made their way along the Crumlin Road. The little girl skipped along. She was happy because she didn't have to go to school. It wasn't a holiday and she hadn't been sick, so she had wondered why her Ma had kept her home. She didn't like school, so she much preferred to stay at home with her Ma and play, or colour books. The other girls at the school didn't like her. She knew it had something to do with her not having a Da. All the other girls had a Da and a Ma, but she only had a Ma. So that had to be the reason that they didn't like her. None of the other girls or boys would play with her. When she tried to join their games, they would push her away. Even when the teacher tried to get the other children to include her in their games, they cried and refused. She hated school. The girls used bad words when they spoke about her Ma. She didn't understand the words, but she knew that they weren't nice. The people on their street didn't like Ma either. They never came to the house for tea, and they looked funny at Ma when she passed by. Maybe it was because Ma was getting fat. She could feel the pressure of her mother's hand on hers. Ma was squeezing her hand tight, and it was starting to hurt. She wanted to tell her Ma to let her hand go, but there was a lot of traffic on the road and Ma had told her that she had to hold her hand, in case she ran out in front of a car. But she was a big girl now, and she understood that she had to stay on the path. Ma could hold her hand when they crossed the road, but she didn't need to be treated like a baby when she was on the footpath. She was aware that the pressure from Ma's hand was increasing, and when she looked into Ma's face, she could see that she wasn't smiling like she usually did when they were together. She loved Ma more than anything else in the world. She loved sitting on Ma's knee with Ma's arms around her. She wondered where they were going. The last time they had made a trip like this was when Ma went to see the doctor. Ma had been crying when she came out of the doctor's surgery, but she said that she wasn't sick or anything. Ma had only been sad and that had gone away quickly. She felt Ma jump a little, and they started to cross the street. They were moving fast now. Ma was pulling her along, and her little legs were moving as fast as they could, but she could barely keep up the pace that Ma was setting. They had almost reached the corner of the street when the big man caught up with them. He pulled at Ma's arm, and she had to stop. The little girl was happy for the rest. She was beginning to get very tired. She looked up into the big man's face. He was ugly and had no hair on his head. He looked like he was angry with Ma. He had hold of Ma's arm, and she was trying to break away from him, but the man was bigger and fatter than Ma. All the time that Ma and the man were talking loud Ma was gripping her hand tighter and tighter. She was beginning to get afraid and she whimpered a little. When she made the crying noise, the man and Ma both looked down at her. Ma smiled, but it was a funny smile not

like the one Ma had when they played together or when Ma
stroked her hair. The big fat man smiled too, but the smile
made his face even uglier. She wanted to tell the fat man that
she didn't like him, and that he should leave her Ma alone. But
she was afraid that he would hit her. Ma never hit her, but her
teacher sometimes hit the children and made them cry. Ma
and the man started talking again, and then they began
walking down the road in the same direction they had been
going. Ma was still holding on to her hand and the big man was
holding Ma by the elbow. They turned a corner, and the man
pointed at a car. She had never been in a car because Ma
didn't own one, and when they went to the doctor, they'd
taken the bus. The little girl suddenly got very excited at the
thought that they were going to go in a car. They stopped
beside the big black car, and she saw that Ma didn't want to go
in the car. The big man opened the back door of the car. Ma
was still holding her hand, and the big man made her let go so
he could put the little girl into the back seat of the car. Ma
looked at her. There were tears in her eyes. The fat man
opened the front door and pushed Ma into the seat. The little
girl wanted to shout out 'Leave my Ma alone', but she was still
afraid. The big man went quickly to the other side of the car
and got in. He started the engine, and they began to move off.
She felt lonely in the back of the car. Why didn't Ma sit beside
her? There was more room in the back than in the front. The
little girl looked out the window at the people walking along
the street. This was way more fun than the bus. She wanted to
wave at the people on the street. The children at the school
would be jealous of her now. Lots of them had never been in a
car. They hadn't driven long before they stopped. Ma was
crying now, and the little girl started crying too although she
didn't know why. The big man took the little girl out of the
back seat, and Ma got out of the car slowly like she didn't want
to. There was a group of women standing in front of the
building they stopped beside. As soon as Ma got out of the car,

two women came forward and held her by the arms. There was a big woman with yellow hair telling the other women what to do. They took Ma and brought her into the big building. The little girl started to cry.

'It'll be alright, dearie,' the woman with the yellow hair said. 'Nancy'll take you away for a wee ice cream. You'd like that wouldn't you? The little girl stopped. She nodded, and took the woman called Nancy's proffered hand. She liked ice cream.

CHAPTER SIXTEEN

I t was one of those times when Wilson didn't really want to go back to the office. The investigation was going nowhere fast, and he would have preferred to be out on the streets trying to drum up a lead than sitting behind a desk waiting for something to happen. It was one of the drawbacks of rank. As a young detective constable, it had all been about finding evidence and learning the game. When he moved up to detective sergeant, he'd taken on some responsibility for the work of the constables, but he was also on a learning curve to become an inspector, and then the exalted rank of chief inspector. It was what he and the other cadets aspired to when they were at police college. Some cadets like Jennings took it to extremes of ambition while others were happy to truck along as constables for the rest of their lives. He knew that among his own team, the only person who had leadership qualities was Moira McElvaney. He had insisted that they make her up to detective sergeant but from now on it would be up to her how far she wanted to go. As far as he was concerned, he was happy to have made superintendent, and he had no desire to climb any further up the greasy pole to the rank of chief superintendent where he would be buried in a mound of bullshit administration. He had recently carried out the annual appraisals of his team and to a man they declared their ambitions satisfied. That didn't mean that they wouldn't like a few extra quid in their pay packets every month but in terms of job satisfaction, they were, by and large, happy. Harry Graham had, he thought, finally accepted the fact that he would never be able to pass the sergeant's exam. He didn't know why Harry continually failed. He didn't think that the man was dyslexic so perhaps it was simply a phobia with exams. Wilson had already put in twenty years on the force. Despite the overt antipathy of DCC Jennings towards him, he had managed to reach a rank he had no desire to go beyond. Ian Wilson was a copper, and that's what he always would be.

Only Ronald McIver was present in the squad room when he returned. The other four members of the team were beating the bushes for a lead. As soon as he was settled behind his desk, he reluctantly opened his computer and clicked the mail icon. A flood of new e-mails filled the screen in front of him. He wondered whether this new technology was a blessing or an affliction. He knew what he thought. He selected one with the subject line 'toxicology'. He clicked on the enclosed pdf and learned that Lizzie was marginally over the legal alcohol limit and Sammy Rice was over by the proverbial mile. He was glad he didn't have Sammy's liver. There was nothing else of interest. The second e-mail contained a revised forensics report. Nothing major there either, only a few more finger-prints were identified. Added to the report were the rap sheets of those additional people. None of them would have been welcomed in heaven judging from their past deeds. He worked quickly through the rest of the e-mails discarding the ones that had been sent simply to show the hierarchy that a particular officer was still alive and working on something extremely important. Then he dumped the e-mails consisting of 'things he should know about' such as new rules concerning the powers of the Chief Super to amend the station organisation chart. Important stuff no doubt, but not very relevant to finding the murderer of Lizzie Rice. By the time he had cleared his e-mails he had done a considerable amount of work but the investigation into the murder of Lizzie Rice hadn't moved forward by one inch. He looked at his watch. It was lunchtime, and he had to choose. He hated eating alone in a pub.

CHAPTER SEVENTEEN

Deane's restaurant in Howard Street is probably the best restaurant in Belfast. The main dining room exudes class with the white linen covered tables contrasting with the deep red of the walls and the dark brown of the wooden floors. Most people are highly delighted to receive an invitation to lunch at Deane's but DCC Roy Jennings was an exception. He felt uncomfortable as he looked around the well-filled main dining room. A senior editor at the *Belfast Chronicle* had invited him and he was more apprehensive than usual at the reason for the invitation. He was not one to shy away from contact with the press. Ingratiating himself with editors and journalists was part of his strategy to attain the office of Chief Constable by establishing a positive press presence. Therefore, the prospect of a decent lunch allied to an opportunity to schmooze with a senior journalist meant that he had jumped at the invitation. When he had arrived at the restaurant to find the table had been set for three, his nose had been thrown a little out of joint. He had assumed that the lunch would be an intimate one where he could easily ingratiate himself with the senior editor. Exchanging confidences at a table for three was a risky enterprise since it reduced considerably the value of deniability. He was even more bothered when the senior editor arrived with none other than Maggie Cummerford in tow. Cummerford had until recently been the crime reporter on the *Chronicle*, but her star had waned after she had been obliged to retract a front-page story concerning a Professional Standards investigation into Ian Wilson.

'Deputy Chief Constable,' James Reilly extended his hand to Jennings, who took it and gave it a Masonic handshake. 'I think that you've already met Maggie Cummerford.'

'No,' Jennings said. 'I haven't had that pleasure. Although, of course, I think I may have read some pieces by her in your paper.' He extended his hand to Cummerford who took it and shook. He noted that she dropped one of those messenger bags at the side of the table before taking his hand. Jennings was not a great ladies' man. He was aware that many people considered him to be a homosexual, and he had done nothing to dissuade them. The truth was as usual somewhat simpler. All of Roy Jennings' concentration was on attaining the highest post in the PSNI. He considered himself to be sexless, a being without desires for either men or women. When he looked at Cummerford he saw a rather petite, mousy haired woman of average stature. Her face wasn't particularly attractive, neither was it plain. All the features were there in the right proportions, but none was striking enough to warrant remark. Her figure was boyish with wide shoulders and a narrow waist. She was, all features considered, the picture of the modern woman making her way in a man's world.

Cummerford looked for something to wipe her hand with as she and Reilly took their places at the table. Shaking hands with Jennings left her feeling that she had just handled a three-day-old slimy fish.

'I thought that we would be dining alone,' said Jennings as he picked up the menu. He never had any problem with weight other than he seemed incapable of putting flesh on his delicate frame. As a boy he had always been the weed of the class. But he liked to think that what he lacked in physical prowess, he more than made up for in intelligence and cunning. He decided to stick to the Linen Lunch and ordered the fish cake.

Reilly and Cummerford also chose from the Linen Lunch menu. 'Drink?' Reilly asked. He was used to his lunch guests abusing the expense nature of the meal, but he didn't think that Jennings was the type.

'Water,' Jennings said.

'Three designer waters,' Reilly instructed the waiter with a smile.

'Roy,' Reilly began when the waiter had departed. 'I can call you Roy.'

Jennings bridled but was obliged to go with the flow. 'Of course, James.' He hoped that Cummerford would have the good sense not to call him 'Roy'.

'You may remember several months ago that we were obliged to retract, with an apology, an article regarding an investigation into Chief Inspector Wilson.'

'Now Superintendent Wilson,' Cummerford added through a mouthful of bread.

'Vaguely,' Jennings said. He remembered it only too well since Wilson used it to turn the tables on him.

The food was delivered, and Reilly began on it immediately. 'So,' he said through a mouthful of pork belly. 'We have a little problem. You see we were not very kind to Maggie since we felt embarrassed that we had to print the retraction, etcetera. For the past few months, she has been rehabilitating herself as you might say.'

'Garden fetes, junior soccer matches, that kind of thing,' Cummerford intoned while screwing up her face.

Jennings played with his food. This was not the kind of lunch that he had anticipated. He wondered when Reilly was going to get to the point.

'But Maggie is a rather clever girl,' Reilly said patting

Cummerford's hand. 'She permitted us to send her to Coventry, as it were, because she had something else in mind, and she was willing to wait for an opportunity to spring back at us.'

Jennings forked a piece of fish cake into his mouth What the hell had all this drivel got to do with him? Had he been invited to lunch so that Reilly could play footsies with his employee. He hoped that his impatience was showing on his face.

Maggie Cummerford bent and took a small recording device from her messenger bag and placed it on the table. She pressed a button, and the voice of Chief Inspector Harrison could be heard loud and clear. After thirty seconds, she switched the recorder off.

'It appears Maggie had irrefutable evidence,' he nodded towards the recorder, 'that the story she wrote, and we published was, in fact, true.'

If Jennings had not already finished eating, he might well have choked on his fish cake.

'We have reacted,' Reilly continued, 'by reinstating Maggie as our crime reporter and there have been some financial repercussions which we do not need to discuss here.'

'And this affects me how?' Jennings asked.

'You lied about the investigation into Wilson,' Cummerford said quickly.

'The investigation was unofficial,' Jennings knew that he was on shaky ground. 'Since it never existed officially then I was quite right in my statement.'

'I assume that a Freedom of Information request will confirm that,' Cummerford said.

Jennings looked at the young woman. He saw something that he missed in his earlier appraisal of her. It was a streak of ruthlessness and ambition. He recognised it because it paralleled his own. His plan to put an end to Wilson's career via the newspapers had not been a bad one, but it was now in tatters. Harrison was a fool to let her record their conversation. 'I assume that Detective Inspector Harrison told you that the information he gave you was off the record.'

'It's not on the tape,' Cummerford said.

"You devious little bitch," Jennings thought. 'You obviously have something in mind,' he said. 'Perhaps you'll be so good as to let me know what it is.'

'I want to do a profile on Ian Wilson.'

Jennings' mouth curled. He didn't want Wilson to have any more profile than he already had. He was aware of Wilson's reputation of being able to charm women out of their pants and he could just see the gushing profile that this young woman would produce. 'You don't need me for that.'

'But I want access to all areas. I want to follow him through an investigation and see how he works. The Lizzie Rice investigation is perfect. I need your OK to tag myself along to the Murder Squad team. I want to be embedded in the team.'

'Out of the question,' Jennings said.

'Then I have no choice but to go in another direction,' Cummerford said. 'You ruined my career by lying. I have proof that you lied, and I have a legal opinion from the paper's barrister that I have a case in law.'

Jennings was now on the horns of a dilemma. He had no doubt that this vicious little bitch was as good as her word. He would be exposing himself to some criticism from the Chief Constable if he acceded to her request, but he would end up in an unsavoury court case that might end his career if he didn't do what she wanted. He concluded that it would be easier to handle the Chief Constable. 'You cannot be allowed to interfere with the investigation. I will need the original tape, and a paper signed by you attesting that there are no copies.'

'Understood.'

'I'll make the arrangements.'

'Today. I don't want to be behind in the investigation.' She stood up. 'I'll hear from you this afternoon. Now I'll leave you two boys alone. I'm sure you have lots to talk about.' She picked up her leather messenger bag and strode out of the restaurant.

'I'm sorry, Roy,' Reilly said watching her head disappear through the front door. 'She had us over a barrel as well. Don't blame me. Blame that stupid fucker who gave her the interview.'

Jennings had already buried Harrison in the bandit country of south Armagh, but he would have to think whether there was something further he could inflict on the stupid idiot.

'We'll just have to grin and bear it,' Reilly said raising his hand to the waiter. 'Fuck this water stuff. I need a whiskey.'

Roy Jennings sipped his water. He was not known for either grinning or bearing it.

CHAPTER EIGHTEEN

The Murder Squad team assembled in front of the whiteboard at two o'clock precisely. Wilson had rarely seen a whiteboard as blank as the one that stared back at him. There was a photo of Lizzie at the top with the indication 'victim' and some murder scene photos beneath it. Wilson noted that Moira had created a timeline on Lizzie's movements prior to the murder on the right-hand side of the board. Apart from that, nothing. 'Moira, run us through the movements,' he said

'Lizzie and her friends have a bingo night every Wednesday. They normally bring a flask of vodka along so it's a combination of gambling and drinking. You can't say that you can set your watch by them because it depends on how they're doing as to how long they stay. This week they did well, or at least they finished up ahead. Lizzie was the big winner with twenty quid. She left the bingo hall at about nine fifteen,' she indicated the timeline on the board. She stayed outside chatting and smoking for ten minutes or so and then headed home on her own. Normally, she might have flagged down a taxi, but obviously she decided to hold on to her winnings. It would have taken her thirty minutes to walk home, so she arrived at approximately ten o'clock.'

'It's a good guess that the killer was watching the bingo hall. He would then have to get ahead of her so that he could disable Billy and be there in time before she arrived,' Wilson said. 'Have we checked the bingo hall for CCTV?'

'Not a sausage,' Peter Davidson interjected. 'The hall is on a major junction, so there's a traffic CCTV which is concentrated on the junction itself. North Street has alleys, and most of the business premises are empty and boarded up. The ones that are still operating are more interested in paying their rent than in installing CCTV systems.'

'Check the traffic CCTV for nine thirty last Wednesday,' Wilson said. 'See if you can spot Lizzie and see if you can see someone following her. With a bit of luck, we might get a lead.' He tried to put more confidence into his voice than he felt. 'What about the house to house?'

It was Davidson's turn again. 'House to house is finished, boss. We've done all the streets in the vicinity and there's not much point going any further out.'

'What have we got?' Wilson asked.

'Nothing to write home about. I haven't collated all the sheets from the uniforms but at a guess I'd say we're goin' to draw a blank.'

'That's not what I wanted to hear,' Wilson said.

Davidson snorted. 'This fucker must be some sort of ghost. It's a tight-knit community, and they're normally on the lookout for strangers. I'm a bit confused that nothing has turned up.'

Wilson pointed to the scene of crime scene photos. 'The living room looks like a slaughterhouse. There's blood and brain all over the place. Please don't tell me that the murderer didn't get blood on his clothes. It's just not possible. Someone walked out of the Rice house covered in blood, and no one noticed him. I don't buy it. Go back to the streets. Interview everybody again. Somebody must have seen whoever came out of that house. There's some auld biddy sitting at her window watching who walks up and down. Find her.'

'You're living in the past, boss. The auld biddy that used to sit by the window, now sits in front of a forty- inch colour flat screen TV provided by the Social.'

The other members of the squad laughed, and the tension was dissipated somewhat.

Wilson slapped his hand against the whiteboard. 'We're under the cosh and the clock here. There are going to be people on the streets tonight and every night until we find who killed Lizzie. Sammy is staying quiet for the moment, but don't count on it staying that way. I don't credit Sammy for a high level of emotional intelligence so this mourning that's going on now is only to shore up his support in his enclave. As soon as Lizzie's in the ground, Sammy is going to be out there competing with us to find the killer. And I don't want him to succeed where we failed. Ronald, how are you doing on Lizzie's background?'

Ronald McIver was sitting on the desk closest to the white-board. 'Lizzie was no saint, as I'm sure we're all aware. Back in the Seventies and the Eighties she was right in the middle of the 'Troubles'. She headed up the women's branch of the Ulster Volunteer Force in the Shankill and by all accounts, she was involved in a lot of unsavoury stuff. She was lifted a total of seven times and questioned about burnings and harassment, but she was never charged. She always produced cast-iron alibis. Most of what I've managed to put together has come for contacts in the press. I tried a few old contacts in the paramilitaries, but nobody wants to talk about Lizzie except to say that she hasn't been involved for the past twenty years or so. In terms of people bearing a grudge against her, you could probably fill the Ulster Hall.'

'It just gets better and better,' Wilson said. 'We need to turn up some leads soon. Which means that you guys are going to have to work your socks off until we develop a definite line of enquiry. Get to it. More interviews, check CCTV, talk to the women who were at bingo with her. Was she nervous? Had she been threatened? Bring me something.' The group broke up slowly and moved back to their desks silently.

WILSON WAS aware that he was transmitting the tension that he was feeling to the rest of his team. But that was part of being a team leader. Creating tension could be a bad thing, but it also could be good. It would depend on the person. Moira would put her back into the investigation, and it would be difficult to get her out of the office. She was also intuitive, which made her the best detective on the team. Peter Davidson would go into his shell until something broke. He was seldom the member of the team that sniffed out a lead. But he was a good solid detective in following up. Ronald McIver would continue to pound the computer keys and man the phones. Every team needed a researcher and that fitted Ronald's character and his fear of the streets perfectly. Harry Graham would plod along making sure that the murder book was kept up to date and ensuring that all the rules and regulations were adhered to. Eric Taylor was the oldest on the team. He knew all the ropes and every copper in every station in Belfast. But he was one year away from retirement, and it was beginning to show. The members of the team had strengths and weaknesses, and it was his job to play to the strengths and minimise the weaknesses. He was hardly five minutes in his office alone when his phone rang. It was an invitation for a second visit to HQ in one day. A second invitation didn't bode well.

WILSON WAS USHERED DIRECTLY into the DCC's office as soon as he arrived at HQ. He was somewhat surprised to find Maggie Cummerford sitting facing DCC Jennings. He remembered Cummerford from her short stint as a crime reporter for the *Chronicle*, but he hadn't seen her in some time. Then he remembered the wave at the press conference. 'I can wait outside,' Wilson said quickly, 'until you're finished.'

'This concerns you,' Jennings said pointing at the second chair in front of his desk.

'I don't understand,' Wilson moved slowly towards the chair and sat with some reluctance.

'It appears that the *Chronicle* wishes to write a complimentary article about the PSNI, and it will be centred on the work of the Murder Squad.' Jennings had his two hands together in a praying manner covering his mouth as he spoke. His voice was strained as though something was caught in his throat.

Wilson looked at Cummerford wondering what the hell was going on. 'Sir, I am involved in perhaps the most difficult and without doubt the most politically charged murder case of my career. Perhaps it would be more appropriate for the *Chronicle* to highlight the work of some other section of the force.'

'The decision has been made,' Jennings said sharply. 'The editor insists that, given your sporting past and the level of name recognition that you have, you are the optimum candidate to represent the new PSNI. I'm not sure that I share his opinion, but I have been prevailed upon to agree.' He bridled at the smirk on Cummerford's face. 'This young lady will have total access to you and your team during the Lizzie Rice murder investigation. That access concludes when the investigation concludes.'

'I'm afraid I must press the issue with the Chief Constable,' Wilson said trying to take in the impact of having a journalist around during an investigation.

'Please be my guest. The Chief has already given his approval. He thinks it will show the force in a good light and to be open and transparent.'

Wilson was loath to give in. 'Things may be said and done

during an investigation that we would not want to reach the public domain.'

Jennings leaned back in his chair. 'As I understand the brief, the focus is on you as an individual and not on the murder investigation. The article will not concern itself with the investigation or with any of your colleagues.'

Maggie Cummerford nodded when Wilson looked at her.

Something was very wrong here. He remembered that Cummerford had mentioned wanting to do a profile on him some months previously, but he had no idea how she or her editor had managed to convince the Chief Constable that having her follow him around during an investigation was a good idea. 'I would like to have my objection recorded, and I will need a written confirmation that HQ has insisted on this action.'

'Done,' Jennings said simply. 'Please wait outside. Miss Cummerford will join you shortly, and you can make arrangements. I have given instructions that Miss Cummerford is to be provided with a visitor's badge.'

Wilson stood and realised that his fists were clenched. If this was another attempt by Jennings to undermine him, it was a damn clumsy one. He turned and made for the door.

'I don't like you,' Jennings said when Wilson had left the room. 'And I don't like having my arm twisted.' He removed the cassette from his desk drawer and pulled the tape out squashing it in his hand as it went. 'You should be careful who you push against. Some people are apt to push back harder. You must take great care of yourself, Miss Cummerford. You may think that you have won a battle, but this was simply a skirmish. The battle is yet to come. Now get out of my office.'

WILSON WAS WALKING up and down outside Jennings' office when Maggie Cummerford exited. 'What in God's name are you up to?' he asked as he towered over her.

'I told you months ago that I wanted to do a profile on you,' she stood staring up into his face. The combination of American and Ulster accents was as soft as a summer rain. 'You should have said yes then. You're an interesting fellow – former sports star, head of the Belfast Murder Squad and partnered up with a leading light of the legal establishment with a baby on the way.'

'Surely to God you could have done your profile without looking over my shoulder during a murder investigation.'

'The opportunity was too good to waste. This case alone is a career maker for a journalist with the inside track. At the same time, I get to know you as well as any human can,' she smiled. 'Not in the biblical sense, although I might be up for that too before we're finished.'

'I need to get back to the station, and we need to establish some ground rules.'

'I'll take a lift. I don't think DCC Jennings likes me.'

'Join the club.'

CHAPTER NINETEEN

Lizzie Rice's body was released at midday. Sammy Rice had barred his father from the mortuary. He was in control of events, and he wasn't going to allow the auld fool to screw things up. Since the night of the murder, Billy had been buried in a whiskey bottle, and every now and then he came out with some shit about murdering ten Taigs for Lizzie. Luckily, nobody was listening to the bastard. The house in Malvern Street was still a mess. The crime-scene tape was gone, but Sammy hadn't had time to have the blood and brain cleaned up. The hearse delivered the coffin bearing Lizzie's body to Sammy's house in Ballygomartin Road. Sammy had moved on from the two up, two down in Malvern Street that he had been born in. The house in which Lizzie body would lie was a three-storey bay-windowed Victorian red brick consisting of five bedrooms, three bathrooms, a large modern kitchen and two reception rooms. Although it was a big step up from the family home, it was well below Sammy's spending power. Sammy Rice could afford to live among the wealthiest in Belfast, but he needed to be close to his people and the source of his power – the Shankill Road. Sammy had arranged for family members to carry the coffin into the large downstairs living room where Lizzie would lie in state. It was a tradition in Ireland to hold the wake with the coffin open. The funeral home had used all their arts to give the impression that Lizzie's head was still intact. Chairs had been placed around the edge of the living room, and Sammy placed himself next to the coffin. Word had been spread throughout the Shankill that Lizzie could be viewed, and food and drink would be available at the Ballygomartin house.

'I want a major kick-off in the Shankill this evening,' Rice said to Ivan McIlroy. 'Last night was only a parade. I want to mark Lizzie's wake with a full-on riot, burning buses, Molotov cocktails, baton charges by the peelers, the whole nine yards. Are you with me? Get every mad fucker out onto the streets.'

'I'll get on it,' McIlroy said.

'What about getting someone close to Wilson?'

'I'm meetin' one of Wilson's team this evenin'.'

'Is it money?'

'Aye.'

'Give him what he asks for. I want the man who killed my mother. Make that clear.'

'I thought that you were connected higher up,' McIlroy smiled exposing a row of rotten teeth.

'Our friend, Wilson, doesn't always play by the book. He tends to keep his cards close to his chest. We need someone who's with him day and night.'

There was a noise at the door and Rice turned and saw a leading Loyalist politician enter. He moved to greet the new arrival. The politician gripped Sammy's hand. 'Sorry for your trouble,' he said. 'Lizzie will be sorely missed.'

'Aye, she will,' Sammy replied. 'Would you like to see her?'

IF THE MOOD at the two o'clock briefing was despondent, by six o'clock desperation had set in. The second level of interviews had drawn a blank and the research into Lizzie Rice's background had added a couple of hundred additional individuals who would like to have done serious damage to her. Moira had managed to add a second trawl through the forensic evidence but aside from the few fingerprints that could not be identified there was nothing new to report.

'It's the perfect fucking crime,' Wilson said as the team completed their reports. 'But then again, we all know that there is no such thing as the perfect crime. The murderer couldn't go through that house, commit a murder and leave without leaving behind some trace. There's a hair, a piece of fingernail, something with DNA on it in that house that we haven't found yet. I just cannot believe that we've hit a brick wall so soon in this investigation.' He looked around at the faces of his team and saw reflected in them a measure of his own despondency. Maggie Cummerford sat in the corner of the squad room beyond the team tapping away on her laptop. Wilson was wrestling with how and why she had been landed on him. It was way outside of protocol to give a journalist inside access to an ongoing investigation. And yet Jennings had been so on board that he had squared the break in protocol with the Chief Constable and issued a written instruction. What was the greasy bastard up to this time? Whatever it was it wasn't going to be good for him. But Cummerford had said that Jennings didn't like her. Was she trying to flim-flam him to get him onside? All he knew was that she was a major distraction. He should be concentrating on finding Lizzie Rice's murderer, but his mind was engaged in trying to divine Jennings' new plan for him. He spent an hour setting boundaries with Cummerford. She was to clear all her reports with him, and she was to leave his private life just that – private.

'Go home, get some rest and for Christ's sake let's pray that something breaks soon. Lizzie is lying in state this evening so maybe one of us should pop round there. Any volunteers?'

No hands were raised.

'OK, Peter you just volunteered. You don't have to stay all

evening. Just drop in and see who's about. The funeral's the day after tomorrow. Moira and I will attend.'

'You think that wise, boss,' Harry Graham said. 'Moira, I mean.'

'Maybe you're right. Peter and I will go.'

Wilson looked at Moira, and she pointed at her watch. Fuck it, he thought, the drink with Guilfoyle.

THE MUTED TELEVISION over the bar of the Crown was showing the news, and the main story was the crowd gathering in the Shankill. The footage could have been taken any time from the early 1970s until the present. The age of the rioters hadn't changed. Most were teenagers out to cause a bit of mischief. They wore balaclavas that had probably been handed down from their rioting parents. The riot police were already assembling in the back streets, their black body armour making them look like an army of giant beetles. There was nothing to show that the footage was current. It could just as easily have been library footage. Wilson turned away from the television. He didn't need the added aggravation. He headed for the lounge where the ubiquitous television was banned. Moira and her boyfriend were already seated at a table in the corner under one of the stained-glass windows.

'Great pub,' Brendan Guilfoyle rose and held his hand out towards the approaching Wilson.

'The Crown is not a pub,' Wilson said taking the hand and shaking it. 'It's an institution.' He looked over the young man much as Moira's father might do. Although Guilfoyle had an Irish name, his look was distinctly unIrish. For a start, his skin was swarthy most unlike the usual alabaster skin colour with which God had endowed the Irish people. He had the dark hair of his father's race but with very clear blue eyes. He was well-built and moved his body like an athlete. Moira had done all right for herself, he thought. A waiter appeared at his side.

'Pint of Guinness,' he said and sat in the vacant chair. One drink. I'm expected at the opening of an art exhibition, and I promised I wouldn't be late.'

'It's great to meet you,' Guilfoyle said as soon as Wilson was settled. 'Moira's told me so much about you.'

It was like listening to those old newsreels of JFK, Wilson thought. Guilfoyle's lilting Bostonian accent washed over you like a warm wave. 'Nothing bad, I hope.' He looked at Moira and smiled.

'Quite the opposite. I'd go into it, but I don't think Moira would appreciate it.'

Both men looked at Moira, and she blushed.

'You want to help out on the Rice murder?' Wilson said when his pint arrived.

'I wouldn't be so presumptuous. I'm here for a year lecturing in clinical psychology but back in the States I also give a course in criminal psychology. I've even written a book on it although according to my publisher, no one seems to want to read it.'

'Maybe I'll make it my one book to read this year,' Wilson smiled and sipped his pint.

'Yeah, guess most people in your business don't get much time to read the musings of guys like me who live in ivory towers. But I do have some experience of working with the FBI and the local Boston police.'

'And what can you tell me?'

'The killer knows your victim real well and has been personally affected by her. The killing is personal, and the killer bears a hell of a grudge. My guess would be that this is a revenge killing.'

'I suppose Moira has made you aware of who Lizzie Rice is or was I should say. You could probably fill a football stadium with people who have a grudge against her.'

'This was no ordinary grudge. The victim did something very bad to the killer or to someone he loved. The hammer and the destruction of the head are significant. I just can't figure out why yet. The question is when did the bad thing happen and why the killer decided to strike now? I don't want to get Moira into trouble, but she tells me that the crime scene was clean. The killer left nothing. My guess is that whoever the killer is, he knows something of police procedure. At least enough to make sure that no evidence was left at the scene.'

Wilson studied his half-empty glass.

'He doesn't believe in profiling,' Moira said.

'Think about what you just told me,' Wilson said. 'The killer bears a deep grudge against Lizzie. Well, you'd hardly kill for no reason. There's always a motive. Like you, I'm interested in the method. There are lots of ways of killing people besides bashing their brains out. I think that the method was chosen specifically. The conclusion on the knowledge of police procedure is interesting, and new. I hadn't got there.' He tipped his glass in Guilfoyle's direction.

'Thanks,' the young man beamed. 'Maybe I'll make you a believer in profiling before the case is over.'

Wilson glanced at Moira. 'Have you ever heard the expression "don't call me, I'll call you".'

Guilfoyle looked downcast. 'You're kickin' me to the kerb?' he asked.

Wilson drained his glass and stood up. 'Maybe we'll talk again. In the meantime, don't do anything I wouldn't do.'

'That's a very short list of don't dos,' Moira said.

CHAPTER TWENTY

G allery One in the Federesky Gallery on North Street in central Belfast is a three hundred square foot room with cream tiles, and white walls bathed in extreme white light from a series of fluorescent tubes attached to the ceiling. Wilson picked up a glass of red wine from a tray held by an attractive young lady dressed in a white blouse and black skirt. It was exactly seven o'clock, and as he glanced about the room, he was pleased to see that Kate had not yet arrived. It was one up for him since she had sworn that she would be on time and insisted that he also be prompt. He didn't bother to take a catalogue since he had no real interest in art. His idea of something that should hang on a wall was a photo of Brian O'Driscoll scoring a try. Still, since he had been given a free glass of wine, it was important to look like he had a passing interest in the paintings, so he ambled around the room stopping at strategic points to gaze at canvases that said absolutely nothing to him. Kate was the art buff, and she generally left these openings as the proud owner of some outlandishly expensive piece of inexplicable art. He hoped that she would turn up soon. He found these gatherings on the upper side of extremely boring. The crowd in the room was made up essentially by what he called the 'cravat gang', pseudointellectuals who could make sense of the series of lines and dots that seemed to be the staple of modern art. Added to his lack of interest was the fact that he didn't move in the art buying circles, so without Kate, he was apt to spend all his time alone.

'Have you seen anything that you like?'

Wilson whirled around expecting to see Kate standing behind him but was surprised to see their new pathologist Professor Reid standing with a wine glass in hand. This was not the Professor Reid of the blue plastic jumpsuit or the hospital scrubs. She was wearing a red silk evening dress that showed off her spectacular figure and contrasted perfectly with her lightly tanned skin. In a word, she looked stunning. 'Professor Reid,' Wilson tried to hide the look of both shock and admiration on his face. 'I've just done a tour of the room and there are several interesting pieces. You're into art?'

'Somewhat, but most of my collection is African. I wouldn't have thought that I'd find you in some art appreciation circle.'

'Appearances can be deceptive,' he sipped wine delicately.

She laughed. 'I would have thought you would have been more at home banging a few heads together at the riot that's taking place in the Shankill.'

'Those were the days,' he smiled as though savouring a memory. 'Thank God the population of the province is so riot prone. I'll probably get a chance to bang some heads together in the very near future. In the meantime, I'm off duty, and I'll have to content myself with art appreciation. I can't keep calling you Professor Reid. I always called you predecessor Charlie.' He was intoxicated by her smell. Her perfume was not overpowering but perfectly understated.

'You were privileged. He always insisted that people address him as Charles. Anyway, my name is Stephanie, but you can call me Steph.'

'Ian,' he said simply.

'I know. You have a way of looking at a woman, Ian. I suppose other people have told you that.'

Other people had told him that, generally just before he had taken them to bed. He looked over her shoulder and saw Kate entering the room. She had come directly from work and was dressed in her habitual black Chanel suit and white blouse. She tossed her head and her perfectly coiffed blonde hair swung from side to side. She scanned the room looking for him. There were now two stunning women in the room. 'Excuse me,' Wilson made eye contact with Kate. 'My partner has arrived. I should go to her before she sees something she likes which is on the expensive side. I'll see you soon.'

'I look forward to it,' she said. 'We really should discuss the Rice case. I've had the technicians in the forensic lab look at issues like the height of the assailant. The report should be with you tomorrow.'

Wilson could see Kate waving from the other side of the room. 'Soon,' he said.

He didn't like the way he was feeling. The pounding in his heart and the erection in his pants were part of the old Wilson, the asshole Wilson, the Wilson that would betray the women he was with for a pair of flashing eyes and a trim body. He had thought that the bad part of him no longer existed, but he knew from experience that leopards rarely changed their spots. The old Wilson had been put aside, but he hadn't entirely disappeared. He knew that he loved Kate, but Stephanie Reid had awakened in him feelings that he thought he had put to bed.

'Who's the blonde?' Kate said as he leaned in to kiss her.

'It's good to see you too,' he said as Kate kissed the air above his cheek.

'That wasn't the answer I was looking for. I leave you alone in a roomful of strangers for five minutes, and you manage to hit on the best-looking woman in the room. Who's the blonde?'

'That, my dear, is Professor Stephanie Reid, Old Charlie's replacement as pathologist. She newly arrived from some Godforsaken part of Africa. She did the autopsy on Lizzie Rice.'

'Beauty and brains, I'm getting more jealous by the minute. And you were discussing her cutting technique with her, I suppose.'

'Just general chit-chat. Art, and the like.'

Kate raised her eyebrows and moved her left hand to her stomach. 'You have stuffed this package into me and day-by-day I'm turning into a blimp. There are times when I resent you for doing this to me. But that resentment would be nothing if I thought that you were casting your eye over a replacement who has the figure of a goddess and the audacity to wear a red dress like that. That thing in your pants would be at serious risk if that small thing in your head doesn't manage to control it. I much preferred the old pathologist. Principally, because he was a man.'

'I love you when you're angry.'

'Oh, this isn't angry. This is tired and emotional. You really don't want to see me being angry.'

He put his hand on her stomach. 'Don't go upsetting junior for no reason. You know they can feel your emotions. And by the way, you're the most attractive blimp I've ever seen.'

'Kate, darling.' A man sporting a cravat and a white linen suit air kissed Kate. 'Let me show you some of my work.' He took her arm and led her away. As soon as her back was turned, Wilson looked at where Stephanie Reid had been standing. He was just in time to see her retreating figure leaving the gallery. He turned back and started to follow Kate and the artist. A feeling of self-hate consumed him. The bad part of him contributed to the death of his ex-wife. If he didn't learn for history, then perhaps he would be doomed to repeat it.

. . .

THE BLACK BEAR was the kind of Belfast pub that could be used in a scene from a spaghetti western. The exterior of the pub hadn't been painted in twenty years and the small amount of blue paint that remained was flecked and blackened by pollution from cars. Inside was a mirror image of the exterior. The ceiling was a dark-brown colour not from paint but from the nicotine deposits of generations of smokers. The plastic covering on the seats that were attached to the walls had long ago split and the foam inside exited like some hidden creature every time a patron sat down. The tables spread around the room were so heavily stained that their original colour remained hidden under layers of cigarette burns and spilt alcohol. The ambiance was completed by the faint smell of ammonia and farts that emanated from the toilet area. Detective Constable Ronald McIver sat in the back room of the Black Bear. He had been to the toilet twice in the last ten minutes, and he felt a third piss coming on. In normal circumstances, he would be worried about his prostate but being in the Black Bear as Ivan McIlroy's guest was apt to make most men nervous. They had been at school together, so he had the measure of the man. McIlroy had been the school bully who ran the establishment in place of the headmaster. Most of the students had celebrated when he decided to leave school early. The celebration was short-lived, however. McIlroy became a fixture at the school gate initially to collect whatever money the students might have and later as the purveyor of illegal substances. The PSNI file on McIlroy was a lengthy one but despite more than a dozen arrests, he had spent no real time behind bars. McIver knew that McIlroy was certainly a sociopath and quite possibly a psychopath. When McIlroy had invited him for a drink in the Black Bear, McIver knew that there was no possibility of turning down the summons. To get to the Black Bear, he had had to run the gauntlet of the rioters in the Shankill, but he was assured a safe passage in McIlroy's company

'Shitty business, eh,' McIlroy said after their drinks were delivered.

'Aye,' McIver decided to keep his contribution to the meeting as short as possible.

'Lizzie Rice I mean. Some fucker waltzes into Malvern, opens Lizzie's head like taking the top off a boiled egg and then just fucks off. Shitty business. Lizzie's lying in Sammy's place at Ballygomartin. Are you goin' to pay your respects?'

'I don't know Sammy.' There was a slight catch in McIver's voice.

'How long have you been a Peeler?' McIlroy scratched at a pimple on his neck.

'Twenty-two years.'

'And you're still a fuckin' constable. Are you dumb or somethin'?'

'No, I'm just not pushy.'

'Your little wifey's a teacher, right?'

McIver could feel a bead of sweat running down his brow. 'Was,' he said simply.

'You've got a nice little life goin' there, Ronald me boy. Especially since you were such a fuckin' wimp at school,' McIlroy sat back and laughed. 'I remember I used to take your lunch money and give you a couple of slaps about the head for good measure.' The laughter expelled a rush of fetid breath. 'You and wifey are lucky I didn't kill you.' The laughing stopped abruptly.

McIver looked into his tormentor's eyes. The pupils were dilated. McIlroy was on something, and it wasn't just Guinness. Ronald McIver wanted to shit very badly.

'Sammy needs a favour and you're goin' to be happy to oblige him,' McIlroy leaned forward. 'He wants to find the fucker who topped his mother and who could blame him? He knows that Wilson wants the same thing, but Sammy would prefer first dip at the bastard. Are you with me?'

McIver nodded.

McIlroy put a wad of cash on the table. 'A little present from Sammy,' he said. 'Take it.'

McIver hesitated.

'I said fuckin' take it, you piece of shit,' there was menace in McIlroy's voice. 'Think about little wifey. I'm sure she wouldn't like bein' raped.'

McIver stretched his hand out to take the money and McIlroy grabbed it. 'Sammy wants to be first. I want to know everything that's goin' on with Wilson. When you find who murdered Lizzie you contact me, understood?'

McIver nodded. McIlroy released his hand and pushed the money towards him. 'Never forget, we own you.'

It was dark when DCC Roy Jennings drove through the gates of the imposing Georgian building in Malone Park, one of the most exclusive addresses in South Belfast. The house boasted four magnificent bay windows at the front, and the garden was well-developed and tree lined. Jennings pulled up before the entrance and exited from his car. The front door had been left ajar, and he walked straight into the living room on the left of the door. Shelves of books lined the walls. A log fire was blazing in the ornate fireplace.

'Worshipful Master,' Jennings said as he entered the room.

Sammy Rice turned away from the fire and looked at the second most important policeman in Northern Ireland.

'I'm sorry that I couldn't attend your mother's wake,' Jennings continued as Rice walked towards him. They exchanged a Masonic handshake, and Rice led his Lodge Brother back towards the fire.

Rice went to a drinks trolley and poured a large brandy. He

held it out to Jennings, who shook his head. 'Don't worry. I understand,' he sipped the golden liquid and sat in a leather wing-backed chair on one side of the fire. He pointed at a similar chair on the opposite side. 'Not too many of our respected Lodge Brothers thought it appropriate to mix with the riff-raff from the Shankill.'

Jennings sat in the chair Rice had indicated. 'It's difficult. Your public reputation conflicts with your position within the craft.'

'We must remember that we are all on the level. Why did you ask to see me?' Rice asked.

'The Chief Constable and I totally understand the reasons behind the riots. Your mother has been callously murdered, and your people wish to express their anger and hurt. However, there are many in the province, who are also members of our Brotherhood, who do not see a value in disrupting economic life.'

'As a businessman I can understand their point of view. The problem is that we have no idea who's behind Lizzie's murder. My colleague on the sectarian divide told me that his crew are not involved in the murder, and I believe him. Otherwise, I would have been organising retaliation. There's always the possibility that the murder was intended to undermine my position within east Belfast. What has Wilson found out?'

Jennings was continually struck by the way in which Rice could change from the street thug to the semi-sophisticated businessman and Lodge leader. Sammy Rice was a dangerous adversary but could be a useful ally. He was a man that Jennings had long ago decided that he needed to have on his side. 'Nothing. I mean it. He has no clue why or who. The forensics came up with nothing. It looks like whoever did it knew what they were doing, but it doesn't look like a professional killing. Professionals don't commit murders with a ball hammer.'

'Ever heard of Richard Kuklinski?'

'No.'

'Aka 'the Iceman',' Rice continued. 'He claimed to have killed more than 100 people. Some of them he killed on the instructions of the Mob in New York, but he also killed people who rubbed him up the wrong way. And he wasn't particular about the method. He shot, stabbed and bludgeoned his victims to death. That's why I haven't excluded a professional hit. Maybe Lizzie is a message for me.'

Jennings leaned forward feeling the warmth of the fire. 'What do you want me to do?'

Rice took a long drink of his brandy. 'Gerry McGreery has been trying to push into my territory. If anyone has an interest in hurting me, it's him. Get Wilson to lean on him. Have the uniforms hassle his people.'

Jennings looked at the Worshipful Master of his Lodge. He was being asked to assist one criminal enterprise by putting the full weight of the PSNI on the other. He had no doubt that Rice was going to use his mother's death to extend his control to another area of Belfast. In policing terms, it didn't really matter whether they were dealing with a single criminal enterprise or with two. 'And the riots?' he asked.

'Lizzie is being buried tomorrow. There'll be no riot tomorrow night as a mark of respect. That could be the end of it. Always assuming that I hear nice things about McGreery.'

You devious bastard, Jennings thought with grudging admiration. Turning his mother's death into a grab for territory was a masterstroke. 'Worshipful Master,' Jennings nodded and rose from the chair. 'It is a pleasure to be of assistance,' he said as he headed towards the door...

CHAPTER TWENTY-ONE

Belfast, 1983

The little girl sat where the woman called Nancy had told her. She had chosen the biggest ice cream in the shop, and she was busy licking it before it defrosted, and lost half of it. Occasionally she heard a scream from the room directly up the stairs. Somebody was very sore because she couldn't remember either her or Ma ever screaming that loudly, and sometimes she felt very hurt. She was left sitting on the stairs alone, although the woman called Nancy came to the top of the stairs and looked down on her from time to time. She looked sharply upstairs every time she heard a scream. She wondered where Ma was and why she was crying when they got out of the big man's car. Ma wasn't normally sad, and the little girl had never seen her crying like she had cried in the street. The screaming stopped, and four women came out of the room at the top of the stairs. They were laughing and happy. The big blonde woman with the hard face took a packet of cigarettes from her pocket and offered some to her friends. They lit their cigarettes and sat at the top of the stairs looking down at the little girl as she finished her ice cream. They smoked and laughed among themselves for a few minutes until they had finished their cigarettes, and then they went back into the room. They were only there a short time when the screaming started again. The ice cream was gone, and the little girl wanted to see her Ma. She had been with the women when they came into the building, but she hadn't been with the group smoking cigarettes at the top of the stairs. "I want my Ma," the little girl intoned to herself, and tears began to fall from her face. The screaming was louder than ever up the stairs, and then it stopped abruptly. The woman called Nancy came out of the room and came down the stairs. The little girl pointed at the blood on Nancy's shirt and said, 'You hurt yourself.' Nancy's face was very white, and she rubbed at the blood on her shirt. She said something with a bad word in the middle. Ma didn't let her say bad words, although the children at school used bad words to her. The other women came downstairs and passed her by. She noticed that none of them looked at her. "I want my Ma," she said a little louder now. The blonde woman hit her on the head and told her to shut up. The other women returned with the big man, and he was very angry. They all shouted at each other, and the little girl got very afraid. She started to cry, softly at first but then louder and louder. The man and the women ignored her and continued to shout at each other. Finally, the big man picked her up. He didn't hold her like Ma did. He put her under his arm and took her out of the building. His car was on the corner, and he opened the very back where it was dark, and he put her in. He closed it, and everything went black. The little girl was crying and screaming for her Ma. She was very afraid, and she felt pee running down her leg. She was a big girl and didn't pee like a baby anymore, but she couldn't stop the flow. The women told her that everything was going to be OK, but deep down, she knew that nothing would ever be the same again. And it was never going to be all right. She lay down across a big rubber tyre and cried until she fell asleep.

CHAPTER TWENTY-TWO

Wilson returned from his morning run and opened the apartment door. There was no smell of coffee, and he hadn't really expected it. Kate had chosen her painting faster than usual, and he could see that her interest in networking was lower than on similar occasions. She put her green spot on the painting, wrote a cheque for the requisite amount and they both headed for home. Not a word was said in the car. Kate had gone to bed immediately they returned, and he was left to nurse a glass of Jameson on his own in the living room. It was happening again and as usual it was his stupidity that was going to ruin everything. It was like he had a self-destruct button attached to his brain that caused him to screw up relationships. He convinced himself that nothing happened. Kate was over-reacting. He had simply been conversing with an attractive woman, and a colleague to boot. It would all blow over, but he would have to give Stephanie Reid a wide berth for a little while. He didn't think about the Lizzie Rice murder for the whole of his jog. Maybe it was just as well because he was far from even starting an investigation. He went into the kitchen and prepared Kate's favourite breakfast, an omelette made with only the white of two eggs and coffee. He covered the omelette pan and popped two pieces of brown bread in the toaster. It was time to brave the bedroom. Kate was sitting up in bed surrounded by legal papers.

'I have your breakfast on the go in the kitchen.'

Kate looked at him but didn't speak.

'I'm just taking a shower,' he announced.

'You do love me,' Kate said from the bed as he was pulling his wet tee-shirt off.

'Totally and completely,' he said sitting beside her on the bed.

'What about that woman last night?' At the gallery, Kate was struck by a bout of *déjà vu*. She was the other woman when Wilson was married, and now she wondered whether the boot was going to be on the other foot.

'I told you she's a colleague from work. Since you hadn't arrived, and since she and I didn't know another soul in the room, we started talking to each other rather than stand around like a couple of idiots.'

'I hate being jealous. We can't deny that you come with a reputation, and I've been in the character assessment business long enough to know that people don't really change. They tell you that they have but in my experience there's little change in people's characters once they're out of their teens. I don't want to spend the rest of my life having to watch you like a hawk or listening to rumours of how you've made a fool of me with someone.'

'If we'd have been talking last night, I would have told you of an additional complication.'

Kate put the legal papers aside and stared at him. 'I don't like the sound of this.'

'You remember that journalist, Maggie Cummerford, the one who broke the story about me being investigated by Professional Services Division.'

'Vaguely. She was fired or something.'

'She was put on the social pages for six months. Somehow,

she is back as a crime reporter, and she's managed to convince HQ to allow her to do a profile on me in the context of the Rice investigation.'

'My God, you attract them like flies.'

'It has nothing to do with me. Jennings has stuck her on me, for some reason or other, and since he's involved, I'm worried that there might be a plan afoot to undermine the investigation and get at me that way.'

'Go and take your shower before some woman or other jumps out of the wardrobe and lands on you. We can mull over the reasons you've been saddled with the journalist over breakfast.'

THE MOOD in the Murder Squad room hadn't improved overnight. On the way to the station, Wilson passed by the detritus of the previous night's riot. Three idiots were stupid enough to leave their cars available for burning. Tear gas canisters had been pushed into the gutters, and he noticed one or two rubber bullets that hadn't been collected as mementoes, just another night of madness and mayhem in Belfast. The nine o'clock briefing was a disaster witnessed by an elfin Maggie Cummerford always tapping away on her damn laptop. The team had reviewed all the evidence or what little of it there was, but they had come up with nothing new. It was beginning to look like Lizzie Rice's killer was going to get away with it. The funeral was scheduled for eleven o'clock.

'Nothing from the phones?' Wilson asked.

'A load of shite,' DC McIver replied. 'We've wasted a lot of resources following up leads to nowhere.

'Anything more on Lizzie?' Wilson looked at Moira.

'Nobody's talking,' Moira said. 'At least not to me. I hate saying it but maybe Peter should be the one pursuing this line. I haven't heard one bad word about Lizzie. "There'd be a bit of a contrast between St Lizzie of the Shankill and the woman accused of assault and abuse of her Catholic neighbours.'

'What about the wake?' Wilson asked.

'The usual suspects,' Peter Davidson said. 'The good and the great of local and national Loyalist politics, community leaders and just about every Protestant resident of west Belfast. I didn't stay long, the procession stretched halfway down Ballygomartin Road. Billy was sober for a change, but he looked like shit. I can't believe that we got absolutely nothing from him. He was there. Maybe he was part of it.'

'I doubt it,' Wilson said. 'If it was the reverse, I'd be willing to buy it. Lizzie was always the hard one. Billy was a bit of a fellow traveller. He did his stint in Long Kesh, but he wasn't capable of much more than leading a riot. Unlike Lizzie, she was capable of anything. That's why her background is so important. Peter, maybe you should talk to some people you know and see if anything useful falls out. According to Moira's profiler friend,' Wilson smiled when he saw Moira redden, 'the crime was very personal. The killer was someone who was hurt very badly by Lizzie, and this is revenge. Lizzie did enough bad things that affected the lives of her victims. This is our usual needle in a haystack search.' He put his hand on Davidson's shoulder. 'You and I at the funeral. We leave here at ten thirty. No need for uniforms. Let's see who shows up.'

Maggie Cummerford joined Wilson as he made his way back to his office. 'I thought journalism was the most boring profession in the world, but I'm beginning to change my mind. Sitting around at a press briefing waiting for some dick to spout inanities can make you feel like eating your head but at least it doesn't really count. 'You guys faffing around day after day digging for a lead is equally mind numbing, but unfortunately it's important.'

'Where did you get that accent?' Wilson asked.

'New York,' she pronounced it New Yoirk as a joke. 'Two

years at Columbia University doing a master's in journalism followed by a year on a free paper in the Village.'

'But you're from Belfast?'

'Born but not quite bred. I left here when I was young and lived in England. Ergo, the accent. Bit of Belfast, bit of middle England and a little New York.'

'How did you end up in England?'

'Long story.'

'Why did you come back to Belfast?'

'Hey, who's supposed to be asking the questions here?'

Wilson smiled. 'Sorry, it's what I do for a living.'

Cummerford stuffed her laptop into her messenger bag and hoisted it over her shoulder. 'See you at the funeral. I must get into position. They're expecting the whole of west Belfast to turn out.'

WILSON LOOKED at the mass of paper on his desk and wondered how he was ever going to clear it. HQ was constantly talking about the 'paperless office' but at the same time requiring more and more pieces of paper to justify every facet of the work. Maggie Cummerford only saw the tip of the iceberg of police work. If she could witness the endless round of paperwork, the constant writing up of records and the assid-uous keeping of notes, then Wilson wouldn't blame her for eating her own head. At least, the paperwork kept his mind away from the Lizzie Rice case for an hour or so. He'd heard a lecture from a psychologist once who claimed that the mind was not capable of concentrating on two things at the same time. He was happy to report that his experience confirmed that conclusion. He had glanced at his watch several times and was finishing up his paperwork when there was a soft knock on the glass door of his office. He looked up to see Stephanie Reid standing at the door. She was dressed in her working clothes of black pants, white blouse and a red jacket.

'Professor Reid,' he said hitting the key to kill his computer screen.

'I thought that we'd gone beyond the Professor Reid and Superintendent Wilson thing,' she said entering the office.

Wilson looked into the squad room and saw that Moira was watching.

'Stephanie, what can I do for you?' Remember what you told, Kate, you randy bastard, Wilson thought to himself.

'Remember I told you that I asked the forensic lab to run a few tests for me,' she slipped easily into the chair in front of his desk.

'Yes.'

She crossed her legs and looked into his eyes. 'I thought that I'd drop by and give you the results personally. It appears that the assailant was somewhere between five foot six and five foot eight. You've got beautiful blue eyes. But I suppose you already know that.'

Wilson decided to ignore the compliment. 'Great. There are probably only one hundred thousand people in Belfast who measure up to that.'

She smiled. 'It's another piece of the jigsaw.'

'A very little piece. Why didn't you pick up the phone to impart this important piece of information?'

She looked around his office letting her eyes dwell on a photo of Kate on his desk. 'I wanted to see where you lived.'

'I'd be a pretty sad individual if I lived in this station.'

'And are you sad? You seemed a bit lonely last night. Your partner was pretty much the centre of attraction, but you didn't seem to know too many people.'

He was beginning to feel a little uncomfortable. 'I didn't know any of the people there. I thought that we'd already established that art wasn't exactly my scene.'

She pouted. 'See, that's sad. Don't you have any friends of your own.'

'It's the reverse when Kate and I watch rugby at the weekend. At the game, we're surrounded by my friends. The fact that we have different interests means that we have a wide circle of acquaintances. Do you have any friends in Belfast?'

'Not really. I'm catching up. Perhaps you could help.'

'I'm sure an attractive woman like yourself doesn't need my help.'

'I'd like you to be my friend.'

'No problem. Charlie and I were friends. I thought that you were from Belfast.'

'Originally, but I've been to a lot of places since then. I got the feeling last evening that you and I could possibly become special friends.'

Sweet Jesus, Wilson thought. Why do you put temptation so much in my way? This woman could possibly have any man she wanted, and she's decided to come on to me. He looked through the glass wall of the office and saw Moira was still staring at them. 'I think we can be friends, but special friends might be out of the question.' He glanced at his watch and was relieved to see the little hand between ten and eleven and the big hand at six. He stood up. 'I've got to go. It's Lizzie Rice's funeral today, and you know the old cliché that the murderer always turns up at the funeral.'

'Why do I get the impression that you're running?'

Probably because I am, he thought. 'I do have a job to do.'

'Can we meet for a drink some time?' she stood up but remained between him and the door.

'I suppose so,' he said putting on his jacket.

'When?'

'I'll get back to you. Maybe when the case is over.'

'Too long.'

'I'm in a relationship where my partner is pregnant. I'm not about to do anything that will upset her so the drink will be in the context of a drink with lots of colleagues. Got it?' He started to push past her to the door.

'The car is ready, boss,' Moira stood at the door.

'I must get back to the Royal,' Reid said moving past Moira. 'If there's any further news from the forensic lab, I'll let you know.'

'Don't,' Wilson said when Reid was out of earshot.

'She's a maneater, boss,' Moira said. 'And in case you haven't noticed it, you're a man.'

'Why me?'

'That's what they all say.'

On any given day, the predominant colour along the Shankill Road is royal blue. However, many of the shops and houses put out black flags. Virtually every shop has its version of the Union Jack and where it was of the flag variety, they were at half-mast to respect the passing of a Protestant legend. All shops and other businesses in the area were closed for the duration of the funeral. The length of the Shankill was crowded. The street along which the funeral cortege made its way from the Ballygomartin Road was lined with men, women and children many holding the obligatory plastic Union Jack flags. The coffin was draped with both the Union Jack and the Red Hand flag of Ulster. A large wreath spanned the length of the hearse bearing the legend 'Lizzie Rice Patriot'. The procession of hearse and mourners moved slowly down the Shankill Road before turning into Townsend Street. Wilson was already standing outside their destination, Townsend Presbyterian Church. The church was a fine stone edifice sandwiched between a building housing the Northern Ireland Post on one side and the Townsend Industrial Park on the other; part of the old Belfast stuck between two buildings representing the new. Wilson noticed that some idiot had painted the word 'KILL' on the red-bricked wall of the industrial park. The exhortation of the graffiti artist hadn't mentioned who should be killed but this was Belfast, and it was left to the spectator to choose their own favourite victim.

The large wooden double doors to the church had been opened, and a crowd had already gathered inside the railings surrounding the church. Townsend Street was cleared of parking to allow the cortege easy passage. Wilson's vehicle was one of the only cars permitted beyond the police-cordoned perimeter. One of the other cars allowed into the cordoned off area was that of Deputy Chief Constable Jennings. Wilson looked around for his big boss but found no sight of him. Jennings, as a representative of the PSNI, was already installed inside among the mourning community leaders. It was another opportunity for the politically adept Jennings to press the flesh of the good and the great. The cliché of the murderer attending the funeral of his victim would be of little use today. Wilson scanned the huge crowd. Men and woman of all shapes and sizes swarmed around the church awaiting the arrival of the funeral party. The buzz created by more than a thousand people fell to a sudden hush as the funeral cortege entered Townsend Road. A group of men wearing sunglasses, black berets and black sweaters suddenly appeared before the church. Wilson recognised Ivan McIlroy and several of the thugs who had stormed the reception area of the station with Sammy Rice. The hearse, led by a piper playing a lament, drew up in front of the church and the crew wearing the dark glasses moved forward. The roof of the hearse was covered in a mountain of floral tributes. The coffin was slowly withdrawn from the hearse and was taken in hand by McIlroy's crew. The crowd had increased to more than two thousand and Townsend Street was packed from end to end. Sammy and Billy Rice stood directly behind the hearse as the coffin was turned and the group proceeded in the direction of the church. Wilson and Davidson stayed outside the church and scanned the faces of the crowd. Wilson noticed Maggie Cummerford standing just inside the cast iron railings with notebook and pen in hand. He also saw camera crews from the BBC and Ulster Television, and he made a mental note to ask for the footage. Peter Davidson joined him at the edge of the crowd.

'Shots fired over the coffin on the way down the Shankill,' Davidson said. 'Well out of the way of our people. The shots were heard, but nobody saw anything. The order is out from HQ, we're to stay well out of the way.'

Wilson wondered whether the senior officer sitting in the pew inside was responsible for keeping his underlings well out of the action. They waited while the service took place and watched as the coffin was loaded into the hearse. Sammy Rice glanced at Wilson and Davidson as the cortege moved off in the direction of Balmoral Cemetery, its final destination. It was not a friendly look.

'WASTE OF TIME,' Wilson said as he finished briefing the team on the Lizzie Rice funeral. 'The usual suspects up to their usual business.' He glanced towards the rear of the squad room where Maggie Cummerford sat tapping on her laptop. Wilson frowned. He didn't like having an outsider, and a journalist, eavesdropping on the discussions between him and his team. He fired off an angry e-mail to the Chief Constable with copies to Jennings and his boss, Chief Superintendent Spence. To date, he hadn't received a reply from any of the recipients. He stared into the faces of the team. The lack of progress was written large on their countenances. 'Let's meet again at six for a final briefing and for Christ's sake try and bring me something we can run with.'

Moira touched his arm as he was about to move away. She hadn't seen him this down since she had joined the team. 'Do you want to talk?' she asked.

He glanced over at Cummerford. 'Only if we can do it in private, I'm afraid to go to the toilet here in case I find her in the stall with me.' He motioned to Moira to follow him to his office.

Wilson flopped into his chair. 'More than two thousand people on the street for the funeral of someone who should have spent time in prison, and I saw more than one murderer in the group outside the church. It makes my blood boil that people caught on camera murdering people can freely attend funerals and be treated as celebrities. There were at least three people there that I put behind bars. They should still be there, but because they murdered in the name of politics, they're out and they can give me the middle finger. What's the bloody point? Meantime, we are scrambling around trying to find a lead.'

'Something will break,' Moira said with an enthusiasm she didn't feel. It was generally Wilson who provided the enthusiasm, but she had noted that he was more troubled that usual. 'Don't let Cummerford get you down.'

'What's she doing here?'

'It's all the rage now,' Moira said. 'Journalists are embedding themselves everywhere. Aren't you following the Afghanistan thing? Every American platoon that goes out has some safari-jacketed idiot along trying to win a Pulitzer Prize or something. The journalists are fed up reporting the news. Now they want to be part of it. Cummerford is just the tip of the iceberg. Her only purpose is to make a name for herself by writing a book on the investigation?'

'Do you believe that? Jennings wouldn't put a journalist in here unless there was a reason. That man could give lessons to Machiavelli's Prince.'

'It might have something to do with that Harrison business. Word was that she was kicked hard because the *Chronicle* had to apologise and retract the story, she wrote about you. Maybe she holds a grudge against you.'

'Something doesn't smell right,' Wilson said leaning forward.

Moira shuffled uneasily. 'I saw Professor Reid in your office. You seemed to be very friendly.'

'And this concerns you how?' He was piqued.

'I'm a woman, and I recognise the type. She's set her sights on you and you'd better be careful how you handle her. It may turn out to be an easy lay, but it'll be an expensive one in the long run.'

'Kate's pregnant, for God's sake. We're about to have our first child.' He knew he was being defensive. He hadn't been able to say that he wasn't interested in Stephanie Reid, and he hated himself for it. Moira was too bloody smart to miss signals.

'All the more reason to give Reid a wide berth.'

'Point taken. And how's your good professor?'

'He's intelligent, funny and sort of good-looking in a quirky kind of way.'

'You're going to marry him?'

'Been there. Done that. Don't much care for a repeat. We'll see how things go. Speaking of Brendan,' they both laughed, 'he asked me to ask you whether you've ever considered a woman for the Lizzie Rice murder. He was talking to some friend of his in Quantico discussing another case in the States and the question of women killers came up. It appears that in many cases the female of the species is more brutal than the male when it comes to killing.'

'I knew that I'd opened Pandora's Box when I agreed to meet the Professor. Call me cynical but I don't like profilers or psychics, and I certainly wouldn't like the professor to be discussing my cases with his friends in Quantico.'

'Glad to see that you're open-minded.'

Wilson could see Cummerford wandering around outside his office. He let out a large sigh. 'Play time is over. Send her in. Let's see what she's up to.'

'Careful, boss, in more ways than one. '

MAGGIE CUMMERFORD LET her leather messenger bag drop

on the floor as she sat in the chair facing Wilson. 'The funeral was a bummer,' she said. 'Nothing happened.'

'What did you want, murder and mayhem?'

She leaned back in the chair. 'Some decent copy; tears, threats of retaliation, old colleagues running for the plane or boat to get away from internecine warfare. Something to titillate my editor and the masses.'

'That's what it's all about, titillating your editor?'

'For now, yes.'

'And I titillate your editor so much that you inveigle yourself into my investigation?'

'You titillate me, and when I'm finished writing about you my editor will be titillated too.'

'And that's the only reason that you're here, there's no hidden agenda?'

'Not on my part, no.'

'Where did this titillation come from?'

'You're a legend, you just don't know it.'

'And neither do the people of Northern Ireland, and maybe that's the way I want to keep it.

'No can do. Ex-rugby star, forced out of the game by an injury sustained in the cause of duty, top cop with a string of high-profile cases behind you, partner to a top barrister flagged for higher things, rubbing shoulders on a daily basis with the top personalities in the province. Of course, the man in the street wants to know about your life. The average man in the street wants your life.'

'Not if they knew how boring it is. Come on, you've seen it yourself. It's just plodding. Look at the Lizzie Rice case. Two days down the line and we haven't a single lead. There are a million and a half people in Ulster and quite honestly any one of them could be guilty of murdering Lizzie Rice. We're exactly nowhere. As far as my partner and I are concerned, you're never going there, and I wouldn't try if I were you. What are you really after?'

'A job on *The Times* or maybe crime correspondent on *Sky News*. But that won't happen unless someone notices me. And you're my path to being noticed.'

Blind ambition, Wilson thought. That would make Jennings and Cummerford bedfellows. 'I hope you make it; I genuinely do,' Wilson said. 'You know the old Chinese curse – be careful what you wish for because you might get it. Now it's time for me to do a bit of plod. Get lost.'

CHAPTER TWENTY-THREE

The squad room was eerily quiet. Ronald McIver was alone in the large room. He opened the drawer to his desk and looked at the roll of notes held together by an elastic band. He counted them several times already. There were ten twenty-pound notes, forty tens and eighty fives. It was his equivalent of thirty pieces of silver, one thousand pounds for becoming a Judas. It was a small enough price. He closed the drawer and sat looking at his computer screen. Although his eyes were fixed on the screen, he saw nothing. He spent the morning enquiring into the life and times of one Ivan McIlroy. Although they had been at school together their lives had diverged in major ways. They became mirror images of each other. He was a police officer and a deacon at the church. McIlroy was a member of the UVF and a thug. He had married Mary and McIlroy had a history of abusing women, lots of women. McIver trawled the databases for information on McIlroy. His police file was substantial citing more than twenty arrests for everything from grievous bodily harm to arson to causing an affray. Then there were the arrests for beating up women, five in all but a lot more suspected. All the cases were dropped due to the victims withdrawing their evidence. However, despite the accumulation of charges, he had only one conviction. He was given six-month's probation for affray. It was justice Ulster-style. Sammy Rice obviously coated his lieutenant in Teflon. Nothing appeared to stick to McIlroy. McIlroy was an evil bastard and no doubt now McIver was inextricably linked to him via the bundle of grubby notes sitting in his drawer. He looked at Wilson's office. He was about to betray his boss and mentor. McIver had never thought of himself as a Lundy, the reviled traitor to the Protestant people of Ulster. Ian Wilson was good to him. He had supported him when he had been having his minor nervous breakdown. And he was about to thank him by working against him for a reprobate like McIlroy. The thought made him feel sick. But what option did he have? McIlroy had a history of violence against women so the threat he had made against his wife hadn't been an empty one. And Mary wasn't just any woman. She was vulnerable and sweet, and she was suffering from early dementia. At first, he thought that she was simply becoming forgetful but the instances of the gas being left on and the keys to the house being mislaid had multiplied. There were the difficulties in reasoning and the impairment in language. The doctor had called it mild cognitive impairment and had suggested tests that had confirmed early onset of Alzheimer's. They had been devastated but at least there were no children. He couldn't bear the thought of her being abused or raped by McIlroy. He looked again at Wilson's office. He'd have to find a solution.

CHAPTER TWENTY-FOUR

Nancy Morison was more than a little tipsy. She'd spent the morning at the funeral of her good friend, Lizzie Rice. She had been one of those who had gone from the house in Ballygomartin Road to Townsend Street Presbyterian and on to Balmoral Cemetery. And her feet could tell the tale. She'd put on her most comfortable shoes, but they weren't snug enough to counteract the hours of standing and walking. Still it was a wonderful service. The pastor had given a beautiful speech, and the singing of the hymns had been heavenly. Sammy put on a spread at the Black Bear public house with sandwiches and plenty of booze. There had even been rousing renditions of the 'Sash' and 'The Protestant Boys'. In all, it had been a lovely day except for the fact that she would never see Lizzie again. They had both been born on Malvern Street six months apart. Lizzie was the elder, and those six months set her out as the senior partner for all their lives. Lizzie led, and Nancy followed. Lizzie was the boss of their class at school with Nancy her able lieutenant. Lizzie always got the best-looking boyfriends. Billy Rice had been the most handsome young man in the Shankill, and Lizzie had set her sights on him. Nancy wanted him too but when Lizzie told her that she was going to have him, she dropped out of the race. She giggled to herself. Billy's looks didn't last long. He took to the lager like it was mother's milk and his slim figure soon ballooned. She'd looked at him at the funeral, and he looked fucked. It wouldn't be long before he'd be following Lizzie. She stumbled a little. How many vodkas had she had? She tried to count back, but the drinks kept flowing so it was all a blur. Sammy must have put a fortune behind the bar, although she'd heard that he owned the Black Bear, so he was really paying himself. She stopped and opened her bag. She had had a packet of ciggies earlier in the day, and she was sure that she still had at least one left. She had a Eureka moment as she discovered a battered cigarette at the bottom of her bag. She pulled it out and stuck it in her mouth. There was no sign of her lighter in the bag. Where the fuck was the stupid little bugger? She swirled her hand into the mass of rubbish in her bag but there was no sign of the lighter. A young man passed her by, and she moved to ask him for a light, but he was past her before she could get the words out. 'Fucker,' she called after him. She stood on the path with the bent and broken unlit cigarette in her mouth. She had difficulty remembering where she was. Her total concentration was on getting a light for her cigarette.

'Hi, Nancy.'

Nancy turned her concentration from the cigarette to the sound of someone calling her. She looked at the road and saw that a car pulled up beside her. A young woman lowered the window and was speaking to her. She smiled although she didn't recognise the figure in the car. She bent her knees slowly and looked inside. The silly bitch at the wheel was wearing one of those hooded things that hid her face. Maybe she could give me a light. Nancy staggered over to the side of the car.

'Get in. I'll drive you home,' the young woman said opening the door for her from the inside.

'Do you have a light?' Nancy said although it came out as

j*ewhavalit.*

'Yes,' the young woman said. 'Get in.'

'Fuck it,' Nancy said and got in the car.

They immediately moved off from the kerb. Nancy's bag was still open, so she closed it. She looked up at the woman driving. 'I don't know you,' Nancy slurred the words. She was happy to be in a car because of her aching feet. 'Whose cub are you?'

'You met me once,' the young woman said and took a Taser from the side pocket of the car and it one movement pressed it to Nancy's side.

A bolt of electricity shot through Nancy. She convulsed and collapsed in her seat.

'Just think about ice cream,' the young woman said giving Nancy a second jolt.

They drove in silence out of Belfast on the B102 through Andersonstown and on to the Stewartstown Road. When they reached the southern suburb of Dunmurray, the young woman turned left into the countryside. She had selected the site over the past few days. It had to be quiet, but the body had to be discovered quickly. They drove for half an hour before they came to the spot she had chosen. She pulled into the side of the road and looked across at Nancy. Seventy kilos, she estimated. It would be a haul, but she would manage it. The house was being constructed twenty yards from the road. The foundations were already put down and concreted. Blocks were stacked around the foundations to facilitate the bricklayers' work.

Nancy Morison began to stir. She looked out the window of the car and saw that she was in the countryside. She was confused and feeling more than a little sick. She could taste bile in her mouth, so a puking session wasn't too far away. She remembered walking along Cambrai Street in the centre of

Belfast. She was desperate for a ciggie. Then she remembered looking for a light. She suddenly became very afraid. She looked beside her and saw the woman in the hoodie with the electrical gadget in her hand then she felt the bolt of electricity hit her again, and she lost consciousness.

The young woman dragged Nancy Morison out from the passenger side of the car and lifted her with difficulty onto her shoulder. She marched along the rough stone path leading to the foundation staggering over the uneven ground. The old woman was a dead weight, but she managed to get her up onto the concrete foundation.

Nancy came round and found herself lying prone on her back looking up at the sky. This was a nightmare. It must be the drink, she thought. She saw dark clouds scudding across her vision. Looks like rain, she thought. She wondered what she was doing here lying on her back on the cold concrete. She remembered the electric shock and felt her bladder collapse and warm pee flood her knickers and form a pool around her bottom. Suddenly, there was a face directly above hers. She had no idea who her tormentor was. 'Please,' she forced the word out of her mouth.

The young woman looked at her as though she were a specimen. 'It's important that you don't move during the next part of the operation,' she said. 'I'm going to have to give you another little shot.' She held up the electrical gadget with the two points like horns and rammed it into the old woman's chest.

Nancy's body convulsed, and she voided herself. The smell of fresh excrement was immediately in the air.

The young woman picked up a large concrete block from the nearest stack and held it as high as she could before smashing it down on Nancy Morison's head.

The concrete block split the old woman's skull as though it were a coconut. The point of impact was the forehead and crown of the head. Brains and cranial blood spilt out onto the concrete foundation. Death was painful but instantaneous.

The young woman looked at the body for a few moments and then smiled. 'By the way, thanks for the ice cream,' she said.

CHAPTER TWENTY-FIVE

The smell in the apartment was heavenly when Kate pushed in the door. It had been a tough day and although she had prepared herself mentally for the rigours of full-time work and pregnancy, she was ready to accept that she was feeling more tired than she had anticipated. She threw her briefcase down in the foyer and made directly for the source of the smell.

Wilson was standing in the kitchen with a tablet opened on the counter in front of him. Several pots were on the go on the stove. He turned quickly when he heard Kate behind him. 'Welcome, stranger,' he said moving towards her and hugging her.

'Tough day at the office?' she asked. Wilson cooking generally meant that he needed a major unwind that could not be attained by his usual jogging routine. She noticed that he had already been at the wine.

'Terrible, you?'

She threw her jacket onto a couch. 'Snap.'

He moved quickly to the fridge and removed a bottle of white wine. 'A glass of Black Oystercatcher will help reinvigorate you.' He poured a glass and offered it to her.

She took the glass and sipped. It was cold and clear and fruity, and it tasted wonderful.

'I have a Thai green curry chicken with sticky rice on the stove. Have a shower and meet me here in ten minutes.' He patted her on the behind and pushed her in the direction of the bathroom.

'You shouldn't make me jealous.'

'You have nothing to be jealous of,' he lied as he pushed her a little harder towards the bathroom. He lied so easily. But then again, he was an expert at it. Stephanie Reid awakened in him that old urge, that old excitement of the chase that he had given up the evening he had seen his wife expire on her hospice bed. The bastard he thought he had banished, was still just beneath the surface. The 'new' Ian Wilson was just a skin-deep version of the womaniser he thought he had cast aside. Perhaps he should expose his real self to Cummerford. He wondered would she be so happy to unmask the rotten truth that he was probably responsible for his wife's cancer. Not totally responsible but not innocent either. And last night he was close to reliving history because of those old urges. He poured himself another glass of wine, this former rugby star, top cop, philanderer, cheater and liar. That might certainly make good copy and titillate Cummerford's editor.

Kate came back into the living area wearing a white terry bathrobe with her hair balled up in a towel. She clinked glasses with him. 'That was wonderful.' She drank and then put her arms around him. 'I love you.'

'I love you too.' He looked for the lie but didn't find it. He really did love Kate.

She kissed him lightly and stood back. She opened the bathrobe to expose her stomach. She was beginning to show. She took his hand and placed it over her naked stomach.

He knew that inside there was the child he had always wanted. 'Our supper will be overdone if we don't make some headway,' reluctantly moving his hand.

'Did you feel anything?' she asked.

He shook his head, then bent and kissed her. It hadn't been such a shitty day after all.

MOIRA MCELVANEY WAS BURNING the midnight oil. Brendan was leading a seminar and wouldn't be free until ten o'clock. They organised to have a late dinner. She hadn't felt like sitting alone in her flat, so she decided to go through some of the boxes that had arrived from the warehouse in HQ where the old files were kept. She asked for files from the Seventies and Eighties relating to the activities of the Ulster Volunteer Force and, in particular, the women's branch of the organisation. Some organ of the security apparatus had penetrated every paramilitary organisation in Ulster on both sides of the sectarian divide. The Royal Ulster Constabulary, the fore-runner of the PSNI, and the Ulster Defence Regiment had links and sometimes, although it would never be admitted, cross-memberships in Loyalist paramilitaries. military intelli-gence was concentrated on the Republican paramilitary groups. The result was that an enormous amount of documen-tation had been generated by the plethora of undercover agents in the various organisations. That was just problem number one. Individuals with divided loyalties wrote much of the documentation so that reports generally contained a small nugget of information hidden in a mass of fictional narrative. That was problem number two. Moira had already ploughed through several documents referring to the women's branch of the UVF only to find that they were so heavily redacted as to be useless. Heavy black lines obscured whole paragraphs. She flipped over move pages and read the inarticulate ramblings of an RUC plant in the Shankill branch of the UVF. Lizzie Rice's name was prominent as were several others while other names had been redacted. It was all very anodyne stuff. Marches were planned; clothes were made from flags; money was collected, and houses were set alight. Anodyne. She glanced at her watch. It was twenty minutes to ten o'clock, and she had managed two one-inch files since seven o'clock. It was too much like hard work. She hoped that Brendan was in the mood for dinner, drinks and a hefty bout of lovemaking. She wondered whether there was any future in their relationship. In six months, he would be heading back to Harvard and she would still be chasing criminals around Belfast. She had been down the marriage road and had seen at first-hand how two people can make a career out of hurting each other. Right now, she would settle for the drinks, the dinner and the lovemaking. Tomorrow would be another day.

CHAPTER TWENTY-SIX

'What sort of day do you have?' Wilson said popping a second capsule into the coffee machine. His head was not exactly in great order due to a combination of Black Oystercatcher and Chianti washed down with Jameson. The good news was that he and Kate were totally reconciled, and he had promised himself to stay as far away as possible from Stephanie Reid within the confines of his job. Kate and their unborn child were his priorities.

'The usual, court, court and more court,' Kate wolfed some toast and marmalade, 'followed by meetings with clients at the office,' flakes of toasted bread flew from the corners of her mouth. 'So, a pretty full day.'

'When can we expect a slowdown?' The coffee was beginning to take effect.

'I'm planning my schedule with the clerk in chambers. I've told him to give the briefs to some of my colleagues who are in urgent need of money.'

'But people are still asking for you?'

'It's nice to have a reputation but not when you're having a baby.'

'And the Truth and Reconciliation Committee?'

'On the back burner as we agreed. Ellie Smith has taken over.'

'What's her interest in Northern Ireland? Doesn't she have enough to do in South Africa?'

'She was born here, I mean Belfast. Emigrated to SA when she was a child, I think. Her father was a mining engineer or something. Anyway, she's a tough nut. She worked with Desmond Tutu on the South African Committee. She has a first in law from Stellenbosch University.'

Wilson's phone started to do a whirling dance on the breakfast bar between them. He grabbed it before it went over the edge and pressed the green button. He listened for a few minutes. 'Tell McElvaney to get a car and pick me up in ten.'

Kate stared at him across the breakfast bar.

'Another older lady found murdered on a building site in Dunmurry. Someone caved in her head with a concrete block.'

'Late tonight?'

'Looks like it.'

'I wonder, will we ever be a normal couple?'

He walked around the breakfast bar and kissed her. 'That depends on your definition of normal,' he said.

THE BUILDING SITE at Dunmurray had already been ringed off by crime-scene tape when Wilson and Moira arrived. Two police cars blocked off traffic on both sides of the road, and a diversion had already been put in place. A small van and a car were already within the cordon, and Wilson assumed these vehicles belonged to the builders. The site was in a secluded area and screened from the road by a row of bushes and trees. The builders had already laid a rough roadway of large stones to allow them to bring lorries directly up to the area where the house would eventually stand. Wilson nodded at Moira, who signed both in. They dispensed with the plastic jumpsuits since the builders, and the local police had already contaminated the scene. A policeman led the two detectives along the stone path to the foundations.

'Where are the builders?' Wilson asked.

'In the van having a cuppa,' the policeman replied. 'They're looking the worse for wear and I don't blame them. I've been on the force for fifteen years, but I've never seen anything like this.'

The woman was lying on the concrete plinth that would eventually hold the house. She was spread-eagled and the concrete block that killed her was still resting on her head. It was delivered with enough force to crush her skull. Blood and brain caked her brown hair.

'The pathologist and the forensic?' Wilson asked.

'On the way,' Moira answered.

'I think it's safe to assume that this has something to do with the Lizzie Rice murder. Looks like we may have a serial killer on our hands.'

'Looks that way, boss.' She was wondering what Brendan would make of this.

The policemen handed Wilson a leather bag. 'One of the builders found this on the stone path. It must have dropped when she was carried here.'

Wilson passed the bag to Moira. She returned to the car where she had left the plastic gloves and evidence bags. He glanced around the area. Not a bad spot for a murder. Not a house in sight and he guessed very light traffic along the laneway. Very little chance of being disturbed and yet a very good chance that the body would be discovered by the arriving builders in the morning. The murderer wanted the body to be discovered quickly. He wasn't depending on someone out walking the dog and finding it accidentally. The question was why did the murderer want the body found so quickly or didn't they care about hiding the body?

'Nancy Morison, late of Malvern Street,' Moira said

joining Wilson at the foundation. 'Nothing out of the ordinary in the bag but I've put everything away nice and neat.'

'Good girl, and I'm being politically correct. OK.'

They smiled.

'Malvern Street again, I think we can assume a definite connection to Lizzie. How old do you think she is?' Wilson asked.

'It's pretty difficult to guess with a concrete block disguising most of her head, but judging from the body and the clothes, I would guess that she's somewhere between late fifties and early sixties.'

'Roughly the same age as Lizzie?'

'More or less.'

'Bit of a coincidence. Both women's heads destroyed, both about the same age and both from Malvern Street. Too bloody much of a coincidence. I wonder what these two were up to that they deserved to die this way.'

'Well there's no doubt that they certainly pissed someone off in a very bad way.'

'Let's talk to the builders.' Wilson turned and made his way back along the rocky pathway. He marched up to the van and slid the side door open. Three men in overalls sat in the van drinking tea from plastic cups. They looked to be in shock. 'I'm Detective Superintendent Ian Wilson,' he held up his warrant card more out of habit than necessity. 'And this is Detective Sergeant McElvaney. Can you please get out of the van?' He moved back to allow the three men to alight.

'I'm Joe Campbell,' said the first man to descend. 'And this here's Jimmy Law and Dick Johnson.'

'Tell me about this morning when you arrived,' Wilson said.

'We come up the lane like we do every morn,' Campbell was taking on the role as spokesman. 'We parked the van and got our stuff together, so we did. We had the blocks put around, the foundation yesterday, and we were goin' to start on the walls today. As soon as we came onto the site, we saw the body on the foundation. I never seen the like. Her head was all blood, so it was. It right turned my stomach. Then we got on the mobile and called you peelers.'

'Did you notice anything strange?'

'Like what?'

'Anything out of the ordinary.'

'There's nothing here, you know. We're only startin.'

'I thought that it was normal to put a fence up to limit access to the site.'

Campbell looked around at his colleagues. 'Aye it is but the main contractor is a mean shite, so he is. That's why we keep our tools in the van. The site is too open, but the mean fucker doesn't want to spend the money to fence it in.'

Wilson looked at the ground outside the site. The excavation had thrown up a good deal of mud, and a series of tyre tracks were visible. He turned to Moira. 'Make sure that forensic get casts of every track. We can easily eliminate the workers' van and the car.' He turned to the three men again. 'If you remember anything, and I mean anything different about this morning I want you to contact me.' He took some business cards from his pocket and handed one to each of the three men.

'How soon will the site be open?' Campbell asked.

'That depends. We're waiting for the pathologist and the forensics team. Not today. You guys are on holiday but leave your contact details with the officer holding the clipboard.'

'No work, no money,' Campbell said. 'We don't take holidays.'

'I'll tell them to get a rush on but they're going to comb every inch of the site. It may take days so if I were you, I'd go looking for a fill-in job.'

'Where have you been lately?' the man named Law said. 'There's a recession on. This is the only job we have at the present. I wish the murderer had chosen another site.'

'I'm sorry for your trouble,' Wilson said. A car was pulling up beyond one of the police cars, and it was accompanied by a meat wagon. 'Looks like the pathologist has arrived.'

'Be still my beating heart,' Moira said under her breath.

Wilson looked at her harshly. 'You're not funny, detective sergeant.' He saw the blonde hair of Professor Stephanie Reid as she stepped out of her car. She strode forward with her blue plastic jumpsuit in hand. She ducked under the crime-scene tape and stepped into her suit.

'Another client,' she said as she joined the group at the entrance.

'You guys can head off,' Wilson said.

The three bricklayers moved towards their van grumbling as they went.

'Another elderly lady,' Moira said. 'Nancy Morison. Head caved in by a concrete block. Not very pretty.'

'Understatement,' Wilson added.

'Superintendent Wilson,' Reid said. 'Pleased to see you again. I better look at the body.' She strode towards the foundation.

Moira put her fingers down her throat and made a sick motion.

'I take it you don't like Professor Reid.'

'Man-eater,' Moira said.

While Reid was examining the body, the forensics team arrived and commandeered the site. Two technicians moved forward with a blue plastic tent and erected it directly over the body.

'The body can be moved as soon as your people are through,' Reid said stripping the top of her blue suit off and jutting her chest out just enough to display her firm, full breasts. 'I'll schedule the autopsy for as soon as possible. I assume you'll attend.

Moira moved off and spoke to the chief of the forensics team.

'Either me, or DS McElvaney,' Wilson spoke loud enough so that Moira could hear him.

'You're being kept pretty busy,' Reid said. 'We'll have to find time to cram in that drink.'

'Like I said when the murderer is behind bars.'

'No rest for the wicked, eh. And I understand you have a reputation for being very wicked.'

'Totally undeserved,' he looked over her shoulder.

Moira re-joined them before she could answer. 'Forensic is in charge, boss. I passed on the message on the tyre tracks and got a rocket from the head boy. Telling him how to do his job etcetera, etcetera. We ready to roll?'

'Let's go see Mr Morison and give him the bad news,' Wilson turned to Reid. 'Let us know when you schedule the autopsy.'

'Looking forward to it,' Reid said as Wilson and McElvaney made for their car.

CHAPTER TWENTY-SEVEN

W ilson sat pondering the latest murder as Moira piloted their car back into the centre of Belfast. There was no doubt in his mind that the murders of Nancy Morison and Lizzie Rice were the work of the same person. There might now at least be a chink in the investigation since they could concentrate on the connection between the two women. There was now also no doubt that the head injuries were a significant element. The killer also transported Morison to the murder site. They would trawl through the traffic CCTV for the previous evening, and he was sure that they would find the vehicle that had been used as transport. The final element he pondered was the fact that the body had been left where it could be easily found. The murderer could very well have dispatched Morison in some leafy glade and buried the body. It might have taken months or indeed years to discover the murder, but the killer would have known that the building crew would be on site the following day. The killer had more than likely scoped out the site before choosing the killing ground.

They drove directly to Malvern Street and parked outside the Morison house. It was a mirror image of the house in which Lizzie Rice had lived – a red-bricked terraced two up and two down. The only difference was the condition of the building. The front door and the window frames had been recently painted. Billy Rice's abode looked like a tip.

They rang the bell, and a man in his early sixties opened the door.

'I'm Superintendent Ian Wilson and this is Detective Sergeant McElvaney,' they held out their warrant cards for inspection. 'I wonder, can we come in?'

Morison's pale face was a picture of confusion and worry-lines stood out on his forehead like ridges on a plain. He opened the door wide enough for them to enter. 'That was quick, 'he said as he closed the door. 'I've just been down to the police station.'

'And why was that?' Wilson asked.

Morison closed the front door behind them, and the three of them stood in the small hallway. 'I thought they sent you from the station,' he said. 'My wife, Nancy went to Lizzie Rice's funeral yesterday but never came home. I phoned around, and folk told me that they saw her at the Black Bear, but since then there hasn't been hide or hair of her. I thought she might have stayed with one of her friends, but she would surely have been home by now.'

Without being asked Wilson walked into the living room. 'Perhaps you'd like to sit down.'

The man sat on a chair and looked up at Wilson.

'Nancy Morison is your wife?' Wilson asked.

'Aye, I'm Joe Morison,' the man replied, and a tear came out of his eye. 'Has something's happened to her? Did she have an accident? Tell me for God's sake.'

'I'm afraid your wife is dead,' Wilson said. 'She was found murdered on a building site in Dunmurray this morning.'

Morison put his head in his hands and wept, his body shaking with every sob. Finally, he stopped and looked up at the two police officers. 'I told her not to go to the funeral of that terrible woman. I was worried sick when she didn't come home or call me. That Rice woman is the cause of her death, mark my words. I want to see her.'

Wilson put his hand on Morison's shoulder. His body was still convulsing. 'She's being transferred to the Royal,' he said. 'We'll arrange for you to see her as soon as possible. Has your wife been threatened lately?'

Morison looked up into Wilson's face. 'What are you talking about, man? Nancy was just a housewife and a good-hearted woman. She didn't have an enemy in the world. It was only when she was around that witch Rice that there was a problem.'

'What do you mean?' Wilson asked.

'All that business during the 'Troubles',' Morison took a paper handkerchief from a box on a small coffee table and dried his eyes. 'Nancy was never political. She didn't have a bad bone in her body, but that Rice woman had some sort of hold over her. She only had to knock on the door and Nancy would be out following her like a stray dog. Why would someone want to kill such a harmless creature?' Morison put his head in his hands again and started to cry.

Wilson looked around the small room. The Morisons didn't live the high life. The television in the corner was several generations old, but he noticed the satellite box under-neath it. Since the husband was still at home, he guessed the couple were on social welfare.

'No overt threats then,' Wilson said when the crying subsided.

'No. As far as I know she didn't have a care in the world.' He blew his nose into the paper handkerchief.

'She wasn't still involved?' Wilson asked.

'Good God, no,' Morison stood up. 'She gave up all that stuff years ago. She didn't attend a meeting or a street demon-stration for more than ten years. As soon as the Rice woman gave up the politics, so did she. A quiet woman, no one had a reason to kill her. What will I do now?' He took a second handkerchief from the box, held it up to his face and cried into it.

'Do you have any family?' Wilson asked.

'Aye,' he said through the sobs. 'Two daughters, but they're in Vancouver,' he pointed at the pictures adorning the wall behind Wilson's back.

Wilson turned and looked at a series of frames containing groups of photos. One showed two young girls photographed together at various ages. 'Good looking girls,' he said.

'Aye, and smart too,' Morison stopped sobbing and put the paper handkerchief into his pocket. The concentration on his children seemed to divert him. 'Got out of here as soon as they could and trained to be nurses. Clever girls.'

Wilson moved to a large frame that contained a series of older photos. 'Do you have a portrait photo of your wife I can borrow?'

Morison went to a small chest of drawers in the corner of the room. He opened the top drawer and began to search inside.

While his back was turned, Wilson removed a photo from the group of old photos. The colours were faded but it showed a crowd of women standing behind a flag of the Ulster Volunteer Force. He slipped the photo into his pocket.

Morison returned from the corner with a six by ten-inch photo of his wife's face. 'It was taken last year for the girls' birthdays. Nancy sent them both a copy in a frame. She was always afraid that they'd forget us.' He handed it reluctantly to Wilson.

'Don't worry, we'll make a copy and return the original to you,' Wilson took the photo and passed it to Moira. 'Do you have anybody who can come to stay with you?'

'I have a sister in Carrickfergus.'

'Why don't you give DS McElvaney her phone number,' Wilson said. 'We'll arrange for a police liaison officer to visit you and to make sure that your sister is informed. We'll call you to tell you when you can see her body and make the formal identification. That will probably be later today. We'll need a statement on your wife's movements yesterday. That can wait as well. Mr Morison we're very sorry for your trouble, and I can assure you that we're going to do everything possible to catch the person that did this.'

Joe Morison extended his hand to Wilson. 'I never thought that Nancy would be the first to go. I'm no good on my own, Superintendent. I can hardly boil an egg. What will I ever do?'

Wilson shook his hand. 'The liaison officer will help you out with organising the arrangements. She also put you in touch with the social and they'll make sure that you're alright.'

'Thank you, Superintendent.' He held out his hand to Moira who shook it.

'THAT CLEARS UP ONE POINT ANYWAY,' Wilson said as they settled in the car.

'Nancy Morison was a camp follower for Lizzie Rice and that's the reason that she's headed for the morgue,' Moira opined.

'Which begs the question.'

'How many more camp followers are there?'

CHAPTER TWENTY-EIGHT

The atmosphere at the team briefing was the opposite of the past few days, and that was down totally to the enthusiasm that Wilson now generated. A new photo of Nancy Morison was added to the whiteboard and a line drawn between it and the photo of Lizzie Rice. The forensic photos would be added later, but Moira had already sketched in what they knew about the latest victim.

'We have several new lines of enquiry,' Wilson said. 'We need a timeline on Nancy Morison's movements yesterday. It appears that she attended the Rice funeral alone and probably hit the bash in the Black Bear afterwards. Peter, you're on this. Talk to people who were at the Black Bear and see if anyone remember what time she left at and what state she was in. Ronald, check the route she would have used on the way home and see if there is any CCTV that we can gather. Check with traffic and see if they have anything. Liaise with Peter so that we can concentrate on the time she was on the road. She was picked up anywhere between the Black Bear and her home. My guess is that the autopsy will show that she was Tasered. We need to know whether she got into a car willingly or did some guy Taser her and then drag her in. Did anyone see an older lady being dragged into a car? Was anything reported to the local stations?' He turned around and pointed at the white-board. Beneath the photo of Lizzie Rice, there were the forensic photos, the photo of the bingo club and the house in Malvern Street. 'We blanked out with evidence on the Rice murder, but we have a lot of leads on this one. One thing bothers me. Lizzie was killed in the house where Billy lay comatose. The killer knew that as soon as Billy came around, the body would be found. Nancy Morison was laid out on a house foundation where the bricklayers had already laid out their blocks and were about to begin work. The killer knew that as soon as the brickies arrived this morning the first thing they'd see would be the body. This killer is smart. He didn't leave a speck of evidence at Malvern Street. He could just as easily have murdered Rice and Morison and hidden their bodies. But he wanted them found. There's a message there. Lizzie Rice's son is a major gangland figure. Is someone trying to give him a message? Think about it and if you come up with any answers, I'd be grateful to hear them. I want to see this whiteboard full by tomorrow. Someone is out there murdering Protestant women of a certain age. I want him. Harry and Moira in my office.'

'Sit,' Wilson said as soon as Moira and Harry Graham were in his office. He produced the faded photo from his inside pocket and put it on the table. 'I've kept the nicest job for you two. This is a photo of the Shankill Road branch of the women's UVF taken some time ago. There are eight women in this photo. In the centre, you'll notice Lizzie Rice and to her right is Nancy Morison. I want to know who the other six women in this photo are, and I want each of them interviewed. I want to know if they're aware of any reason why someone would want to murder at least two of their number. I want a motive for these killings so that I can stop them.'

'OK, boss,' Harry Graham said. 'Finding the identities of the women will be difficult enough. It'll be harder to get them to spill what they know about Lizzie Rice. You know the scene here, *omerta* is the rule. Anyone who puts the finger on Lizzie Rice will have to deal with Sammy. Right now, she's being portrayed as a Loyalist icon. Interfering with that image is going to be very dangerous. Assuming we do get something from them, which I seriously doubt, and there is another planned victim or victims, we have no chance of protecting six people long term.'

'You're right, Harry,' Wilson said. He could just imagine the overtime bill that would be associated with 24-hour protection for six women. 'When we discover the motive, we're going to have to identify the killer at the same time.'

Moira picked up the photo. The women wore their best dresses and their sternest faces for the photographer. Each had some element of the Union Jack about their person, either a scarf, a bag or a blouse. They really were the Loyalist heroines. 'I've been ploughing through old PSNI files,' Moira put the photo back on the desk. 'It's worse than pulling teeth. Most of the reports are written in primary school English and even then, there are lots of errors. There are five boxes of files, and I don't really have the time to help with identifying the women. Harry needs help from someone who has street-credibility in the Shankill. That's not me. Maybe I can assist with the interviews when he locates the women.'

'Sounds like a plan,' Wilson said. 'But we should be moving on it rather than sitting here talking about it.

'Yes, boss,' Moira and Graham said together.

You've made a bloody mistake; Wilson thought to himself. That's the part he didn't understand. Someone who is clever enough not to leave a trace at a murder site but wants the bodies discovered immediately. What's the message? And who is it for? If it's Sammy Rice, then this could be the start of a gang war that could leave a dozen people dead. But where did Nancy Morison fit into a message to Sammy Rice? Perhaps Lizzie was the message, and Nancy was collateral damage.

Perhaps she saw something she shouldn't have or said something that was better kept to herself. In Belfast, you never really knew. Sammy Rice was a dangerous man to send a message to. He looked out on the squad room. The latest killing galvanised the team. He was wondering whether the killer was a professional when the phone rang.

'Hold for the DCC,' a haughty female voice said.

'Wilson,' the DCC Jennings' voice was sharp and unfriendly. Nothing new for Wilson.

'Sir.'

'I'm waiting for a briefing on this morning's murder.'

Wilson put on his subservient hat. Now was no time to rock the boat. 'I've just returned to the office from interviewing the husband of the murdered woman, and I was about to brief Chief Superintendent Spence. I assume that in due course he will brief you.'

'Things are getting out of hand, Wilson. Two murders, and one the mother of a prominent citizen. Several interested parties who feared an escalation in killings after the Lizzie Rice murder have approached me. This business smacks of a gang war. And I want it stopped forthwith.'

'When I find the killer, sir, I'll tell him he is so instructed.'

'Don't get smart with me, Superintendent. Because of my position, I sometimes receive intelligence that is not available to people like you on the lower rungs of the force. I am privy to information that McGreery might be behind the Lizzie Rice killing. I want him brought in for questioning. '

'Do you think it's wise to announce a gang war? We might very well get one. Things have been peaceful since 2011.'

'You do understand the system of rank, don't you superintendent. I am a Deputy Chief Constable. I tell you to jump, and you ask how high and add sir. Bring McGreery in for questioning and any other member of his gang that you consider might be involved. I want the body count stopped at two.'

The phone went dead in Wilson's hand.

. . .

WILSON KNOCKED and pushed in the door of Chief Superintendent Spence's office.

Donald Spence sighed and said, 'Come in.'

'Sarcasm doesn't suit you,' Wilson said sitting down on the other side of Spence's desk. 'I've just had the DCC on the phone.'

'That must have been entertaining. Fill me in on the Morison situation.'

Wilson ran through the discovery of the body and his briefing of the team on the Morison murder.

Spence was silent for a few moments when Wilson had finished. 'You don't think that Jennings could have a point? There are some people out there who would like to bring Sammy down.'

'And where does Nancy Morison fit into that theory? Killing Lizzie could have been aimed at Sammy but as far as we know Nancy Morison has nothing to do with him.'

'As far as we know. Let's humour the DCC. Bring McGreery in. You don't need to give him the rubber hose treatment. A nice cup of tea and a chat.'

Wilson stood. 'You're the boss.'

Spence smiled. 'It doesn't feel like it sometimes.'

CHAPTER TWENTY-NINE

B elfast, 1983

THE MAN DRIVING the car searched frantically for a spot to drop the little girl off. He chose a quiet housing estate in the north of the city. He didn't like it, but you didn't fuck around with Lizzie Rice. He pulled up on an empty road, got out of the car and looked around. It was early afternoon, and the street was deserted. He moved to the boot. The little girl was asleep on an old tyre. The man had never purposely hurt a child in his life and certainly never a Protestant child. He lifted her out of the boot and shook her awake. He placed her on the footpath.

'Where's my Ma?' she asked him through a flood of tears. He told her to wait where she was, and her Ma would be along soon. He got back into his car and drove away quickly. The little girl looked down the row of houses. This wasn't where she and Ma lived. All the houses had front gardens surrounded by brick walls with gates leading to the house. It must be nice to live in a house like this. She sat on the wall of one of them.

She missed her mother. Why did Ma leave her alone with the other women? She started to cry again. She repeated,' I want my Ma,' again and again. It was getting dark when the police car pulled up beside her. The policeman was very nice and took her in his car to a big building. He told her that he was going to find her Ma. They gave her some sandwiches and tea. After a while, a nice woman came and talked to her. She told them that she had lost her Ma, and that Ma had gone into a building with some other women and hadn't come out. She told them about the woman who had bought her the ice cream. A policeman came into the room and spoke with the nice woman. She listened and heard him say that there was no sign of Ma. Must have run off, he said, unmarried, pregnant and dealing with a small child. The nice woman said that she was going to take care of her. She was going to live in a place where there were a lot of children, and she would like it. It sounded nice.

CHAPTER THIRTY

S ix o'clock briefing of the Murder Squad and there was a buzz from the team as Wilson took his place in front of the whiteboard. Maggie Cummerford took her place at the back of the room and tapped away on her laptop. 'Lizzie Rice,' he said simply. 'She's the core of the killer's motive. That is, unless we find out something spectacular about Nancy Morison.'

'Still ploughing through the intelligence files, boss,' Moira said. 'There are boxes and boxes of the bloody stuff. It's going to take weeks. She was a very active lady.'

'Everybody on Malvern Street and the surrounding streets has been re-interviewed,' Peter Davidson said. 'We've done our best to shake up a few memories but nothing so far. Sorry.'

'Search of the area turned up nothing on the blunt instrument,' Harry Graham said. 'Either he still has it, or it's been dumped.'

Wilson looked at Ronald McIver, but he seemed to be a million miles away. He switched his gaze to Eric Taylor.

'I've interviewed Lizzie's friends and former colleagues. Not many words and none of them bad,' Taylor said. 'I've written it up but it's a dead end.'

'Let's move on to Nancy Morison,' Wilson looked at Peter Davidson.

'She attended the Lizzie Rice funeral and the after-funeral bash at the Black Bear. I've spoken to half dozen of the attendees and while most of them remember seeing her, there's no consensus on what time she left. Some people say they didn't see her after five o'clock while others say they saw her at seven. If I was to guess I'd say she left sometime between five and seven.'

'We've got the traffic tapes, boss,' Harry Graham said. 'And we're checkin' to see what CCTV is available for the route from the Black Bear to Malvern Street. It might take a while, but I'm sure we'll turn up something.'

'She was a nobody,' Ronald McIver seemed suddenly awake. 'I went through the records. Nothing. She was never picked up. No record, like I said nothing.'

Wilson tried to hide his disappointment. 'The autopsy is tomorrow morning, but I don't expect that we're going to learn anything new. The cause of death will be a concrete block dropped on her head, full stop. Forensics have the murder weapon but if our killer is as intelligent as I think he is, we won't get anything there.' He let his gaze run across his team. 'We have to keep at it. We need a break.' He looked directly at McIver. 'Ronald can I see you in my office?'

'Boss,' McIver said and followed Wilson to his office.

Wilson noticed Maggie Cummerford packing up her computer but not leaving the squad room. The bloody woman was always hovering about.

'Shut the door,' Wilson said as soon as they had entered the office. 'I've noticed that you're a bit out of sorts lately. Is there something bothering you?'

'Just some home issues, boss' McIver didn't bother to sit. 'Nothing for you to get concerned over.'

'You're a member of my team. That just doesn't mean

work. If there's some way that I can help with whatever the matter is, then I want to do it.'

'It's medical. There's nothing you can do. It'll work out.

'Do you need some leave?'

'Not in the middle of two difficult cases. Maybe if things get a bit quieter.'

Wilson liked McIver. He was the quietist member of the team but one of the most experienced and reliable. He was sad to see him so down. 'Just remember that I'm here to help. You tell me what you need and I'm going to do my best to get it for you.'

'Thanks, boss. It's appreciated.' McIver started to move toward the door.

'See you tomorrow, Wilson said.

He was about to turn to his computer when Maggie Cummerford entered his office. 'Two cases for the price of one,' she said dropping her messenger bag on the floor and sitting down.

'I'm not up for this right now. In case you didn't notice, I'm a bit busy.'

She smiled and waved her access badge at him. 'Access all areas the big boss said.'

'What have you got on him?'

'My editor and him are big pals. They both see the value of turning you into a hero. The general population has almost forgotten that you once played rugby for Ireland, and Jennings is an expert at taking the credit for successful murder investigations. You should learn not to look a gift horse in the mouth.' She bent and removed a file from her messenger case and put it on the table. 'That's the amount of press cuttings I've located on your rugby career.' The file was nearly two inches thick. 'You really were something back in the day. It must have hurt when you had to give it up.'

It still bloody hurts, he thought. When he had moved in with Kate, he had cast aside his previous life. He still had photos of Susan, but he never looked at them. They only evinced guilt. He had presented all his old rugby parapher-nalia to his club, and they had auctioned it off for prices he couldn't believe. It had been like losing a vital organ, but he had decided that his life was about Kate and the future and not about pining for the past. 'Yes, it hurt,' he said simply.

'You're an amazing guy. A lot of people would have used the sympathy element of a brilliant career cut short by an injury sustained in the line of duty to lever themselves in a cushy number commentating or being a pundit on television. But when you recovered you immediately returned to the police job. Why did you do that?'

'I'm a copper not a pundit or a commentator.'

She smiled. 'You're a strange guy. That's why I wanted to profile you. You don't want publicity. You just want to do what you want to do.'

'You got it in one. And if you have any sense, you'll leave me alone.'

She thought for a moment then replaced the file in her bag. 'We'll see about that,' she said before moving to the door.

CHAPTER THIRTY-ONE

S ammy Rice spent most of the day in bed. As the grieving son, he had been obliged to drink alcohol for most of the previous day and night and despite his Irish heritage, an excess of alcohol did not sit well with him. The pains in his stomach were only matched by the headaches. Every time he thought about crawling out of bed a fresh burst of pain would convince him that he wasn't yet ready to confront the world. It was almost five o'clock in the afternoon before he felt sufficiently human. . He managed to get some food down, but the day was totally wasted as far as getting things done. Every now and then, his mind wandered to the question of how Lizzie managed to get herself murdered right in the middle of his holiday. He had splurged on a five-bedroom villa with swimming pool on the Costa del Sol and he wanted to enjoy his new toy. He'd clear things up in Belfast as quickly as possible and then get back to the sun. Sammy's wife didn't bother to join him in Belfast. She never got on with Lizzie and didn't want to be a hypocrite. Either that or she was more intent on peddling her arse to the young Spanish pro at the golf club. He was going to sort that situation out as soon as he got back to Spain. He walked into the living room to find his father spread-eagled in an armchair surrounded by empty beer cans. One of his gang members was in another chair watching snooker on the television.

'Get that auld fucker up to bed,' he said.

His man moved reluctantly to Billy and pulled him upright. He tried to lift him but couldn't manage it. 'Fucker's a dead weight. I'd need a forklift or a crane to get him upstairs.'

'Well, if you're going to be as useless as a snowball in an igloo, fuck off home.'

The young man shuffled. 'Ivan told me to stay here and look after things.'

'And I'm telling you to piss off. Now piss off if you still want to have two knees at the weekend.'

The young man made for the door and left quickly.

What the fuck is going on here, Rice thought. I've been away two weeks, and the fucking hired help thinks that they should obey Ivan fucking McIlroy before they obey me. And some asshole thinks that he can dig a hole in the back of my mother's head, and nothing'll be done about it. Then they don't know Sammy Rice. I'm goin' to hang the bastard that did Lizzie by the balls from a lamppost on the Shankill. That'll show them who's still running things around here. He flopped into the chair recently vacated by the idiot McIlroy left to take care of things. The standard of criminal must be going down seriously when they were taking on village idiots.

'You're up,' Ivan McIlroy stood in the doorway. 'The gobshite I left here's run off home. You threatened to kneecap him,' McIlroy burst out laughing.

'Keep it down. My head is still a bit fragile.'

'I'm not goin' to help it. You remember an auld biddy that used to pal around with Lizzie called Nancy Morison?'

Sammy thought for a while. 'A little auld one, fond of the gargle, used to hang around Lizzie like a pet dog. I think I saw her at the Black Bear yesterday.'

'Aye, that's the one. Someone did her in last night on a

building site out Dunmurray way. They dropped a concrete block on her head. Made a right mess of her.'

'What the f . . .' Rice stood up and struggled into the kitchen. Where was that bitch of a wife when you needed her? He pulled at a series of shelves becoming more irate and destructive as he went. By the time McIlroy joined him in the kitchen, the floor was covered in the contents of the shelving units. 'Fucking Solpadine,' Rice said. 'Where does she hide the fucking Solpadine?' The contents of another shelf hit the floor. He noticed the red package in the corner of the next shelf and pulled it out. He picked up a glass and filled it full of water before dropping two tablets into the glass. He drank the whole lot down as soon as the tablets had dissolved. 'Now run that past me one more time,' he said as he made his way back to the living room.

McIlroy repeated the message concerning Nancy Morison.

Rice could feel a small improvement in his headache. 'Did I change planets when I came back here this week? I can understand someone takin' Lizzie out. She could have filled Windsor Park with the people who had a grudge against her, but some stupid auld biddy. There's something very strange goin' on here. Where did the Morison woman live?'

'Malvern Street, the other end from your old house.'

'Was she married?'

'Aye, old codger used to work in the shipyard.'

'Connected?'

'Wasn't interested. Maybe he's Jewish or something,' McIlroy smiled.

'It's no jokin' matter, Ivan. People around here look to us to make sure they're not killed in their beds. We're the ones that do the killin' around here and not vice versa. Two auld dolls with their heads bashed in, in as many days, doesn't do our reputation any good.'

'The peelers are on it.'

'The majority of them fools couldn't find their own arse-holes with a map and set of instructions.'

'What are we goin' to do about it?'

Rice's head was pounding again. 'You've got someone in Wilson's team.'

'Aye.'

'Lean on him. I'll go higher, but I want information from the horses leading the charge not just from the owner in the stands watching the race. Something that affects us is going down, and I want to know what it is. And I want the bastard behind it.'

CHAPTER THIRTY-TWO

The hostess ushered Wilson to the table. The other seven guests were seated and had already started on their meal. Kate looked up from her plate and raised her eyes to heaven. It wasn't the first time he'd been late for a formal dinner, and it probably wouldn't be the last. These kinds of networking dinners were a feature of Kate's life but not his. For him, listening to the lawyers, doctors and politicians drone on was on a par with a visit to the dentist. And Ian Wilson detested his visits to the dentist.

'Apologies,' he mumbled as he took the only vacant set at the table. 'Busy day.'

Each guest had a place card set before them with their names printed on it. The host and hostess had the seats at the top and bottom of the table with the other six guests arraigned on either side. Wilson quickly glanced at the place names and saw that this evening's guests were from the legal and political milieu. How Roy Jennings would love to be in Wilson's seat. It was a mark of the difference between the two former cadet colleagues. Jennings would squeeze every ounce of benefit from a relationship with a woman as well connected as Kate. He turned to the lady to his side and recognised her dark features and brooding demeanour. Her place card said Ellie Smith.

'No riots tonight?' his host said from the top of the table. He was a judge, who had put many rioters in jail.

'They appear to have run out of steam,' Wilson answered and started on his plate of smoked salmon. He thought about where he would prefer to be, and it was almost anywhere else.

'Ian is more concerned with the two murdered women than with the riots,' Kate interjected.

'Lizzie Rice,' the judge said absent-mindedly. 'Had her up before me once but the prosecution case fell apart. Horrid woman. You must be awash with suspects.'

The other guests at the table laughed except for Kate and Ellie Smith.

'We're working our way through them,' Wilson said.

'Ah, so an arrest is imminent?' the judge remarked.

'I wouldn't say that. However, I am hopeful that you'll get the opportunity to pass judgement on the murderer.' Wilson ducked his head toward his plate.

The host moved the conversation on smoothly to the next subject involving some raucous goings-on at the Stormont Assembly. Kate was actively involved in giving her opinion on the latest political fracas. Wilson relaxed. He was now fully integrated into the conversation, and the concentration would no longer be on him.

'Are you following the rugby?' Ellie Smith asked.

'As much as I can. We're pretty busy right now.' The main course of roast lamb, scalloped potatoes and steamed vegetables arrived.

'I've been reading about the murders,' Smith said. 'They're quite gruesome. Reminds me of the last days of apartheid. People can be incredibly cruel. I'm sure you've heard about the Soweto necktie?'

'It made the papers, although in description only,' Wilson looked up the table and saw Kate in animated conversation with the host. She really was a phenomenon. The combination of brains and beauty was terrifying. He stared at Ellie Smith. She certainly would not have been called beautiful and there was a kind of sadness in her eyes. He wondered what had happened to cause it. 'How are you enjoying Belfast?' he asked.

'I could do without the weather,' she laughed, and it animated her face. 'But I'm enjoying trying to help Kate progress this idea of a Truth and Reconciliation Commission. I understand that you don't approve of the idea.'

'I think it's a lost cause. People here don't want to rehash the past. We've already had the principles on television doing the *mea culpa* bit. There are still a lot of bodies out there that people don't want to talk about.'

'Don't you believe that those who were involved in atrocities should be punished?' she asked.

Wilson laughed. 'This is Northern Ireland. We have people who committed murders sitting in pubs drinking pints of Guinness while they should be languishing in jail. '

'It was part of a political settlement,' said the politician sitting across from Wilson.

Wilson looked around the table and realised that the other dinner guests were listening to his conversation with Ellie Smith. 'I'm a policeman,' he said. 'That means that I uphold the law and gather evidence that puts criminals before the courts. What happens after I pass the file to the Director of Public Prosecutions is not my business. But it burns me up when I see people that I know have broken the law in the worse possible way living like normal citizens.'

'You don't believe in rehabilitation?' the judge said from the top of the table.

'My views are simple,' Wilson said. 'I investigate crimes, and I catch the perpetrators. If you or our political friends think that it is expedient to let them go, that's your business.'

'The murders you're investigating now, where do you

think they come from?' Smith asked. 'The method is quite cruel. You may feel like murdering someone, but you don't generally want to cave their heads in. There's obviously some unresolved issue behind the murders. A Truth and Reconciliation Commission might have resolved whatever pain is causing the killer to react.'

Seven pairs of eyes stared at Wilson. He was uncomfortable being the centre of attention. 'I have no doubt that the two murders have their genesis in the past. The Rice murder was carefully planned and carried out, the Morison one less so. There is undoubtedly a motive. As there is in most murders. This isn't a bar room brawl that ends in a stabbing. There is someone out there who wanted these two women to die. When we find the why, we'll find the who.'

The main course plates had been removed by a waiter and dessert plates distributed. It was all very civilised. Murder among the educated classes was a topic of dinner conversation not an everyday reality despite at least three lawyers being present. 'You cannot transpose an idea from South Africa to Ulster. You have to be from here to understand the context,' Wilson said.

'But I am from here,' Smith said quietly.

'But you spent most of your life in South Africa,' Kate said from down the table.

'That's right. I went there when I was very young. But Ulster still means something to me. That's why I'm so interested in helping out here.'

The desserts were passed around.

'I have to side with Ellie on this one,' Kate said. 'We will never have real peace in the province until we fully understand and accept our responsibility for what happened during the 'Troubles'.'

Seven pairs of eyes looked at Wilson again. 'No comment,' he said and started on his blueberry tart.

. . .

'WE COME FROM DIFFERENT WORLDS,' Wilson said as they settled into Kate's car. She was always the designated driver since she had reduced her alcohol consumption to almost zero since becoming pregnant. Although he had wanted to attack the judge's fine whiskey, he had refrained for Kate's sake. 'Those people wouldn't last a day on the streets.'

'Well it's lucky for them that they'll never have to go there. We can't all be white knights tilting at windmills.'

'But ultimately they belong to the class of people that free the murderers I catch.'

'And I belong to that class too?' There was a tremor in her voice.

'You're the most beautiful and intelligent woman I've ever met and most days I wonder why the hell you hooked up with me. You're at home with judges and Members of the Assembly. I'm a home with criminals, junkies and paedophiles. Your friends exude power. The people I deal with generally have broken lives.'

'I wouldn't like it if you were a barrister,' she said softly. 'You're worth ten of the people I deal with every day principally because you have integrity and empathy. They think only of themselves and how they can get ahead. I don't want the fact that I must live in that world to come between you and me. I want our child to have two parents who love each other but who can reconcile the fact that they are different.'

He put his hand on her knee. 'Loving you is the easiest thing in the world. I know that we have to mix with your colleagues and the people who can advance your career, but I sometimes feel that they're slumming when they're looking at me and talking about what I do.'

'Why don't we have that nice female sergeant of yours and her boyfriend over for dinner and what about Donald Spence?'

He smiled. 'Forget the dinner. Next time we're having a pub thing I'll give you a call. You should meet them in their natural habitat.'

She pulled into their parking space and manoeuvred herself out of her seat belt. She leaned over and kissed him. 'I love you and so will our child.'

Wilson kissed her and smiled. In his mind, he was wondering what would happen on the day that his world and Kate's would collide.

CHAPTER THIRTY-THREE

'I hated this fuckin' dump,' Ivan McIlroy moved through the corridor which ran through the centre of the building that used to be East Belfast Comprehensive School. The walls of the corridor were covered in graffiti, and the doors had been stripped from the classrooms. There was an acrid smell of stale urine and faeces in the air. 'I'm glad they closed the bastard, and if they need someone to burn it down, then I'm their man.' He turned and looked at Ronald McIver, who was walking directly behind him. 'Happy days, eh!'

McIver didn't answer. He wanted to get this meeting over as soon as possible so that he could get back home and relieve his sister-in-law who was babysitting his wife. The circle of life was completing for the woman he loved more than anything. After coming into the world, she had been babysat and now on her way out she required babysitting again. It was a sad reflection on life.

'What was wrong with the Black Bear?' McIlroy asked when McIver remained silent. 'Do you want to relive our schooldays?'

'I don't want to be seen talking to you,' McIver said his voice deadpan.

McIlroy laughed. 'Fuckin' peeler. I'm a busy man. What have you got?'

The two men stood facing each other on either side of the corridor. 'Nothing,' McIver said. He took the roll of notes McIlroy had given him at their previous meeting from his pocket and tossed them across the corridor.

McIlroy caught the roll and looked at it. 'You're doin' it for nothing?' He tossed the roll of notes into the air, caught them and put them in the pocket of his donkey jacket.

'I'm not going to inform on the work of my team,' McIver said putting as much steel as he could muster into his voice.

McIlroy frowned. 'I thought that I made myself plain in the Bear. It's like the Taigs. Once in, never out. You're my man and no matter what you say you're goin' to feed me what Wilson is up to.' His smile exposed a row of brown teeth. 'I don't give two fucks about you. I could hurt you real bad like I used to when you were a wain. But I prefer to do a bit of business with your old lady.'

McIver threw himself at McIlroy. The two tussled for a moment before McIlroy punched McIver hard in the stomach. McIver doubled over, and McIlroy was about to launch a right cross to his head when he stopped. He didn't want to mark his face, in case he would have to explain the injury to Wilson.

McIver leaned against the wall of the corridor. He was struggling for breath. A tear of frustration came out of the corner of his eye. He was about to betray a man who had been nothing but only good to him. His wife was going to be used to coerce him into helping a group of criminals and thugs. He looked at McIlroy's smiling face. He remembered that same smiling face in this corridor as its owner extracted lunch money from the few children whose parents could afford to give it to them. He had been a thug then, and he was a thug now. He fished around in his pocket and came out with his service pistol, a Glock 17.

'Put that fuckin' thing away, or I'll tear your fuckin' head off.' Despite the bravado there was a tremor in McIlroy's voice.

'No,' McIver raised the Glock and pointed it at McIlroy.

'Let's be reasonable about this,' McIlroy held his hands out and took a step forward. Something over seven feet now separated the two men.

'No more steps forward,' McIver said. McIlroy's eyes were dilated. They reminded McIver of a rat's eyes when it's cornered. He remembered that a rat is at its most dangerous when it's cornered. He held the gun as steady as his hand and his heightened emotional state would permit.

'Put the gun away,' McIlroy said. He was about to piss his pants. He pushed the little bastard too far. Shouldn't have threatened the wifey, he said to himself. The wee bastard has nothing else in his life. 'I was only kiddin'. I wouldn't harm you. After all, we go way back.' He looked around the derelict building. 'We had some great times here.'

McIver's brain was racing. He was in a very bad place. McIlroy was vicious, and he wouldn't forget that he had pulled a gun on him. Something very bad would happen to him when his usefulness was over. He couldn't betray Wilson, and he wasn't about to put his wife's life in danger. He didn't care about himself. He should have gone to Wilson before it went this far. They could have pulled McIlroy in. But he would have been out as quickly, and then he would come looking for McIver.

McIlroy could almost see the wheels spinning in McIver's brain. This could go either of two ways. McIver could put the gun away, or he could pull the trigger. If it was him that was holding the gun, it would only go one way, but the wee man didn't have his balls. There was still a chance that he could get out of this. He opened his arms wide in a peace gesture. 'OK, pal. We'll forget about you bein' our man in Wilson's team. Think about it. There's nothing wrong with Sammy wantin' a few minutes with the man that murdered his mother before handin' him over to the peelers.'

McIver suddenly realised that he was the rat in the corner and not McIlroy. There was only one way out. Although he had possessed a gun since the first day he had joined the force, he had never thought that he would ever have to use it. His life was over whichever way he jumped. McIlroy and the Rice gang would murder him and his wife as quickly as they would drink a cup of tea. Killing McIlroy would remove that threat but would ultimately lead to him being caught and jailed. But maybe not.

McIlroy prided himself on his ability to read people's faces. It had saved his life before. The wee man was coming to a conclusion, and it wasn't going to be a good one. There was only one possibility, and that was if he could cover the seven feet quicker than McIver could fire. He tried to see whether the safety was still on, but it was obscured from his view. It wasn't much of a chance, but it was his only one. He launched himself forward.

The gun bucked in McIver's hand. He moved to the side and fired again. The sound reverberated around the corridor, and he wanted to put his hands over his ears.

The bullet caught McIlroy in the chest and stopped him dead. He looked down and saw blood already staining his shirt. He looked up and saw McIver. Fuckin' little rat, he thought. Killed by the biggest wanker in the school. A second bullet hit his chest, and he fell to the ground.

Detective Constable Ronald McIver moved forward in a daze. He bent and put his fingers to McIlroy's neck. There was no pulse. He searched McIlroy's pockets to see if he had a weapon. McIlroy was unarmed. He stood and looked down at the body at his feet. He realised that he had visualised this situation in the past. McIlroy had been his tormentor at school, and he now had a vivid memory of imagining how he would kill him. He had just murdered his tormentor in cold blood bringing to life his imagination. There were extenuating circumstances. McIlroy went for him. In the end, it had been self-defence, but he had been the one holding the gun. He should call it in. He would be banged up. They might buy the self-defence, but they might not. That would mean jail time. Then there was the question of Sammy Rice. Would he be prepared to let bygones be bygones? Or would he wait for the right moment and have some inmate plant a knife in his chest? And who would take care of Mary during all this? He bent down and checked McIlroy's pulse again. Nothing. He took the roll of notes from the pocket of his jacket. A sudden thought struck him. What if McIlroy had told Sammy about him? His body shook involuntarily. He put the gun into his pocket and added the roll of cash. He noticed the two ejected shell casings in the corner. He picked them up and put them in his pocket. He leaned against the wall of the corridor and wept.

CHAPTER THIRTY-FOUR

Wilson flopped onto his ergonomically designed office chair and opened the newspaper. Maggie Cummerford made the front page, surprise, surprise. The PSNI was stumped on the Lizzie Rice murder, but they were developing some lines of enquiry on the Nancy Morison case. There was an interview with Morison's husband who declared his wife to be a paragon of virtue, a regular churchgoer and a visitor to the sick and destitute. He could think of no possible reason someone would want her dead. Join the queue, Wilson thought. There was an article on the Lizzie Rice funeral decrying the continued practice of turning what should be a family affair into a political event. There were pictures of the flag-draped coffin and the funeral cortege. The shots fired were glossed over. Nobody wanted to admit that decommissioning didn't really mean decommissioning. There were still plenty of guns out there, and they were in the hands of people who really shouldn't have them. This was Ulster. Of course, there was the normal crime. Husbands killed wives, usually their own, and vice versa. Lovers killed their partners. Idiot teenagers stabbed other idiot teenagers. The crimes would be solved quickly, and some smart-arsed barrister would dredge up a nefarious political motivation for the crime. Political crimes could lead to early release as had already been proven by the various amnesties tagged on to political settlements. A secondary article discussed the riots. They were a bit of a damp squib according to the correspondent. Twenty-two people had been arrested, and four policemen were in hospital, the result of a mini-riot Ulster style. Some damp squib for the injured. Wilson slowly turned the pages of the newspaper bringing himself up to date on the life of the province. He stopped dead on page eight. A picture of Kate dominated the centre of the page. 'Brilliant Young QC in Line for Top Job' was the headline. He quickly ran through the article. It was a resumé of Kate's life and career. Thankfully, he didn't appear in it. She was being touted as a candidate for Director of Public Prosecutions. If she succeeded, she would be the youngest person to have attained the post. Kate and he had never discussed money since they had lived together. He stuffed as much as he could into a jar in the kitchen each month, and Kate used it as she saw fit. The apartment was Kate's, and she had steadfastly refused to accept that he should pay for the privilege of living there. He knew that she made a lot of money but when he saw her supposed annual income published in the article, he almost fell off his chair. Kate earned a multiple of his salary. He picked up the telephone and called her private number.

'Hi,' her voice was cheery. 'You've seen the newspaper.'

'You should have warned me. I wasn't aware that you were going to hit such heights.'

'I'm not. I'm on a list, but it's a pretty long one. I'm ten to twenty years away from having a real chance. But you know the way the members of the Fourth Estate behave. I'm the youngest candidate, so I'm the story.'

'Why didn't you tell me?'

'We haven't talked that much lately. You've been busy and

quite honestly I prefer to talk about our impending child than my boring job.'

'According to this article your job isn't so boring.' And incredibly well paid, Wilson thought but did not say.

'Paper talk, I was following your normal instruction on anonymity when I gave you a cursory mention and then only in the context of my pregnancy.'

'It's appreciated. There's no impending possibility that you are going to be even more busy, than you are now?'

'Absolutely, I've told my clerk that as of the end of the month I am not accepting any new briefs. Although I know you don't believe it, I'm as committed to having a healthy baby as you are. Now get back to work and find that damn murderer so we can spend a bit more time together.'

'When this case is over, we're going to spend a few days in a hotel. I'm beginning to realise that there are sides to you that I've never explored. It might even mean introducing a little shop talk into our relationship.'

'That sounds interesting. Forget the hotel. Let's just lock the door of the apartment and make believe that we're the only people left on earth.'

'I can't wait. See you this evening.'

Wilson looked up and saw Moira on the other side of his glass door. She was holding a copy of the newspaper pressed against the glass partition, and she was smiling. He motioned her in.

'Nice article,' she said noticing the paper in front of Wilson.

'My partner the superstar,' Wilson smiled.

'She's the woman who has everything,' Moira said and reddened when she realised that it could include Wilson. 'Successful career and about to have a baby. What more can you ask for?'

'How's Brendan?' Wilson asked.

'As crazy as usual. Now that he's met you, he's fixated.

He's taken to nicknaming me Watson. All his university friends have followed his lead. It's funny and it makes me laugh, but I wish they'd continued calling me Moira.'

'I'm glad you're happy, but I'm afraid that I might lose you at some point.'

'How so?'

'Brendan's on a sabbatical. Sooner or later, he's going back to Boston and maybe you'll go with him.' He noticed her frowning. It looked like she was hearing something that she told herself, but that she didn't like the sound of.

'Possible but not probable,' she noticed the team gathering at the whiteboard for the morning briefing. 'I think they're waiting for us.'

Wilson stood before the whiteboard. 'Where's Ronald?'

'Sick, boss,' Harry Graham said. 'Had him on the phone, and he sounded like he was about to croak.'

'Not convenient,' Wilson said. 'We need someone who can work the magic machine, aside from Moira that is. Peter, any movement on the photograph?'

'Not a lot, boss,' Davison said. 'But it's early days. It's definitely the Shankill branch of the women's UVF early 1980s. There are eight women in total in the photo. Lizzie is in the middle with Nancy Morison beside her. I'm told that they were inseparable at the time. I've been around the houses in the Shankill, and I've identified two more of the women, both deceased. That makes four. The four others are a bit of a mystery. It looks like a couple have moved away, possibly to England while the other two may be somewhere in the province but as yet address unknown.'

'Nancy Morison's movements, Harry?'

'Nothing particular in the past few days. She attended the wake at the Ballygomartin house accompanied by her husband. She was at the funeral and then the graveyard. She went back with the crowd to the Black Bear, and that's where the timeline gets fuzzy.' Graham pointed at the timeline on the whiteboard. 'We're concentrating on the two hours between six to eight o'clock. Traffic has already sent us some disks, and we're collecting what available from businesses in the area. It's going to be a thankless task going through all those tapes.'

'That's what they pay us for,' Wilson said. 'Moira, how's the research on Lizzie going?'

Moira smiled. 'It's an education, boss. I wasn't up to speed on the activities of our undercover colleagues during the Seventies and the Eighties, but I'm learning fast. The material is copious and heavily redacted. There are lots of mentions of Lizzie, and I've only just started to include Nancy Morison in the search. The files are so heavily redacted that sometimes I must guess at what's behind the black strikeouts. It's going to take a while, and it may have absolutely nothing to do with the case.'

'Keep on it,' Wilson looked at the rear of the squad room. No sign of wee Maggie. 'Eric, you help Harry on the tapes. Find me something. And Eric, get Jimmy McGreery in here for twelve o'clock and book the soft interview room. We don't want Jimmy to get the wrong impression.'

'OK, boss,' Taylor said.

Wilson glanced at his watch. 'Nancy's autopsy is in one hour. Moira, you and me. The rest of you get at it, time's passing. We have someone out there bashing in old women's heads. I want to find the bastard.'

The group broke up. Moira joined Wilson. 'Are you sure that you want me along? Three's company and all that.'

He looked at her. Both her eyes and her mouth were laughing. Brendan Guilfoyle was having a positive effect on her. 'I definitely want you along.'

CHAPTER THIRTY-FIVE

Detective Constable Ronald McIver sat on a chair in his living room. He hadn't slept a wink. He had returned to the small house that he occupied with his wife at ten o'clock the previous evening. His sister-in-law was already gone, and his wife had been put to bed. Ever since his wife's mind had begun to slip, he had moved into the spare bedroom so that neither one would disturb the other's sleep. His wife was often confused and switched on the light at all times of the night. He left the door of the spare room open so that he could follow her movements when necessary. There was, therefore, nobody who could or could not corroborate the actual time he had returned home. He wasn't a big drinker but there was always a bottle of Bushmills on hand in case someone visited. He hit the bottle as soon as he returned home but was unable to get more than three glasses down. Deep down, he knew that he was screwed. He had killed a man, and he was going to have to pay the price. He had played the scene in the derelict school over and over in his mind. Each time he tried to find the salient point that would lead to his arrest for murder. Nobody knew he was there. Unless McIlroy had told someone, and that wasn't certain. On the surface, he didn't leave a trace. He thought about what kind of evidence he might have left. He hadn't touched anything in the school that he could remember. Collecting evidence in a place that had been used by junkies and dossers would be a Herculean task. He picked up his coat and felt in the pocket. The shell casings were there. He had been in a fugue state when he had picked them up, but he now realised that it had been a smart move. He rubbed them on his jacket and dropped them back in his pocket. He had cleaned the Glock as soon as he had returned home. He had also burned every stitch of clothing he had been wearing. He scrubbed his hands with paraffin and soap in the hope of getting rid of any gunshot residue. Since the 'Troubles' started, there were more than five thousand unsolved homicides in Northern Ireland. Why couldn't the death of Ivan McIlroy be just another unsolved murder? Then it hit him. There was only one piece of physical evidence against him. McIlroy called his mobile phone number early in the day to set up the meeting. His number was on record at the station. Somehow, he was going to have to come up with an explanation for that phone call. He looked across the room to where Mary sat. Her eyes appeared to be watching him intently, but they were dead. He wondered whether she could take in what she had seen him do. 'How are you, love?' he said. 'What about a nice cup of tea?'

No response. Mary was on planet Mary.

He'd called in sick, but he would have to face work sooner rather than later. Sammy Rice and his gang would soon miss McIlroy. Maybe they'd already missed him. They would begin scouring Belfast. It would be better if the police found the body first. A call to the confidential police number was in order, but it would have to be made from an outside phone. And he would have to find some way to disguise his voice. Wilson would ask to hear the tape and might recognise him. It was strange thinking of ways of escaping from his boss. The crime seldom caught the villain, but the cover-up almost always did. He was going to have to be super careful. He stood up. 'I think I'll get you that cup of tea now, love,' he said to the unresponsive figure at the other side of the room.

CHAPTER THIRTY-SIX

They parked in virtually the same spot outside the mortuary at the Royal Victoria as they had two days previously. Wilson got out of the car slowly then he, and Moira made their way into the mortuary building.

Stephanie Reid was already gowned and waiting. 'I thought that you were in a hurry with the autopsy,' she said as Wilson entered. 'I have several clients today, and I was tempted to make a start on some of the others.'

'You're in a happy mood this morning,' Wilson said accepting a surgical gown from Reid's male assistant. He nodded at Moira, and she made her way to the observation room.

'Does she go everywhere with you?' Reid asked.

'She happens to be my sergeant and a bloody good one she is too,' he said pulling on his gown.

'I suppose it's no harm that she's also attractive,' the smile in Reid's eyes was mischievous but was not accompanied by a smile on her lips.

'Already spoken for,' Wilson put on the green gown. 'The lucky lad is a visiting professor at Queen's.' He glanced toward the observation room and saw that Moira was busy with her notebook. He realised that without the microphone she couldn't hear what was being said in the theatre.

'From what I've heard that never bothered you before,' said Reid as she whipped a white sheet off the corpse and handed it to her assistant. The naked body of Nancy Morison was fully exposed. Reid clicked the overhead mike. 'The body is that of a female of approximately sixty-five years of age. 'She did a rough examination of the body noting the marks left by the Taser. Then she picked up a small circular saw and clicked it into life. She started work on what was left of the head.

One hour later, Reid picked up the shower attachment and sluiced the blood off the metal table. While she worked, she spoke for the microphone. 'Nancy Morison died from a blunt trauma to the head. Pieces of a concrete block were still present in the wound. At least three points on the body have marks consistent with an electric shock being administered. An examination of the skin around the mark would indicate that the shock would have been of such a level as to render the deceased powerless. 'Fluids have been gathered and will be sent for a toxicity screening. The contents of the stomach indicate that the deceased ingested a considerable amount of alcohol in the hours preceding her death. Death would not have been instantaneous. Time of death was between eight and ten in the evening. 'She clicked the microphone off.

'Same killer?' Wilson knew it was a rhetorical question.

'Undoubtedly,' Reid came and stood beside him. She glanced up to ensure that the microphone was off. 'I saw the article on your partner in the newspaper.'

Wilson didn't respond.

'She seemed very professional, very antiseptic. Is she good in bed?'

Wilson made a grimace.

'Gentleman to the end. I'm told that I'm very good in bed, very professional but certainly not very antiseptic. You know that we're going to screw each other.'

'It's not going to happen,' Wilson said staring into her blue eyes. His penis was telling him he was a liar. He was trying to ignore its opinion.

'I'm not looking for a relationship. I won't interfere with your little Miss antiseptic and the future genius she's about to produce. I just want to screw.'

'I'm sure you'll find someone who feels the same.'

'I know that you feel the same, but you're trying to deny it. Why bother? What about that drink tonight?'

'No thanks,' he looked toward the observation room and saw Moira packing up her stuff. She glanced into the theatre, and they locked eyes before she exited.

Reid smiled. 'Looking to your attractive sergeant to save you from the big bad lady who wants to screw your brains out?'

Moira opened the door and walked towards them. 'Got it down, boss,' she said holding up the notebook.

'We done here?' Wilson asked Reid.

'The autopsy's finished. Sorry I can't make it for that drink.'

Sneaky bitch, Wilson thought. The idea was now planted with Moira that he had asked Reid for a drink.

'Just as well,' Wilson said making for the door.

'I'm almost afraid to ask but what that was all about?' Moira said as they walked to the car.

'Nothing,' Wilson said.

'Never kid a kidder. I told you that woman is a man-eater and she's decided that she'd like to take a few bites out of you. I couldn't hear the words, but I was watching the body language. Are you sure there isn't something you'd like to tell me?'

'I'm sure. I think that Brendan is Americanising you. Either that or you're watching too much daytime television.

We've got some bugger out there who is killing former members of the Shankill branch of the women's UVF. We know that there were at least eight members in the group. Two of them died naturally, and two have been murdered in the past few days. I think it's time we got our skates on and found the missing four. Any one of them could be the next target.'

Moira pressed the alarm release button on the car key. She respected Wilson, but he was a man and men sometimes followed their small friend instead of their brains. Wilson had already proved that he wasn't the exception to the rule. Maybe she would have to have a word with Professor Stephanie Reid before too long.

CHAPTER THIRTY-SEVEN

Jimmy McGreery was already organised with a cup of tea and a plate of biscuits. Wilson had no idea where the biscuits had come from but assumed the desk sergeant had a secret stash that could be produced for special visitors. The godfather who ran the drugs, prostitution and protection rackets in central Belfast was certainly a special visitor. McGreery had been involved in Loyalist paramilitary activity virtually all his life. He had marched on his first twelfth of July at the age of three and had done his first stretch for petrol bombing a Catholic family out of their home at twelve. McGreery had been a footballer in his youth and had played for Linfield, the Protestant team in Belfast. In those days, he was known as 'Slim Jim'. The man that sat before Wilson in the soft interview room weighed in at one hundred and forty kilos, or twice the weight at which he had played football. Throughout the 'Troubles', he had climbed the paramilitary ladder and had played his part in sectarian murders and intimidation. Nothing had ever been proven against him, but the British Government considered him a sufficient threat to intern him in Long Kesh along with other suspected terrorists. When he exited detention after the signing of the Good Friday

Agreement, he found that he was at the head of his local para-military group. Peace had brought with it a dividend for McGreery in that he could concentrate his efforts on his criminal activities.

'Mr Wilson,' McGreery said through crunching biscuits. 'I'm right fond of this new kind of policing.' He looked around at the soft furnishings. 'It's no like the peelers of old. It's like being invited to tea at the Europa. Big improvement, big improvement.'

'I didn't realise it had been so long since we'd had a chat on the premises,' Wilson said taking a seat directly across from McGreery.

McGreery slurped noisily at his cup of tea. 'My lawyer wanted to come along, but sure I told him Mr Wilson only wants to have a wee talk.' He raised his eyebrows.

'That's pretty much it,' Wilson said. 'Just a friendly chat, for the moment.'

McGreery smiled but made no comment.

Wilson looked at 'Slim Jim' McGreery. With his rotund stomach and fat florid face, he could have been used as the poster boy for Santa Claus. He had grown a beard since Wilson had last seen him and added a few pounds as well. He may have looked like a genial character from a Dickens novel, but it would be a huge mistake to expect even a drop of the milk of human kindness from Jimmy McGreery. He had been ruthless on the football field, and he carried that ruthlessness into his criminal activities. 'You know that I'm investigating the deaths of Lizzie Rice and now Nancy Morison?'

'Aye, it's a rum business,' McGreery nodded and slurped his tea.

'We've pretty much discounted the sectarian angle, and we're wondering whether Lizzie's death had anything to do with Sammy.'

'Lizzie was a wild wee bitch,' McGreery laughed. 'We used to say that she give it away with Smarties. I often wondered whose Sammy is. He might even be my auld fella's. I know he had more than one go at Lizzie. There're lots of people who have something against Lizzie, but the other wee bitch is a bit of a mystery. I've never even heard of her.'

'What about somebody moving against Sammy?' Wilson asked.

'Bollox,' McGreery pushed his empty teacup away. The plate of biscuits was already devoured. 'Sammy's a vicious wee tyke. He's also fairly well connected if you know what I mean.' McGreery rubbed the side of his nose with his right index finger. 'Big in the Lodges is our Willis. He's nobody's fool. If someone is out to mess with him, they'd better be prepared. Sammy doesn't take prisoners. You could say that Sammy and me are bound to remain friends.'

'Nobody in the 'life' was involved in Lizzie's death?' Wilson asked.

'What 'life' are ye talkin' about, Mr Wilson?' McGreery sat forward with his ample stomach resting on his knees. 'I'm a small businessman who runs a couple of snooker halls and pubs. I'm not in any 'life'. You peelers have your heads up your arses about me. Lizzie Rice is yesterday's news. Nobody gave a shit about her when she was alive and nobody much cares now that she's dead. Maybe dying the way she did gives Sammy and you some ideas but if someone wanted to give Sammy a message, they'd go closer to home.'

'Lizzie is close to home.'

McGreery smiled. 'Aye, Sammy will cry a few crocodile tears at the funeral, but he hasn't been involved with Lizzie for years. Sammy only cares about Sammy, and if I wanted to strike at him, I'd go for his business. That's the thing that's closest to Sammy's heart. If he has one.' McGreery pushed hard on the two side of the chair to lever himself into a standing position. 'Now it's been pleasant having a cuppa with you, but I've some business issues to attend to. I'd be grateful if you're finished with me.' He stood up and waddled towards the door.

'WASTE OF BLOODY TIME,' Wilson said as soon as he returned to the squad room.

Moira looked up from a pile of files. 'No sign of a Loyalist feud then?' she asked.

'Loyalist feuds tend to leave a lot of male bodies strewn around. I've seen a few of them so far, and they manage to be an exclusively male preserve. McGreery said that he'd never heard of Nancy Morison, and I believe him. I'm becoming more convinced that her death might be linked to membership of that group of women in the photo. We can't check that theory until we talk to one of them. Peter really needs to locate one of the four missing women.' Wilson walked over to Harry Graham's desk. CCTV footage of cars and pedestrians was playing on his computer screen. Graham was busy watching grey time-elapsed stills of people walking along a road. 'Anything?'

Graham shook his head. He held up five DVD boxes. 'Early days.'

'No sign of Ronald?'

Again, a shake of Graham's head.

Wilson went into his office. He sat down at his computer and scanned his e-mails. None had the red tags that denoted urgent. He opened a scanned copy of the preliminary forensics report on the Morison murder site. The result of the cast taken of the tyre tracks was not included. There were prints on the concrete block, but it had been handled by the bricklayers on the site and by the workers in the builder's providers yard and possibly where it had been manufactured. There was a cost estimate for establishing a series of elimination prints with an assessment of the utility of such an exercise. There was a request for budget approval that required approval by an officer higher than his pay grade and stood a snowball's chance in hell of being agreed. He often wondered why there was never any talk of budgets in television series concerning crime scene investigation. He opened his word processor and typed a short report of his interview with McGreery. He concluded that there was virtually no possibility that McGreery was involved in the deaths of Lizzie Rice and Nancy Morison. He sent the report by e-mail to Spence and Jennings with a copy to Harry Graham for inclusion in the murder book. Having completed his priority work, he turned to his e-mails. It was the equivalent of diving into a barrel of shit.

CHAPTER THIRTY-EIGHT

Ronald McIver had spent the morning cleaning and recleaning his gun until he was sure that a cursory examination alone would not be enough to show that it had been fired recently. Across the room, his wife watched him at his work without showing a flicker of life. When he had finished reassembling the Glock, he loaded it and noticed for the first time his wife's eyes widening. She thinks I'm going to shoot her; he thought. Or maybe she thinks that I'm going to shoot myself and leave her to fend for herself. Neither course of action had come into his mind as he was cleaning the gun, but both had their attractions. Mary was *compos mentis* for less and less time and withdrawn for more and more of the time. Her mother had suffered the same disease, and he had watched her disintegrate when she was put into a care home. He remembered one occasion when he would gladly have shot the old woman to put her out of her misery. Despite what those who speak of the sanctity of life may think, there is no dignity in a life of incontinence, incoherence and mindlessness. He looked across at his wife and wondered how she would fare if his crime was discovered, and he was put into prison. He wondered how he would fare if he was put into prison. His former Superintendent, Joe Worthington, took the easy way out by putting the Ruger into his mouth and blowing the top of his head off. He looked down at the Glock. He didn't think that he was capable of taking his own life. At this time yesterday, he hadn't thought that he could take another person's life, but he had done so. It was strange what we're capable of when put to the test, he thought. He wasn't thinking about time when he was cleaning the gun, but he would soon have to report the dead body in the deserted school. There was little or no chance of the body being found and although McIlroy was a mindless thug, it was unfair to leave his body undiscovered and his loved ones worried about him. That was if such a man had any loved ones. He might be a murderer, but he wasn't a monster. McIlroy needed to be found. He wondered where he might find a public telephone. They were few and far between these days. And quite a few of them were in the range of CCTV cameras. He would have to buy a new SIM card, make the call and then throw the card away. There would be no way they could trace it to his mobile phone. He rubbed his temples. There were so many things that he had to think of in order not to be caught. Maybe he should throw himself on Wilson's mercy. There would be a lot of suspects for McIlroy's murder. The case could very easily remain unsolved. All he needed was his boss's help in the cover up. He could make a case about having to look after Mary. But that wasn't going to happen. Wilson was a straight shooter. The best plan was to keep covering up. After all, he would be central to the investigation. He would know where it was going, and he would be able to take appropriate steps to keep himself out of the frame. He put the Glock back in the holster. For a second, he thought that he could see a look of relief in his wife's eyes. He put the gun on top of the bookcase in the living room. He put on his jacket and kissed his wife goodbye. 'I'm just going to the corner shop,' he said by way of explanation. 'I'll be back soon. I'll get some cakes, and we can have a real afternoon tea.' His wife's lips were limp to his kiss, and she continued to stare into space.

The local shop was only a few minutes away, but he would have to walk a considerable distance to find a shop selling SIM cards. He walked along trying to erase from his memory the prone body lying in the corridor of his old school and his part in putting it there. He eventually found the shop he was looking for and bought the SIM card he needed. He didn't bother to look up at the ceiling directly over the cashier's head. If he had he would have seen the small camera taking a perfect picture of his face.

CHAPTER THIRTY-NINE

'Where's the fucker?' Sammy Rice was feeling human again, and he wanted to get on with the search for the killer of his mother. He had given that task to Ivan McIlroy and suddenly there was no sign of the bastard. He looked at the two young men in the front room of his house in Ballygo-martin Road.

'No idea, chief,' one of McIlroy's minions answered.

'Wrong fucking answer.' Rice grabbed the young man by the throat and forced him back against a wall. 'You're telling me that he's disappeared off the face of the earth?'

The man's head was forced up, and his voice croaked. 'We've tried all the usual haunts, and he's not answering his mobile.'

Rice removed his hand from the young man's throat. 'You don't want to get me angry. Get out on the streets and find him. I want McIlroy here now.'

The two men quickly left the room, and Rice heard the outside door closing. The quality of his men had gone through the floor. Five years ago, the people he hired looked like they could go twelve rounds with Joe Frazier. The current crop looked like they'd have difficulty going one round with Woody

Allen. Lizzie was in the ground, and Billy was back in his hovel in Malvern Street. He stuck two hundred quid into the auld man's pocket before he left. The off-licence would be ringing up the till for the next week or so. He flopped into one of the armchairs situated on either side of the bay window. Billy was fucked. The drink was killing him, and he didn't have the sense to kick it. It wouldn't be long before he'd have to plant him too. His mind was only semi-clear, but he knew he was going to have to solve the riddle of Lizzie's murder. It was something to do with him. He remembered the state of the auld bitch when he had picked her up from the mortuary. They didn't just kill her; they'd almost left her without a head. The people he dealt with usually put a bullet into someone. The business with the head was strange. He thought about Jimmy McGreery. The fat bastard could come up with something like that. Their territories were banging up against each other. McGreery grabbed the most lucrative area of central Belfast. Now that peace reigned the centre of Belfast had taken off. Despite the recession, business was booming and the yuppies, or whatever they called them these days, flooded into the upmarket developments close to their work. They had the money, and they had the need for recreational drugs. The visiting businessmen had the need for female companionship, and the businesses needed additional security. McGreery stole his pot of gold. Lizzie's death could have been a feint against him, a pinprick to see how he would react. He tried to remember whether McGreery had a mother. He had never seen or heard of one. How to react? That was the problem. A turf war was out of the question. McGreery and he had similar numbers of men. They'd just end up pissing the peelers and the politicians off. He needed McIlroy. Ivan wasn't the sharpest knife in the drawer, but he was a gutter rat. Now he disappears just when he needed him most. Rice lifted his head slowly. He began to think the unthinkable. Perhaps McIlroy had gone over to the other side. McIlroy on McGreery's crew would spell the end of him. He had no doubt that the next few days would be the defining moment for him as a criminal boss. The streets of Belfast would run red with blood before he would go down.

CHAPTER FORTY

Two police cars were pulled up outside the derelict building in the dock area of east Belfast when Wilson arrived. The phone call had come in just after two o'clock in the afternoon. The uniforms had contacted him as soon as they had verified that there was a body. Wilson picked up two white jumpsuits and threw one of them to Moira. She caught it while she was still signing them both in.

'Maybe we should think of investing in a couple of these things for ourselves,' Wilson said slipping the jumpsuit on. He pulled his shoulders in to accommodate the XXL version of the suit and told himself that not only was increased exercise necessary but so was a diet. The takeaways would have to go but considering his and Kate's lifestyle that would be difficult to accomplish.

'Is this our man again?' Moira asked climbing into her suit.

'Let's go and find out,' Wilson led the way into the building. He looked around the entrance. The foyer looked like a hurricane had hit it. Bits of masonry had been gouged from the walls, and some of the ceiling had collapsed. Where plaster still existed on the walls the graffiti spray painters had done their work.

'It used to be a school apparently,' Moira said as she joined him in the foyer.

'I remember something like this,' Wilson said looking around. 'But it was before education became important.'

A uniform appeared at their side. 'He's down there,' he pointed the length of the corridor.

'Were you the first on the scene?' Wilson asked.

The young officer nodded.

'Give your name to DS McElvaney. We'll need to talk to you later. and forensic will need to have elimination prints and DNA.'

Moira pulled her notebook from inside her suit and wrote the officer's name.

'Let's take a look,' Wilson said. He could see the shape of the figure halfway along the corridor. The ground was littered with masonry, broken glass and plastic bottles interspersed with used syringes and condoms. The building had probably been used as a squat until it disintegrated to such a state that it was unliveable even for junkies. The forensics team were going to have a merry old time going through this mess. The body was lying on its side. He wouldn't disturb it until forensics had photographed the scene. He removed a pen flashlight from his inside pocket and shone it on the face of the corpse. He bent to get a better view of the face. 'Oh, shit,' he said and cut the light off.

'You know him?' Moira asked.

'Ivan McIlroy, he's Sammy Rice's right-hand man. If Lizzie Rice was bad, this is a disaster. We could be looking at a body count in double figures before we're finished here.' Wilson stood up straight.

'His head looks to be in one piece,' Moira said.

'He's been shot,' Wilson said simply. 'Two by the look of it. We'll confirm when we flip him over. Ivan lived by the sword, so I suppose it's no surprise that he died by the sword. Sammy has lost his mother and his right-hand man in the past few days. He's not going to be a happy bunny, and he's not the kind of man who'll spend a lot of time sitting around wondering what to do next. That means we're looking at a hell of a lot of trouble.'

A noise at the end of the corridor indicated the arrival of the forensics team. 'You people are keeping us busy these days,' the team leader said.

'Tell me about it,' Wilson moved aside, and he and Moira retraced their steps back along the corridor. His mind was racing. It didn't compute. Three murders in as many days, two of elderly women on whom excessive violence was enacted. Now a third more classical Belfast hit. Something was going on, but he had no idea what it might be. If McGreery was to be believed, there was no turf war. Lizzie was ancient history, and Nancy Morison was a nobody. But Ivan McIlroy was a heavyweight, and he was current. He was looking into Lizzie's background for the motive, but perhaps he had been mistaken after all. Maybe it was about Sammy after all and McGreery had sold him a dummy. Perhaps Jennings was right to have McGreery pulled in. If so, it would be the first time Jennings called it right. Wilson's hypothesis regarding the murders of the two women would be in tatters. His whole team would be following a line of enquiry leading nowhere.

'We have to stop meeting like this,' Stephanie Reid's voice cut into his thoughts. 'I can see why Charlie needed a sabbatical. Although I've never heard of people calling Africa a sabbatical.'

Wilson smiled. 'Just trying to keep you busy.'

'Or trying to avoid that drink and what might follow.'

Moira joined them and Reid made a cat hissing sound.

'I think they're ready for you inside,' Moira said sharply.

Reid hissed again and made her way into the building carrying her small leather bag.

'I really do not like that woman,' Moira said. 'I always trust my first impressions, and that woman turns all my alarm bells on. And if she hisses like that at me again, I'll give her a punch she won't forget.'

'And she'd have you for assault, and she would have won.'

'Have you ever wondered why she's not married?'

'We know nothing about her,' Wilson said watching Reid climb into her plastic suit. 'Maybe she was and is no longer.'

Moira reddened. It was a remark too close to the bone. 'I put mine in jail. I wonder what she would have done with hers. Perhaps she's a black widow.'

'And maybe she's just a diversion, and we don't need to be diverted right now.' Wilson turned back to Moira. 'As soon as they're finished, I want to look at the body again. In the meantime, I'm going to find somewhere locally that serves a decent coffee. I've had my full dose of Stephanie Reid for today, and I don't want to be around when she exits. Don't let them take the body away until I've taken a second look at it. '

'What about time of death, cause of death, stuff like that?' Moira said.

'Your business,' Wilson made a cat hissing sound as he walked away.

WHEN WILSON RETURNED HALF an hour later Reid had already left. The crew from the mortuary were loitering beside their van having a cigarette. Moira was in the foyer of the building.

'So,' Wilson said as he joined her. 'Time of death, cause of death, stuff like that.' He smiled.

'Certainly last night, two shots to the chest, she won't have anything exact until she does the autopsy.'

'Let's go look,' he motioned over his shoulder. 'We don't want the body crew getting antsy.'

Ivan McIlroy was lying on his back. His shirt and jacket were stiffened with blood from his wound. Wilson looked at the face. No marks. He wasn't tortured. He picked up the corpse's hand and looked at the wrists. No ligature marks. He wasn't tied up either. 'He wasn't brought here,' he said more to himself than to Moira. 'We'll need to know from Reid, whether he was killed here or was he moved. My guess is that we're standing on the murder spot, but I want to be sure. The question is, why would McIlroy come here alone with somebody who wanted to kill him?'

'Maybe it was a meeting between the second level of the Rice gang and some other gang,' Moira said.

'These people own snooker halls, pubs and bingo halls. That's where they hold their meetings. Places they control and where it doesn't matter if they're seen. This smacks of either a punishment shooting or an abduction. Since there are no marks on the body, I'm inclined to discount both. Let's wait until Reid digs the bullets out and we'll see if the weapon has been used before. Call the body crew in. We're done here. Forensics will collect a dozen refuse bags of rubbish, and I pity the poor devil that has to sift through it. '

CHAPTER FORTY-ONE

Wilson went straight to Chief Superintendent Spence's office as soon as he returned to the station. Spence was in a meeting, but he finished immediately and invited Wilson in.

'Tell me the rumour I just heard isn't true,' Spence said as soon as Wilson settled himself in a chair.

'I don't know what the rumour is, but I can tell you that it's true.'

'Ivan McIlroy, for Christ's sake. Killing McIlroy is tantamount to declaring war.' Spence opened the top drawer of his desk and took out a small white cylinder. He shook two pills into his hand and slapped them into his mouth.

'I thought you were off the pills.'

'I'm back on now that I know McIlroy is dead. Tell me about it.'

Wilson outlined the phone call followed by the discovery of the body. He explained their visit to the derelict building.

'Have you heard the call?' Spence asked.

'Not yet. They said they sent me something on the computer. The techs are also tracking the phone. The call was made from a mobile. If the guy who made it knows what he's doing, it'll probably end up as a dead end.'

'Ivan McIlroy, for Christ's sake.'

'You already said that,' Wilson smiled. 'Do you want to pop a few more pills?'

'Wait till Jennings hears.'

'You think that he hasn't. He's probably had to change his beautifully pressed bottle green uniform trousers twice since he heard the news. A feud between two Protestant groups is not a pretty sight.'

'We've got to keep a lid on this.'

'I think that might be a little difficult. Too many people are now aware that Ivan is no longer in the land of the living. It may be that Sammy hasn't heard the news, but I'd be willing to wager my next month's pay that he has. What did you have in mind in terms of keeping a lid on it?'

'We're screwed. Sammy's the kind of idiot who'll react without thinking. I won't even make a guess at the number of bodies before the tit for tat can be stopped.'

SAMMY RICE WAS in the back room of the Black Bear. He gathered together his four most trusted men. The news of McIlroy's death shook him to the core. He could ignore Lizzie's death as a one-off, but McIlroy was central to his business, and his murder was highly significant.

'Any of you jokers have any idea what Ivan was doing in that school?' Rice asked.

Four blank faces looked back at him. These men had already seen examples of Sammy Rice's famed temper, and none of them wanted to be the butt of it.

'Somebody must know what the fucker was doing there,' Rice leaned forward and shouted.

One of the men coughed. 'Ivan was a solo operator,' he said hesitantly. 'He didn't clear things with the likes of us.'

Rice looked at the four men around the table. Together they wouldn't equal one Ivan McIlroy. They were foot soldiers in his organisation. McIlroy was an officer capable of running things in his absence. He was beginning to feel that he had allowed business to slide over the past year or so. His new villa in Spain and the lifestyle on the Costa was deflecting him. His business was in Belfast, and that's what he should have been concentrating on. There were only two possibilities: either McGreery was making a move on him by taking out his No 1 lieutenant or McIlroy had decided to go solo and had tried to make a deal which got him killed. In any event, Sammy Rice was in trouble, and his reaction would be the same as always – someone was going to pay. He didn't like making moves in the dark. Lizzie's murder was a complete mystery. That was until he had received news of McIlroy's murder. He had been racking his brains, but he could see no connection between Lizzie and McIlroy's murders. 'OK,' he said. 'We need to find out if McGreery's behind Ivan's murder. I want you jokers to lift one of McGreery's top guys.'

The four men looked at each other. 'Which one do you want?' one of them asked.

'Anyone'll do for the moment. All we want is some information. Lift one of the fuckers and bring him to me.'

'McGreery won't like it,' one of the men said quietly.

'I don't give a flying fuck what McGreery likes or doesn't like,' Rice shouted. 'I want one of his boys lifted, and I want him here yesterday.'

'It'll start a war,' said the oldest of the men facing Rice.

'If McGreery had Ivan topped the war has already been declared. Now get to fuck out of here and bring me back someone. We'll use the warehouse in the Harbour Estate. Let me know when you have him.'

The four men stood up slowly and headed toward the bar area. None of them looked happy. It was generally the soldiers who ended up in the coffins during a turf war, and they knew it

Rice sat alone thinking through the possibilities. If it came to an all-out war, it would be difficult to pick a winner. Maybe they'd both be losers. "I didn't start it," Rice said to himself.

CHAPTER FORTY-TWO

Moira McElvaney was still hunched over her desk when Wilson left his office at eight in the evening. He already texted Kate on his late arrival home, and he hadn't received a reply probably indicating that she would be late home herself. He stood behind Moira and saw that she was still wading through old police reports and intelligence documents.

'Time to go home,' he said. 'I need you fresh for tomorrow. You're doing the McIlroy autopsy.'

She turned and smiled. 'Professor Reid will be disappointed,' she pointed at the papers in front of her. 'This lot would make interesting reading if we weren't under such time pressure. Despite the level of redaction, there were a lot of very nasty people out there during the 'Troubles'.'

'Kate's trying to revive the Truth and Reconciliation Commission idea,' he said. 'What do you think?'

'I think that people would be appalled if they could see even the sanitised reports that I'm reading. Maybe we need to face up to the past before we can go forward. Flags and marching are totally unimportant against the terrible waste of life represented in these pages.'

'I'm convinced that the motive for Lizzie's murder is in there somewhere. Most of the the non-family murders in this province have their genesis in our violent past. I don't want Kate to get mixed up with the Truth and Reconciliation Commission because I'm afraid that as a society, we're not mature enough to see it as a process for moving on. Some will see it simply as an opening of old wounds that might lead to more problems. Anyway, you can have a philosophical discussion with your professor boyfriend. Finish up here and get yourself home.'

'These documents should all have been scanned and collated. Then I would simply have to type in Lizzie Rice, and I'd have all the reports relating to her. As it is, I'm reading reams of paper just to find her or Nancy Morison's name.'

'That's why they call us the Plod. We have to look at the resources tomorrow to see how we can manage the Rice/Morison cases and the McIlroy murder.'

'You don't think that they're linked?'

'They may be, but I'm worried by the MOs. The man who killed Lizzie and the Morison woman wanted their heads crushed. Whoever killed McIlroy did it Belfast-style with a pistol. If it's the same killer, we need to know why he switched MO for McIlroy. We also need to know how McIlroy is tied to Lizzie and Morison. It's all about motive. I'm bushed. See you tomorrow.'

Moira watched his back as he walked toward the door to the squad room. His shoulders appeared more hunched, and he moved like a man with a lot on his mind. She closed the file she had been reading. If the motive was in there, she was going to find it.

WILSON SMELLED dinner as soon as he entered the apartment. He walked into the open-plan living room and saw that the table was set, and two candles were inserted into Waterford Glass candleholders. He smiled when he saw the effort that Kate made. He went into the kitchen. She was at the cooker stirring some gravy, and she hadn't heard him enter. He put his arms around her from the back and kissed her on the neck. 'What's the occasion?' he asked.

'I'm trying to soft soap a pissed-off partner,' she turned, embraced him and kissed him hard on the lips. 'Also, I was listening to the evening news, and I heard about the latest murder.' She broke off the embrace. 'I reckoned that you would need a pick me up, so I invested in a bottle of Middleton.' She opened the boxed bottle of whiskey and showed it to him before pouring them both a double measure. She handed him a glass. 'Cheers,' she said touching her glass to his. They both drank. 'I'm sorry about that bloody newspaper profile,' she said. 'They were supposed to tell me when it was being published. I was going to warn you it was full of crap.'

'It showed me another side of you,' Wilson said switching off the gas under the gravy and leading her away from the kitchen. 'What made me angry was that it's an important side and for some reason, or another, I didn't explore it. You're a high-flying barrister with a brilliant future, and I'm a police officer with a brilliant past.'

'Maybe that's the fit. Both our lives are a bit intense. When I heard the news this evening, I realised how much it impacted on you, and therefore, it impacted on us. I know the stress that you operate under. That's why the special dinner.'

'You're more thoughtful than me obviously. I don't even know what cases you're working on. But this evening I want to know.'

'My version of the law would bore to tears someone like you. I don't want anything to come between us. I just don't want our relationship to mean that I have to give up the law.'

'I would never ask you to do that. But there are things which we will have to discuss and one of them is how we're going to arrange our combined finances.'

'That's out of the question,' she said. 'Money right now is not an issue. When it becomes one, we can get into that discussion.'

'There's also the fact that I'm uncomfortable in your world. I'm just a copper. I don't socialise with judges and top legal eagles.'

'We don't need them if that's what you want. But you should know that they lap up being in the company of someone who represented his country at a sport they love. I want you to be honest with me. If the finances or the schmoozing bother you, let me know. We'll sort things out.'

He could see that she was in earnest, but he was also aware that her future depended on maintaining her network. She was intelligent enough to know that eventually the schmoozing would be a large part of her future life. Was he ready for that? He downed his whiskey and started toward the kitchen.

She pulled him back. 'Dinner and a conversation about films, books and our child. Your murder and my wife battering case can wait for another day.'

CHAPTER FORTY-THREE

The woman who had killed Lizzie Rice and Nancy Morison sat in her flat. Six women were responsible for her mother's death. Two of them had died of natural causes, and she had killed two principles. She had never considered herself capable of murder. But there was something inside her that wouldn't allow her mother's murderers to go free. She researched her mother's death with a lot more attention than the police. The police investigation was, at best, cursory at best. Her mother was unimportant. The body had never been found. The police reports at the time concluded that she had run away and left her young daughter to be placed and taken care of by the state. Just another unmarried mother for whom the pressure of bringing up a small child was too great. The woman she had known as 'Ma' was lying in a shallow grave in some Godforsaken part of Ulster. She had long ago given up hope of bringing her bones back and interring her properly. She had contemplated asking Lizzie or Nancy or one of the others where they had dumped her mother's body, but she knew it was pointless. Her mother was simply one of the many casualties of the 'Troubles' who would never be found. Wilson was good but so far, she had managed to escape detection.

However, the more she advanced on her crusade of revenge the greater the chance of discovery. She realised that she had left more evidence during the murder of Nancy Morison. Sooner or later, they would find a fragment of CCTV that would identify the car. That would be a dead end since she had stolen it specifically for the murder. But that fragment of CCTV would lead them on. Ian Wilson wasn't a fool. Eventually, he was going to connect the dots and when he did, he would start on the trail that would lead to her. Maybe if she could complete her programme before he found her, she could metamorphose again. She had already done it once when she had changed from the lost waif in Belfast into the woman she was now. But she was used to change. She had murdered. She was no longer the same person who had come to Belfast seeking revenge. She felt the change deep in her breast. Although she was avenging her mother, she was losing something of herself. You don't destroy the heads of two women without changing yourself in some way. You don't feel a life force disappearing at your hands without change. She didn't consider herself to be abnormal. Killing was the only way she could think of to avenge her mother. She had considered all the other possibilities but, there had only been one; hunting down and killing the perpetrators. She didn't feel psychopathic or even sociopathic. She was simply a daughter. The funny thing was that she hardly remembered her mother, and she had no idea, whether she had been a good or a bad person. The memory of standing outside the romper room eating an ice cream while her mother had been murdered inside had stayed with her throughout her childhood. It was that memory that had fuelled her need for vengeance. She wondered whether the need to avenge her mother would have been sated if the murderers had been brought to justice. It was a moot question. For almost thirty years, she had fed on the thought that one day she would avenge her mother. It was that thought that kept the wound of her mother's death raw. The need for revenge was the main driver of her life. That feeling was as old as mankind itself. It was the basis of the eye for an eye and tooth for a tooth. It was the basis of literature from Shakespeare to Mario Puzo and drove characters as diverse as *Othello* and *Don Corleone*. According to the saying, it was best served cold. Many times, in the course of her relatively short life she had fantasised about how she would avenge her mother by killing those who murdered her. As she sat in her apartment, she was thinking that the fantasy far outweighed the reality. In the fantasy, she could kill the Rice woman again and again. She was only able to kill her once. Perhaps it would have been better for her to stick to the fantasy. Although she had thought through and visualised the killings something was wrong. She had played the scenes of death so many times she fully expected the reality to be ten times sweeter than the fantasy. That it wasn't so bothered her. The deaths of the women were supposed to restore the equilibrium of her world that had been disturbed by her mother's death. So far, that wasn't the case. She erred somewhere along the line. Then a thought struck her. Rice and Morison died without knowing why they had to die. She almost cried with frustration. They should have known that they were dying because they killed her mother, and they should have known that it was she who was about to kill them. They should have known that they were dying because they'd hung a young woman upside down from the ceiling and dropped her until her head was mush. There was still time. There were others to kill. But Rice and Morison were the important ones, and they didn't know why she killed them. That fact would live with her beyond the current programme of revenge. It was a lacuna that she would put right with the next killing.

Two MILES AWAY, Ronald McIver was cleaning up the kitchen in his small house. He'd already deposited his wife in

bed. It was a particularly bad day with Mary. It was the first
time that she had not had at least some minutes of lucidity. It
probably marked the beginning of the end. She was still
capable of taking a bath and dressing herself, but she was
beginning to rise in the middle of the night. He wondered
would he be able to cope much longer. He didn't like the idea
of putting her in a home. But soon there would be no alternative. He suddenly found himself sobbing uncontrollably. He
moved to the sink and started to wash the dishes. He heard a
sound behind him and spun around. There was nothing. He
was becoming paranoid. His mind had played and replayed
the scene in which he had killed McIlroy. He felt that he
should be tired, but he had no desire to go to sleep. There were
a lot of questions that he had no answer for. Why had he
brought his gun along for the meeting? Had he intended to kill
McIlroy all along? Was he trying to convince himself that it
had been self-defence? IT was McIlroy who made the first
move. Or had he? He replayed the scene again. How had the
gun arrived in his hand? Did he already have the gun out
when McIlroy moved towards him? Why did he pull the trigger? Why had he fired the second shot? It had all happened so
fast and each time he replayed the scene it was slightly different, as though he were all the characters in *Rashomon*. Deep
down, he hated McIlroy and wanted to kill. He was a
murderer. He felt sweat prickling on his brow, and he let a
plate slip from his hand into the sink where it hit a cup and
broke it into pieces. He picked out the broken cup cutting his
hand in the process. A thin line of bright-red blood streaked
across his palm. He watched it fascinated then heard the
sound behind him and spun around. There was nothing. He
ran his palm under the cold tap. The cut was miniscule and
was already closing. He took a handkerchief from his pocket
and held it to the cut. The kitchen clean-up could wait until
tomorrow. He would have to go back to work. Wilson would
want to know why he had stayed off sick. Tears were running

down his cheeks. They were going to catch him and put him in jail. Nothing was more certain. A wave of fear washed over him. How would he survive in prison? How would Mary survive without him? He went into the living room and took his gun from the top of the bookcase. Worthington dodged prison by putting a bullet in his brain. The same option was open to him. He thought about it for a moment and then returned the gun to the top of the bookcase. He wasn't caught yet. He'd give Wilson a run for his money before he considered suicide.

'JIMMY IS GOIN' to have your guts for garters,' Davie Best, one of Jimmy McGreery's lieutenants, was trussed up in the back of a van speeding towards east Belfast. His hands and feet were bound with thick plastic tape. 'Let me go now and I'll forget all about it. No harm's been done.' He was ignoring the gash in his temple where he had been pistol-whipped. He looked at the man sitting opposite him cradling the Browning Hi Power pistol. The bugger was only just out of short trousers.

'Shut the fuck up or we'll do you here,' the boy with the pistol said. He jumped up and put the pistol against Best's head. 'I'll blow your fuckin' brains over the back of the van if you open your trap again.'

Best stopped talking and saw that the eyes of the three men in the back of the van with him were dilated. These boys were on something, and he hoped to God it wasn't crystal meth. What he didn't need now was a couple of fools who thought they were supermen. The three men continued to fidget while he stayed quiet. Best was an old-timer and as such he knew that his only chance of staying alive was to remain calm. The whole of Belfast had heard the news about Ivan McIlroy and everyone in the 'life' fully expected some reaction from Sammy Rice. Jimmy had put everyone on alert, but it was just blind bad luck that this group of junkies had picked on him. He was sure that they didn't have orders to snuff him. Sammy wouldn't go that far unless he knew for sure that Jimmy had ordered Ivan's death. Sooner or later, he would be delivered to Sammy, and he would be able to negotiate his way out.

CHAPTER FORTY-FOUR

W ilson pulled into his spot outside the police station. He was not surprised to see DCC Jennings' car directly in front of the door. The desk sergeant's index finger pointed upwards as he said, 'Good morning, boss.'

'Aye, good morning it is,' Wilson replied and made his way to the squad room. DCC Jennings would be in Spence's office having an early-morning coffee and undermining Wilson while he was at it. Either he was about to be called upstairs or Jennings and Spence would be joining the nine o'clock briefing. Wilson used all his detecting skills to arrive at the latter alternative. His full team were already at their desks. Wilson said, 'Good morning,' and went directly to his office noting that McIver was back and looking much the worse for wear. He either hadn't shaved or he was growing a beard. Wilson would put his money on the former. He switched on his computer and opened his e-mails. He had twenty minutes before the briefing. The usual rubbish, he thought as he scanned the thirty or so e-mails that arrived overnight. Only one was marked urgent, and he didn't instantly recognise the name of the sender. However, he did note that the e-mail had been sent at eleven thirty the previous evening. He clicked the mouse and opened the mail. The message simply read: 'Please contact me urgently re Rice case'. The name at the bottom was George Tunney and beneath it was Senior Scientific Officer, forensics service of Northern Ireland. Another one of those guys, who's been watching too much CSI, Wilson thought. He picked up the phone and dialled the number at the foot of the e-mail. The voicemail was as terse as the e-mail. George Tunney wasn't at his desk but leave a message, and he would get back as soon as he returned. Wilson left a short message. He started deleting e-mails and had dealt with the majority before he looked at his watch and saw that it was five minutes to nine.

DCC Jennings and Chief Superintendent Donald Spence were resplendent in their green uniforms as they entered the squad room. They both had their hardest faces on, so the situation was indeed serious. Neither man spoke to the team but made straight for Wilson's office.

Jennings pushed open the door. 'We've come for the briefing,' he announced. 'You can begin.' Jennings and Spence positioned themselves in front of the whiteboards.

There were now two separate whiteboards. One had photographs of Lizzie Rice and Nancy Morison on it while the second had a police photo of Ivan McIlroy on the top with a series of crime scene photos, a short biography of the victim and the basis of a timeline beneath. Wilson's team stood directly behind Jennings and Spence. Maggie Cummerford had slipped in quietly and sat at the back.

'Moira has been examining old police records and reports from the Seventies and Eighties when Lizzie was active.' He nodded in Moira's direction.

'I'm up to 1980,' she said. 'However, the material is so heavily redacted that I might have already missed something.'

'We've linked Lizzie and Nancy Morison to a women's branch of the UVF,' Wilson said. 'For the moment that link appears to be the best area to produce a motive. That's always assuming that there is a specific motive.'

'You mean there may possibly be a serial killer out there picking on sixty plus year old women?' Jennings said.

'Unlikely,' Wilson was getting bored contradicting the DCC, and he could see streaks of red on Jennings' neck. He continued quickly. 'The two women were involved in para-military activity during the 'Troubles', and they were both murdered in a similar fashion. I'd guess that Moira might eventually stumble onto something that might have got them both killed. Peter, any news on the missing women in the photo?'

'I've found two more, boss. One woman moved south ten years ago, and the other woman lives in north Belfast. I've arranged to go to see her this afternoon.'

'Anything on the traffic and CCTV, Harry?'

'We have Nancy Morison on her way home and a yellow Datsun picking her up,' Graham said. 'The figure inside the Datsun is wearing a hoodie, so we can't get a good look at him. We're looking at the traffic footage now to follow the car to the murder site.'

'Good,' Wilson said. 'We're making progress. Get whatever footage you can on the car. Try for a registration plate or a clear view of the driver.' He let his gaze run across his senior officers and his team. 'You are all now aware that we have a new murder,' Wilson pointed at the second whiteboard. 'Ivan McIlroy was found shot dead yesterday in a disused school in east Belfast. He's up for autopsy this morning, but I can tell you that he was shot twice in the chest at fairly short range.' He went on to describe the finding of the body and his and Moira's examination of the crime scene. 'We'll have the bullets after the autopsy, and we'll try some comparison. With luck, we'll get a hit. So far, we have no idea what McIlroy was doing in the school. The amount of shit and syringes lying around indicates that junkies regularly visited the school. Was he there on drugs-related business? Did he go there to meet some-one? Who might that someone be? We need answers to those and any other questions you can come up with.'

'Perhaps the three murders are connected,' DCC Jennings interrupted.

'That's possible, but unlikely,' Wilson said. 'The MOs are so different. I still think that the crushed heads are significant in the Rice and Morison killings. There's a message there. We just don't know what it is for the moment. McIlroy was shot in gangland style. However, we're not excluding any possibility for the moment.'

'Lizzie Rice was Sammy Rice's mother, and McIlroy was one of his lieutenants,' Jennings said. 'Is that not a good enough connection for you?'

'Again, that might be where the investigation will go,' Wilson wanted to tell Jennings to stop with the stupid questions, but he opted to play along. It was interesting to see the DCC playing at policeman. 'We need a motive for all these killings.'

'A takeover of Rice's criminal enterprise, perhaps?' Jennings said.

'Again, possible but unlikely,' Wilson said. 'I had Jimmy McGreery in here yesterday, and I don't think a takeover was on his agenda.'

'You don't think,' Jennings said with a sneer.

Wilson ignored the remark. 'The pathologist estimates death occurred the evening before last between eight and ten. We need to know what, if any, connection exists between McIlroy's murder, and the two women killed earlier this week. We need to develop a full timeline on McIlroy's movements for the day before last and we need to know who he met with in the past few weeks. Was he about to jump ship and go over to another godfather? We need answers to questions.' Wilson produced a small tape recorder from his pocket and pressed play. The phone message lasted less than twenty seconds and identified the corpse and its location. 'And we definitely need to know who made this call. The voice is disguised so I've already asked for forensics to look at it. I've also asked for a trace on the number. It's likely a throwaway SIM but we still have to follow up.'

'I go back to one of my previous points,' Jennings said. 'This looks like a turf war, and it looks like it's being started by Jimmy McGreery. We need to put pressure on to stop it in its tracks, and that means keeping McGreery out of circulation.'

'I might be wrong,' Wilson said. 'But I believe McGreery when he says he isn't behind the killings. The Rice and Morison murders show no signs of a paramilitary or gangland style hit. I'm not totally convinced that he's innocent of the McIlroy killing. We'll know more tomorrow. I'd like to take advantage of the presence of the DCC and the Chief Super to talk over the resource situation. Two murders had us stretched to the limit. Three pushes us over the top. Since I'm pretty sure McIlroy is a stand-alone crime, there are two separate investigations. We should really have two teams.'

'Out of the question,' Jennings said. 'We live in a time when everyone has to do more with less.' He glanced at his watch. 'I hope that my input into the briefing proves useful'

'As usual your comments have been pertinent and insight-ful,' Wilson said smiling. 'We'll be following up on all your suggestions.'

Chief Superintendent Spence's smile was cut off by a sharp look from Jennings. Wilson turned to his team. 'Peter, you're on McIlroy's timeline. Eric hit the usual McIlroy haunts and find out who he's been talking to lately. Harry, you're going to end up with TV eyes because I want you to get what-ever CCTV there is around the area of the school. We'll follow up with Traffic if you hit something. Moira, you're at the autopsy. Ronald, you take over from Moira on the search through the reports on Loyalist paramilitary activity.'

'What about asking military intelligence if they have anything on Lizzie?' Moira asked.

'Try but I can guarantee you'll get nowhere,' Wilson said. 'We're done. Ronald, in my office.'

'What about you, boss?' Moira said.

'By the look of things, I'm off to the forensics lab. Some genius there sent me an urgent e-mail this morning.' Wilson glanced towards the rear of the squad room and noticed that Maggie Cummerford was no longer present.

'You look like shit,' Wilson said as soon as McIver closed the door of his office. 'Are you still sick or what?'

McIver moved from foot to foot. 'No, boss, I'm all right. It's just Mary. Things have been difficult lately.'

'Sit down, man.'

McIver sat on the chair before Wilson's desk.

'You look like you haven't slept in days. I can't use someone who's suffering from sleep deprivation. What's the problem?'

'The wife's getting worse. The medics warned that the dementia could accelerate. I don't know whether I'm up to dealing with it.'

'Take some time off and go to Social Services. They'll help you get organised. You don't have to handle this alone.'

Tears started rolling down McIver's face and try as he might he couldn't stop them. Wilson would assume that he was crying for Mary, but in effect, he hadn't been able to stop crying since the impact of the killing of McIlroy had hit him. How long could he carry the guilt without spitting out the truth?

Oh God, Wilson thought as he watched McIver's attempts to stem the tears. The man is having a breakdown. McIver was unravelling before his eyes. Right now, he needed his full team, and he was about to lose an asset. 'Ronald, you have to pull yourself together for Mary's sake. You don't have to shoulder the burden yourself. There are people out there who are paid to help in situations like this.'

'You don't understand,' McIver sobbed.

'I know I don't, and I want to help,' Wilson said quickly. 'Take a couple of hours off and sort things out.' The telephone rang as Wilson was about to dismiss McIver.

'George Tunney for DS Wilson,' a deep voice said.

'Mr Tunney,' Wilson cupped his hand on the receiver. 'Let me know how it goes,' he said to McIver, who was already on his feet.

'Sorry,' Wilson said. 'I had someone in my office. Your e-mail intrigued me.'

'No problem, I'm George by the way. I did some tests recommended by Professor Reid, and I was wondering whether you'd like to take a look.'

'Can you send me a report?'

'I can but I think you should come over here. It'll only take an hour or so,'

'Now?'

'Now would be good.'

'I'm on my way.'

RONALD McIVER WENT BACK to his desk. He had to pull himself together. He was a few seconds from blubbing that he killed McIlroy. Only Wilson's swift intervention stopped him. He was not the first man who had killed another human being in cold blood. But his blood wasn't cold. He was motivated by fear. The problem was that there was no road back. He could have gone to Wilson and told him that McIlroy was threatening him. That would have been the smart thing to do. Now he was on a road and he would have to stay on it until either he was found out or he escaped. At the moment, he didn't care. He looked up and saw Moira McElvaney staring at him.

CHAPTER FORTY-FIVE

Davie Best lifted his head at the sound from the other end of the warehouse. He was taped to a wooden chair and both sides of his face hurt where Sammy's boys had laid into him. He wasn't worried about the pain or the bruises he would carry for the next week. He needed to get himself out alive. Sammy's goons could be dealt with later.

'Did you sleep well, Davie boy?' Sammy Rice asked as he stood directly before the chair.

'Well enough, Sammy, you know the score,' he winced when he tried to smile. 'I'm glad to see you. The idiots you sent to pick me only know how to talk with their fists.'

Rice pulled over a chair and sat down. 'We're all a bit upset about Ivan.'

'Understandable.'

'I had to identify the body, Davie. Someone planted two rounds in his chest.' He made his right index finger and thumb into the shape of a gun and pointed at Best. 'Bang, bang. No way out, dead as a doornail. The questions are why and who?'

'I can't say that I liked Ivan,' Best said. 'We weren't exactly best mates. During the 'Troubles', we organised a few things together. That being said, I would never have hurt him. So why me?'

'Never say never, Davie boy. This week I lost my mother and my head boy. Some people tell me that it's a coincidence. Maybe that's so but maybe someone is tryin' to give me a message. If that's the case, I have to respond. That's where you come in.'

Best looked directly into Rice's eyes. Sammy had the reputation of being a crazy bastard, but he also was an astute businessman. He didn't need trouble. 'Meet with Jimmy,' Best said. 'He'll tell you to your face that he had nothing to do with either your mother or Ivan. He'll even help you find the bastard who did both.'

Rice stared into Best's eyes. He fancied himself as someone who could tell when a person was lying, and so far, he could see no lie in Best's demeanour. Best was as cool as a cucumber. 'You remember that scene in *The Godfather* when they have the meeting in the restaurant, and the gun gets hidden in the toilet. I don't think that Jimmy and I should meet right now.'

'We were all in this together at one time,' Best said.

'But we also slaughtered each other from time to time.'

'They were the hotheads, the psychopaths. You and Jimmy are about makin' money. Think about it. There's no real reason why Jimmy would want Ivan out of the way.'

'Maybe he wanted Ivan to change sides and when he wouldn't, bang, bang.'

'It doesn't gel. Up to now, no harm has been done. You top me, and you'll start a war.'

'I top you and I sink you in a bog hole, and no one can prove anything. Then Jimmy starts a war, and the peelers rip his arse out. How does that sound to you?' Rice stood up and moved to the back of the warehouse where four of his men were standing. 'Food and water for now. Did he have a mobile?'

One of the men took a smartphone from his pocket and handed it to Rice.

'And no more rough stuff. If we have to top him, we will.'

THE FORENSIC SERVICE OF NORTHERN IRELAND is not a branch of the PSNI. It is an independent organisation that works for the Police Service but also for clients, such as defence solicitors, who require forensic work to be carried out. The laboratory buildings are located on the Belfast Road just south of the town of Carrickfergus. Wilson took the M5 out of Belfast and drove alongside the Irish Sea. It was a pleasant journey with the slate grey waters of the sea on one side and the abundant foliage on the other. It was still possible to find countryside just a few miles from Belfast city. In twenty-five minutes, Wilson pulled into the short lane leading to the FSNI Lab. The double gates were festooned with signs – ALL VISITORS MUST SIGN IN – ALL VISITORS MUST REPORT TO THE MAIN OFFICE – RESTRICTED ACCESS. They were only short of putting up a sign for abandon hope all who enter here. Wilson flashed his warrant card and was admitted by a security guard who motioned him in the direction of the main office. Even a detective superintendent from the PSNI was required to sign in. Wilson was told to leave his car where it was. The receptionist phoned George Tunney, who said he would pick him up within five minutes.

Five minutes later a short rotund man wearing a white lab coat entered the main office and made straight for Wilson. 'Superintendent Wilson I presume,' Tunney's eyes sparkled behind his thick spectacles.

'George,' Wilson said taking his outstretched hand. 'You can call me Ian.' Tunney gave him a Masonic handshake that Wilson didn't return.

'Please follow me,' Tunney led him out of the office and

towards a series of large barn-like buildings and the rear of the complex. 'Like I said on the phone,'

Tunney legs were short, and Wilson had to adjust his pace downward to stay beside the scientist.

'The pathologist, Professor Reid, asked us to perform a series of tests. They were quite simple tests really, but I thought I should show you the results. It's always better to see with one's own eyes rather than read some report or other. Don't you think?'

It was one of those subjects upon which Wilson didn't have an opinion, so he didn't bother giving one.

Tunney pushed open a door of one of the large buildings and led Wilson into a small lab at the rear. 'I've done a simulation of the Lizzie Rice murder,' Tunney began as they entered the lab. 'From the photographs taken at the autopsy, I have created a three-dimensional representation of Elisabeth Rice's head.' He tapped on a computer keyboard, and Lizzie Rice's head appeared on the screen. It was lifelike enough, and the injuries were very clearly represented. 'Then I've used the additional photos to create a three-dimensional representation of her body.' Some more tapping on the computer and Lizzie Rice stood on the screen. 'The pathologist had identified a hammer as the murder weapon and from the indentations in the skull, I have definitely established that it was indeed a ball hammer.' More tapping and a ball hammer appeared in the corner of the screen. 'Now we try to fit the ball hammer to the injuries.' The ball hammer moved and lined up with one of the indentations on Lizzie's head. 'Now, let's assume that a hand is holding the hammer.' More tapping and a hand and arm appeared holding the hammer. 'Now, let's add a body.' A few keys were tapped, and a body gradually grew out of the arm. 'You see where we're going,' Tunney turned and looked at Wilson who was staring at the screen.

'Are you sure about this?' Wilson asked.

'It isn't rocket science. It was quite a simple exercise.'

'What height would you say the assailant was?'

Tunney tapped a few more keys, and the answer appeared on the screen.

'Five foot two to five foot four,' Wilson read off the screen. 'It was either a woman or a very short man.'

'I did some calculations of the force exerted on the head by the ball hammer and extrapolated that data to give an idea of the strength of the person wielding the hammer. The calculations are a bit rough and ready, but my conclusion is that the person who murdered Lizzie Rice was certainly a woman.' Tunney let out a chortling laugh. 'Either, that or a fairly weak man.'

'Can you run this stuff off for me? I need a series of screen shots. Yesterday.'

'They'll be on your computer before you get back.'

'I might have a job for you on another case.'

'We're here to serve. Where should we send the bill?'

'Send it to PSNI, usual address.'

'I did this without a work order,' Tunney said. 'Next time make it official.'

'You've met Professor Reid, I assume?'

'Ah, yes,' Tunney reddened.

CHAPTER FORTY-SIX

A woman, Wilson hadn't thought of that possibility, and he could have kicked himself. He remembered Reid saying something about it, but he couldn't remember why he had excluded the possibility? Probably because women didn't kill with a high degree of violence. Bashing in a victim's head with a ball hammer was not a typical *modus operandi* for a woman. Wilson pulled in and stopped his car as soon as he got outside the gate of the FSNI complex. He took out his mobile phone and called Moira McElvaney. 'Where are you?' he asked when she replied.

'On the way back to the office. The autopsy finished about fifteen minutes ago. Reid retrieved two bullets, both nine-millimetre Parabellums. They're a bit messed up, but I'll get them over to forensics to see whether we have something on record. The injuries are classic. The first shot damaged the lung and chest wall causing a hemopneumothorax,' she stumbled over the pronunciation. 'He might have survived with immediate medical attention, but the second hit the heart and that was curtains for McIlroy.

'If forensics find that the gun was used before, we'll at least have a lead.'

'Is there anything else?' she asked.

'No, I was hoping to catch you are the mortuary. I'll just have to call Reid.'

'Careful,' Moira said and closed the line.

Wilson sat back in the car and looked at his mobile. He scrolled through his contacts and chose Stephanie Reid. He pressed the green button and waited.

'Reid,' the voice was terse and agitated.

'It's Ian Wilson.'

'It's old scaredy-cat,' she laughed. 'Afraid to come to the autopsy, were we? Sent along our female Rottweiler instead. '

'I had other business. That was a smart move of yours to ask FNSI to look at the height of the assailant. I've already kicked myself in the pants for missing that one.'

'Modesty becomes you.'

'It made me think about the McIlroy shooting. Have you looked at the angle of entry and exit of the bullets?'

'I've marked it on a chart of the body.'

'Anything unusual or should I make a request to FNSI?'

'I didn't note anything. But if you are as thorough as your reputation, you'll get FNSI to rig something up. They have all sorts of rubber dummies. It's no big deal.'

'Thanks for the advice. I'll get on it. Scan the autopsy report and get it over to me.'

'Already requested by Miss Rottweiler. I suppose it is Miss, since I reckon I'm not alone in having designs on your body.'

'She's very efficient. I've got to go.'

'We make a good team, Ian. See you soon.'

Wilson didn't know whether he should smile or frown, so he did neither. Stephanie Reid was becoming a distraction, and he didn't need a distraction. He started the car and headed back to the station.

. . .

'I HAD to put him in there,' the desk sergeant pointed at the 'soft' interview room as Wilson entered the station. 'An agitated Jimmy McGreery in the entrance hall is not something the average citizen necessarily wants to see.'

'Send me in a cup of coffee,' Wilson said as he made his way to the interview room.

Jimmy McGreery immediately terminated the mobile phone call he was making when Wilson entered the room. There was no point in telling him that the room was wired for sound and vision. Wilson would check the tape later.

'Mr McGreery, what can I do for you?' Wilson said as he sat down.

'One of my boys has been lifted,' McGreery said. 'That wee bastard Rice thinks that I had something to do with McIlroy bein' shot. Davie Best was lifted on his way home last night, and he hasn't been seen since. If I don't get Davie back in one piece,' he let the sentence trail off.

'The normal time period for reporting a missing person is twenty-four hours. At what time was Best last seen?' Wilson asked.

One of the constables from the front desk entered and deposited a plastic cup containing a dark hot liquid vaguely resembling coffee in front of Wilson. He took one look at the contents and decided to forgo the pleasure.

'As far as we can tell sometime around eleven o'clock last night.'

'So technically he's not a missing person until eleven o'clock tonight.'

McGreery leaned forward. 'I'm not waiting for twenty-four hours. If we don't do something now, he won't just be missing at eleven o'clock tonight. He'll be dead.'

'And he wouldn't just have wandered off? Maybe he met a friend on the way home, and they're spending some time together.'

'Aye, Davie a good lad, who always stays in touch. The smart money says that he's been lifted.'

'Have you spoken to Sammy Rice?' Wilson asked.

'Sammy's gone to ground. He's not answering his mobile, at least not the mobile number I have for him. I've put feelers out but so far nothing. It's up to you now, Mr Wilson. You get to Sammy and tell him to let Davie go.'

'You have absolutely nothing to do with McIlroy's death?'

'Believe me or not. I have no interest in starting a turf war. I've seen what happened in this city when two groups go at each other. It just means wailing women and funerals. That kind of shite was for the mad dogs.'

'McIlroy was autopsied this morning, and the pathologist pulled two nine-millimetre Parabellums out of his chest. Those bullets were fired from the weapon of choice of the paramilitaries.'

'I swear on my mother's grave that I had nothing to do with Ivan's death. We didn't always see eye to eye, but that was just business. I'll have a drink at his wake like everyone else.'

'Then where should I look?'

McGreery sat back and thought. 'I'm stumped,' he said finally. 'McIlroy was an experienced operator. He wasn't the kind of guy who'd walk into a trap. My guess is that he knew the fellah who shot him, and he trusted him. Otherwise, he would never have been alone with him in that school.'

'We're looking for someone McIlroy knew well and who he trusted. Why should someone like that want him dead?'

'You're the detective. Maybe it was Sammy who organised the hit. It's no secret that Sammy's been spendin' more time in Spain than in Belfast. Maybe Ivan thought it was time he took over the reins. But this isn't getting us any nearer to saving Davie's skin.'

'Sammy's no fool. He knows if he harms Best, he's declaring war, and I'm supposing that he doesn't want a fight either. I'll try to get to him and get your man back. I don't suppose that there'll be any recriminations.'

'I understand where Sammy's coming from. If Davie was found shot in some deserted spot, I might be reacting like Sammy. He wants to know what's going down, and he thinks that Davie might have some of the answers. The problem is that he doesn't.'

'OK,' Wilson said. 'I'm on it.'

McGreery pushed himself out of the chair. 'I'll keep trying to get to Sammy.'

Let's hope that we get to him before Davie Best is added to the list of corpses, Wilson thought.

CHAPTER FORTY-SEVEN

As soon as Wilson returned to his office, he arranged for FSNI to carry out an examination of the McIlroy shooting. He wanted to know what height the shooter might be. There was no need for a return visit to Carrickfergus; a simple report would suffice. He rushed off a report on his visit to FSNI and his conversation with McGreery. He had already added 'shot by someone he trusted or knew' and 'why the deserted school?' to the whiteboard containing the information on the McIlroy murder. He looked through the glass window and saw that only Moira and McIver were at their desks. His watch said eleven thirty, and he would expect the team to assemble at midday. He kept his gaze on the squad room until he caught Moira's eye, and he motioned for her to join him.

'That was one pissed-off pathologist this morning,' Moira laughed as she entered his office. 'She must have spent an hour getting herself made up to knock your socks off, and then I turn up. Not a happy bunny as they say.'

'I spoke to her on the phone.'

'And she didn't bite your head off?'

'You're making a mountain out of a molehill.'

'Just make sure you don't trip over that molehill.'

'That's not why I wanted to talk to you. I want you to keep an eye on Ronald.'

'The guy has just recently moved to another planet,' she said. 'He opens his desk drawer, looks in it and then closes it twenty times a day. If you look at him, he breaks out in a sweat, and he's developed this faraway look. What's going on?'

'Trouble at home. His wife has early dementia, and I think it's beginning to get to him. He looks like shit. I think that he may be unravelling. I suggested that he look for help for Mary, but I'm beginning to think he's the one that needs to see a shrink.'

'We need all hands on deck right now. What do you want me to do?'

'Just keep an eye out. If he starts to go off the wall, we might have to look for a replacement.'

'Good luck with that.'

Ronald McIver's ears were burning. He watched the boss and the DS talking in the boss's office, and he was sure that he was the subject of their conversation. McElvaney was a dead giveaway. She had glanced twice into the squad room where he was the only occupant. He knew how important it was to remain normal in this situation. But since killing McIlroy his emotions were all over the place. In the twenty years that he'd been a police officer he'd never had occasion to draw his gun, never mind shoot another human being. He had qualified on the shooting range every year in order to continue to hold a personal weapon, but he never imagined that he would have reason to use it. He'd heard it said that you are never the same after killing, and they were right as far as he was concerned. If he'd killed in the line of duty, his weapon would have been confiscated, and he would be having a dozen sessions with a shrink. He still had his gun, and the sessions with the shrink were out of the question. His only possibility of staying out of jail was talking to nobody about McIlroy. But the guilt was eating him up inside. He'd joined the Murder Squad to catch people who had done what he had done. The knowledge that he was as bad as some of the bastards he put away ate at him. The boss and his pal were on to him. It wasn't possible, but he didn't like the way they looked at him. Behaving off beam would only raise suspicion. But he always had Mary's condition to fall back on. A tear crept out of the corner of his eye, and he quickly wiped it away.

THE TEAM WERE all assembled for the midday briefing. Wilson noticed that Cummerford had taken up her usual position at the rear of the room. The tone of her articles on the Rice and Morison killings was measured, and she hadn't descended into too much speculation. Also, it was clear that she wasn't using a lot of the information she was picking up at the internal briefings, and that she was sticking to the line being put out by the PSNI press office. So, all in all, she wasn't the impediment to the investigation that Wilson assumed she would be. Wilson stood in front of the whiteboards where amendments had already been made following his visit to FSNI and Moira's attendance at the autopsy. 'So,' he started. 'We now have a vital piece of new information. The killer of Lizzie Rice and Nancy Morison was most probably a woman. That changes the direction of the investigation.' He pointed to a copy of the photograph of the Shankill branch of the UVF appended to the whiteboard. 'We need to find all these women, now. One of them may be the killer or the killer may be after the whole group. Peter will be talking to Joan Boyle, the woman we've identified from the photo this afternoon, and it's important that we get information on the activities of the group but also on the whereabouts of the other women. Eric, anything further on the car that lifted Nancy Morison?'

Eric Taylor moved forward and stuck a photo on the whiteboard. 'This is the best enhancement we can get of the person driving the car. It's about as useful as a midget in a basketball game in terms of identification. We can't even tell for sure whether it's a man or a woman. The hood of the fleece is covering most of the head. My guess is that this person was very well prepared for the abduction.'

'What about the traffic cameras?' Wilson asked.

Taylor took another photo from a file and stuck it on the board. 'This is the best shot of the interior of the car taken by a traffic camera. It has been enhanced. You'll note that the passenger is clearly identifiable as Nancy Morison, but you'll also notice that the driver's face is a blur. The best guess I can get from the traffic guys is that there was some kind of privacy tape put in strips across the driver's side which allowed the driver to see out through the gaps, but which blurred the image for the camera. We're dealing with someone who's pretty smart here.'

Wilson looked at Moira. 'Anything on the background check?'

Moira said. 'I'm still searching through the police reports on UVF activities in the Seventies and Eighties which covers Lizzie's involvement. Nothing so far.'

Wilson turned and looked at Ronald McIver who seemed a million miles away. 'Ronald?'

'Boss,' DC McIver jumped as though he had been startled.

'Anything?' Wilson asked

'No, boss. I'm drawing a blank.'

Wilson looked at Moira and she raised her eyebrows as a signal of understanding.

'OK, let's move on to McIlroy. Moira the autopsy.'

Moira put down the coffee cup she'd been drinking from. 'Ivan McIlroy was shot twice in the chest at close range; the estimate is two to three metres. In other words, by someone at the other side of the corridor in which they were standing. The pathologist removed two bullets.' She walked forward and stuck a photo of the two bullets on the whiteboard. 'These are two nine mm Parabellum slugs. They are currently with forensics for comparison testing and for identification of a possible weapon.'

'I've asked FNSI to look at the trajectory of the bullets to give us some indication of the height of the shooter,' Wilson said. 'That way we'll be able to say for sure that the Rice and Morison killings are a separate crime from the McIlroy killing.'

'The killers might be different, but the motive might be the same,' McIver said.

'What?' Wilson said.

'Well, for example,' McIver continued, 'if the killings are intended to put pressure on Sammy, they could be carried out by a group which had both a male and female assassin.'

'That's possible but a bit in the realm of conspiracy theory,' Wilson said, and he wanted to add that perhaps McIver was reading too many Dan Brown books. 'We won't separate the killings until we have all the information.'

'Forensic will be back on the bullets by this afternoon,' Moira said. 'I put a rush on the testing.'

Wilson frowned. This would be reflected in the cost and would impact on his budget. 'Last point. We have a possible abduction.' He explained his conversation with McGreery. A look at the change of expression on the faces of his team was enough to tell him that they all understood the implication. 'This is only hypothetical now. I've asked the uniforms to keep a look out for either Sammy or members of his inner circle. I've put the word out that I need to speak urgently to Sammy.'

'Jesus,' Peter Davidson said softly. 'Back to the bad old days. If Davie Best is murdered, that's it. It'll be tit-for-tat killings until they run out of foot soldiers.'

'I'm aware of that,' Wilson said. 'I want all of you to spread the word. I need to speak to Sammy, and I need to speak to him today. So far, Best is not even technically missing, and we have no evidence to confirm that he has been abducted. If we can nip this thing in the bud, it will be better for all concerned especially for Sammy and the goons that carried out the abduction. We need to get Davie Best back alive and in the best condition possible.'

WILSON WAS JUST SETTLING himself in his office when Maggie Cummerford knocked on his door and entered.

'Interesting briefing,' she said sitting in his visitor's chair.

'And confidential,' Wilson said.

'I stick to my agreements,' she pulled out a series of pages from her messenger bag and tossed them on the desk in front of him. 'My profile of you. Not quite so gushing as that piece on your partner but probably more positive than you expected. Over the past week, I've spoken to people who played rugby with you and worked with you and even quite a few who claim to have slept with you. I don't know how my editor will react. I think he might consider my views on your personal life might need to be toned down, but I do have sources for every statement.'

'And I thought that I was universally popular,' Wilson said picking up the pages. 'When can I expect to see this in print?'

'That's my editor's decision. There's even a chance that he may not publish it at all. But my guess is that he will. Possibly if you manage to solve either the Rice and Morison case, or the McIlroy case.'

'You sound a bit downbeat. I thought the action of two concurrent cases to report on would be a reporter's dream.'

'I'm getting bored with Belfast. It rains too much, and everybody is hung up on religion. It's like living in the Bible Belt in the States without the compensation of the weather.'

'No place is perfect.'

'But some are better than others.'

'Are you ready to tell me how you got Jennings to permit you to have such access to our investigation?'

'Not yet.'

'You're an interesting person, Maggie.'

She smiled. 'After researching you, I'm really worried that's a come-on.'

He laughed. 'No, I mean it.'

'You don't know the half of it,' she said and picked up her bag. 'Let me know what you think of the piece.

CHAPTER FORTY-EIGHT

K ate McCann sat at the defence table in Belfast Crown Court and adjusted her gown while listening to the opposing barrister rip into her client. Lunch had been a tuna sandwich and a coffee, the lot consumed in five minutes so that she could attend a client meeting in the middle of what was a difficult trial. Her client, an Irish woman of thirty-five, was seeking a Crown Court writ for the return of her two sons who had been abducted and taken to Latvia. Her husband was fighting the writ and had used the well-worn technique of blackening his wife's character in order to resist the issuance of a writ that Kate would then try to internationalise. She had warned her client that her character was going to be dragged through the mud and to be prepared for the vicious attack from her husband's barrister. Despite the warning and considerable preparation, her client was becoming increasingly emotional as charge after charge was laid against her. This was the part of the law that Kate hated most, the vilification of one party, usually the innocent one. The emotional garbage that was being stored up by the attack on her client would linger long after this case was settled. She looked up and saw that the line of questioning of the opposing barrister equally perturbed the female judge. The problem was that Kate had sometimes behaved in a similar manner as her esteemed colleague. In representing the interests of her client, it was often necessary to destroy someone's character. It was not the most pleasant of tasks, but she was committed to helping her client recover her children. The opposing barrister was winding up as Kate looked through her notes. By the time she glanced up, she saw that the judge was looking at her. She couldn't remember her opponent's last question, but that didn't matter. She was suddenly very warm, and she could feel sweat on her forehead. Something was happening that she didn't understand. Her stomach cramped. She knew that something bad was happening, and that she needed to get out of court and into a hospital. She stood up and suddenly the room started to spin around her. She looked up at the judge and saw her through a fog. Then everything went black, and she fainted.

WILSON RUSHED into the gynaecology ward at the Royal Victoria and went directly to the reception desk. 'Kate McCann,' he said breathlessly.

The receptionist looked at her computer and then picked up her phone. She spoke into the receiver for a few minutes. 'The consultant is with her now. Perhaps you could take a seat, and we'll call you when she's through.'

Wilson reluctantly moved away from the reception desk and took a seat in the waiting area. The message he'd received was that Kate had fainted during a court case and had been brought to the Royal Victoria as a precaution. He'd been told not to worry, but that was ridiculous. His pregnant partner had fainted and been rushed to hospital, of course he was going to bloody worry. It was at moments like this that Wilson wished that he hadn't given up smoking. He looked at the other people in the waiting area and considered bumming a cigarette from them. What was he thinking of? He glanced at the wall and saw the no-smoking sign. He would have to go outside to smoke and there was no way he was leaving the waiting room until he found out what was happening. He stood up when he saw Kate's gynaecologist coming towards the reception area.

'Ian,' she made directly for him with her hand outstretched. 'It's great that you're here. Would you please come with me to one of the family rooms?'

The 'family room' didn't sound good. 'Is she OK?' Wilson asked grabbing the consultant's hand.

'I really need to speak to you in private,' she said quickly. She took him by the arm and led him back along the corridor. The gynaecologist pushed open a door, and they entered a room with a comfortable couch and a coffee table. There were magazines and newspapers strewn across the coffee table.

'I'm sorry, Ian,' the gynaecologist said as soon as she closed the door. 'There's no easy way to say this. I'm afraid Kate has had a miscarriage. She's lost the baby.'

'What!' Wilson shouted. 'She was fine this morning.'

'Ian, please sit,' she guided him to the couch. 'This is not unusual. Fifty percent of pregnancies end in miscarriage. Luckily, most of them occur before the woman realises that she's pregnant. Fifteen percent of recognised pregnancies end in miscarriage.'

Wilson was too stunned to speak. He realised that the gynaecologist was holding his hand.

'The causes of miscarriage are not well understood,' she continued. 'Most miscarriages that occur in the first trimester are caused by chromosomal abnormalities in the baby. Chromosomes are tiny structures inside the cells of the body that carry many genes. Genes determine all a person's physical attributes, such as sex, hair and eye colour, and blood type. Most chromosomal problems occur by chance and are not related to the mother's or father's health. There's no reason why Kate and you won't have a successful pregnancy in the future.'

'How's Kate?' Wilson asked.

'As you can imagine, she's distraught. Like most women, she blames herself, but nothing could be further from the truth. The problem was with the embryo. The miscarriage was a way of clearing up that problem.'

'Can I see her?'

'Yes, but remember there is no blame here, and you are a strong and sympathetic man. You're going to need those traits in the coming days. The pain of losing the baby will pass.' She stood up. 'Let's go.'

They stopped outside a door to a private room. 'Kate's physically fine. I want her to stay overnight. We have to do a short surgical procedure called dilation and curettage to remove tissue from the uterus. I've told her she has to take it easy for a while.' She pushed opened the door and ushered Wilson in.

Kate was lying in a hospital bed with her head away from the door. Wilson walked to the bed and sat. He put his arm around her and hugged her. She immediately began to sob uncontrollably. He held her tighter. 'It's all right,' he said kissing her on the neck. 'It's part of life.' He tried to turn her towards him, but she resisted.

'I lost our baby,' she said haltingly through the sobs.

'It had nothing to do with you,' he said. 'It was just nature's way of telling us that there was something not quite right.'

She turned towards him. Her face was paler than he had ever seen it, and her eyes had dark circles under them from crying. Her blonde hair was wet and lank on her head. 'That's what you say now. But tomorrow when you realise that there's no more baby, you'll sing a different tune. You told me so. You said I was working too hard. Maybe you were right.' She buried her head in the pillow.

He lifted her head up and held it in his large hands. 'I love you. The gynaecologist said there's no reason we can't have a successful pregnancy. We'll get over this together.'

'I'll never get over this,' she said through sobs. 'And neither will you. Every time you look at me, you'll remember that I'm the one that lost your child.' She pushed her head into his breast.

'Don't be silly. We're not unique and there are lots worse things that could have happened.'

'Promise me that you'll never blame me,' she said looking up at him.

'I'll never blame you,' he said and kissed her forehead. The phrase 'never say never' came to mind.

She looked into his eyes. 'And promise me that nothing will change between us.'

'Nothing will change between us,' he said.

She slumped back on the bed.

The door opened, and the gynaecologist entered with a nurse. 'We need Kate for a few minutes, Ian,' the gynaecologist said. 'She won't be receiving visitors for a while, but you can come back this evening.'

Wilson lifted Kate's head and kissed her on lips that seemed lifeless. 'I love you,' he said before placing her head gently on the pillow. 'See you this evening.'

CHAPTER FORTY-NINE

The small estate of Archvale lies in the townland of Newtonabbey in the north of Belfast. Peter Davidson arrived in the labyrinthine housing estate after a short twenty-minute drive from central Belfast. The estate consisted of interlocking streets all containing similar small bungalows. This was the opposite of the rabbit warren of Victorian houses constituting both the Catholic and Protestant areas of west Belfast. Each of the bungalows was detached, and most had a small garden in front. Others had eschewed the garden and created an off-road parking space. Davidson took the precaution of printing out a map from his office computer, and he piloted his car to a spot directly outside the house he was seeking. Without the map and street numbers, it would be impossible to identify a particular house. The residence he was looking for resembled every other house in the street except that Davidson noticed it was a little more rundown than its neighbours. He parked his car and made his way up the short driveway.

'Yes,' the woman who opened the door to Davidson was in her sixties with short curly grey hair and a pleasant face. Her blue eyes stared at him across the chain holding the front door at an angle. She was dressed in a housecoat over a pair of jogging pants, and a heavy-knit sweater.

'Detective Constable Peter Davidson,' he held his warrant card extended. 'I called you yesterday.'

The woman made a show of examining the card before unlatching the chain. 'Aye,' she said. 'You can't be too cautious. Although it's safe around here with so many people on the streets and all, I'm careful who I let in.'

'Quite right too,' Davidson said as he crossed the threshold.

As soon as he was in, she closed the door and slipped the chain back on. 'I'm Joan Boyle, by the way,' she said leading him into the living room.

'I'm pleased to meet you Mrs Boyle,' Davidson sat in the chair that Boyle indicated. The living room was neat and tidy but in need of redecoration. The carpet covering the floor was threadbare and a couch and two easy chairs that had seen better days dominated the small room. A petite coffee table was placed directly in front of the couch and a 32inch flat-screen TV sat in one corner.

Joan Boyle sat on the couch facing Davidson's chair. 'I have no idea what the police want with me, don't you know? I've been fretting all night thinking that I might have done something wrong.'

'There's no need to worry I'm part of the Murder Squad, and we've been looking into a series of crimes that I'd like to talk to you about.'

'Oh my God,' she brought her hands up to her cheeks. 'What would I know about murders? I hardly ever leave this little house.' She seemed to be thinking of something. 'You'll be wanting a cup of tea, I suppose.'

'I wouldn't say no,' Davidson smiled in order to reassure Boyle that she had nothing to worry about. As soon as she left the room he stood up and examined the photographs that stood on the mantelpiece above the fireplace. There were photographs of Joan Boyle and a man who could have been her husband taken in Malvern Street. A small boy stood between them. There was a series of photographs of a young man, one in Army dress uniform and others drinking with friends. The door opened behind him, and he quickly retook his seat.

'I hope you like banana bread,' Boyle said moving to the coffee table and setting down a tray holding a teapot, two cups, a milk jug, sugar bowl and a plate holding two pieces of cake. She poured two cups of tea. 'I'll let you do the milk and sugar yourself.' She sat and watched him as he put two spoons of sugar and a dash of milk into his tea. 'Now that we're settled, how can I help you?'

Davidson sipped his tea. 'You're originally from the Shankill?'

'Aye, born and bred,' she put sugar and milk into her own tea and sipped.

'You knew Lizzie Rice?'

There was a slight pause. 'Faith and everybody in the Shankill knew Lizzie. It was terrible what happened to the poor woman.' She looked up sharply as though something had suddenly dawned on her. 'You're investigating the murder of Lizzie and that unfortunate Morison woman.'

'I'm one of the team investigating those murders.'

'Who could have done such a terrible thing?'

'Don't worry we'll find them.' He produced the photograph of the women's UVF group. 'Do you recognise this photograph?' he asked.

She took the photograph from his hands, took a pair of glasses from her housecoat and put them on and then examined the photo. 'I don't think that I remember this.'

'Look at the banner. It says, 'Shankill Women's UVF branch'. That's you, third from the left.'

She smiled. 'Aye, I was a bonnie lass. All the boys were after me.'

'Can you think of any reason from those days why

someone would want to kill Lizzie and Nancy Morison?'

She thought for a moment and then looked down to the left. 'I don't know why anyone would want to kill Lizzie and Nancy. Sure we were only supporting our men back then. We made tea and sandwiches and things like that.'

And Molotov cocktails for burning Catholics out of their homes, Davidson thought. 'The feedback we get from the people we talked to in the Shankill is that your group was a little more active than that.'

'Then you've been told lies.'

'You didn't go to Lizzie's funeral?'

'I haven't been back to the Shankill in years. We moved out here more than ten years ago. My husband, God rest him, won a couple of pounds, and we managed to buy this wee place.'

'Do you remember any of the women in the photograph?'

'It was years ago. I've lost contact with everyone.'

'You've read about Lizzie and Nancy's murders. Both of their heads were crushed in. Do you have any idea why someone should kill them like that?'

Joan Boyle's face went white and her hands shook. The photograph dropped from her hand and fell on the floor.

Davidson bent to pick it up. He put it on the coffee table facing Boyle.

'I'm sorry,' she said. 'I have a bit of Parkinson's, and you're beginning to upset me.'

'There're eight women in that photograph. Two of them have died naturally, and two have been murdered. We think that the reason those two women were murdered has something to do with this group of women. We think that the four women still alive are in danger. It's vitally important you tell me anything you might know that will help us find the person who killed Lizzie and Nancy.'

Boyle removed her glasses and rubbed her hand through her hair. Then she looked left again. 'I know nothing. Now I'd be grateful if you'd leave me alone. I'm an old woman, and you've upset me.'

'I'm sorry,' Davidson said standing up. 'Whoever killed Lizzie and Nancy is still out there. They may be finished, but we don't think so. If you remember anything, I suggest that you call me immediately.' He took a business card from his pocket and left it on the coffee table at the same time he lifted the photograph and put it in his pocket. 'My mobile number is on the card so you can reach me day and night.' He started toward the door of the living room. 'Thanks for the tea.'

She followed him out of the living room and opened the door for him. 'I'll call if I remember anything,' she said before closing the door.

Davidson walked down the short drive and stood beside his car at the pavement. He looked back at the house in time to see the curtain flutter from the window of the front room. Joan Boyle had a secret all right. It might just be the secret that's getting her old friends killed, but she wasn't about to give it up yet. That meant that the secret was deep and dark. He wondered just how deep and dark it might be.

SHE WATCHED the car pull away from the pavement. She hated the peelers. At one time, they were all for the Loyalists, but now they were licking up to the Taigs. An independent police force, my arse. She moved to a small desk in the corner and opened the top drawer. She took out the same photograph that Davidson had shown her. Those were the days. They ruled Belfast with Lizzie as their leader. Now the Taigs were part of the Government. She spat out of the corner of her mouth. If only they hadn't killed the bitch. That was the beginning of the end. The bitch deserved to die, but it pissed off the top brass in the organisation. There was no way she was going to inform to the Peelers on her comrades. Even if it cost her life.

CHAPTER FIFTY

W ilson's mind was in turmoil when he reached the station. He made his way to his office and closed the door. Moira, Ronald and Harry were in the squad room but the look on his face was enough for them to give him a wide berth. His and Kate's child was dead. That wasn't quite true. Their child had just never existed. He was neither a philosopher nor a doctor, so he wasn't about to argue with himself about whether the child comes into being at the moment of conception or at the moment of birth. The reality was simple. There would be no child. Well not this time anyway. Time would heal the hurt. Kate must be feeling dreadful. This morning when she woke, she had life growing in her womb. This evening all traces of that life would have been scraped and washed away. He held his head in his hands. He had told Kate that nothing would change but deep inside, he knew that things would never be the same again.

'Boss,' Moira had opened the door and stood in the gap.

He looked up and could see from her face that she was seeking some explanation for his mood. 'Kate lost the baby,' he said. 'A miscarriage, I'd be grateful if it didn't go any further.'

'Sorry, boss,' she came inside and closed the door behind her. 'Poor Kate, she must be devastated, how is she?'

'They're keeping her in overnight. She's distraught. Blames herself but according to the gynaecologist it happens all the time. Nobody's to blame.'

'I know,' Moira said. 'I've been down that road myself. I didn't even know I was pregnant, so I suppose that's a plus for me. There was no anticipation, just the loss. She'll get over it.'

'That's what worries me. I know Kate, and I know her response will be to throw herself into her work even more than before. Kate doesn't accept failure easily, and for her, she's failed to hold on to her child.'

'Don't get me wrong,' Moira said. 'It's going to hurt like hell. When I miscarried, I went over everything I'd done in the preceding days to see whether anything I did was responsible for the miscarriage. They told me the same; that it happens all the time, but I still wanted to blame myself. If she wants to talk to someone who's been there, I'd be happy to help out.'

'Thanks, the offer is appreciated.'

Moira looked at the big hulk sitting behind the desk. He looked strong and weak at the same time if that was possible. Not weak maybe, but vulnerable. She'd never thought of him as vulnerable, but now she saw that he was just as human as everyone else. If he had been a friend instead of her boss, she would have hugged him. But he wasn't a friend. He was one of her heroes. She supposed that eventually all heroes turn out to have feet of clay. 'I'd better get back to examining those documents,' she turned and left the office.

Wilson contemplated going home but dismissed the thought. His second thought was to head for the Crown and bury himself in a bottle. That wouldn't help either him or Kate. He would hang on in the office and wait until it was time to go to the hospital. Work was the immediate answer. He would take a leaf out of Kate's book and bury himself in his work. The pointless plodding might help to erase the memory of the child that never was. He was wiping a tear from the corner of his eye when the phone rang.

'I hear that you've been looking for me,' Sammy Rice's voice came over the air. Wilson immediately threw off his grief like an old overcoat and became professional. He had stood up to fifteen New Zealand giants doing the Haka and he was a superintendent in the PSNI. He proved he was a man, and it was time to start acting like one and to stop acting like a wounded animal. 'I want to have a word with you. Can we meet?'

'We're talking now and that's as good as it's going to get for the minute.'

'I hear that you lifted Davie Best last night. I hope to God nothing has happened to him.'

'Maybe, it's not me that has him.'

'Let's say that you lifted him because you think McGreery had McIlroy hit. In that case, you'd probably torture him until you got something, then shoot him and bury him in a bog somewhere.'

Rice laughed. 'That might be a plan. If it was me that lifted him.'

'If that were to happen, it's likely that tonight or tomorrow one of your men would end up in an adjacent bog hole, and on it would go until the whole bog was used up and there's only you and McGreery left to go at it mano a mano.'

'Sounds plausible.'

'I'm going to find whoever killed McIlroy. If McGreery ordered it, I'm not going to rest until I put him in jail. But if Davie Best doesn't reappear soon, and I mean very soon, it won't only be McIlroy's killer who will be enjoying Her Majesty's pleasure.'

There was silence on the line.

'You fuck this up, Wilson, and the someone that will end in a bog hole might be closer to home. I understand your Mrs is some hotshot barrister. We wouldn't want anything to go wrong, now would we?'

Wilson felt the hairs on the back of his neck stand up. Red mist floated around his eyes. Rice was a lucky man that he wasn't standing in front of him. Wilson would gladly have gone to jail just to pound that evil face to a pulp. He used all his powers to pull himself back from the brink. 'I'm going to give you a pass on that threat on account of your grief for your mother. But if you ever threaten either me or a member of my family again, I'll throw away my warrant card and come looking for you. Davie Best free tonight.'

'I'll pass the word along.' The line went dead.

The miserable little git, Wilson thought as he put the phone on the table. A muppet with a bouffant blond hair and a fake tan, he would tear the rotten bastard limb from limb if he even approached Kate.

'WILSON WON'T BRING me in even to consult?' Brendan Guilfoyle was sitting cross-legged on the bed in Moira's flat.

'No chance,' Moira said lying back on the pillows. 'He has you in the same bracket as mystics and fake psychics. You know his mantra, plod, plod, plod. He doesn't believe in intuition, female or otherwise, and he doesn't believe in hunches.'

'I wouldn't have guessed that a woman was involved in the two murders of the women. It's not a woman's MO. A woman might stab or shoot, but she'll generally prefer some quiet method like poison. A woman who likes caving in the heads of her victims. Damn but this is an interesting case. The MO is very important to this person. In fact, the MO is central to the motive. You don't just wake up one morning and decide to go knocking the top of someone's head off like you would a boiled egg.'

'I sometimes wonder whether you're with me because you

like me or because you want the inside track on our investigations.'

He jumped up and threw himself at her kissing her liberally about the face. 'I don't just like you, Munchkin. I loves ya.'

She pushed him away. 'Get off. You've had your ration for today. I'm just wondering where we're going with this thing.'

He fell back on the bed and lay beside her. 'You're the detective. You tell me.'

She turned her head and looked at him. She really did love him, but she also loved her job. Right now, she didn't want to think that someday she might have to give one up for the other. 'But you're the psychologist and profiler. You know everything about me and those things you think you don't know you've worked into my profile. So where are we going with this thing?'

'I can't say that I haven't been thinking about it. I think you'd love Boston. It's full of Irish. It would be just like being at home for you. That is if you were willing to try it. '

'And what would I do for a living?' She crooked her elbow and put her head in her hand so that she was looking directly into his face.

'We have cops in Boston too. You, being a sergeant and all, they'd probably jump at the chance to recruit you.' He ran a finger through the edge of her flaming red hair.

'I'd be a detective like I am here?'

'Probably not at first, you'd have to retrain and do the beat for a while. Every cop wants to be a detective. You'd have to compete.'

'And I'd have to wear a gun?'

'What the hell is that fucking great big Glock 17 on top of the closet?'

'How did you know where I kept my gun? Have you been snooping?'

'Look around. This place is smaller than Mickey and Minnie's mousehole.'

'Point taken. I'd have to give up my job and move to

another country where I don't have the right to reside. I'd have to apply, retrain if accepted, walk a beat for how many years and compete for a job I already have here. Sounds like a deal.'

'Yeah, I've been thinking about that.'

'And what did you conclude?'

'We need another plan.'

WILSON WASN'T USUALLY a clock-watcher but today hadn't been a usual day. As soon as the small hand hit the seven and the large hand the twelve, he dropped everything and made his way to the Royal. Kate's room was on the third floor, and he went there directly. He pushed open the door as quietly as he could and entered the room. Kate was lying on the bed with her head turned away. She was making soft sleeping noises. He walked quietly around the bed until he could see her face. A certain amount of colour had found its way back into her cheeks and the bags that had been around her eyes in the afternoon had all but disappeared. However, there was something new in her expression. Maybe it was just his imagination but there was a tinge of sadness etched on her beautiful features. There was a chair on the side of the room close to the door. He took it and placed it where he could see her face. Then he sat quietly and watched her. He had been in the room for about an hour when the door opened, and a nurse entered.

'Oh,' she said when she saw Wilson.

'I'm Kate's partner,' Wilson said. 'She's been sleeping since I arrived.'

'The doctor gave her something.' The nurse picked up the chart and examined it. 'I don't think you can count on her waking this evening. She'll be ready to leave first thing in the morning so maybe you should think of coming back then.'

'I think I'll stay a bit longer, if that's all right.'

'Of course.' The nurse moved silently to the door and left them alone.

CHAPTER FIFTY-ONE

The evening light was disappearing over Belfast as she sat in her car in Archvale Gardens. For the first time on her trail of vengeance, she was hesitant. Her kit bag lay on the passenger seat beside her. It contained the same range of equipment she had used on Lizzie Rice. The ball hammer was new, but the poncho had been washed and was ready for use again. The Taser was charged, and the tear gas canister refilled. She had been sitting in the car for over an hour. She remembered a saying she had heard: 'a weak man has doubts before a decision; a strong man has them afterwards.' Was she beginning to have doubts or was it just her abhorrence at the sticky black-red liquid that poured from the heads? Or was it the coppery smell? There was no doubt that these women deserved to die. They had murdered her mother in cold blood, and the police had done nothing about it. She had the police file on her mother. It was easy to classify her as a missing person, easier than looking for her body and bringing her killers to justice. That role was left to her. Initially, she took on the mantle gratefully. Her mother loved and cared for her. It was the least that she could do to return that love by wreaking vengeance on the people who murdered her. She glanced at her watch. It was approaching ten o'clock. Joan Boyle lived less than one hundred metres from where she was sitting. Boyle was guilty of murder. The question was whether she had the stomach to kill once more? Wilson was flailing around in the dark. As things stood, she wondered whether he would ever find her. Perhaps like the Shankill Butchers she was going to get away with murder. Except she wouldn't call it murder. It was retribution. She would have to face the sticky liquid and the copper smell again. She picked up the small kit bag from the floor at the passenger side of the car and stepped onto the pavement.

JOAN BOYLE WAS WATCHING TELEVISION. Since the death of her husband, she had watched more television than she had watched in her whole life before his death. Her son told her to get out more. She should join clubs and meet people. After all, sixty wasn't such a great age. She knew a woman down the road who had recently remarried at seventy. Her son wanted her to find someone who would be a companion for her in her old age. While she might have valued companionship, she wouldn't have minded having a little more sex. She had tried to concentrate on the television, but she was disturbed by the visit from the detective. There had always been a chance that what they had done would come back to haunt them. She always assumed that when it did come it would have been in the shape of the law. She followed the newspaper reports on the disappeared in Northern Ireland but never saw a report on Francis McComber. She had no idea where the body had been interred. The boys had taken it away and that had been the end of it as far as they were concerned. The sound of the door-bell startled her. Who could be calling at this time of night? She stood up slowly. It was probably some group of ruffians. She'd heard that they pushed lighted newspaper containing dog shit through the letterboxes of old people. Maybe she should get herself a man after all. She stood up and started for the door. There was no lighted newspaper with dog shit in the hallway. She moved to the door and made sure the chain was on. She opened the door and saw a young woman on the step.

'Good evening,' the young woman said. 'I'm collecting for the poor in Africa. If you can't afford money, I'd be happy to take any old clothes that you can donate.'

Joan Boyle looked into the young woman's eyes. They were deep and blue and earnest. 'Wait here, I'll be back in a minute.' She left the door ajar and went towards the back of the bungalow where her bedroom was.

The young woman slipped her hand around the corner of the door and released the chain. She entered the hallway and closed the door. She quickly took in the surroundings. The living room was on the left and the kitchen and dining room on the right. The bedrooms were to the rear. She removed the Taser from her bag and moved stealthily towards the back of the house.

Boyle was rummaging through her old clothes when she felt an incredible pain in her neck, and her legs collapsed under her. She tried to shout, but she found that she had no voice. She had fallen on her side and all she could see were a pair of shoes. Gradually, the pain subsided, and she was able to turn her head. The young woman was standing above her. 'Bitch,' she squeezed the word out of her mouth.

'That's the kettle calling the pot black,' the young woman said. She had withdrawn a plastic poncho from her bag and was slipping it over her head.

Boyle was slowly coming back to herself, but her arms and legs wouldn't obey her brain. She wanted to lash out but as hard as she tried, she couldn't move her limbs. 'You're her cub,' she said through bared teeth. 'You killed Lizzie and Nancy.'

The young woman smiled and nodded. 'I wished they had known why they died, but I was new to this killing business. At least, you know why.'

'Your mother was a skank who opened her legs for anyone. And you're a murdering bitch.' The young woman pressed a black thing against her neck, and she felt a jolt of pain running through her. She was still looking at the woman when she saw her removing a hammer from her bag. The scream she let out was internal.

'Enough of the social chitchat,' the young woman said. 'I'm afraid this is going to hurt.'

RONALD McIVER SAT on the toilet in the small bathroom of his house. His Glock 17 sat on his lap. It had already made two trips into his mouth, but he had been unable to pull the trigger. He couldn't leave Mary with the mess of blood and hair to clean up along with the detritus of his life as a policeman. He wondered whether they would pay his pension if he topped himself. It wasn't exactly the kind of question he could ask Human Resources. On the other hand, he didn't know how long he could play the hiding game. He stood up and looked at himself in the mirror. Christ, he thought, you won't have to pull the trigger soon. He looked like death warmed over. His eyes were sunken in his head, and black bags had suddenly appeared under them. His skin was pale and lifeless. There were only two choices. He could either hand himself over now and end the torment, or he could brazen it out and hope that the whole affair went away. The latter choice was perhaps wishful thinking but up to now there wasn't a scrap of evidence against him. He had thrown the shell casings away after wiping them clean. Nobody had seen him, and the gun had been cleaned and recleaned. Maybe, just maybe, getting away with it wasn't wishful thinking after all.

CHAPTER FIFTY-TWO

W ilson arrived at the Royal at 8 a.m. and went directly to Kate's room. He found her sitting on the bed fully dressed. He moved towards her but saw on her face that now was not the time for hugs and kisses.

'The bloody doctor left an hour ago to prepare my discharge papers,' Kate's tone was angry. 'One hour to prepare a single sheet of paper letting me out of this place. No wonder the Health Service is in crisis.'

'How are you feeling?' Wilson asked. He was totally unprepared for Kate's anger.

'That's a stupid question. I've just terminated my first pregnancy and had the last vestiges of my child scraped from my womb. How the hell do you think I feel? I need to get out of here and back to work. I'm due in court at ten o'clock.'

'Don't you think that you should at least take the day off?'

'That's the last thing I want to do. If I had to sit at home, I'd only spend the day feeling sorry for myself. A fat lot of good that would do. If you want to make yourself useful, you could find out where that bloody doctor has got himself to. Probably down in the cafeteria scoffing bacon and eggs.'

Wilson went down the corridor. There was a single nurse

manning the station. 'Miss McCann is waiting for her discharge letter,' he said.

'I'll find out what's the delay.' The nurse picked up the phone and dialled a number. She spoke quietly into the receiver before replacing it. 'They're having a team meeting at the moment. They should be finished in twenty minutes or so.'

Wilson conveyed the news to Kate.

'I'm out of here,' she said standing up. 'They can send the discharge letter later. I phoned my PA and the office is sending a car for me.'

'I'll drive you,' Wilson said.

She stood facing him. 'There's only one rule. We don't talk about what happened yesterday. It's over. The gynaecologist explained everything. It was nobody's fault. It was just nature at its most evil. We'll continue as we were before I got pregnant, but we will not speak of the miscarriage for a long time.' Tears began to stream down her face. 'At least, until the pain is gone. The drama ends here.'

Wilson held her in his arms and kissed her wet cheeks. He wanted to tell her that the pain would pass, but he knew it would sound trite. He could feel her arms squeezing him.

She released her grip on him and pulled her head back. She took a handkerchief from her handbag and dried her cheeks. 'I'm going to look a sight in court this morning,' she said. 'I don't want this getting out. Sympathy from my colleagues would be just too much for me.'

The nurse from the station entered the room and handed Kate a white envelope. 'I told them you were insistent.'

'Thank you,' Kate said graciously. She turned to Wilson. 'Now let's get to hell away from this place.'

WILSON SAT in his car outside the station for more than an hour. From the outside, it looked like Kate had already assimilated the experience and was ready to move on. Deep in his heart he knew that this was a camouflage of her true feelings. Regaining an even keel was not going to be an easy exercise.

The desk sergeant called him over as he entered the station. 'Message for you,' he said. 'Bloke named Davie Best walked in here last night and said to tell you that he wandered off for a couple of days, but he was headed home.'

'How did he look?' Wilson asked.

'Like he went ten rounds with Mike Tyson.'

Wilson shook his head and made for the squad room. The team, minus McIver, were busy at their desks. McIver was a problem in the making, and he wondered whether he should advise upstairs that some action might have to be taken soon. He knew that McIver liked working with the Murder Squad but there was obviously a personal problem, and a change of duty might be in order. 'Briefing in ten,' he said as he entered his office. He switched on his computer and checked his latest e-mails. A short message from forensics told him that the gun used to kill Ivan McIlroy did not appear on any of the databases. The bullets were indeed 9 mm Parabellums and the gun could have been any that used that calibre. It was another dead end on top of all the other dead ends he'd experienced lately. He deleted a series of e-mails that he was required to read concerning new procedures for setting budgets and appraising staff. When he screwed up using the old system, someone would come and show him how the new procedures worked. It saved having to bore himself to death reading the meanderings of some accountancy geek. He was satisfied with his morning's venture into the world of administration by the time he took his place in front of the whiteboards. McIver had made it to the office, and it looked like he had managed to shave, an advance on his appearance of yesterday. However, the razor didn't manage to remove the haggard look from his face. 'No news, or indeed bad news on the bullets retrieved from McIlroy's body,' Wilson began. 'There's no match for the gun in the database. We're looking for a 9-millimetre pistol.' The assembled team laughed. 'I know it's a needle in a haystack. It's the favourite handgun in this part of the world. Belfast is full of them, etcetera, etcetera. Eric, how are we doing on McIlroy's timeline?'

Eric Taylor came forward and pointed at the timeline he had sketched on the whiteboard. 'We have a pretty good idea how he spent his day. His colleagues are not so happy to fill in the gaps because some of those gaps might incriminate them. We're pretty sure that he was meeting someone on the business level. He was asked whether he wanted someone along, but he was very dismissive of the need to have a minder. This leads us to believe that he didn't recognise the person he was meeting as a threat. However, he didn't tell any of his colleagues who that person might be. One item we haven't located is his mobile phone. That would have given us direct information on the people he called, but we're working with his provider to see what calls were made to and from his mobile. We've returned to look at his movements the day prior to his death, and we'll go back further, if you think it's useful.'

'If he met the killer alone,' Wilson said, 'it's logical that if they had earlier meetings, he would have done those alone as well. Check back and see who he met during the past week on his own.'

'OK, boss,' Taylor said. 'But the guys we're using for information are not the most open, or we have to suppose not exactly trustworthy.'

'I don't suppose anyone has come forward who saw people around the school on the evening in question?'

Again, Taylor stood towards the front. 'We put out a request for witnesses using the police confidential line, so far nothing. The school is in an area that's up for redevelopment. The only people around at night are gangs of youths up to no good. I wouldn't expect too much.'

'OK, we need to concentrate on the timeline and the calls. People like McIlroy don't use paybill phones, and they scatter

SIM cards around like confetti. Forensic get anything on the call?'

'Nothing from voice recognition,' Harry Graham said. 'They can't even tell if it's a man or a woman. They're concentrating on identifying the number the call was made from. It's a long shot, but it might pay off.'

Wilson turned to Peter Davidson. 'Peter, your visit with Joan Boyle?'

'I've written up a report, boss.' Davidson was sitting on a desk facing the whiteboard. 'It should be in your e-mails. She knows nothing. She doesn't recognise the photo of the women's UVF group, and she lost contact with Lizzie Rice and Morison years ago. All they ever did was make sandwiches and bake cakes. It sounded cut and dried, but I didn't believe a word of it. She tries to come across as a little old lady but there's a bit of steel about her. She knows something, and she wasn't about to tell me. It's a secret, and that's the way she intends it to remain.'

'If we bring her in can we crack her?' Wilson asked. He looked towards the end of the room and saw the desk sergeant waving at him. When Wilson caught his eye, the desk sergeant pointed upwards. The message was clear.

'Maybe or maybe not,' Davidson swung his legs. 'She's a tough old bird. Whatever she knows concerns them all. It's just a matter of how deep and how dark the secret is.'

Wilson was aware he would have to wrap things up quickly. 'I trust your nose, Peter. We'll take a second crack at Boyle. If she won't open up, bring her in. Moira, you go with Peter this time. I'd like your opinion of this tough old bird. What's the story on the police files?'

Moira cleared her throat. 'I'm up to the 1980s. Lizzie was a heavyweight in those days. Very involved but nothing could ever be pinned on her, lots of innuendo. If we get a lead from Boyle, I can hone in on the time period and see what your predecessors wrote.'

'It's looking like Boyle is the key. Get out there straight away and break her. We need a motive, and we need it yesterday.'

'And what will you do, boss?' Moira asked. 'A visit to the mortuary at the Royal?'

'You are a very bold lady,' Wilson said. Reid had been the furthest thing from his mind over the past eighteen hours. 'In fact, I'll be communing with my betters.'

'YOU MANAGED to get Best back safe if not totally sound,' Chief Superintendent Spence said as Wilson planted himself in a chair in his superior's office.

'You heard?'

'A flea doesn't fart in this station that I don't hear about. That's what they pay me the big bucks for.'

'Listening to flea farts. I thought you were paid the big bucks for dealing with bad boys like me.'

Spence smiled. 'The DCC wasn't best pleased that it was you that managed to get Sammy on side. I wonder whether he would have been more pleased if Rice and McGreery launched World War Three. By the way, you look like shit. Anything I should know about?'

Kate's admonishment was at the front of Wilson's brain. 'Nothing much. A serial killer has bashed in the heads of two sixty-odd-year-old women. Oh, and let's not forget the lieutenant of a major crime boss has been found with two slugs in his chest, and we've narrowly avoided a turf war. Other than that, everything is hunky dory.'

'How are things downstairs?'

'The team is working its collective butt off and my overtime budget is going ballistic.'

'Get a result and everybody will forget about the overtime.'

'Don't get a result and Jennings will pillory me.'

'I trust you so much I told the DCC that you'd close both cases in a couple of days.'

'Thanks heaps, we're royally stuck on the Rice and Morison killings, and we have no idea who McIlroy was meeting at the school. That means we're nowhere on both cases. A couple of days was perhaps a little bit optimistic.'

'Like I said I trust you. Well done on the Best issue. Please try to make me look good to the DCC.'

TWENTY MINUTES after the end of the briefing McElvaney and Davidson pulled up outside Joan Boyle's small bungalow in Archvale. They made their way to the front door and pressed the bell. No answer. Davidson pushed again only harder. There was no answer and no movement from inside. Davidson walked to the side of the house and looked in the window of the living room. He could see a light coming from the television in the corner. 'The television's on but there's no sign of Boyle.'

'I'll go round the back,' Moira skirted the side of the house. There were two large-sized windows at the rear. She looked in the first one. The curtains were closed but there was a gap in the middle. The room contained a single bed, a wardrobe and a small chest of drawers. There were football posters on the wall. This wasn't a lady of a certain age's bedroom. She moved to the second window and pressed her face against the glass. The first thing she saw were the streaks of blood, which seemed to cover every wall. She looked down and saw a pair of feet protruding from the edge of the double bed. 'Oh Christ,' she said and ran quickly around to where Davidson was standing in front of the door. 'Break it down,' she shouted.

'What?' Davidson said.

'Break the fucking door down,' Moira shouted. 'Joan Boyle is in the bedroom and from the amount of blood, she's fucking dead.'

Davidson pulled out a pack of skeleton keys from his pocket and started working on the lock. It clicked open within twenty seconds. He pushed it in noting that the chain was no longer on the door. They were completely fucked. He led the way along the hallway towards the rear of the house treading carefully as he went. He pushed open the door to the bedroom and looked at the body of Joan Boyle spread out on the floor. The top of her head was a bloody mess, and the room was covered in blood. 'Oh, fuck. Better call the boss.'

Moira pulled her mobile phone out and dialled Wilson's number. 'Boss,' she said breathlessly when he answered. 'It's all gone to shit. Joan Boyle's been murdered. You don't have to ask, yes her head's been caved in.'

CHAPTER FIFTY-THREE

The squad cars started arriving within minutes of Moira's phone call. Crime-scene tape was immediately set up around the house. Moira and Davidson stood at the front door and allowed the uniforms to get on with their job. Forensic and the pathologist were already informed so there was nothing to do but wait for their superior.

When Wilson arrived in Archvale, he looked along the rows of small bungalows. He was reminded of the song *Little Boxes* by some American folk singer. The only difference here was that the little boxes were all painted in various colours. The street on which Joan Boyle lived was a mass of patrol cars and police Land Rovers. The car dropped Wilson at the edge of the gathering, and he walked slowly to where Moira and Peter stood in front of the house. This death answered some of the questions that had been running around inside his head. The motive was the Shankill branch of the women's UVF. Three of the women in the 1980s photograph had now met their deaths violently. That clarified the issue. It was about them, and something they were involved in. There were only two more questions to answer. What had they done and who wanted to avenge it? What they had done must have been serious if the aggrieved person thought that they had to die like this.

'Boss,' Moira came forward as he approached the house. 'What a fuck up.'

'Stupid woman,' Wilson said taking a white plastic jump-suit from a uniform at the edge of the tape. He slipped into the suit. 'If she'd opened up to Peter yesterday, she might be alive today.' He looked toward the edge of the police perimeter, where a group of onlookers had already assembled.

'Maybe it was coincidence,' Moira said. 'I mean Peter's visit yesterday and her being murdered. Maybe the killer had her on the list all along.'

'She was certainly on the list, but I'm not so sure about the coincidence. Maybe she was watching Boyle and when Peter turned up, she decided to move up the plan to kill her.' He moved past Moira and into the house. 'You and Peter stay out. You've already contaminated the scene.'

'We were very careful, boss,' Davidson said.

'I know but let's make life as easy as possible for forensics,' Wilson entered the small hallway. The inside of the house was neat but a little run down. The doors needed painting, and the flowery wallpaper was from another era. The front of the house consisted of two rooms, a living room and a separate dining room leading to a small kitchen at the rear. Wilson walked through the three rooms without seeing anything out of the ordinary. He looked in the empty single bedroom at the rear. The football posters were faded and curled up at the corners, and the duvet cover on the bed had a football motif indicating that it had been bought for a child or a teenager at the most. It had been some time since anyone had used the room. He walked gingerly across the hallway avoiding drops of dried blood on the floor. The trail of blood led to a door at the back of the hall. It was a small bathroom. He could see drops of water on the bath. He closed the door and moved to the main bedroom. Joan Boyle lay on the floor on her back. The top of her head had been demolished and a mixture of dark cranial blood; bits of skull; brains and hair had spilled out onto the worn carpet on which she lay. A large pool of blood ran from her head to the edge of the bed where a bundle of old clothes had been thrown. He bent down and saw the burn marks on her neck. The Taser had been applied several times. He stood up and looked round the room. There were strips of blood on the ceiling and on the walls. Moira was right; it was a complete fuck up. Wilson retraced his steps, and he went into the small living room. There was a series of photos on the mantelpiece over the fireplace. Joan Boyle had a husband and a son. There was no sign of either in the house. The next of kin would have to be informed. He went to the small sideboard near the door and opened the top drawer. It was full of photographs, most of them turned sepia from age. On the very top was the photograph that Peter Davidson carried in his pocket. He picked it up. It was the group of eight women. Peter had shown her the photograph, and she disavowed any knowledge of it. Yet, it was on the top of the pile. Wilson replaced it.

The forensic team had arrived by the time Wilson had carried out his cursory examination. He prayed that this murder site would yield more than the previous two. At least, he now knew where he had to concentrate. He joined Moira and Davidson on the driveway into the house and slipped out of his jumpsuit. A uniform took it from him and placed it in a refuse bag. 'Peter, we'll need to carry out a house to house. At a wild guess, I'd say we're looking at some time last night. Round up a few uniforms and start now while the iron's hot. You can start with that lot,' he nodded at the group of onlookers. He noticed Maggie Cummerford in the middle of the group taking notes as she talked to what he assumed were neighbours. He caught her eye and beckoned her to the crime-scene tape.

'When you didn't turn up at the briefing this morning, I thought we were finished with you,' Wilson said.

'Since the profile's finished, and I didn't get anything that the other reporters had except for the woman angle.' She pulled a small recorder from her pocket. 'Do you have any comment on the latest murder? On the record of course.' She clicked the button and shoved the recorder towards his mouth.

Wilson stood quietly until she pressed the button shutting the recorder off. 'How did you get here so fast?'

'Radio tuned to the police frequency. Is there a serial killer murdering old ladies? Did this old lady know the other old ladies? Is it open season on old ladies in Belfast?'

Wilson yawned. 'Not trying to start a panic, are we?'

'Am I boring you?'

'I'm sure my superiors will be holding a press briefing later today. Don't forget all those questions about the serial killer. That's what sells papers. Got a name for her yet?'

Cummerford laughed. 'Why not the old-lace killer? By the way, my editor is not so impressed with my profile of you.'

'Told you I was boring.'

'I wonder is there any way that we can make you more interesting?'

'I'll leave that with you.' he looked along the road and saw the blonde mop at the top of Stephanie Reid's head bouncing along with her business-like stride. He moved away from the tape and met her as he was entering the gate. Reid was already suited up in her blue jumpsuit.

'Who's your little friend?' she asked.

'Journalist.'

'Close friend?' she smiled.

'No. The body is in the back bedroom. Time of death exact as possible would be useful.'

She looked to where Moira and Davidson were standing. 'Oh my God, the Rottweiler's here.' She made a growling sound as he walked up the short driveway and into the house.

'Is there any chance that Reid is on the killer's list?' Moira said as she joined him. 'If not, I might be tempted to bash in that head myself.'

'We have our line of enquiry,' Wilson said. 'Those eight women or even a smaller group of them were involved in something pretty nasty. They pissed off someone so badly that more than twenty years later, somebody has come back to seek revenge. We need to find out what the nasty deed was, and who it affected. Those documents that you're making such heavy weather of must contain some, or all of the answer.'

'Look, boss,' Moira didn't like defending herself, but she was busting a gut for him. 'During the Seventies and the Eighties half of Belfast was informing on the other half who were themselves at times informing on the other half. So just about everybody was saying something about somebody. It was like the Salem witch thing. If you didn't like someone, you put out a story about them. The documents are full of crap and if there's any mention of someone with a bit of power the heavy black pencil has been used. In other words, I'm doing my best.'

'I wasn't criticising,' He put his hand on her shoulder. 'I know you've been burning the midnight oil on this one, but now that Boyle is no longer with us that's where our best chance lies. Peter can handle things here.'

Moira pursed her lips. 'I get to spend my day reading twenty-year old rumour and innuendo.'

'If that's where the answer lies, you'll be the first to crack the case.'

'Meanwhile Peter will be out here doing the real detective work. Who said that it isn't a man's world?' Moira noticed Reid exiting from the front door of the house. 'Tell Peter I'm taking the car.' She strode down the road.

'Did someone take away the Rottweiler's bone,' Reid said as she joined Wilson.

'I always think that it's a mistake to make an enemy when one doesn't have to,' he said. 'And I certainly wouldn't want to have DS McElvaney as an enemy.'

She laughed. 'OK, forget the crack about the bone.'

Wilson smiled. He liked women with a sense of humour.

'See, I can make you laugh.'

'Time of death?'

'Working solely on temperature I would say somewhere between nine and eleven o'clock last night. I may be able to give a more exact time when I examine the contents of the stomach. It appears to be raining older ladies.'

'That and our friend McIlroy.'

'They're connected?'

'I doubt it. Except that it's a bit of a coincidence him being gunned down this week, and I don't really like coincidences.'

'I'll autopsy her tomorrow. I'd love you to attend. I feel we're really getting to know one another. But I suppose I'll get the Rottweiler again.' She walked off in the direction of her car growling as she went.

CHAPTER FIFTY-FOUR

D etective Constable Eric Taylor was a methodical policeman. He was the epitome of Wilson's commitment to plodding. In his ten years in the Murder Squad, he had never actually broken a case, but he had generally provided some nugget of information that allowed Wilson and his old sergeant George Whitehouse to catch the criminal. He spent two days digging away at the Ivan McIlroy murder without turning up anything that might be considered a nugget. He revisited the crime scene and spoke to many of McIlroy's friends and acquaintances and still nothing. He spent an hour listening to the phone messages on the Crimeline and nothing. His primary objective was to develop a timeline of McIlroy's movements prior to the murder. However, criminals didn't exactly advertise their movements. McIlroy's circle was made up of people in the same business, and they were reluctant to discuss whether they had seen or met with the dead man in the two days before his death. Taylor read and reread his notes. He examined the crime scene photographs and the forensic evidence. The obvious conclusion was that McIlroy's murder was the result of a falling-out among thieves. Wilson had discounted the possibility that

McIlroy had been the first casualty in a gang war. Taylor had spoken to McIlroy's wife and two of his girlfriends, and they had all ruled out a crime of passion. McIlroy didn't display or attract passion. The women were universally scared out of their wits by him. Where to go next? While Wilson, McElvaney and Davidson had gone to the latest crime scene, Taylor had decided to take a second trawl through the denizens of the Black Bear public house. All conversation stopped as he pushed in the front door of the pub. He looked behind the bar. There was no sign of a coffee machine. 'No chance you have a coffee machine, I suppose?' he asked the barman

'Yes,' said the barman as he picked up a jar of instant coffee and a kettle from the back of the bar. 'This do you?'

Taylor sighed. He was a bit of a fanatic about coffee. 'Aye, make me a cup.'

The barman opened the jar of instant coffee. 'I think it's been about two years since anyone asked for a coffee.' He scraped at the jar with a spoon. 'I don't suppose it's gone off.' He deposited the spoon of dubious coloured granules into a cup and plugged the kettle into an electricity socket. 'It was an American tourist on a 'Troubles' tour. He sipped the coffee and left it on the bar. I don't think he liked it.'

'Forget the coffee,' Taylor said, the sight of the granules had been enough. 'Give me one of those yuppie waters and open the bottle in front of me.'

'We don't often get peelers in here.' The barman flipped the top off a bottle of water and put it and a dirty glass on the bar. 'Two in one week, are you guys turning this into one of your haunts? That'd be some fucking joke.'

Taylor ignored the glass and drank from the bottle. He wondered who else had been to the pub. It was his job to research the timeline. 'Fat chance of that. When was the other peeler in?'

'Two or three days ago, having a right old natter with Ivan.'

'Gerry, need you a minute,' a man wearing a leather jacket called from a corner table.

The barman immediately left and went to the corner. Taylor looked into the mirror at the back of the bar. The leather jacket had pulled the barman down to him by gripping his collar and was whispering in his ear. He watched the barman nod and then make his way back to the bar.

'That'll be two pound fifty,' the barman said when he had taken his place behind the bar.

Taylor finished the contents of the bottle and tossed three pounds in coins onto the bar. 'Keep the change.'

'No,' the barman scooped up the coins and sent them into the till. He returned with a fifty pence piece making sure the other customers in the pub saw him returning the change.

'Pity about the coffee,' Taylor said. 'I think you and I are going to meet again very soon.'

RONALD MCIVER SAT ALONE in the squad room. The other members of the team were either out at the Boyle murder site or following up on the Rice and Morison cases or trying to find him. He knew he needed psychological help. Perhaps a couple of visits to a shrink would get the snakes out of his head and make him whole. Maybe. He wasn't sleeping, and he couldn't stop his eyes from darting from face to face wondering whether they could detect in his face that he was a murderer. His concentration was gone to pieces. He'd tried to focus on the tasks that Wilson had given him, but he found his mind wandering or maybe not even wandering but not there at all. Eric Taylor was on the McIlroy case full time. There was very little to work on, but Eric was methodical. He would eventually find a scrap of evidence, and he would prod away at it until he opened it fully. It would lead to another piece of the puzzle and so on until it arrived at him. There was a sense of inevitability about it. He leaned forward and held his head in his hands. He was so bloody tired. He wanted to confess and go to sleep. But if there was a chance that he could get away with killing McIlroy, he was going to take it. The chance might be slim, but it existed. He needed to get out of the office. He was convinced that Wilson was watching him. No, he was sure that Wilson was watching him. Maybe Wilson already knew. But, how could he? There was no evidence. He was in the centre of the investigation, and he knew that they had found nothing to incriminate him. McIlroy was already on his way to being designated as another unsolved killing. There were hundreds maybe even thousands of them in the province. He turned as the door to the squad room opened, and he watched Eric Taylor enter and move to his desk.

'How's it going?' he asked when Taylor sat down.

Taylor looked up as though the question had woken him from his thoughts. 'Still faffing about with the McIlroy time-line. Pity the bloody bugger didn't keep a diary in his pocket.'

'You'll get there,' McIver said because he knew that was what he was expected to say. He was hoping for the opposite. 'I'm off home early for lunch. The wife's not well. If the boss asks, I'll be back this afternoon.'

WILSON NEEDED some time to think and assimilate the latest happenings, so he decided to take a walk around the Archvale estate. He wandered along the labyrinth of roads each containing small bungalows of the same type. His mind was totally concentrated on his job. Kate was right. The time for drama was past. They could spend weeks or months going over the whys and wherefores of the miscarriage but in the end, it was what it was. The baby was gone and if the gynaecologist was to be believed it was probably better off never having been born. It was time to move on and concentrate on real life. Three women had been murdered in a most violent fashion. All three were members of the Shankill branch of the women's

UVF during a particularly troubled period of Ulster's chequered history. They had made progress but not enough to point at either the motive or the murderer. He meandered along the peaceful roads. This was the Ulster that most of the residents wanted. Streets clear of burnt-out vehicles, rows of neat houses with well-tended gardens and tarmacadam driveways. The problem, as exposed by the Boyle murder, was that beneath the façade of peace there existed the potential for violence. Maybe Kate and her friends who wanted a Peace and Reconciliation Commission had the right idea. Perhaps the evil of the past needed to be brought out into the light and exposed for what it was. Maybe people who hated each other simply because they had different religious beliefs might understand that they shared a common humanity and a desire for a better life for all. He turned a corner and saw the police cars ranged across the road. This was the reality. The past revisiting the present and an elderly lady lying in her bedroom with her head caved in. He walked toward the vehicles and saw Peter Davidson standing with a group of uniforms. He nodded at him and moved to the side. 'Any news from the house-to-house?' he asked.

'Old guy a few doors down thought he saw a young woman at the door sometime around ten o'clock. She was holding a bag. He can't remember what she looked like, but I think another go around with him might produce more. Other than that, nothing.'

Just then two mortuary attendants wheeled out a body bag containing the remains of Joan Boyle and put her into an ambulance.

'I think we're done here. Forensic inside?' Wilson asked.

Davidson nodded.

'Tell them to pay special attention to the bathroom?'

Davidson sighed. 'Yes.'

'Ok, I'm out of here,' said Wilson moving in the direction of his car.

'Any chance of a lift back to the office?' Davidson called after him.

'Get the uniforms to give you a lift.' Wilson had no intention of returning to the office. The office equalled administration and right now he wasn't up to dealing with some idiot's version of organisational management. He took out his phone and called Kate's office.

'Kate McCann and Company,' the secretary said.

Wilson identified himself.

'Miss McCann is in court, but I can get a message to her if you want,' the secretary said.

'Don't bother, does she have a lunch appointment?' He heard the shuffling of papers.

'It doesn't look like it, and her order for a sandwich is here.'

'Cancel it and tell her I'll pick her up at twelve thirty.'

SHE WAS SITTING in her favourite café on Botanic Avenue. She had taken a seat by the window so that she could watch Belfast go by. She hadn't been able to believe that they had found Joan Boyle's body so quickly. She had planned a phone call later in the day and had fallen off her chair when she heard the police radio call that a body had been found in a house in Archvale. After the exertions of the previous night, she would have preferred an extended stay in bed, but she supposed that would be impossible. The ball hammer she used was at the bottom of the Lagan. The poncho, the clothes and shoes she had worn had been burned to a crisp. She even destroyed her underwear. Then she showered in hot water and scrubbed her skin until it almost bled. If she had left even a smidgen of Boyle's blood on her person, she deserved to be caught. She knew that there was no such thing as the perfect crime. Criminals, no matter how smart they thought they were, leave behind some clue that eventually leads to them ending up behind bars. She had carried out three murders and as far as the smartest detective in Belfast was concerned, she hadn't left a single clue. Wilson and his team were flailing around in the dark. They were now aware that a woman was possibly the murderer, but it could also be a small man. How many people fitted that description in Belfast? Hundreds, possibly even thousands. She thought about the Boyle murder and realised that she had made a serious error with Lizzie Rice and Nancy Morison. Joan Boyle had died knowing why she had to die. It was amazing to see the change in her face when she knew that she was dying in revenge for the death of a woman she considered to be a 'skank'. At the door, Boyle had looked like a kindly old woman but lying on the carpet knowing that she was about to die for her crime, she turned into a spitting crone. She saw her reflection in the window glass. She didn't look like a thoughtless murderer. Then again, murderers didn't have a specific look. If that was the case, a lot more people would be in jail. She'd read the research about the areas of the brain that lit up like Christmas trees when the psychopath did his work. Killing made her feel powerful. Men and women out in the street moved across her vision. She wondered what secrets lay hidden behind their faces. Some of them had to be liars, others cheaters and some even possibly, like her, murderers. She was that blind lady holding the scales in her hand. In a society based on justice, the organs of state would have avenged her mother. But they failed miserably. She didn't even have a grave to visit. Which one of those men and women rushing past the window of the café would not harbour vengeance for the killing of a loved one? How many of them would be capable of carrying that vengeance to its ultimate conclusion? How many were like her? Remorse was for the weak, and those without a valid crusade. The McIlroy murder was a magnificent distraction. She could not have planned it better. It muddied the water. They had to decide whether it was linked to the Rice, Morison and Boyle killings and confused the issue of motive. It bought her more time. And her work was done. It was almost time to get out of Dodge. She drained her café latte and waved at the waitress to provide her with a refill.

THE OFFICES of Kate McCann and Company were in an office building on Oxford Street just around the corner from the Royal Courts of Justice on Chichester Avenue. Wilson pushed open the door to the reception area on the second storey. Kate's office covered the whole of the second floor and consisted of the reception area, three offices on one side of a corridor that ran the length of the building, and a large conference room occupied the other side. Studded walls enclosed the offices while the conference area was an all-glass affair. This was not the traditional law office with walnut panelling, antique partners' desks and dusty cupboards. The office was one hundred per cent Scandinavian chic. Glass and plastic were the dominant materials. Wilson could see one of Kate's juniors working away inside the conference room that also doubled as the company's library. Rows of leather-bound law books covered the solid walls of the room. Wilson glanced at his watch. It was almost twelve thirty. Kate's office door opened abruptly, and he looked up to see Sammy Rice and a short man wearing a suit standing directly in front of him.

'Mr Wilson,' Sammy Rice said. 'Didn't expect to see you here.'

'Nor I you, Sammy.' Wilson stood up to his full height, which was some four inches taller than Rice. 'I thought that you and I had an understanding.'

Rice looked like he was thinking deeply. 'You have me there, Mr Wilson.'

'Oh, ye of short memories,' Wilson waved an admonishing finger. 'Remember I advised you to stay away from certain people.'

Rice smiled. 'Oh that,' he looked at the suit beside him. 'My solicitor and me are here on business. We're looking to change our legal representation and my man here suggested that I talk to Miss McCann. Wonderful woman by the way, attractive and brilliant, what a combination.'

Wilson looked beyond the two men and could see Kate readying to leave. 'I've taken enough of your time,' Wilson said extending his hand to Rice.

Rice took Wilson's hand and was not ready for the pressure that was immediately exerted on his fingers. He tried to resist, but he was too late. Wilson continued to squeeze, and it was all Rice could do to resist from screaming.

'I think I remember that understanding now,' he said slowly through clenched teeth.

'Good I was hoping that you would.' Wilson released his grip.

Rice shook his hand to re-establish circulation and made for the door. 'You're fucked,' he said under his breath as he passed Wilson.

'What was all that about?' Kate asked as she left her office.

Wilson kissed her lightly on the cheek. She had recovered most of her colour. 'Mr Rice is an undesirable character. He's been on the wrong side of the law since he was strong enough to heave a Molotov cocktail.'

She smiled wanly. 'You could say that about most of the people who cross the threshold of this office.'

'But Mr Rice is a special case. He operates a diversified business that involves drugs, prostitution, protection and loan sharking. He could be described as a social entrepreneur since he was operating a system of payday loans long before the term became respectable. I have no desire to waste time discussing Mr Rice when my stomach is rumbling.' He could almost touch the elephant in the room, but he could see that they were both ignoring it. It would become the subject that could never be discussed.

'Good,' Kate pushed him towards the door. 'I concur. He just wasted half an hour of my time bullshitting me on how he wishes to change his legal representation. I got the distinct impression that his objective was something else. Perhaps it has something to do with that pissing contest in reception.'

Wilson held the door open for her. 'You're the local here. Where are we going?'

'You invite a girl to lunch, and you haven't even made a reservation,' she said as they walked onto Oxford Street.

He hung his head. He felt they were playing a scene from a movie.

'Just as well. I'm due back in court at two o'clock, so I suggest we make our way quickly to the Garrick on Chichester Avenue. They serve a mean pie.'

He held out his arm, and she took it. 'I heard the news you've got another body. I hope that's the reason for the belated lunch invitation.'

'I couldn't face the office,' he said, as they turned left on Chichester Avenue. 'Three dead women and a dead gangster and I haven't got a single lead. I can just imagine Jennings bending the Chief Constable's ear. There'll be lots of "I told you not to promote him" going down and there is absolutely no doubt that if I don't produce the goods in the next few days, there'll be a move to get me off the case.'

'So is this a working rather than a recreational lunch. Have you any idea what my time costs?'

One of his problems was that he did have some idea. 'Let's try both. You're a lot smarter than me so let me run a few things by you.' He pushed open the door of the Garrick and ushered her in. Every head in the room turned when they entered. Most waved at Kate. 'Legal colleagues?' he asked.

'By and large,' she said and steered him in the direction of the back bar.

CHAPTER FIFTY-FIVE

The team assembled, again minus McIver, at two o'clock in front of the whiteboards. A photograph of Jean Boyle was affixed to the board bearing the pictures of Lizzie Rice and Nancy Morison. A line of black whiteboard markers connected the three photographs. The essentials of what they knew about Joan Boyle had been written beneath her name. Davidson was busy during lunch.

Wilson was feeling re-energised after spending just over an hour with Kate. The miscarriage wasn't mentioned, and their embryonic child was dispatched to the dustbin of history. Wilson wondered what had happened to the embryo but decided that he really didn't want to know. He found comfort in the philosophical argument that life didn't exist until the child was born. He found it strange to converse so naturally with Kate. She was so compartmentalised that she had already put the event behind her. He'd always admired her incisive brain, but he was again reminded that there were other aspects of her character that he had not yet probed. He appreciated her grasp of detail as she questioned him about the facts of the three cases. He realised that he had been foolish trying to keep their worlds apart. It wasn't always cataclysmic when worlds collide. Sometimes they coalesced to form something bigger than the sum of their parts. 'Joan Boyle,' he tapped the photo. 'Former member of Lizzie Rice's group, Peter interviewed her yesterday and called it right when he said that she was hiding something. Moira, your briefing on finding the body.'

Moira stood forward and ran through the events of the morning up to the arrival of Wilson.

'Thanks,' Wilson took over again. 'The pathologist thinks she died sometime between nine and eleven last night. We'll have a better idea after the postmortem. Peter, the house-to-house?'

Davidson explained the extent and results of the house-to-house investigation. 'I intend to return to interview the couple who saw the young woman at the door sometime around ten. Hopefully, they've been talking about the earlier interview, and something else may come to light.'

'Do we think that Boyle was killed because she was about to tell us something?' Harry Graham asked.

'Good question, Harry,' Wilson said. 'It's certainly a coincidence, and I don't generally like coincidences. It's something that we must bear in mind. It could mean that someone was watching yesterday when Peter interviewed her.'

'Or she could have spoken to someone on the phone,' Moira said.

'Harry, check the phone records. Any calls in or out. I don't anticipate a timeline problem with Boyle. Harry and Peter will liaise to produce a timeline from yesterday morning until her death.'

Graham and Davidson nodded and took notes.

'Things are beginning to crystallise,' Wilson said. 'We still don't have a motive, but the Boyle murder allied to the Rice and Morison killings point to the activities of the eight ladies in the photograph. Three of these ladies are still alive and despite our best efforts, we have been unable to locate them. I don't know what that means but we can't count on their help in establishing the motive.' He turned and looked at Moira. 'That makes the police files the only avenue we have.'

'I wouldn't hold out much hope, boss,' Moira said. 'I've already been through two boxes.' She pointed at two Xerox boxes sitting on her desk. 'I've still got two to go but quite honestly so far it's been mostly rubbish and heavily redacted rubbish at that.'

'It's all we've got for the present. We need motive, if we're going to catch the killer and without it, we're just moving around in the dark hoping to stumble over something. You know the mantra, plod, plod, plod.'

'I'm on it, boss,' Moira said.

'Eric, where are we on the McIlroy case?' Wilson asked.

Taylor hesitated before speaking. 'Still on the timeline. Nothing new.'

'Maybe all four killings are connected,' Moira said.

'Almost certainly not,' Wilson said. 'The women are certainly connected both through the photograph and the MO of the murders. McIlroy is not. I'm not saying that the same person didn't kill all four but certainly if they did, the motivations are different. McIlroy could have known the killer and been prepared to expose her, and maybe he died for that. However, I doubt he had anything to do with the motive for killing the women. Anyone else?'

The team shook their heads.

Wilson noted that McIver was absent. He was going to have to decide what to do with him sooner rather than later. 'OK, let's keep at it.' He turned and walked towards his office.

WILSON FLOPPED INTO HIS CHAIR. They were making progress, but it was painfully slow. He leaned back and closed his eyes. Four murders in one week, probably a record even for peacetime Belfast. They uncovered very little real evidence at any of the murder sites. He flayed the chief of the forensics team, but he knew that they couldn't find what wasn't there. Whoever was murdering the women was incredibly careful. The level of violence would have left her covered in blood. She couldn't just walk around with blood-streaked hair and clothes. That meant that she had some means of covering herself. He would see what forensics came up with from the Boyle house, but he wasn't hopeful. The McIlroy shooting posed a different problem. There was too much evidence. The derelict school was used by junkies and teenagers as a drug den and probably also for illicit sex. The forensics team had a hell of a time collecting samples and the report had run to thirty pages, but there was no evidence of any known felon being in the corridor. He tilted his chair forward and noticed Taylor at the door.

'A word, boss,' Taylor said closing the door behind him.

Wilson pointed at the chair in front of his desk. 'What's up, Eric?'

'I wasn't exactly telling the truth at the briefing. About the timeline, I mean.'

Wilson sat forward and opened his hands. 'Tell me.'

'I visited the Black Bear this morning trying to tie up the timeline. It's been a bitch because none of McIlroy's gang will open their mouths about his movements. The barman made me for a copper and then let slip that McIlroy was in conference with another policeman a few days ago.'

'And,' Wilson said.

'Some of McIlroy's people were sitting at a table and as soon as the barman mentioned the policeman, he received the signal to shut up.'

'It would be naïve for us to think that people like Rice and McGreery didn't have contacts in the force. The questions are who exactly was meeting McIlroy and why?'

'The barman is off at six. I was thinking I could have another chat with him. Bring him in if necessary.'

'That doesn't sound like a bad idea. Try to be circumspect.

The poor bastard is probably shitting himself, so try not to put him in more trouble than he's in already. I'll be here late. I have a mountain of paperwork to go through. Get back to me on this.'

'OK, boss, will do.' Taylor stood up and left.

Wilson sighed and looked at his watch; two-forty. Four hours of paper pushing. He didn't know whether he was ready for this. He pulled a file towards him and opened it slowly. He had just started to read when his phone rang.

'Press conference at HQ at three-thirty.' Chief Superintendent Spence was sparse with words.

'That should be fun,' Wilson said.

'The DCC wants a briefing paper on the Boyle murder and the state of the investigation by three o'clock. Joe Public wants to know why someone is murdering people who are already in the waiting room for Heaven. And he wants to know what we're doing about it. The Chief Constable is shitting bricks, and the politicians are ringing his phone off the hook. The DCC thinks it's time he paraded the officers who are responsible for the debacle, so you and I are to be in attendance. We'll leave here at three-fifteen. Send the brief directly to the DCC with a copy to me. Be careful, Ian, there may have to be a sacrificial lamb on this one.'

'Understood,' Wilson said and broke the connection. He looked through the glass surround of his office until he caught Moira's eye and beckoned her into his office. 'I have need of your excellent skill in composition,' he said when she entered.

CHAPTER FIFTY-SIX

Wilson considered most police briefings as a monumental waste of time. He had some respect for the briefings that consisted of showing the public a photofit of some miscreant they were searching for and enlisting their aid in apprehending him. He could not abide the farce where they appeared before the public ostensibly to seek the aid of the public simply because they didn't have a clue themselves. The latter type of press conference only served to verify for Joe Public that in this case, they had their heads up their arses. Therefore, it was with great reluctance that he had allowed himself to be coerced into appearing on the podium next to his superiors. DCC Jennings led their little parade into the press-room followed by Chief Superintendent Spence with Wilson bringing up the rear. His two superiors were in green dress uniform, while he was in civilian clothes. About a dozen journalists were assembled before them and television cameras from the main television channels were already set up. When they reached the podium, DCC Jennings took the centre chair with Spence on his right and Wilson on the left. The force's press officer introduced them, and Jennings read from his script. The crimes they were examining were horrific, they were following certain lines of enquiry, and they were expecting an arrest soon. Wilson noted that the word 'imminent' had not been used. As soon as Jennings had finished, he threw the meeting open for questions.

'I have a question for Superintendent Wilson,' Maggie Cummerford had jumped up immediately Jennings had finished speaking. 'What connection do you think there is between the murders of the elderly women and the murder of Ivan McIlroy?'

Jennings reluctantly pushed the microphone towards Wilson. 'I'm not sure that there is a connection and if there is one, it's tenuous. We have a very definite line of enquiry in the case of the murders of Lizzie Rice, Nancy Morison and Joan Boyle. We are still examining the evidence in the case of Ivan McIlroy.'

'Does that mean that you think the same person is responsible for all four murders?' Cummerford asked before any of her colleagues could ask a question.

'The killer may be the same person or there may be two separate individuals.' Wilson pushed the microphone back to Jennings.

The DCC launched into a long monologue on the value of the PSNI, much of which had no relevance to the crimes under discussion, but which would delight his political masters. The hierarchy, the Minister, the Chief Constable and himself were doing their utmost to bring the criminal, or criminals, to book. If they were unsuccessful, it would obviously be because their underlings had failed them. Wilson and Spence were firmly staked as the sacrificial goats. Jennings wound up the proceedings in order to show that he had pressing issues to attend to.

'What was that about?' Maggie Cummerford said as she joined Wilson in the group trooping out of the pressroom.

'I think it's called ass-covering in the States,' he replied.

'Do you have time for a drink?

'Not right now, I have to travel back to the office with my boss. I have to reassure him that in case of a catastrophe, I'll fall on my sword.'

'Come on, it's not life or death.'

He smiled. 'Of course not, it's much more serious than that.'

MOIRA CLOSED the buff cover on the file she had been reading and placed it on the pile she had already examined. She tried to remain dispassionate as she read. The files catalogued the atrocities carried out on the Catholic population of Belfast. Moira had given up the religion of her birth during her teens and if requested to state her religion in a questionnaire, she would have oscillated between 'none' and 'lapsed Catholic'. She knew that police files relating to the activities of the IRA and the INLA mirrored the files she was examining. However, something in her upbringing made her consider atrocities against her co-religionists as somewhat graver than those against another group. She wondered whether the change had been brought about by her relationship with Brendan. Unlike her, Brendan had never cast off the religion of his birth. Jesuit schooling consolidated his faith. He was a regular Sunday attendee at Mass, and he had even succeeded in dragging her, not exactly kicking and screaming, to church for the past two Sundays. She supposed that he was hoping for a renaissance of her faith that might earn him God knows how many indulgences and ease his way into the Kingdom of Heaven. There was a possibility that he was succeeding. She had banished the old religion to the back of her mind and hadn't thought of resurrecting it until Brendan came along. Maybe it would be one of the things she would have to thank him for when he boarded the jet back to the States. She picked another file out of the Xerox box and was about to start when she took up the file she had been examining earlier. She flicked through to near the end and read through a heavily redacted report by one of Wilson's predecessors concerning the activities of Lizzie Rice and her lady friends. Something about the tone of the report grabbed her attention. It was not so much what was written but the way it was expressed. The writer didn't like Lizzie Rice and was convinced that she was behind several attacks on Catholic families. He also intimated that Lizzie might have been involved in more serious crime. She looked at the name on the bottom of the report and removed her note-book from her bag. She wrote 'DI Jack Armstrong' and circled the name several times with her pen. She looked up and saw that only she, and McIver were in the squad room. McIver was staring into the open drawer of his desk. She noticed him carrying out a similar action several times a day. He was either concentrating very heavily on the contents, or he was on 'planet McIver' again. She watched as he closed the drawer and locked it. Maybe it was her female inquisitiveness, but she was intrigued by what might be in that drawer. She put the buff folder back on the pile and pulled the new file towards her. She started to read.

'What the fuck are you up to?'

The question shouted behind her back startled her. She closed the file and turned around to see McIver standing behind her. 'What?' she said.

'You're fucking watching me,' McIver shouted. His eyes were wide and glassy and there were streaks of red running up his neck and into his face. 'Every time I look up, I see your beady little Fenian eyes staring at me.'

'You've got it wrong, Ronald. Sometimes I look up just to get a break from reading.' She looked at his hands and saw that they were balled into fists. He looked like he was about to explode.

'Don't you fucking Ronald me, you Fenian bitch. Ever since you arrived here you, and Wilson have been getting it on. That's why you made it to detective sergeant while better men had to watch. You're his little sneak. Watching what everyone does and reporting back.' Spittle flew out of his mouth.

'That's quite enough, DC McIver. One more word and I'm going to put you on a charge.' She tried to put as much steel in her voice as she could but was aware of a quiver.

'Fuck you and your fucking charge. You stop watching me or you'll be sorry.'

They both turned as the door into the squad room opened and Harry Graham entered. He quickly assessed the situation and moved sharply to Moira's side. 'What's up?' he asked.

'Fucking Fenian bitch has been watching me,' said McIver as he wiped spittle from his mouth. 'You're all watching me, but she's the worst.'

'Take it easy, Ronald.' Graham moved Moira back behind him and faced McIver. 'You're coming apart at the seams. Look at yourself. You look like shit. I bet you haven't slept properly in days. You need help. This job eats people up. That's why we top the divorce league and our kids get to disown us when we're older because we were never there. Nobody's watching you. It's just your imagination.'

'You're one of them, you fuck,' McIver shouted. 'Protecting the Fenian bitch. Fuck you all.' He turned and stormed out of the squad room.

'You all right?' Graham turned and looked at Moira. He could see the tears welled up in her eyes.

'Yes,' she shivered. 'That was unexpected. For a minute there I thought I was going to be hit but I was prepared to hit back. McIver's gone. He's completely unravelled. The man's a basket case.'

'Don't be too harsh on him.' He put his hands on her shoulders and pushed her back into her chair. He went to his desk and pulled a bottle of water from a six-pack on the ground and brought it to her. 'Drink this!'

Moira opened the bottle and tilted it to her mouth. She realised that her lips were completely dry. She was shaking. If

McIver's condition was what this job did to you, she wondered whether it was really what she wanted. She took another deep drink from the water bottle and then offered it back.

'Keep it. As soon as the boss gets back, we have to inform him. The decision is his, but I think we may have seen the last of Ronald for a while. The shrink will have a field day on him. You sure you're OK?'

'Thanks Harry, it's appreciated.'

He tipped his forelock. 'All part of the service, sergeant.'

CHAPTER FIFTY-SEVEN

'What was he about to let slip?' Sammy Rice sat in an easy chair in the front room of his house in Ballygomartin Road. One of McIlroy's men stood in front of him.

'This gobshite peeler was askin' questions about who Ivan was meetin',' the man said. 'And the fool of a barman let slip that Ivan had been talkin' to some guy he marked as a peeler in the Black Bear a day or so before he was topped. The guy askin' the questions got a bit excited about that. I tipped the barman to keep his big gob shut.'

'Where's the barman now?' Rice asked.

'He's still at the Bear. He doesn't finish his shift until five.'

'Pick him up and bring him here.'

'And if he doesn't want to come?'

Rice smiled. 'He'll come.' He sat back in his chair. A peeler. He remembered telling McIlroy to buy someone on Wilson's team. That must have been the guy. Could it possibly be that the peeler had offed Ivan? No, nobody killed the goose that laid the golden egg and Ivan would have already passed one golden egg, across. However, it did answer the big question. His men had beaten every bush in west and east Belfast for a lead on whoever had offed Ivan. He'd been sure that

McGreery had been behind the killing, but he was slowly changing his mind. They had given Davie Best a fair old beating but so far there had been no retaliation. McGreery had gone to ground. Who the hell had Ivan tapped on Wilson's team? He had no idea. He left it up to Ivan. He pulled out his mobile and searched through his contacts. He pressed the green button and waited. The phone at the other end rang out.

'I'm busy,' the man at the other end said.

'How many people on Wilson's team?' Rice asked.

'Five.'

'How many men?'

'Four.'

'I need their photographs by fax yesterday. You have the number.'

'I'll do my best.'

'No, just do it. Urgent.'

The line went dead.

WILSON RUBBED AT HIS TEMPLES. He didn't need additional aggravation. Moira and Harry sat across the desk from him.

'He was totally out of control, boss,' Graham said.

'I've got the picture.' Wilson looked at Moira. 'Are you all right?'

'I'm pissed off with myself that he managed to shake me up, but otherwise I'm OK.'

'We've all seen him disintegrate over the past week or so,' Graham interjected. 'He's essentially a good copper but something has flipped a switch in his brain, and he's lost it. You've got to get him some help and when he's better, I doubt he'll be able to come back to this part of the job. They'll find him something in records.'

'He hasn't been right for a long time,' Wilson said. 'I blame myself for holding on. I should have arranged for him to move on some time ago, but I didn't want to break up the team.'

'It's like football, boss,' Graham said. 'You have to freshen up the team every now and then. That means that some new people are added, and some others have to leave.'

'Where is he now?' Wilson asked.

'He left here mumbling to himself,' Moira said.

'Probably in a pub somewhere lashing back as much booze as he can handle,' Graham said.

'We need to get his warrant card and his Glock. We don't need a repeat of the Worthington affair.'

'I don't think we're there, boss,' Graham said. 'Mary's heading downhill fast. He wouldn't leave her like that.'

'Tomorrow morning, we collect the warrant card and the gun. I'll get on to Human Resources and arrange for some counselling and a change of job. I'll also try to fill the gap, but my guess is that I'll be told to do more with less.'

'One more thing, boss,' Moira said. 'Every now and again I've seen Ronald open his desk drawer and look inside. Then he closes it carefully and locks it. Maybe we should have a look inside before he gets back.'

'I don't like it, boss,' Graham said. 'So far, Ronald's behaved a bit whacko, but he hasn't done anything that deserves us prying into his personal affairs. It sets a bad precedent if people feel that their privacy can be invaded at a whim.'

'I don't consider threatening the DS to be a whim,' Wilson said.

'Look, boss,' Moira said. 'Ronald knew that you, and me were watching him. Yet five or six times a day he pulled that drawer out and looked inside. Then he had that spaced-out look before closing it up again. Call me nosey but I really think we should look. It could help sort things out.'

'Harry has a point though,' Wilson had a lot of respect for Moira's intuition. He was beginning to think that maybe she was on to something. However, Harry's point was valid. McIver had done nothing wrong apart from threatening his sergeant. He had abrogated his role as team leader by failing to decide on McIver. He was now in a position where he could compound that bad decision by doing nothing. 'Let's look.' He pulled a set of lock picks from his desk drawer. 'If there's nothing we just leave things as they were. Harry, I want you along on this thing just to make sure it goes according to the book.'

They left the office together and went to McIver's desk. There was paper strewn over the top, and it was plain to see that little work had been done. Wilson fidgeted with the picks until he found one that would fit the lock. He manoeuvred the picks, and the lock clicked in a matter of moments. He put a pick on the edge of the drawer and slowly pulled it open. Three faces moved directly over the drawer containing mostly office rubbish; pens, post-its, a box of staples. Six eyes fell on the roll of notes bound with a rubber band sitting in the back of the drawer.

'Evidence bag,' Wilson said simply.

Graham went to his desk and pulled out a roll of evidence bags. He tore one off the top.

Wilson took the evidence bag and using a pencil lifted the roll of bank notes through the centre and carefully placed it in the bag.

'I don't like this, boss,' Graham said. 'This could be his savings, and we're making more of this than we should.'

'Don't worry,' Wilson sealed the bag and handed it to Graham. 'If there's a simple explanation, I'll readily accept it.' He wasn't about to mention his earlier conversation with Eric, but he was connecting the dots in his mind. What if McIver was the police officer who McIlroy had met in the pub and what if the roll of notes was some form of payoff? That was already a lot of 'what ifs'. He was running a little ahead but there were questions that McIver was going to have to answer. 'Put the bag away for the moment.' A bell was ringing in his head, and he was wondering whether he should answer it.

There was a good chance that Ronald McIver was rotten. Proving it wouldn't be his job. The arseholes from Professional Services would be rubbing their hands together for a chance to blacken one of his team. He would have to do this by the book. First, he would have to talk to McIver. If he couldn't explain the money, he would have to hand him over to Professional Services. That was the protocol. If that was all there was, why was the bell in his head still ringing?

CHAPTER FIFTY-EIGHT

Ronald McIver whistled as he crushed the sleeping tablets in the mortar and pestle. The Fenian bitch was on to him. He wondered whether she had told the boss that she suspected him. He would have to deal with her. It was the only way that he could remain safe. He stared into the mortar at the white granulated powder. There were more than thirty Nambutal tablets. He had been saving them for ages, but he couldn't remember why. That should be enough although he wasn't sure whether their potency had been reduced over time. He was having difficulty keeping his thoughts together. He wasn't even sure as to why he was grinding the tablets. He remembered coming home from the station and letting Mary's minder go. He'd spent some time with Mary telling her about killing McIlroy and how the Fenian bitch was watching him. Mary had been bugger all use. He wanted her to advise him. She used to be the clever one. Now all he had was a stone wall. Something had snapped inside, and he needed someone to tell him what to do. The problem was that he didn't feel like himself anymore. He could hardly remember the person he'd been. It was like living inside a skin that he didn't recognise. Then he remembered getting the idea about the tablets. It was time to clear up the mess he had created. But could he go through with it? He knew in his heart of hearts that Mary wouldn't like to descend into the abyss that was facing her. His plan was formulated out of kindness. They'd seen her mother descend into that black hole. Twenty people sitting around in a circle, no one watching the television in the corner, incontinence pads, soft food, dribbling, and nothingness. Mary had often told him that she would prefer to die than exist as a vegetable. He tipped the white granulated powder into a glass. He poured in the water and dissolved the granules slowly using a spoon to swirl the solution. He brought the glass into the living room. Mary was still in her chair staring into space. He put the glass on the table beside her and sat down facing her. He took her hand in his, but she didn't respond to the squeeze he gave it. He started crying. They'd been together thirty years. For some reason, there were no children. Perhaps it was better that way. They'd had their ups and downs. There was nothing really to bind them except perhaps their fear of loneliness. He had his job in the RUC and then the PSNI. Mary took care of the house. He looked around the small room and wondered how she had amused herself during the day. It hadn't been all cleaning and cooking. As far as he knew she didn't have any friends. However, he was slowly realising that he knew very little about a woman he had spent half his life with. He dried his tears with the sleeve of his jacket. He picked up the glass and opened her mouth. He poured in the liquid looking for the signs of muscular activity in her throat as the solution went down. He thought he saw something in her eyes; some flicker of life or perhaps fear, but it disappeared as quickly as it had materialised. He wondered if she knew what he was doing and whether she approved. It was all very well saying that you couldn't live as a vegetable, but it was a different matter when the time came. He looked again into her eyes but saw no emotion. She swallowed the solution. He put the glass on the table and took her hand again. Within five minutes, her eyes began to flicker and then closed. She fell back in the chair and within minutes, she was fast asleep, her slack mouth pulling in gasps of air. He went into the kitchen and opened one of the drawers. He took out the roll of large plastic bags and pulled one off. He replaced the roll in the drawer and returned to the living room.

GERRY HEALY LIT up a fag as soon as he left the Black Bear. He had four hours off, and he was going to spend them in front of the TV with his feet up. He'd taped a film the previous evening, and he was looking forward to seeing it. He was about to head home when a black cab containing a couple of the heavies from the bar pulled up beside him.

'Gerry,' the guy known locally as 'Big George' hailed him from the passenger seat when the cab drew level. 'How're they hangin'?'

'OK,' there was a catch in Healy's voice. Being hailed on the street by two of Sammy Rice's mob set his heart racing.

'A man wants to meet ye,' Big George said. 'Hop in the back.'

'Which man wants to meet me?' Healy contemplated running. The only thing that stopped him was the knowledge that it would be futile. If they wanted him, they'd get him. It was best if he played along.

'The man,' Big George smiled. 'No need to shit yer pants. We're not takin' you for a ride. You'll be home in fifteen minutes with your fist around a cold one. Now hop the fuck in the back before you annoy me.'

Healy opened the back door, and the car moved off.

Ten minutes later, they stopped in front of the Ballygo-martin house. Big George opened the back door and led Healy up the short drive. They knocked on the front door. A man of equal dimensions to Big George opened it. They two men nodded, and Healy was led into the living room. He immediately recognised Sammy Rice and felt an urgent need to pee.

'Gerry Healy,' Big George said by way of introduction.

'Gerry,' Rice didn't bother to stand. 'Nice of you to come around. Sit down,' he pointed at a chair. 'I only need a few minutes of your time and then the boys will drop you wherever you want to go.' He took four sheets of paper from the table and handed them to Big George, who passed them to Healy. 'You remember the peeler who was talking with Ivan a few days ago?'

Healy nodded.

'Look at the pictures and tell me if one of them was the man.'

Healy examined the four photos. He immediately recognised McIver as the man who had been talking with McIlroy.

Rice had been watching Healy closely and saw that he recognised one of the photos. 'Give it to me.'

Healy handed over the photo.

'You've been a good boy,' he stared at the photo. 'George, drop this fucking idiot off somewhere and get back here. You, Gerry, or whatever the fuck your name is, forget you were ever here.'

Big George put his hand on Healy's shoulder and ushered him from the room.

Rice took out his phone and hit the green button. 'An address for Ronald McIver,' he said when the phone was answered.

A half a minute later, he had the address of the man who might have killed Ivan McIlroy.

ERIC TAYLOR WATCHED the two goons pick up Healy and followed their car to the house in Ballygomartin he knew belonged by Sammy Rice. He parked down the road and waited while Healy was marched into the house. A few minutes later, Healy and one of the goons that Taylor knew as George Carroll left the house and got back in the car. He followed them back into central Belfast and saw Healy being dropped off on the Springfield Road. As soon as the car and the goons had sped away, Healy removed a cigarette from a packet and lit up. Taylor eased his car into a space close to Healy and got out. He wasn't about to replay the scene outside the Black Bear because he was certain sure that Healy would bolt if hailed again from a car.

Healy puffed on his cigarette, and gradually his hands stopped shaking. He knew that he had been in the company of one of the most dangerous men in Belfast. He decided to forget his earlier plan about the television. He needed a drink. The Orient Bar was the nearest watering hole, so he made his way there. He went inside and ordered a pint of Guinness and a whiskey chaser. He was beginning to breathe easier when a man sat down beside him. He turned and saw it was the peeler from the Black Bear. He was about to stand up when he felt the peeler's hand on his shoulder.

'Detective Constable Eric Taylor,' the man said. 'Time for us to have a little chat.' He told Healy that he had been waiting from him to finish his shift and had seen him being lifted by George Carroll. He knew about the trip to the Ballygomartin house, and he wanted to know what had happened inside.

'Do you know who owns that house?' Healy asked.

'Sammy Rice,' Taylor said calmly.

The barman of the Orient approached.

'Do you have a coffee machine?' Taylor asked.

The barman nodded.

'Americano, please,' Taylor said.

'You're going to get me killed,' Healy looked furtively around the bar but recognised nobody.

'Nobody's getting' killed. Just tell me what happened in Ballygomartin and I'll be out of your life.'

'What if I say nothing happened?' Healy took a long slug of his Guinness.

'Then I'll be forced to invite you to accompany me to the station. Now that might definitely succeed in getting you killed.'

The barman returned and put a coffee in front of Taylor. There was even a ginger biscuit on the saucer. Belfast was becoming continental, Taylor thought. He sipped his coffee and watched Healy agonise with his conscience.

'OK,' Healy said finally. 'McIlroy met this guy a few days ago in the Black Bear. I made the guy out to be a peeler. You get to know the type. I have a good memory for faces so they brought me to Rice, and he showed me four photographs. I recognised one of them as the guy who met with McIlroy.'

'Only four photos?' Taylor was surprised. Why only four, Belfast has hundreds of coppers?

'Only four,' Healy repeated. 'And you were one of them.'

MOIRA LOOKED up from the file she was reading. Her concentration was all over the place. At first, she thought that the altercation with McIver was the cause but the more she thought about it the more her mind came back to Jack Armstrong. It wasn't so much what had been written in the report on the activities of Lizzie Rice and her merry women but what hadn't been said. It was obvious that Armstrong felt that Lizzie was a criminal who should be closely watched, but he didn't outline any evidence as to why he should feel that way. The next file covering 1984 was completely different. Lizzie was beginning to fall off the radar already. Something had gone down between her and the hierarchy of the UVF so that she had to be side-lined. Lizzie's group had been all but disbanded and its activities really did correspond to Joan

Boyle's assertion that they provided sandwiches and drinks. That must have been one hell of a climbdown for someone like Lizzie who in earlier files was portrayed as the Protestant hero. What happened in the early 1980s that forced the UVF to effectively shut Lizzie Rice and her friends down? Moira looked at her notebook and the name she had circled so many times. She picked up the phone and prayed that there was still someone working this late in Human Resources.

WILSON WAS HAVING similar concentration problems. He had already sent a text to Kate explaining that he would be late. She hadn't bothered to reply, which was unusual. He wondered whether the silence was ominous. He had made the decision that McIver was out of the squad. He would tell him in the morning. He could have just sent him across to Human Resources, and some guy with a psychology degree would break the news, but that wasn't the way he operated. Ronald had been one of his team, and he wasn't going to finesse the bad parts of the job. He would collect his warrant card and his gun, ship him off to the head doctor and hope for the best. He wished he had been out and about that evening instead of trying to staunch the flow of administration. His finger seemed to hover constantly over the computer keys. He was aware of a knock on his door and he looked up to see Moira standing there.

'A word, boss.'

'Come in and sit down.'

Moira told him about the change in the files regarding Lizzie Rice. 'Something happened around '83 or early '84 that turned Lizzie from a first division player into an also ran. There's nothing in our files, and since we can't access military intelligence files, we're going to have to discover it ourselves. One of your predecessors, DCI Jack Armstrong, had severe reservations about Lizzie. He was pushing for a full investigation into her activities but since at that time King Rat and Mad Dog were actively murdering people, I assume Lizzie wasn't the first priority. The push to have Lizzie investigated ended when Armstrong moved on.'

'You think he was on to something?'

'It's never said but it's there in the subtext. Lizzie is dangerous. She's done bad things. We need to stop her.'

'Where's Armstrong now?'

'I just got off the phone with Human Resources.'

Wilson's eyebrows rose and he glanced at his watch. 'No kidding.'

'They're usually away by five but there was someone still there. Armstrong is alive. He's living in the old people's home in Portaferry.'

'And you called them?'

'Yes. I made an appointment to see him at ten o'clock tomorrow morning.'

'We'll go together. I think that you should go home now. You look exhausted. I want you to forget the things that McIver said. He's unhinged.'

'Maybe it was a case of *in vino veritas* except instead of vino there was some kind of mental breakdown. Maybe I am the Fenian bitch to most of the staff, but nobody will come out and say it.'

'I can tell you everybody in this station respects you and what you stand for. You're an officer in the PSNI, and you have the rights and obligations of any officer irrespective of religion or colour. You've done an outstanding job here and you fully deserved your promotion. In fact, I think that you'll go far.'

'Thanks, boss, but I don't need the pep talk.'

'That's what they pay me for. To pep talk people like you. Now get the hell on home. Tell that boyfriend of yours that you're in sore need of a drink. Home, no arguments.'

'Night, boss.'

He watched her as she turned and made her way into the squad room. She turned off her computer and picked up her bag. He saw her fiddle with her mobile and assumed that she was following his instructions. Not for the first time he thanked God that Moira McElvaney had landed in his squad.

CHAPTER FIFTY-NINE

Big George Carroll had left school at fourteen and had been working for Sammy Rice ever since. His reports at school never read 'can do better', principally because most of his teachers realised that the only thing between George's ears was fresh air. George liked working for Rice. The boss did the thinking, and he had the brawn to carry out instructions that generally involved some level of violence to be meted out. And nobody did violence better than Big George. Sammy told him to pick up the peeler in the photo and pick up the peeler he was going to do. He stood on the stoop of the small house occupied by the McIvers and rang the bell. There was no answer. George moved to the window and looked in the front room. There was an old doll sitting on an easy chair directly facing him. He would have assumed that she was asleep if it wasn't for the plastic bag over her head. He turned his gaze to the left and saw the back of the head of a man sitting in a similar easy chair but facing the old doll. That had to be the guy Sammy had sent him to collect. He went back to the front door and rang the bell again. Nothing. George looked to the right and the left. To the right, there was a small gap beside the garage leading to the back garden. He wondered whether there was a back door and made for the rear of the house. The back garden was small and covered in grass. There was not a flower or tree in sight. George moved to the back door and tried the handle. It was locked. He was running out of options. Two glass panes constituted the top of the door. George hit one of them with his hand, and it shattered. He cleaned out the broken glass and put his hand into the gap feeling around for the lock. The key was in the lock. He turned it and the back door swung in.

McIver heard the glass shatter at the back of the house. He walked across to Mary and removed the plastic bag from her head. She looked so peaceful sitting there. He stroked her cheek. It was already turning cold. He had almost forgotten about the sound of the shattered glass that had brought him out of his reverie. He turned and saw that a huge man was blocking the door to the living room. 'What the . . .?'

Big George had spent thousands of hours in the boxing club, and although he was a big man, he moved like a cat. Before McIver could finish his question, he had covered the distance between them and had landed a punch to McIver's jaw. The PSNI man collapsed in a heap at his wife's feet. George put his fingers on the old doll's neck like he saw them do in the cop shows. There was no movement and he could see that she was already cold. The lousy bastard topped his own wife. He picked McIver up like he was some collapsed Pierrot doll. He lifted him over his shoulder and started for the front door. He opened it and left. Job done, he thought as he deposited McIver in the back seat of the Volvo Estate he'd used for the job.

THE FORENSIC REPORT from the Boyle house was in. While not a lot had been discovered, Wilson was right about the bathroom. They found two stands of foreign hair, identical and certainly the hair of a woman. At least, it was something. All he needed now was to match a suspect to the hair. He was contemplating leaving the office when his mobile phone rang.

'Boss,' Eric Taylor's voice came over the line. 'Where are you?'

'Still at the office.' Wilson could hear the tension in Taylor's voice. 'What's up?'

'Do you know where Ronald lives?'

Wilson gave the address.

'I'm there. We've got a problem.'

'I'm listening.' The pit of his stomach ached. It was the Joe Worthington affair all over again.

Taylor explained quickly his conversation with Healy, who had given a fair description of McIver as the man he saw talking with McIlroy in the Black Bear. 'I came over to see whether I could talk this out with Ronald.'

'And.'

'The front door was open. Mary is dead in the living room. I'm no expert, but I don't think it was natural. There's no sign of Ronald. I haven't contacted anyone yet; I think you should get over here as quickly as you can.'

'Call it in and put an APB out for McIver.' It was all gone to shit in a basket. He called down for a car. It was too late to call Moira. She was probably in a bar somewhere winding down. Eric and he could handle whatever had to be done.

Two squad cars were pulled up on either side of the McIver house when Wilson arrived. A uniform was busy setting up crime-scene tape around the house, and the usual gaggle of spectators had started to arrive. Wilson met Taylor at the door.

'I'm confused, boss,' Taylor said. 'The glass at the back door has been broken from the outside, but the front door was open when I arrived.'

Wilson entered the house and went immediately into the front room. Mary was lying back in an easy chair as though she was asleep. There was a glass on the side table. A plastic bag lay on the floor. It wasn't necessary to be a stunning detective to see what happened. Forensics would find traces of a strong barbiturate in the glass and traces of Mary McIver's saliva on the inside of the plastic bag. It was murder, but Ronald's barrister would call it a mercy killing while his client's mind was disturbed. He might get away with three years in an open prison while they worked some miracle with his brain. Or he might just disappear into himself. Wilson had seen both results. However, Eric hit the nail in the head about the crime scene. The broken window didn't fit in with the scenario that Wilson had imagined. Had Ronald been forced to break in? He doubted it. There were no signs of violence in the house. Mary was more than halfway to being a vegetable. But he couldn't deny that Ronald had run. The uniforms would pick him up sooner or later wandering along the side of the Lagan or sleeping rough in some doorway. He wanted to pity him, but he had taken his wife's life, and that wasn't his prerogative. It was against the law, and he would have to pay the price. He looked again at the woman sitting in the chair, and he wondered whether she would thank her husband for taking the initiative. Ronald was off beam but perhaps that's what it took to make the final decision. Wilson looked around the room. His eye caught the edge of a leather holster sticking out at the top of the bookcase. He walked across and reached his hand up to pull McIver's service pistol from its hiding place. He slipped the Glock into his pocket. It was good news that McIver wasn't rambling around Belfast with a loaded PSNI- issued weapon in his possession. There was nothing more he could do here. He went to the front door and almost ran into Stephanie Reid. She was dressed for a night out in a black chiffon dress that showed off her ample bosom and a pair of tanned legs.

'Like what you see?' she said noticing the way his eyes ran over her body.

'Did we catch you at the theatre?' he said ignoring her comment.

'I was out for a very expensive meal with a man who hopes to get into my pants. You'd love to have seen the expression on his face when I was called away. All that money gone for nothing.'

'Why are you always so blunt?'

'Three years in the Kivus changes you forever. I don't have to read books about living in the now. The monsters roaming around in this world already taught me to grab at what I want while I'm still able. I've already met some monsters face to face once, and I survived. Next time I might not be so lucky. In the meantime, there's life, and I intend to enjoy it.'

'It was in the Congo?'

'Oh yes. What do we have here?'

'Wife of one of my team. My guess is barbiturates followed by a plastic bag. She had early dementia, or maybe Alzheimer's.'

'Mercy killing?'

'Murder. You'll be out of here in ten minutes. Time of death is all that interests us. It's pretty recent.'

'My date has gone home, and I'm still hungry. It would be a shame to waste the hour it took me to get made up. You could even take his place for the afters.'

'Thanks, but no thanks. I'm heading home.'

'I'm dying of envy,' Reid said and started for the living room with her bag in hand.

Wilson watched her enter the house. For a second, he almost accepted her invitation. The problem was he wasn't quite sure what he was heading home to. He took out his mobile and called the station. If Donald Spence was still in the office, he'd need to be informed. 'The boss still at home?' he asked the desk sergeant. 'Good, tell him I'm on my way.'

CHAPTER SIXTY

'We are royally fucked,' said Chief Superintendent Donald Spence as his pacing had almost wore a hole in the already threadbare carpet of his office. 'There is no possibility whatsoever that it wasn't him.'

'None,' Wilson said simply. He was sitting in the visitor's chair in front of Spence's desk. He had gone to Spence's office as soon as he had returned. 'Things could get worse.' He explained about the meeting between McIver and McIlroy.

'You have his gun?' Spence asked.

'I already passed it on to forensic.'

'I don't believe this is happening,' Spence continued pacing and rubbing at his temples. 'You've done it this time, Ian.'

'Hold on a second, I didn't kill Mary McIver, and I hadn't anything to do with the McIlroy murder, so don't let's get this thing out of perspective. You and I need to be on the same page here, or we really are fucked. Mary McIver was descending into Alzheimer's, and her husband couldn't handle it. It can easily be sold as a mercy killing. After all, PSNI officers are just human beings.'

'And how will we sell McIlroy?'

'We'll cross that bridge when we come to it. We need to talk to McIver.'

'And if he did it?'

'Then you and I are going to have to sit down and see how we're going to spin it. If McIver did it, it may have been self-defence. We need to know what happened before we develop a scenario.'

'And McIver, where might he be?'

'Anybody's guess, possibly off his head rambling around Belfast. We know that Sammy Rice is looking for him and there were signs of a break-in at his house. We have an APB out on him. The uniforms will pick him up sooner or later. If Sammy has him, he won't risk harming him. McIver's not exactly Billy the Kid. If he did McIlroy, something went seriously wrong.'

Spence stopped pacing long enough to pull a bottle of whiskey out of the bottom drawer of his desk. He pointed the bottle at Wilson, who shook his head. Spence poured himself a large measure. Glass in hand he resumed his pacing. 'Any press present?'

'Not when I was there. It went across the radio as a domestic. They might get interested later if it turns out to be a cluster fuck.'

'Christ, Ian, this could finish us. Jennings will be all over this like a rash, and the fickle finger of fate will be pointing directly at us.'

'Calm yourself, we both know that if anyone is going to pay a price here, it'll be me. I just don't want you to run out on me.'

Spence took a slug of his whiskey. 'I have less than a year left before I get my pension. There isn't a lot they can do to me, so I won't be running out on you but we're going to need a damn good explanation for why we didn't act when McIver went off the rails.'

Wilson pushed himself out of his chair. 'I've had enough for today. We need to talk to Ronald.'

'THAT BAD,' Kate said when she looked up from her desk into his face.

'Worse,' he forced a smile. He went to the desk and pulled her up from her chair. Her features were still pallid, and he hadn't seen her smile lately. He hoped that the pallor, and the sad demeanour would leave soon.

'I was worried about you.' She held him tight.

'It's nothing that a few whiskeys won't cure,' as he kissed her lightly on the forehead. He thought he could feel the absence of the bump in her stomach pressing against him. He reflected on the woman in the flower dress lying back in the chair at the McIver house. She entered the world an innocent. He had no idea of the journey that brought her from that innocent baby to dying with a plastic bag over her head.

Kate closed the legal papers she had been examining. 'OK, first the whiskey and then you're going to walk me through it.' She eased him away aware of his reluctance to let go. He looked tired. Maybe he was as tired as she was. She didn't like to look at her face in the mirror these days. When she found out that she was pregnant, the thought of the baby frightened her. The law was her life. Wilson fitted rather neatly into that life, but she had been afraid that a child might not. She sometimes thought about her own upbringing. Helen McCann was never going to win mother of the year. She had been packed off to Victoria College as soon as humanely possible, and her mother was not exactly a constant visitor. Helen was too busy making money for herself and her friends to mother her. The law became her mother and father. She had no desire to inflict the same childhood on someone else. So, all in all, the miscarriage was probably not such a disaster. Perhaps she had even willed it on herself. It was not a thought she was comfortable with. She went to the bar and poured them both a liberal shot of whiskey. When she turned, she saw that he was standing at the picture window looking out over the city. She didn't need to offer him a penny for his thoughts. Maybe his thoughts were as dark as hers. She came behind him and held his whiskey out. He took the glass from her hand and turned to face her.

'Cheers,' he touched his glass to hers and drank the contents in one gulp.

'Cheers,' she said sipping her whiskey. 'That's what I call a drink.'

He walked to the bar and poured another large measure.

'It isn't a solution,' she said joining him.

'There isn't a solution. I get to swim around in a bowl of shit every day, and I'm supposed to remain sane. One of my team has been unravelling for weeks, months maybe. I don't know. I missed it because I'm so bloody bound up in my own life. This evening he went home, fed his wife a glass of barbiturates and then put a plastic bag over her head. Have you any idea what it takes to do all that?'

'While you're swimming around in the shit, I get to clean up the aftermath. Yes, I do have some idea of what it takes because I must listen to and defend the people who do those horrible things. I must look at the reasons they set their house on fire with their children still inside. I get to hear their rambling about why they had to decapitate their partner because there was a snake coming out of their head. I get to make sense out of the senseless. I get to defend the indefensible. I feel your hurt because I've felt it myself. The problem is that this is the life we chose. The problem is, we're both good at what we do.'

Wilson finished his drink and went to the bar to replenish his glass. 'It's all so bloody pathetic. I can still see her sitting in that chair with her mouth hanging open. I know I'm not guilty of that poor woman's death. I even think that she might be better off. I'm just pissed that I didn't see it coming. I didn't see

McIver unravelling to this extent.'

'He'll get help. Talk me through what happened and let's see if I can help.'

He sipped his whiskey. 'What the hell will become of us?'

'*Che sera sera*, there'll be plenty of time to worry about that. Let's forget tonight then tomorrow we both have to get back in that bowl and swim.'

MOIRA WAS SITTING in Bar 12. Brendan was late, something about a tutorial. She'd seen the way some of his female students looked at him and wondered if he was seeing someone else. She was so tired that she didn't care. She was on her second drink, and she knew there would be more. The Fenian bitch in her was rising to the surface. She was getting the eye from two guys sitting at one of the tables. She hadn't returned their 'come on' looks, and she was only short of taking her lipstick from her bag and writing 'fuck off' on her forehead. After two days of ploughing through the shit of the past, she didn't need to listen to some arsehole's chat up line. She glanced at her watch, eight o'clock. If Brendan didn't turn up soon, she was going to head home for a long hot bath and a bottle of wine. She had picked up a brochure from a travel company, and she laid it on the bar in front of her. She opened it at the long-haul section and looked at the photograph of a beach somewhere in Thailand. The water was azure blue and the sand a crystalline white. There was nobody on the beach, and a hammock hung from two trees in the corner of the picture. That's what I want. No, that's what I need. She tried to remember whether she had any holidays coming. Two weeks of nothing. The thought was so appealing that she wanted to rush out and book right at that moment. One of the guys at the table decided to try his luck. She caught him rising from his seat out of the corner of her eye, and she turned her full bitch look on him. It was enough to cause him to swing around her and look for an imaginary friend outside the front door. She smiled inwardly but kept the bitch face on.

'I do not like that look,' Brendan said from behind her back.

'And I don't like people who sneak around,' she swivelled on the barstool. 'Did you get tired of being adored by eighteen-year-olds?'

'Tough day, eh,' he motioned to the barman. 'Pint of Guinness and whatever the lady is having.

The two guys who had been eyeing her were throwing dagger looks at Brendan. She decided to increase their pain by giving him a big wet kiss. 'You don't know the half of it,' she said.

'Hey, you try fighting off five or six eighteen-year-olds who want your body. Now that's my idea of a tough day.'

The waiter put a pint in front of Brendan and a double vodka and a bottle of tonic in front of Moira. Brendan looked at her, and she held up two fingers.

'I mean it's my third,' she laughed.

'Don't worry I got it,' he said, sipping his drink. 'Now tell.'

Once he had turned on the tap, Moira couldn't stop. She told him about Joan Boyle, ploughing through the old police files and the altercation with McIver. By the time she was finished, they needed another drink, and she motioned to the barman for a refill.

'You're going to feel like shit in the morning,' Brendan said.

'It won't be any more shit than I feel now.'

Brendan motioned to the barman and cancelled the drinks. 'What have you got in the fridge?'

She laughed. 'Who do you think I am? I'm a working girl. The fridge is empty.'

'I've got a plan. There's a store down the road. I'll pick us up the Penne arrabiatta, and a bottle of wine. You take a hot bath, and by the time you're finished dinner will be on the table.'

She finished the dregs of her drink. 'I could get to love you.' She picked up her bag unaware that on her mobile phone was the text of the APB for Ronald McIver.

BIG GEORGE DEPOSITED the peeler at the warehouse in east Belfast. Two of Sammy's men wearing balaclavas pulled McIver from the back seat of the Volvo and carried him inside. They strapped him to the chair recently vacated by Davie Best. There were blood spots on the floor under the chair, but McIver didn't bother with them. He put up zero resistance. He didn't really care whether he lived or died. He was aware at some level that he had been abducted and there was a good chance he would end up in a bog hole somewhere. It didn't matter. Mary was dead, and he didn't have anything else to live for. He assumed he had been lifted by members of Sammy Rice's gang meaning that they now knew he had killed McIlroy. They might kill him for that. If they didn't, he'd be arrested for killing his own wife. It was six of one and half a dozen of the other. The lights were switched off in the warehouse as soon as the men in balaclavas left. McIver let his head fall forward. He was tired right down to his very bones. He was caught. There was nothing to fear now except death, and he had no fear of that. Maybe now he could sleep. He closed his eyes, and he saw Mary in front of him. In his mind's eye, she was young and vibrant and alive. He slept for the first time in days, and he was unaware of how long he'd slept when he was shaken awake. He looked up and saw three men wearing balaclavas staring into his face. One of the men moved behind him and pulled his hair back roughly.

'Tell us about Ivan,' said one of the men as he stood forward.

'It was an accident,' McIver said. His throat and lips were dry. He was amazed at how calm his voice sounded. 'Didn't mean it. I only wanted to get out. McIlroy wouldn't let me, and he was going to hurt me, so I pulled my service revolver.' He swallowed hard. 'Gun went off. Two shots one after the other at close range. Fucking accident.' He started laughing. 'All this mess because of a fucking accident.'

'Where's the gun?' the man asked.

'My house. Are you going to kill me?'

Nobody spoke.

'Please kill me. I don't want to live. I've nothing left to live for.'

The man holding his head back took a carpet knife out of his pocket and looked at the man asking the questions. The man shook his head, and the carpet knife went back into the first man's pocket.

The man who asked the question signalled to the other two that they were leaving. The man behind McIver let his hair go, and his head fell forward.

As soon as they were outside the warehouse, Sammy Rice whipped off his balaclava.

'Want us to do it?' one of the men asked.

'No. If it has to be done, I'll do it myself,' Rice said. McIver put him off his game. He thought they were going to have to beat a confession out of him. Normally, people who were beaten to a pulp begged to be killed just to stop the pain. McIver begged to be killed without taking a punch. 'Leave him. I'll deal with him tomorrow. There's someone I have to talk to.'

MAGGIE CUMMERFORD WAS in the newspaper office when the message came in that the body of a woman had been found in a house in south Belfast. The first transmission was closely followed by a police APB for Detective Constable Ronald McIver. She quickly checked the address and saw that the woman was found in McIver's house. The police were even getting in on the killing act, she thought. She wondered whether she should go there. Wilson would be at the house. A little additional taunting might do him some good. She decided that there was no point. The poor man was up to his ass in corpses and there wasn't even a gang war to blame for it. She had made her contribution, but it was almost time to disappear and leave him with his mystery cloaked in an enigma. She enjoyed her little joust with Wilson. In a way, he was a worthy opponent but this time the deck was stacked against him. Two more days and she would be on a flight to the States. There was no better country in the world to disappear in than America. It was big and full of people who didn't want to be found. For God's sake, they were still looking for weathermen, who disappeared themselves during the 1960s. She gave her mother some degree of justice. All the women present should have suffered the same fate as Rice, Morison and Boyle. But she was not a psychopath. She laughed. At least, she didn't think so.

SAMMY RICE SWIRLED a snifter of brandy and took a sip. He was sitting in the front room of his house in Malone Park, and DCC Roy Jennings was seated directly across from him.

'Are you sure he wasn't involved in your mother's death?' Jennings asked.

'I don't think so, but he did kill Ivan. He blabbed like a baby, and we didn't even lay a hand on him. Guilt is eating the poor bastard up. He wouldn't have been much use in our business.'

'What do you intend to do?'

'I'm going to take the fucker out into the woods and put one into the back of his head. Then I'm going to bury him. It's what my people expect. I can't allow him to kill one of my men and walk away.'

'You mentioned something earlier about Wilson.'

Rice related the incident at Kate McCann's office. He

could still feel the pain in his hand and the indignity of wilting under Wilson's pressure grip. 'I want that bastard.'

'I detest him, and I've tried to nail him on several occasions, but he's got more lives than a cat. However, with a little bit of thought we may have him this time.'

'How so?' Rice sipped from his snifter.

'McIver is a member of his team. McIver has murdered an upstanding citizen and his wife. The case will be all over the papers, and a few judicious words to a journalist would be enough to cast aspersions on the man responsible for monitoring McIver's actions. The McIver case could be used to shine a spotlight on Wilson. I might be under considerable pressure to require his retirement.'

'You're a devious bastard. I'm glad you're on my side, and you'll stay on my side, as long as I outrank you in the Order,' he thought. 'What does that mean?'

'You have to cut McIver loose tomorrow morning. There's an APB out on him. Drop him off where there's a police presence, and he'll be picked up in no time. We need a court case to see Wilson off.'

Rice sat back. 'My people expect me to take care of this. You don't kill one of my men and not end up in a hole in the Mourne Mountains. That's normally non-negotiable. This is going to be a difficult one for me to square. McIver's going to get what, fifteen years for the two murders. He'll plead diminished responsibility. I've seen what's left of him, and he'll get it. He might be out in five after a couple of years of psychiatric care.'

'McIver isn't the target.'

Rice nodded and drained his glass. 'I'll do it.'

CHAPTER SIXTY-ONE

Wilson slept fitfully and had risen at six o'clock. He had been sitting at Kate's desk for two hours drinking coffee and sketching on a writing pad. Some things were clear while some required clarification. McIlroy and McIver knew each other. How they knew each other needed to be clarified, but Wilson would bet that they had been at school together. Their ages made that conclusion possible. McIlroy recruited McIver to report on the Lizzie Rice investigation. That was confirmed by the presence of the roll of bills in McIver's drawer. The big question was whether McIver had had his finger on the trigger when McIlroy was shot. After examining all the possibilities, Wilson had concluded that he had. The Glock would test positive and that would confirm that Ronald McIver, a detective constable in the PSNI, had shot and killed Ivan McIlroy. McIver had gone to ground but would be caught eventually. The case would be spectacular. A double murderer, one from whatever motive his barrister would ascribe and the second a mercy killing under extreme stress. It would be a circus and a perfect case for Kate McCann. However, the stain on him and his team would be harder to wash away. He didn't hear Kate, but he smelled an omelette from the kitchen.

'Breakfast is ready. Have you worked it out?' she asked.

'More or less,' he folded the papers he had been scribbling on and turned to face her. 'It isn't pretty, and I may not come out of it unscathed.'

'Just remember, you didn't do anything.' She moved towards the breakfast bar.

'That's the point,' Wilson stood and followed her. 'If I'd been on the ball, I would have noticed McIver going downhill. Maybe I'm not fit to lead a team.'

'Don't talk rubbish. Nobody could have seen McIver killing his wife coming.' She put a plate containing an omelette in front of him.

He dug his fork into the omelette. 'There are those who will not take such a charitable view of my actions. They've been waiting for me, and now they have a chance of getting me.'

'Maybe that's what you want. Our minds work in mysterious ways. Maybe you're being forced in a direction you really want to go.'

Wilson put a forkful of omelette into his mouth. Maybe he was tired dancing the dance. He couldn't see an alternative, but the image of Mary McIver had been added to the catalogue of horrors imprinted on his mind. The job ate people. It had eaten Joe Worthington, and it had eaten Ronald McIver. He wondered who it would eat next.

THE NINE O'CLOCK briefing was a morose affair. Eric Taylor briefed the team on the events of the previous day ending with the discovery of Mary McIver's body at the house. There had been no sign of Ronald McIver, but the uniforms were on the lookout. Wilson took over with his theory on McIver being the shooter in the McIlroy murder. McIver's Glock had been handed over for examination to see if it had been the gun that had killed McIlroy.

'Eric,' Wilson said. 'You stay on this one. Find me the link between Ronald and McIlroy. My guess is it's the school, but I might be wrong. I put you on the docket for the examination of the gun, so forensics will get back to you. And I also want you to liaise with the uniforms in the search for Ronald. We need to find him as soon as possible. I don't like the idea of him rambling around out there. Moira has some ideas on the Rice/Morison/Boyle murders.'

Moira came forward and explained her examination of the police files. 'One of the boss's predecessors, DI Jack Armstrong, seems to have taken a particular interest in Lizzie and her gang. The boss and I are going to meet him at ten-thirty. We should be on our way, boss.'

Wilson glanced at his watch. It was nine-thirty.

PORTAFERRY IS a small town located approximately thirty miles from Belfast at the southern end of the Ards Peninsula, near the Narrows at the entrance to Strangford Lough. It is the kind of pretty seaside village that attracts the elderly and holidaying families. Wilson and Moira were lost in their thoughts during the hour-long drive along the shores of Strangford Lough. A stiff wind was blowing a fine mist of rain across the grey waters of the Lough when they arrived at the Haven Nursing Home on the Shore Road within sight of the marina. They entered along a tree-lined drive and pulled into the parking lot. The Haven was a purpose-built home comprising three red brick two-storeyed buildings. Wilson gazed out over the finely manicured gardens and saw the waters of the Lough in the distance through the trees. He could imagine spending the end of his days in such a peaceful setting. He followed Moira through the door with the large white 'Reception' sign over it.

Moira moved to the reception desk and spoke to the lady behind the hatch. 'We have to sign in,' she said when she returned to where he was standing.

'Are they afraid we'll run away with somebody?'

She raised her eyebrows. Wilson's and her phones rang simultaneously. They both grabbed at them and answered.

Wilson listened wordlessly and then cut the line.

'Thanks,' Moira said and turned her phone off. 'They've got him.'

'Aye, thanks be to God. He's being taken to the station.'

'No mobiles inside,' the receptionist said from the hatch. 'It bothers the guests.'

'Armstrong is waiting for us in the sunroom at the rear.' Moira pressed a button on the wall, and the door sprang open.

They entered a large room where a dozen 'guests' were arranged in a semi-circle around a television. Only two guests appeared to be concentrating on the programme, the rest displayed no interest. An old lady stopped Moira as she moved round the edge of the semi-circle.

'Have you come to take me home?' the old lady asked pleading in her voice.

'Yes,' Moira said gently. 'But first we have to take our tea. I'll come and find you when we're ready.'

'Oh, thank you,' the old lady said and moved on.

'My granny was in a place like this,' Moira said by way of explanation. 'I hope Armstrong isn't gaga.'

Two people sat at either end of the sunroom. One was an old lady of indeterminate but extreme age, and the other was a man of perhaps seventy-five.

'DCI Armstrong?' Moira said as she approached.

The man in the wheelchair laughed. 'Been a long time since someone called me that.'

They introduced themselves and flashed their warrant cards.

Wilson pulled two chairs over and he and Moira sat

down on either side of Armstrong. 'How long have you been retired?' he asked. He could see how slight Armstrong was even though he was wrapped in a blanket. His body appeared to be tiny, and his head was large in comparison. He was almost completely bald, and his pate was a mass of liver spots.

Armstrong thought for a second. 'Twenty-five years, I suppose. I did a bit of private work when I left but then the wife died suddenly, and I wasn't much at looking after myself. There was some drinking and health problems, and here I am. What can I do for you?'

'You've read the newspapers about the spate of murders,' Wilson said.

'Aye, and I've seen you on the television. You're the SIO. I see old Donald Spence is still about. He was a kid when I ran the murder squad.'

'We have three dead women, Lizzie Rice, Nancy Morison and Joan Boyle,' Wilson said. 'We've been back through the files, but we can't come up with a motive. The only lead we have is that they were all members of the women's branch of the UVF in the Shankill at the same time. We're hoping that you can help us.'

'Morison and Boyle were in the gang with Lizzie?' Armstrong asked.

'Yes, we found a photograph of all eight members of the Shankill branch of the Women's UVF. All three are in the photo.'

Armstrong's face hardened. 'That crowd were worse than a witches' coven. They had more evil in them than a group of Satanists. I tried as hard as I could to pin something on them, but Lizzie was like Teflon back then. You could get her behind bars, but the politicians would have her out before you could say Jack Robinson.'

'She disappeared off the scene pretty quickly,' Wilson said.

'That's what alerted me,' Armstrong coughed into his

hand. 'She was a fixture for more than ten years then poof she was history. It doesn't happen like that.'

'You have a theory?' Wilson asked.

Armstrong wheezed and when he spoke it was like the words were passing through a gravel bed. 'I had a dozen of them at the time. I looked at every crime that occurred about the time she fell from grace. We had a couple of well-known sectarian serial killers active at the time, so we were pretty much overloaded. Although I tried, I couldn't tie Lizzie to any of the active murder cases.'

'But you didn't stop there?' Wilson wanted to give the old man a chance to draw his breath.

Armstrong smiled. 'I heard about you. You didn't need to be a copper. You had all that rugby stuff going for you until you walked into a bomb.'

'Shit happens,' Wilson said.

'Your rugby mates could have fixed you up. Got you a nice well-paid job, but you went back to the force. They say you're good. Maybe even as good as I was.' His lined face cracked into another smile.

'You found something that might have been linked to Lizzie being closed down?' Wilson said.

'You are good,' he wheezed. 'A disappearance, a woman called Francis McComber, a Protestant and a single mother without any connection to the paramilitaries. She was walking along the street one minute with her little girl in tow, and she just vanished into thin air. The little girl was found on a housing estate just outside Belfast.' Armstrong drew a long breath. 'It was assumed the mother couldn't deal with the child and had skipped across the water. The girl was questioned but at six years of age, she didn't make much sense.'

'Why did you link the disappearance to Lizzie?'

'The husband of one of Lizzie's gang was a bit of a lad. There was a rumour that he was having a fling with the McComber woman. There was talk of a baby.'

'Tenuous,' Wilson said.

'I know, but when I put the rumour together with the wee girl's statement, it started to make a little sense.' He gave a gravelly cough. 'She talked about a lady with straw-coloured hair and her friends hurting her mother. That could have been Lizzie and the coven.'

'Maybe they gave a message to lay off the husband, and McComber disappeared because she feared the worse.'

Armstrong leaned forward. 'Don't you think that I thought of that? I was as good at the job as you are. I spoke to everyone who knew McComber. Every one of them said the same thing, she was totally dedicated to her little girl. She would never, and they insisted absolutely never, have abandoned her.'

'Did you follow up with the young girl?'

Armstrong shifted in the wheelchair. 'This was a couple of years later. The wee girl was put in care. I went to the orphanage looking for her, but she had already been fostered. Apparently, she was a sweet wee thing and children like that get taken quickly.'

'Which orphanage?' Wilson asked.

'It'll be in my notes.'

'I haven't come across any notes from you,' Moira said.

'I left all my old notebooks at the station for filing.'

Moira and Wilson exchanged glances.

'Anything else you'd like to tell us?' Wilson asked.

'I did my best to nail Lizzie. I launched missing persons' searches for McComber for years. Nothing. I'm convinced Lizzie, and the coven murdered her. The body was never found, and at this stage never will be. I tried to get justice for McComber, and I didn't succeed. I'm right sorry about that.'

Wilson took a card from his pocket. 'If anything, else occurs to you, I'd be grateful for a call.' He left the card on the table beside Armstrong.

'Home for Little Girls,' Armstrong said lost in thought.

'Something like that. If you find whoever killed Lizzie, tell them I'm praying for them.'

'Thank you,' Wilson said standing. 'You've been a great help.'

Armstrong watched them as they left. The policeman in him wanted Lizzie's killer caught, but the human being wanted him to escape.

'WHAT DO YOU THINK, BOSS,' Moira asked as they sped back towards central Belfast.

'I think we need to review the McComber file and find out where we can locate her daughter.' Wilson could feel the tingle he normally got when the case was coming together. 'It's a long shot, but it's all we've got for the moment.'

'I'm not clear on the figures, but I know that more than a thousand people go missing in Northern Ireland every year. Most of them return home, but a fair number are never traced again. Why should McComber be any different from the others? She was a single mother probably living on the Social in a city that was tearing itself apart. That's a pretty good set of reasons to disappear.'

'She might have disappeared, but I agree with Armstrong that she would probably have taken the child with her. Some of the missing who don't return, do so because they're already in a hole in the ground somewhere. Francis McComber could be one of them.'

'But what good will the file of a disappeared person do for us? Surely we need to find a body?'

'First step will be to examine the file. Someone must have investigated the disappearance. We need to see what the investigating officer found. That's going to be your job.'

'And what will you be doing?'

'I will have the great pleasure of interrogating our former colleague, McIver.'

. . .

WILSON WENT to the interview room directly he arrived back at the station. He met Harry Graham at the door, and they entered together. Ronald McIver looked like a blow-up doll with all the air let out. He was dishevelled and had a two-day growth of beard. His eyes were sunken in his head, and his face was a pasty pale colour. His wife probably looked more alive than he did.

McIver looked up as Wilson and Graham entered. His eyes didn't seem to register them. There was an untouched plastic cup of tea before him on the table.

'Has he been cautioned?' Wilson asked.

'Not by me, boss,' Graham said.

'Do it.'

Graham issued the normal caution.

'How are you, Ronald?' Wilson sat across from McIver.

McIver 's head came up slowly and there was a confused look on his face. 'Boss, I'm all right I suppose.'

'Harry is going to start the recorder, and the interview is being videoed. Did you understand the caution?'

'Yes,' McIver' s voice had a mechanical tone.

'Tell me about Ivan McIlroy,' Wilson said.

'He was a bully when we were at school. Stole my lunch money whenever I had lunch money to steal. I hated him.' McIver's hands were in his lap and he was rubbing one hand against the other absentmindedly.

'Is that why you killed him?'

McIver laughed out loud. 'God no.'

'But you did kill him?' Wilson asked.

'I suppose so. The gun went off by itself, boss. I didn't mean to kill him. I met him to tell him that I wasn't going to spy on the team like he wanted me to. I brought the gun in case he wouldn't let me off the hook. I only wanted to threaten him.'

There was a knock on the door and the desk sergeant entered. He bent and spoke into Wilson's ear.

Wilson sighed. 'Interview suspended at twelve-ten,' he said and looked at Graham, who switched off the recorder.

They followed the desk sergeant out of the interview room.

Jennings' face was red with anger when Wilson entered Spence's office. It was clear to Wilson that his boss had been taking a tongue lashing.

'What in God's name do you think you're doing?' Jennings shouted.

'I'm interviewing a suspect in a murder case,' Wilson said calmly.

'You are interviewing one of your own subordinates. Have you lost your reason?' He turned and stared at Spence. 'Are you totally out of control? You cannot have thought it was correct for his superior officer to interview McIver.'

How times have changed, Wilson thought. A few months previously it was perfectly all right to instruct him to interview Joe Worthington, his superior officer at the time. However, now wasn't the time to throw that back in Jennings' face. 'I'm the SIO on the McIlroy case, and it's my duty to interview individuals suspected of being involved in that murder.'

Jennings came forward and stood directly in front of Wilson. He had to raise his head at an angle to lock eyes. 'You're lucky I stopped the interview when I did. I'm having McIver transferred to another station. He'll be interrogated by officers from that station, or indeed I may ask for officers from another force to take over this investigation.'

'You don't trust us to be impartial?' Wilson asked.

Jennings turned and walked to Spence's desk. He held his thumb and first finger of his right hand close together. 'I am this far of charging both of you with misconduct. The only thing that's stopping me is that this event will cause enough bad press for the force and dragging you two over the coals will only exacerbate that situation. Superintendent Wilson, you are no longer Senior Investigating Officer on the Ivan McIlroy murder case. You will prepare to hand over the murder book, and all pertinent evidence to an officer designated by me.' He turned to Spence. 'Chief Superintendent, I will be issuing you with a letter of reprimand which will be added to your personnel file. Nobody from this station speaks to McIver. Understood?'

Neither Wilson nor Spence responded.

Jennings turned and stormed out of the office.

Spence made the action of wiping his brow. 'I suppose he has a point,' he said when Jennings had gone.

'Ronald is a mess. Right now, he'd confess to killing JFK and Martin Luther King. The only chance he has of getting justice is if we have all the preliminary interviews done here. Jennings doesn't just want him transferred to another station. He wants him transferred to somewhere he can control the situation. Somehow or other he's looking for a way to turn this situation against you and particularly me.'

Spence put his head in his hands. He could see his pension flying out the window. 'I suppose there's nothing we can do.'

'Maybe there is,' Wilson took out his mobile phone, flipped through his contacts and rang. 'It's Ian Wilson, is she available.' He waited for half a minute or so. 'Kate,' he said finally. 'I need a favour.'

CHAPTER SIXTY-TWO

Wilson oversaw the packing up of the murder book and the collection of all the papers relating to the Ivan McIlroy murder. Eric Taylor was particularly pissed off at handing over all the good work that he had done on the case. Wilson had Eric take a photo of the whiteboard containing all the information on the McIlroy case before dismantling the board and scrubbing the writing. The case was no longer his. The dissatisfaction of the team was palpable as they bundled up the information they had collected. No policeman is happy when handing over an almost completed case. It was even worse when the culprit was someone they knew intimately.

'What'll happen to Ronald, boss,' Harry Graham spoke for his colleagues as they completed the packing of the evidence.

'My guess is the DPP will come to some arrangement with his legal team. From what we heard today the crime wasn't premeditated. That means the most he'll be charged with is manslaughter. I'm sure that his legal team will have some head doctor or other look at him. They'll decide that he was out of his tree when he committed the McIlroy manslaughter, and he'll be sent away to get his marbles put back in.'

'What about the wife?' Taylor asked.

'Different case,' Wilson said, 'acting while the balance of his mind was disturbed would be my guess. He'll be off to the funny farm on that one to.'

'Come on, boss. You can't kill two people and not do time,' Taylor said.

'Depends on his legal representation,' Wilson said. 'Some people say that O.J. Simpson murdered two people, and he walked out of the courtroom a free man. That's a hell of a precedent.'

'Do we concentrate on the Lizzie, Morison and Boyle murders now?' Taylor asked.

'We do, and we regroup quickly,' Wilson said. He briefed them on the meeting with ex-DCI Armstrong. 'Moira has gone to pick up a copy of the missing persons' investigation.'

The door to the squad room opened, and Moira entered carrying a buff folder. She marched to where the team were assembled around the whiteboard. She didn't look happy. 'This is a bloody joke,' she said opening the folder and taking out four A4 pages.

'That's it?' Wilson asked.

Moira held up the four pages. 'The investigation into the disappearance of Francis McComber.'

'What about Armstrong's notes?' Wilson asked.

'Disappeared, thrown out. Nobody remembers him leaving any notes behind.'

'We shouldn't read too much into that,' Wilson said. 'Every now and then the uniforms are told to spring clean. That means trash everything that's not nailed down.'

'I'm not as charitable as you,' Moira said. 'I think someone wanted this file buried. They couldn't just get rid of all the paper, so they left a few sheets in case anyone came back later. This all went down thirty years ago. They thought it was buried.'

'I presume you've already read the four pages?' Wilson said.

She closed the folder. 'Three witness statements all leading to the conclusion that McComber hit the road of her own free will and a copy of the child's statement. The latter is the only document that I'd believe.'

'So,' Wilson said. 'We start by reinvestigating the disappearance of Francis McComber in . . .?'

' 1983,' Moira said.

'Boss,' Harry Graham said, 'thirty years ago, and that's not our territory. We should pass this to the Historical Crimes team. They have the resources for this type of investigation.'

'They've also got a caseload of several hundred murders,' Wilson said. 'Do you really think that they're going to concentrate on a missing person's case? We're not trying to find Francis McComber. We're looking for a motive for three particularly violent murders, and McComber may, or may not, help us establish that motive. It's the only lead we've had since the beginning of this investigation.'

'Ok, boss,' Moira said. 'What's the plan?'

'Let's look at the three victims again. Peter, did you notice any pictures of Joan Boyle's husband at the Boyle house?'

'No, boss,' Davidson said.

'I wonder why. And why did they move away from west Belfast? The house is still a crime scene?'

'Yes, boss,' Davidson said.

'Get back there and find me the answers to those questions. Eric, you take Morison. Maybe he knows more than he's letting on. Pump him. Don't take any old crap from him. Bring him back thirty years and put Francis McComber in front of him. Moira will look for McComber's daughter while Harry and I will take our good friend Billy Rice. We meet here at six.'

MAGGIE CUMMERFORD WAS BRINGING her life in Belfast to

a close. She had already deposited her notice with the *Chronicle,* but the asshole editor had insisted that she work a couple of days while he interviewed some hopefuls for her job. He was already buffing up his couch before she'd left his office. She had checked her apartment with Luminol to make sure that not a trace of blood could be found. She had scrubbed until she was satisfied that there was nothing that could tie her to the murders of Rice, Morison and Boyle. She was happy that she had avenged the death of her mother. Three for one was not a bad average. It might have been more but there was no point in being greedy and getting caught into the bargain. She thought about dropping by Wilson's office to wish him farewell, but he was a smart bastard and that would be something out of the ordinary that might pique his interest. She'd already dumped fifty per cent of her clothes into a charity shop. Her landlord squeezed a month's rent out of her, and she had closed her utilities as from the end of the week. She hadn't yet decided on her destination; somewhere warm where she could get the cold and humidity of Belfast out of her bones. But also, somewhere well out of the way. It was either the US or Luang Prabang in Laos. It was possible to disappear in places like that and re-emerge as someone else. She'd make up her mind at the last minute. She opened the locket that hung around her neck and looked at the photograph of her mother. She would have liked to have known her better. Lizzie Rice had made sure that she would never have the chance. She sighed. It was strange to be at the end of the revenge trail. It was a bit like leaving school or university. A weight was lifted off her shoulders. She was finally free of an event that had haunted her for thirty years. She was free to become Maggie McComber.

THE ARCHVALE ESTATE was quiet as Peter Davidson pulled up beside the house formally occupied by Joan Boyle. He parked outside the house and slipped under the crime-scene tape. He produced a set of keys taken from the evidence room and opened the front door. The house smelled differently. The overriding smell was a sick sweet coppery odour. He went to the rear bedroom where Joan Boyle had been murdered and saw that the room had not yet been cleaned. He closed the door, but it had little effect on the smell. He put on a pair of surgical gloves and went into the living room. The forensics team had already been through the house, but they had been searching for evidence relevant to the crime. He was looking for items of relevance to the life and times of Joan Boyle. He looked around the living room. The boss was right. There were hardly any photos. The walls of his parents' home were covered in photographs of them and their children. In the Boyle living room, there was only one photograph of their only son. He picked it up. The young Boyle was a handsome lad with a full head of fair hair, high cheekbones, a well-proportioned face and full lips. He would have caused increased heartbeats in the female population of wherever he was located. He opened the chest of drawers positioned directly behind the open door. The first thing he saw was Joan Boyle's copy of the photo of the Lizzie Rice gang. He picked out a handful of photos and looked through them. He recognised Lizzie and some of the other gang members. He also recognised some of the locations and judging from the amount of fading of the colours they were mainly from the time the Boyles lived in west Belfast. He dug further into the drawer until he found a photo album. He took it out and opened it. A large photo dominated the first page. It was a wedding photo of a much younger Joan Boyle. The face of the man standing beside her was scratched out with something sharp. He turned the page to another set of photographs. In every .one, the man beside Boyle was defaced. He continued through the book and on each page, the defaced man appeared. He replaced the album and picked up another bunch of photographs. This time they were photos of a young boy gradually growing into a man. The photographs of the boy alone or with his mother were complete. However, there were some photos where the person standing beside the boy had been removed with a scissors. Things were obviously not well in the Boyle household. He heard a noise at the front door and quickly closed the chest of drawers. He went to the hallway in time to see a man retreating from the front door.

'Can I help you?' Davidson asked the retreating figure.

'Oh,' the man turned and faced him. 'I'm Jim McGillon, the next-door neighbour. I was just wondering what was going on.'

Davidson held up his warrant card. 'If you're wondering what's going on again, call the police. I could have been anyone. Did you know the Boyles well?'

'I was here when they bought the place. That doesn't mean that I knew them well. They kept pretty much to themselves.'

'Get on well, did they?'

The question seemed to confuse McGillon. 'Funny you should ask but the wife and I had the feeling that Joan hated his guts. She was positively over the moon when he was diagnosed with pancreatic cancer. Terrible death the poor man had.'

'What was he like?'

'Affable sort of a bloke. Good-looking fellah as well.' He smiled. 'I had to keep an eye on my Geraldine when he was about.'

'What about the son?'

'Nice boy. Got out of here as soon as he could. There was something toxic in that house. I suppose he'll be back to sell it?'

'I suppose so.' There was no point in saying that they hadn't managed to contact the son. His mother would be on ice until they could locate him.

'Do you have any idea of why they moved here?'

'They never said but somehow I got the impression that there had been some trouble, and it involved the husband. There was trouble for everyone back then. It wasn't polite to ask. Everything is all right then?' McGillon said making for the driveway.

'Yes,' Davidson was a million miles away. 'Yes, everything is all right.'

ERIC TAYLOR SAT in the front room of the Morison house in Malvern Street. George Morison had managed to make a cup of tea and had rustled up a packet of ginger nut biscuits.

'I don't know whether I'm comin' or goin',' Morison said pouring two cups of tea. 'I've had to delay the funeral for a week so that Nancy's sister can come from Australia. I haven't seen the woman in nearly twenty years and now she's dictating to me when I can bury my wife. I don't suppose you've come to give me any news.'

Taylor took the proffered cup of tea and shook his head. 'We need a little more information.' He sipped the tea but ignored the biscuits which had little blue marks on them.

'Anything I can do to help?' Morison sat back.

Taylor put down his teacup and resolved not to take it up again. How could a grown man have no idea how to make a cup of tea? 'We've established that your wife, and the two other murdered women were members of a women's group in the Shankill. That group was disbanded in the early 1980s. Can you tell me why?'

Morison lifted his head from his teacup. 'I've never been interested in politics. The 'Troubles' went on around me and I did my best to stay out of it.'

'That must have been difficult considering where you live.'

'It was, but I managed to a certain extent. Nancy was a little more involved. I don't know how she got into the local

UVF, but she did. She also did her best to get me involved, but I didn't want to go down that road. It was my opinion that the working people should stick together and not be at each other's throats.'

'The disbanding of the group that Nancy was in?' Taylor took out his notebook and put it on the coffee table in front of him.

'There was some trouble. Nancy never discussed the details with me, but I know that it badly affected her. She didn't go out for a week or more. It was very unusual. Those women lived in each other's ears. Normally, she couldn't see a day go by without meeting one of them. Then in a flash it all changed.'

'And you've no idea why?'

'I didn't ask, and she didn't tell me. Around that time, I could find her sitting alone saying 'the poor wee girl' again and again. When that stopped, she switched her focus to religion. Not the sectarian kind but the fanatical kind. She spent hours begging God's forgiveness.'

'Have you ever heard of a woman called Francis McComber?'

Morison's brow furrowed. 'Not that I can think of.'

'She disappeared at the time your wife's group was disbanded.'

'I don't think I ever heard of her,' Morison cast his eyes down to the left.

Taylor noticed the movement. 'Your wife died a violent death, and the PSNI is committed to bringing the person who killed her to justice. But we can't do that if people hold back information on us. I have a feeling that you've heard of Francis McComber, and I think you know more about the reason the group was disbanded than you're telling me. Your wife's dead. Nothing you say can harm her now.'

A tear forced its way out of the corner of Morison's left

eye. 'Nancy was never the same,' he said. The first tear was followed by another and another until he was forced to raise his hands to his eyes to staunch the flow down his cheeks. 'She didn't die this week,' he sobbed. 'She died thirty years ago.'

Taylor watched as Morison shook from the sobbing. He had been there before. He picked up his pen as the floodgates were about to open.

Moira hoped that Armstrong's memory was good as she entered the Haven for Young Girls orphanage on the Ormeau Road. The building had seen better days, and like much of old Belfast had been constructed during Victorian times. Attempts had been made at modernisation, but as Moira stood in the vestibule, she had a vivid picture of little girls running about in grey skirts and blue pinafores. The woman in the reception was like the building, a leftover from Victorian times. She was dressed in herringbone long skirt and jacket. Her brown hair was pulled back in a bun and her face a strict mask that looked like it had never seen a smile.

'Detective Sergeant Moira McElvaney,' she smiled and produced her warrant card.

'Emily Strachan, how can I help you?'

'I'm trying to trace a young girl who was put in care in the early 1980s, Margaret McComber.'

'A young Protestant girl?'

'Yes, she came from somewhere around the Shankill Road.'

Strachan's nose turned up. The people of west Belfast were not her kind of people. 'You have a warrant, of course.'

'No, I assumed that we could do this without becoming too legal. After all, it was thirty years ago.'

'It doesn't work like that. Time is not the issue. The young girl in question may not wish to be found.'

'I can see where that works with a relative. However, I am

a police officer investigating a series of murders, and I have no intention of disclosing anything that you might tell me to a relative.'

'Come with me,' Strachan led the way along a corridor and opened a door close to the end.

The small office contained a series of filing cabinets. The Haven for Young Girls eschewed the computer era. Moira could feel the musty air in the room.

'Margaret McComber, you said.' Strachan moved to a file cabinet and shuffled through a row of hanging files before withdrawing one. 'McComber, Margaret,' she said handing the file to Moira. 'You may examine the file in this room and take whatever notes you wish, but you will not remove any of the contents.'

Moira took the file and opened it. Pinned to the inside cover was the picture of a six-year-old girl. She was a handsome child with curly blonde hair and a pixie look. Moira wondered what she would look like as a thirty-five-year old woman, but she was not good at projecting people into the future. There were several sheets of A4 paper in the file. A doctor's report on the child indicated that she was in perfect health on arrival and departure. A report from Social Welfare explained the circumstances of her placement in the Haven. The final paper was not an adoption certificate but a letter indicating that young Margaret had been fostered to a couple living in Finaghy named Glynn. She wasn't adopted. Moira took the details of the couple and their address of thirty years before. She passed the file back to Strachan slipping the photograph of the McComber girl from the file as she passed it over. 'Thanks for your assistance,' she said and hurried from the building.

WILSON PUSHED OPEN the door to the public bar of the Black

Bear and adjusted his eyes to the gloom inside. It took him several moments before he saw Billy Rice sitting in the corner. Wilson and Graham walked over and sat down on stools facing Rice. The barman moved to the telephone, but a look from Graham made him drop the receiver.

'Mr Wilson,' Rice picked up the remnants of a pint of Guinness from the table between them and emptied the glass. 'Nice to see you,' he laughed sarcastically.

Wilson never liked Billy. The older Rice was a vicious thug who should have spent most of his life behind bars but had escaped that fate due to his commitment to the Loyalist cause. But the Billy that sat in front of them was far removed from the young firebrand of yesteryear. Billy grew fat on too much booze and too little work. At three o'clock in the afternoon, he was already on his way to Guinness-fuelled oblivion.

'Still in mourning, eh Billy?' Wilson said.

'Fuck you,' Rice signalled to the barman. 'Nothing for the peelers,' he shouted. 'No drink while they're on duty.' He smiled showing nicotine-stained teeth. 'Did you catch the bastard that did Lizzie yet?'

'Not yet,' Wilson said simply.

'Well get up off your fat fuckin' arses and find him.'

The barman dropped a pint of Guinness in front of Rice and left quickly.

'The Queen,' Rice toasted and drank a quarter of the Guinness. 'State your business or fuck off.'

'We're looking into Lizzie's background to see why someone wanted her dead,' Wilson said. 'How come her group was disbanded in the early Eighties?'

Rice thought for a minute. 'Can't remember,' he said finally.

'We're going to find out sooner or later,' Wilson said.

'Be my guest,' Rice took another slug of his Guinness. 'I told you I can't remember.'

'Ever hear of someone called Francis McComber?' Wilson asked.

Rice's eyes opened wide. He laid the glass on the table slowly. A nerve just beneath his left eye hopped. 'What's that?'

'Francis McComber,' Wilson said loud enough for the other drinkers to hear.

'Never heard of her,' Rice said.

'How did you know it was a woman? Francis could have been a man.'

'OK, never heard of him.'

'She disappeared in the early Eighties. One of my predecessors, Jack Armstrong, was sure that Lizzie had something to do with the disappearance.'

'Don't tell me that auld cunt is still alive?' Rice spat on the ground.

'Are you sure you don't remember her?'

Rice seemed lost in thought for a moment. 'I'm sure,' he said finally.

Wilson stood up slowly. 'I'm going to find out what happened back in 1983. I've got a strong feeling that both you and Lizzie were involved in disappearing Francis McComber. If I get to prove it, I'm going to make sure you spend the rest of your days in prison.'

Rice lifted his head, and his eyes were hooded. 'My son knows where you live.'

'Bring it on,' Wilson said as he turned and left the bar.

MOIRA HAD RETURNED to the station from the orphanage and started on her search for Margaret McComber. She had spent the next hour on the telephone and learned that the Glynns had later adopted Margaret after her mother had been missing for five years. She also learned that the Glynns no longer lived in Finaghy but had moved to England. There was no forwarding address. The next stop was the Department of

Social Welfare where she located a family called Glynn who had established a home in Mold in Flintshire one week after the Glynns left Belfast. It had to be the same family. She looked up the address and called the local police. Mr Glynn died, and his wife had moved. The trail looked to have gone cold.

THE TEAM ASSEMBLED at six in front of the whiteboards. Every space was now covered with information on the crimes. Harry Graham had located a photograph of Francis McComber from the Social Welfare and Moira had added a blown-up version of the photo she had removed from the young girl's file.

'We're almost there,' Wilson said as he began the briefing. 'Francis McComber, single mother, has an affair with Joan Boyle's husband who is a bit of a Jack the Lad. Francis also has one in the oven. Lizzie and the gang find out and decide to chastise the woman who is cuckolding their friend. The chastisement gets out of hand, and they kill McComber. Lucky for them their boss is connected, and her husband probably has experience in getting rid of unwanted bodies. The McComber girl is dumped on a housing estate where she's sure to be found, and her mother is removed to a shallow grave somewhere she won't be found. Our killer is on the revenge trail. Lizzie is gone because she was the boss, Boyle because her husband was the cause and Morison for some reason we don't know. Anyone want to argue with this hypothesis?'

The team remained silent.

Wilson turned to Moira. 'We have to find the girl.'

Moira said, 'She was adopted by a couple called Glynn who subsequently moved to the mainland. The husband died a few years later in Cheshire, and the wife moved on. The question is where to. I've put requests out to our colleagues on the mainland. Maureen Glynn was about thirty-five when her husband died so it's likely that she remarried. I'm trawling through the marriages from the date of her husband's death.'

'Good,' Wilson said. 'We've all had a tough day, and we're almost there on this theory. If it's the right one we're close to nailing the case. First priority is to find where the girl is today.'

CHAPTER SIXTY-THREE

The e-mail from forensics was in his in-box when he returned to the office. McIver's Glock 17 fired the bullets that killed Ivan McIlroy. Forensics had sent him a copy although he was no longer SIO. He supposed it was a question of professional courtesy. He had lost someone who had not only been a colleague but a friend. His mind filled with pictures of Ronald, sitting studiously at his desk, or in the back bar of the Crown his head tilted backwards laughing at a joke at the closure of a case. That was the way he wanted to remember him. Not the dishevelled man with the sunken eyes and the two-day old beard. If he needed any further evidence of what this job did to people, it had been before him in the interview room. Maybe he didn't need this anymore. How many more colleagues would he see needing their heads retuned before he took the hint? The job chews people up and spits them out. Only bottom feeders like Jennings thrive. Bottom feeders, bag carriers and paper pushers, they were the new lords of his universe. He looked at his phone. No message from Kate. They hadn't had sex since the miscarriage, which he totally understood. It was a road that she didn't want to tread for some time. He remembered what he had said in the hospital room. It was inevitable that things would change. The question was how much and in what direction. He looked out into the squad room and saw Moira hunched over her computer terminal. He didn't want to lose her but there was a part of him that hoped she would follow Brendan. Sooner or later, the job would get to her and he didn't want to be around when that happened. He picked up his jacket and switched off his desk lamp. He was dog-tired. When this case was over, he was going to take a few days off. Get up late and watch old films on TV all day.

MOIRA WAS ON A ROLL. She was running through reams of certificates of births, deaths and marriages. This was a crash course in genealogy. If she ever decided to ditch the PSNI, she could apply for a job with those agencies that find heirs to their inheritance from long-lost relatives. She had searched high and low for the Glynns and finally discovered that they'd moved to Cambridge. Then it was a question of going through every marriage certificate in the area of Cambridge for the ten years after their arrival. Plod, plod and more bloody plod.

WHEN WILSON LEFT THE OFFICE, he was on his way home. However, his car seemed to find its way to a parking place beside the Crown. He sat in the car for several minutes trying to decide and then switched off the engine. As he pushed in the door of the Crown, he entered a different world. Nobody here was murdering anyone or contemplating putting a plastic bag over the head of their comatose spouse. Well, not on the surface anyway. He glanced at the bar and a barman was waiting for his order. It was one of the advantages of being a local. This really was decision time. He signalled for a pint of Guinness. He would just have one pint, and then it would be home.

. . .

MOIRA GLANCED AT HER WATCH. It was eleven o'clock, and light from her desk lamp was casting an eerie glow round the squad room. She might be a Fenian bitch, but she could get the job done. Two more years of marriage certificates to go through. It had to be there. Pages flashed across the screen. Then she pressed stop. Maureen Glynn married to a Joshua Cummerford. It was a Eureka moment. Margaret, Maggie, now it made sense. Margaret McComber was Maggie Cummerford. Her hands were shaking when she took out her phone.

'Boss.'

'Aye,' Wilson's voice was soft on the other line.

She could hear the noise of a public house in the background. 'I found her,' she couldn't keep the excitement out of her voice. 'The wee girl, the McComber girl is Maggie Cummerford.'

'You're sure,' Wilson's voice was suddenly alert. 'You know where she lives?'

'Not yet.'

'Find out. Send a car for me to the Crown. Call Harry and get him in.'

IT WAS ALMOST midnight when they assembled in the squad room. 'Show me the papers one more time,' Wilson said. He had consumed what seemed like a gallon of coffee since Moira's phone call. Just when he needed all his wits about him, he decided to run off the rails.

Moira printed off copies of all the papers, the fostering document, the adoption papers, the death certificate for Mr Glynn, the marriage certificate for his wife and Joshua Cummerford and the *piece-de-resistance* the change of name certificate for Maggie Cummerford nee Margaret McComber.

'Outstanding work,' Wilson patted her on the shoulder. 'You must be exhausted. Go home, Harry and I can take it from here.'

'You've got to be joking, boss. You think I could sleep without being in on the collar.'

'Harry, any news on the tactical team?'

'They'll be ready by one o'clock.'

'Are we sure she's inside?' Wilson asked.

'Two uniforms saw the lights go out about midnight. Nobody's left since then. I would never have believed it, boss. That skinny little woman beating the heads off people.'

'They don't normally have 'murderer' tattooed on their foreheads, Harry. You've been around long enough to know that.'

'When do we do it?' Moira asked.

'As soon as the tactical team is ready.'

MAGGIE CUMMERFORD WIPED the sleep from her eyes. The knocking on the door of the house was incessant. She heard the shouts of 'police, open up' but she had no realisation that they were intended for her. She picked up her mobile phone and looked at the time. Ten minutes past one o'clock in the morning. What the hell was going on? She stumbled from her bed and was on her way downstairs when the front door was literally knocked off its hinges. In seconds, the hallway was full of armed policemen.

'On your knees,' the lead policeman shouted pointing his gun directly at Cummerford. 'Hands behind your head!'

She knelt and put her hands behind her head. A woman officer came forward and frisked her then nodded to her colleagues who holstered their guns. She looked up and saw Wilson entering the house followed by McElvaney and Graham. She smiled.

'Good morning, Maggie,' Wilson said. 'Moira, would you do the necessary, please?'

Moira stood forward. 'Margaret Cummerford, I am arresting you on suspicion of the murder of Elizabeth Rice, Nancy Morison and Joan Boyle. You do not have to say anything, but it may harm your defence, if you fail to mention, when questioned, something that you may later rely on in court. Anything you do say may be given in evidence. Do you understand?

'Yes,' Cummerford said. 'May I get dressed?'

'You will be given clothes at the station,' Wilson said.

'I'm innocent. You'll be sorry you did this,' Cummerford said.

WILSON STOOD in the squad room and watched Maggie Cummerford on the CCTV. She was dressed in a white jump-suit and seated at the table in an interview room. Wilson had left her in the room for an hour to allow her to stew in her own juice, but she seemed completely calm, outwardly at least. Moira and Harry had done a quick and dirty recce of her apartment but had come up with nothing. Forensics were about to arrive, and the apartment would be taken apart piece by piece. If there was any evidence there, they were going to find it. The question was whether Cummerford had left anything to find.

Moira walked into the squad room. 'I hope forensics have more luck than us.'

'Time to have a word with Maggie,' Wilson said. He pointed at Moira. 'You're with me.'

Maggie Cummerford looked up when the two police officers entered the room.

Wilson and Moira sat across from her. Moira switched on the recorder and went into her rigmarole of date, time and who was present.

'Well, Maggie,' Wilson said. 'It's been a long road but here we are. We know everything.'

Cummerford smirked but said nothing.

'Maybe I should call you Maggie McComber.'

'Call me what you want.'

'Margaret McComber was the name you were born with.'

'If you say so.'

Moira took a paper from a file and placed it on the table. 'A photocopy of your birth certificate,' she said.

Cummerford ignored it.

'Your mother was Francis McComber, father unknown,' Wilson read from the photocopy.

No reaction.

'Your mother disappeared on April 25th, 1983 according to our records. Was that the day she was murdered?'

Cummerford smiled.

'You were there when she was abducted,' Moira placed another paper on the table. It was a copy of the statement made by the six-year-old Maggie McComber. 'Nobody believed you.'

No reaction.

'When did you find out that your mother was murdered?' Wilson asked.

Cummerford sat back in her chair and crossed her legs.

'It won't help not to answer questions. We have the motive and we have you,' Wilson said.

'But you have no proof,' Cummerford said. 'Remember I attended all your briefings.'

'Except for those relating to the Joan Boyle murder. That one was a real mess. The clean-up must have taken forever.'

Cummerford's eyes suddenly looked sharper.

'Yes, Maggie, we found something that links you to the house and the murder. Now is the time to spit it all out because we have enough to hold you and in the coming days, we'll add to that. Now that we know who you are, we only have to track your movements. We'll place you at Malvern Street, somebody will have seen you torching the car, and we'll even place you at Archvale. It's over.'

'You're bluffing,' Cummerford said.

Moira took a plastic evidence bag from the file and laid it on the table.

'It's hair,' Wilson said. 'And it's got Joan Boyle's blood on it but it's not from her head. Now who else do you think that hair might belong to? DS McElvaney removed some hair from a hairbrush in your apartment. The DNA test is being done as we speak.'

Cummerford squirmed back. 'You can't do this.'

'You are charged with a capital crime. We can do anything we bloody well like. Now let's go back to the beginning. When did you find out that your mother was murdered by Lizzie and her gang?'

Cummerford slumped in her chair. 'I want a lawyer.'

'You will have a lawyer when you are charged, but we have some time before we have to do that. We've had a long day, and we're ready to have an even longer one if that's the way you want to play it. Wake up, Maggie. It's over. The only thing that you can do now is to come clean and gain some brownie points with the system. Because if you don't, you're going to bring a shit storm down on your head the like of which you've never seen.'

Cummerford stared at the small plastic sleeve on the table containing the hair and sighed. 'One of Lizzie Rice's gang sent me a letter via the orphanage last year. I always checked in with them on the off chance that my mother made contact,' she laughed. 'I half believed the bullshit about her running away. The old bitch who wrote was dying of cancer, and she was afraid to die with such a big sin on her soul. She described how they had hung my mother by her feet from a beam in their romper room and dropped her until her head almost hit the floor. Then one time they didn't catch the rope in time, and her head smashed into the floor. That was much more fun. They dropped her again and again until the top of her head was mush. Then they wrapped her body in bin bags, and one of their husbands disposed of her.'

'That wasn't so hard,' Wilson said. 'You decided to avenge her death.'

'I came back to Belfast thinking that I could get the case reopened. I got the files under the Freedom of Information Act and saw that there wasn't a hope in hell of getting anyone to believe what was in the letter.'

'What about Historical Crimes?'

'My mother disappeared. She was never murdered. The murderers were getting old and dying off naturally. I had to do something. I decided to speed up the natural process.'

'So, you admit that you murdered Elizabeth Rice, Nancy Morison and Joan Boyle.'

'No. I executed them like the state should have done if it was doing its job.'

'You picked a particularly nasty way of executing them,' Moira said.

'I gave them the same death as they gave my mother.'

Wilson leaned back in his chair. He needed a coffee. No, he needed a pot of coffee. The next bit was going to take time. He signalled to those watching on CCTV for a drink to be brought in. 'OK, Maggie,' he said. 'Talk us through the murders.'

CHAPTER SIXTY-FOUR

Wilson had been awake for more than thirty hours by the time the first interview with Maggie Cummerford was completed. There was a lot of backslapping as he walked through the station on his way to the squad room.

'There's a car waiting for you outside,' Harry Graham said as soon as he walked into the squad room. 'You're wanted at HQ.'

Wilson wheeled around without a word and headed for the parking lot. He slept in the back of the car during the twenty-minute journey to Castlereagh. He flashed his warrant card at the entrance and made his way to the top floor and the office of the DCC. Chief Superintendent Donald Spence was sitting on a chair directly outside the office.

'Been waiting long?' Wilson asked.

'Long enough,' Spence replied. 'You look like shit.'

'Nothing that a sleep, a shower and a fresh shirt won't put right,' Wilson cracked back. 'Pain or pleasure?'

'My guess is pain,' Spence stood up and straightened his uniform.

They entered the outer office together, and Jennings'

secretary pointed at the door of the inner office. 'He's waiting for you.'

'I suppose you think I'm going to congratulate you about the Cummerford woman,' Jennings began as they entered his office. 'Well I'm not. I just received the file on the interrogation of McIver. We are going to be pilloried in the press. A long-serving police officer murdered two people, one of whom was his wife. Questions are going to be asked.' He looked at Wilson. 'I notice that he has already engaged a senior member of the Bar to represent him. I suppose he can thank you for that.'

'He can hire who he likes I presume,' Wilson said.

'Sir,' Jennings shouted. 'You will address me as sir.'

'Yes, sir,' Spence said quickly cutting off any possible reply from Wilson.

Jennings thumped his fist on his desk. 'I'm not going to carry the can for your incompetence. I have every intention of speaking to the Chief Constable concerning the level of dereliction of duty on both of your parts.'

'I don't think that would be wise,' Wilson said and added 'sir,' as an afterthought.

'You don't think, so do you?' Jennings stood up from his desk. 'If you're still in the force after this fiasco, I'll make sure that you're pounding a beat.'

Wilson stood at his full height and looked down on his superior. 'In defending ourselves, we may be obliged to explain that you gave permission for a serial killer to have access to the station and worse to attend briefings of the team investigating murders for which it appears she was responsible.'

Jennings' face went white and his mouth flapped open and closed without making a sound.

'I wonder who'll be pounding a beat when that piece of news hits the airwaves,' Wilson said.

Jennings fell back into his chair as though he had been punched in the chest.

Wilson could almost see the wheels in Jennings' mind trying to turn and grapple with the threat. Wilson continued, 'McIver's legal representative has no desire to drag the PSNI over the coals. It might be wise for you to deal with her directly to ensure that the force receives the minimum amount of negative publicity. Perhaps she has already considered how McIver's deeds might reflect the difficulty experienced by PSNI officers and the stresses they are forced to work under. Then the Cummerford issue would have no need to see the light of day.'

'Get out,' Jennings' voice was shaking. 'Both of you, get out.'

Wilson looked back over his shoulder as he left and saw that Jennings was sitting forward with his head in his hands.

'My God, Ian,' Spence said when they were outside the office. 'I thought Jennings was the most devious bastard I'd met, but you're up there with him. It's a side to you that I hadn't realised before.'

'Spend a few months living with Kate McCann,' Wilson said. 'Some of the deviousness rubs off.'

THE TEAM and associated hangers on from the station were assembled in the back snug of the Crown. The mood was initially morose. The McIver affair was still a raw wound but as the drinks began to flow the mood became more jovial.

'There's money behind the bar,' Wilson said. 'And I'm paying for taxis home for all. Nobody drives home tonight.' He was fighting back sleep himself, and he could see that Moira and Harry were not going to last the pace.

'Does that include me? After all, I am a member of the team.'

Wilson wheeled around and saw Stephanie Reid standing at the door of the snug. She was dressed in her working clothes of white blouse and black skirt. 'I suppose so,' he said.' He looked around the assembled policemen and saw the effect Reid was having on them. They were just short of drooling. His gaze finally rested on Moira who wasn't exactly drooling. She looked like her favourite dog just died.

'Double gin and tonic,' Reid sat beside Moira. 'Us girls are going to have to stick together. The boys look like they're about to get drunk.' The waiter deposited a gin and tonic in front of her. 'Good result,' she clinked glasses with Moira

'You're wasting your time,' Moira said through clenched teeth.

'Only time will tell,' Reid said. She turned to Wilson. 'Now who's going to start the sing-song?'

# # #

AUTHOR'S NOTE

I hope that you enjoyed this book. As an indie author, I very much depend on your feedback to see where my writing is going. I would be very grateful if you would take the time to pen a short review on Amazon. This will not only help me but will also indicate to others your feelings, positive or negative, on the work. Writing is a lonely profession, and this is especially true for indie authors who don't have the backup of traditional publishers.

Death to Pay is the third novel in the Wilson series. It follows on from Nothing but Memories and Shadow Sins.

Please check out my other books on Amazon, and if you have time visit my web site (derekfee.com) and sign up to receive additional materials, competitions for signed books and announcements of new book launches.

Dear Fee is a former oil company executive and EU Ambassador. He is the author of seven non-fiction books.

. . .

DEREK CAN BE CONTACTED at http://derekfee.com.

Derek Fee©2014

Publisher's Note: This is a work of fiction. Names, characters, places, and incidents are a product of the author's imagination. Locales and public names are sometimes used for atmospheric purposes. Any resemblance to actual people, living or dead, or to businesses, companies, events, institutions, or locales is completely coincidental.

UNTITLED

DARK CIRCLES

DEREK FEE

CHAPTER SIXTY-FIVE

Big George Carroll drummed his fingers on the steering wheel of the black taxi. He cast a glance at the rearview mirror, and hoped that his passengers didn't notice. Two pairs of cold lifeless eyes stared back at him. Neither man had spoken a word since he'd collected them at the arrivals gate of Belfast International Airport. He wished that Sammy had given this job to someone else. However, Sammy trusted him and that made George happy. Big George shivered. His mother would have said someone had just walked over his grave. The two men in the back seat were an ill-matched pair. They reminded Big George of the Mutt and Jeff cartoon characters that he loved. The one that reminded him of 'Mutt' was tall and thin with the pale face and demeanour of a professional mourner. The second man was considerably smaller standing no more than five feet four inches. His face was as bland and pallid as his colleague's. George doubted that either man spent much time in the sun. Mutt and Jeff incited something in Big George that was unusual – fear. It wasn't a feeling he was used to. George was six feet seven and weighed in at one hundred and forty kilos, most of which was muscle. Big George didn't do fear. The people he dealt with did. Except for the two in the back of the cab. There was something about them that sent the shivers up his spine. The instructions from Sammy were clear enough. Pick up two guys at the airport and drive them to an address in the University area of Belfast. A parking place would be blocked off with traffic cones; he was to remove the cones and park. He was not to converse with his passengers and when instructed he was to move on to a second address. It was a simple, no-brainer driving job. But Sammy had said nothing that could have made George feel the way he did. The three men sat in the car in silence and waited.

BRIAN MALONE STOOD up to leave his office at the Northern Ireland Infrastructure Agency at exactly five thirty. Although he contemplated having a drink before heading home, he decided that he'd wait and have a stiff one at the flat instead. He looked around and saw that barely sixty per cent of his colleagues were heading for the exit. It was not a good strategy to quit on time if you wanted to make it in the NIIA. Members of the hierarchy would be striding along the corridors checking out who was still at their desks. Meanwhile, the pile suckers would be spending their time playing Solitaire on their computers, or checking their Facebook pages. It was so damn pathetic. Malone didn't like to think about climbing the greasy pole. He didn't like to think about spending the next thirty years doing it either. There had to be more to life than shuffling papers about. He dreamt about skipping out on cold and miserable Belfast and heading to Cyprus. He was a diving fanatic and had a long-term plan to open a diving school on the island. He'd chosen Cyprus because it was English-speaking and had a regular throughput of English tourists. The question was how long term was his plan. He'd tapped his parents for a loan, but they were not receptive. Anyway, they needed the money for themselves. He'd looked at the costs, and he needed fifty grand. Said in one breath it didn't seem like a lot but for a junior civil servant, it would require more than ten years of concentrated saving. By then he might be married with a child on the way and the fifty grand would always be a mirage that he could see in the distance, but was fated never to reach. It was a fine evening so he decided to walk to his apartment. Belfast was almost bearable on an evening like this. Awnings had been installed on bars and restaurants so that when the light rain that was a constant visitor to the city made its appearance, the customers could still enjoy the continental lifestyle without getting drenched to the skin. As he walked along, he smiled at the after-work groups enjoying their drinks. Life didn't seem so bad and maybe even the fifty grand wouldn't turn out to be a mirage. You never really knew what was around the corner.

JEFF SAT in the rear of Big George's cab with a photograph on his lap. The face in the photograph was etched in his brain, but he was a professional and it was better to be sure. There was not going to be a fuck-up. He was in the zone. He knew what had to be done. Two men were to be murdered, and nobody would be the wiser. Both would be made to look like natural or accidental deaths. 'We're on,' Jeff said softly as Malone turned a corner and walked slowly in the direction of their cab.

MALONE TOOK no notice of the black cab parked on the street where he lived. He was whistling and looking straight ahead as he approached the door of the house containing his apartment. He didn't notice the two rear doors of the taxi opening or the shapes of the two men exiting. He slipped the key into the front door and turned the lock. As he pushed the door open, he was shoved from the rear and stumbled into the small hallway, just ahead of the two men dressed similarly in black polo neck jumpers and dark trousers. He turned to remonstrate, and as he did so was struck on the side of the temple. The blow didn't appear to be hard. It was more of a sting than a blow, but it was sufficient to turn his lights out.

MUTT CAUGHT him before he hit the carpet. Jeff removed the keys from his hand, and together the two men carried him to the door at the end of the hall where a plastic '2' hung upside down. Jeff inserted a key and turned the Yale lock. They carried the prone body inside.

'First things first,' Jeff said in a soft Glaswegian accent. He removed a small box from his side pocket and opened it as his colleague sat Malone into the only easy chair in the room. He removed a large hypodermic syringe from the box and slowly pulled the plunger down, filling the glass body of the syringe with liquid from a vial. He opened the young man's mouth and lifted his tongue. He plunged the syringe into the underside of the tongue and pushed the plunger. 'Instant heart attack,' he said to his colleague.

Mutt turned and looked at the figure slumped n the chair.

Malone moaned and looked like he was about to come awake when he shuddered, fell off the chair and lay on the floor. His eyes opened, and he saw the two men looking at him. He remembered that he was hit on the head, but that wasn't where the pain was. His chest was aching, and he was having difficulty breathing. He tried to get up but found that he couldn't move. The pain in his chest was excruciating. He tried to speak, but no words came from his mouth. He lay back.

Jeff dismantled the syringe and put it back into the box. He slipped the box into his pocket and then felt the neck of the man lying on the ground. The pulse was still there. He went around the small flat opening drawers and examining the contents, making sure to replace them in their original positions. He looked over at his colleague who held up a plastic bag containing a laptop computer. From the corner of his eye, he noticed the man on the ground convulse. He abandoned his search and stood directly in front of the dying man. He had seen many men die. Some he had sent to their Maker, whilst for others he had simply been an observer of their last moments. He watched the man convulse again. He was not a religious man, but he carried out an experiment every time he saw someone die. He tried to identify that moment when the soul left the body. He put his fingers on the young man's neck. There was still a pulse, but it was weak. The potassium chloride was doing its job. Without immediate medical attention, death was just around the corner. He would have preferred some other method of murder but the instructions were that it had to look natural. There was nothing more natural than a heart attack. He went back to his observations. Although he was convinced that the soul did not exist, he was ready to change his mind if on even one occasion the dying person did not go from a living breathing entity to a waxwork figure in an instant. The man on the ground convulsed one last time and expired. Jeff placed two fingers on the side of his neck and felt no pulse. Brian Malone had left the building.

The two men glanced at each other and took one last look around the flat. Jeff dropped the keys on the dining table, and they let themselves out.

CHAPTER SIXTY-SIX

'David, for Christ's sake put your hand up for the vote.'

David Grant suddenly came out of his reverie due to the sharp pain in his side. He looked to his right and saw that his colleague had jammed an elbow into his ribs. 'What? Vote?' Grant said absentmindedly.

'Put your bloody hand up.' His colleague grabbed his right jacket sleeve.

Grant raised his hand and looked into the chamber of Belfast City Council. All the members of his party had their hands raised, as had been agreed with their leader. The Chairman made a piece of theatre out of counting the hands before declaring that the vote had been passed. Grant had no idea what he had just voted for, but he would have followed his colleagues anyway.

'What the hell's up with you?' Grant's colleague asked.

'I was away with the fairies,' he answered.

'You've been away with the bloody fairies for the past two weeks.'

Grant dropped his hand down to the edge of the bench and felt the briefcase sitting beside his right leg. It was a crocodile skin case that had been a gift from his brother who worked for a development agency in Madagascar. He'd seen similar cases in a shop in Royal Avenue and there was no way he would have been able to afford one. The contents of the case were the reason why Grant had been so distracted over the past several weeks. He had no idea why the local Deep Throat picked on him. He assumed it was because he was the only Jewish member of the City Council. Whatever the reason, the documents were of such an import that they were certain to change his life. The question was whether it would be for the better or the worse. One of the City Councillors had launched into a speech about flag days or marching or some such other issue that was of no consequence to Grant. He wasn't very religious and hadn't been in a synagogue in years but being Jewish in Northern Ireland had its advantages. As a young solicitor, he was expected to join the Masons, but he was spared the more or less obligatory membership of the Orange Order.

'You look shot.' His colleague was staring into his face. 'You're either burning the candle at both ends, or you're coming down with something very nasty.'

Grant was well aware that he looked dreadful. His normal pallor accentuated the dark circles under his eyes. He had spent the past two weeks examining documents that would have an explosive effect on the very fabric of Northern Ireland, and on his career. He remembered the part of the Bible where Jesus had knelt in the Garden of Gethsemane and wished that the chalice would pass. As he had struggled to make sense of the papers that had been entrusted to him, he wished he had never accepted them. He was also sorry that he had involved one of his friends in the exercise of understanding what were extremely complicated documents.

'Maybe you should see a doctor,' his colleague suggested.

'Just overworked,' Grant said because he realised that his colleague was waiting for a reply.

'Take a rest,' the colleague said. 'The Council takes a break in the next few weeks. Most of the issues on the table are facile anyway, so you don't even have to turn up here for this bullshit.'

The Chairman was attempting to bring a speaker to a conclusion but was encountering a high level of resistance.

'Any more votes this evening?' Grant asked.

His colleague looked at the order paper. 'Nothing. As soon as the extremists have had their say the Chair will wrap us up.'

Grant cleared the space in front of him and dumped the documents into his briefcase. It was time to go home.

CHAPTER SIXTY-SEVEN

Mutt and Jeff sat in David Grant's small house. The lock on the front door had presented no problem to them and there was no alarm. They waited patiently and silently in the dark. The house had been searched from top to bottom. Although both men knew it was getting late, neither had looked at his watch. They would wait until they had finished their job.

GRANT PUSHED in the door of his house. He had opted to renovate a modest two-up two-down dwelling in the Ashley Avenue rather than go for an upmarket new-build apartment. He had tried to maintain the character of the property and felt that he had succeeded. As he entered, he dropped his briefcase on the floor and made his way to the kitchen at the rear. He plugged in the electric kettle and opened the door of the American-style fridge. The remnants of a lamb rogan josh and some sticky white rice stared back at him from the middle shelf. He didn't feel like facing a reheat, so he took a packet of cheese slices and a tomato from the upper shelf. He pushed the door of the fridge closed and saw a small man standing on the other side.

'What the ...,' Grant dropped the cheese and tomato on the floor. He saw the small man's hand move, but it appeared to flash very quickly to a point on his head. He felt dizzy for a second and then hit the kitchen floor.

Mutt appeared at the door and without speaking moved to the prone man. 'We'll need help,' he said simply.

Jeff nodded. 'The Hulk in the cab?'

'Has to be.'

'Shit.'

'I'll get him.'

Jeff nodded. He never thought about his lack of stature. He had a set of skills that did not depend on physical prowess. However, the man lying on the kitchen floor weighed in at perhaps one hundred kilos and there was no way he and his colleague could manhandle deadweight of that size.

Big George and Mutt appeared at the door of the kitchen.

Jeff handed George a pair of surgical gloves. 'Put those on and help me get him into the hallway,' he said.

George looked at the prone man. Sammy had told him to stay out of the way, but he didn't want to get into an argument. He took the gloves and put them on before picking up Grant's feet. Mutt had chosen his shoulders, and together they lifted him. They walked through the kitchen door and into the hallway.

Jeff had already placed a small case on the ground and was removing an item of female clothing. 'Undress him.'

George was wondering what was going on. He knew the two boys were heavy metal, and that they had come to Belfast to do some kind of special job. The guy on the floor was out for the count and the man who had helped him carry him into the living room was taking the guy's jacket off. George removed the man's shoes, noting the level of wear, and then removed his socks. His partner was removing the shirt so George loosened the belt on the man's trousers, and pulled them down. The guy was wearing a pair of white Y-fronts which had turned grey from washing. George hesitated. 'Everything?' he asked.

Jeff looked at him.

George pulled down the guy's Y-fronts. The man was lying naked on the floor. George examined his tackle and saw that he was both circumcised and fairly well endowed. He looked away and saw that Jeff had already laid out a pair of ladies' fancy knickers, a brassiere, a garter belt and a pair of ladies' stockings. He didn't like what the two men were doing. It wasn't nice to dress a man in women's clothes.

'Out of the way.' Jeff pushed George aside and picked up the garter belt. With a quiet efficiency, he dressed the man on the floor in the female items. Mutt lifted the guy up so that the brassiere could be affixed to his torso. Jeff slipped a camisole over the stunned man's head and put a pair of red high heels on his feet before standing back to admire his work. He smiled and turned to George. 'Get him up.'

They lifted Grant up into a vertical position. An open wooden staircase ran to the upper floor with a short return on the landing. Jeff climbed the stairs and tied a rope to the post at the top of the stairs. He dropped the noose-end of the rope down to his colleague who put it around the semi-conscious man's neck.

'Keep him up,' Mutt said to George. He went into the kitchen, returned with a chair and placed it directly under the stair post.

Together they hauled the prone figure up onto the chair.

Grant moaned as he was manhandled into a vertical position. His eyes began to open. Jeff, at the top of the stairs, immediately put strain on the rope, and Grant was in a semi-hanging position with his feet just about able to reach the seat of the chair. He suddenly opened his eyes and began to choke.

Mutt kicked the chair away making sure it fell in a natural position.

Grant swung in the air and started to kick his legs. He hit Big George in the face with the heel of one of his shoes and opened a cut in his cheek.

'Hold the bastard's legs,' Jeff called from above.

Big George lunged at the flailing legs and grabbed them. He held them tight. He could hear the noise of the man choking above him, but held on to the legs for dear life.

'Pull down, you big fucking oaf,' Mutt shouted.

George did as he was told and the force in the legs gradually reduced until there was one final kick, and they went quiet. He released his grip and looked up into two bulging eyes. He stood back. He hadn't bought into this. He was only the driver. He put his hand up and felt the blood running down his cheek.

Jeff descended the stairs and joined the two men below. They stared up at the body. Jeff rearranged the chair. Grant had kicked off one of the red high heels, and they left it where it lay. Jeff pulled down the top of the panties Grant was wearing and took his penis out. He moved Grant's hand over and rubbed it on the penis.

Big George looked away. He didn't mind the heavy stuff, but this was bloody sick. He didn't know what had happened with the poor bugger at the flat, and he didn't want to know. 'You need me?' he asked.

Jeff shook his head.

George made for the door.

Mutt and Jeff made a final appraisal of the hung man. They nodded at each other and made for the front door. Jeff noticed the briefcase in the entrance hall and nodded at it. Mutt picked it up and took it with him.

George was already behind the wheel of the black cab. He started the engine as the two men exited the house.

Jeff pulled the door of the house closed behind him. The

two men retook their places in the cab and it pulled away from the curb.

'Where to?' George asked.

'Belfast International,' Jeff said.

'It's night,' George said. 'There are no flights.'

'Belfast International.'

AUTHOR'S PLEA

I hope that you enjoyed this book. As an indie author, I very much depend on your feedback to see where my writing is going. I would be very grateful if you would take the time to pen a short review. This will not only help me but will also indicate to others your feelings, positive or negative, on the work. Writing is a lonely profession, and this is especially true for indie authors who don't have the backup of traditional publishers.

Please check out my other books , and if you have time visit my web site (derekfee.com) and sign up to receive additional materials, competitions for signed books and announcements of new book launches.

You can contact me at derekfee.com.

ALSO BY DEREK FEE

The Wilson Series

Nothing But Memories

Shadow Sins

Death To Pay

Deadly Circles

Box Full of Darkness

Yield Up the Dead

Death on the Line

A Licence to Murder

Dead Rat

Cold in the Soul

Border Badlands

Moira McElvaney Books

The Marlboro Man

A Convenient Death

ABOUT THE AUTHOR

Derek Fee is a former oil company executive and EU Ambassador. He is the author of seven non-fiction books and sixteen novels. Derek can be contacted at http://derekfee.com.

Made in the USA
Las Vegas, NV
21 February 2024